CATCHING

NETTIE

GORDON

BY

JEAN JEGEL

Published by Emery Press at Kindle Direct Publishing

ISBN: 978-1732411968

Discover other titles by Jean Jegel at jeanjegel.com

This book is a work of fiction. Any references to historical events, real people, or real places are used fictitiously. Other names, characters, places and events are products of the author's imagination, and any resemblance to actual events or places or persons, living or dead, is entirely coincidental.

Scripture quotations from The Authorized (King James) Version. Rights in the Authorized Version in the United Kingdom are vested in the Crown. Reproduced by permission of the Crown's patentee, Cambridge University Press. Read more at:
http://www.cambridge.org/bibles/about/rights-and-permissions/#bxs1vegcPkJMbMpk.99

Cover by Dave Simmons

To Mom and Dad
For providing a wonderful, imperfect beginning

CHAPTER ONE
Los Angeles, 1905

"You simply must come, Nettie. I told them I'd help set up chairs. This is the most exciting time for women in the history of the world!"

It was plain to see Eula was caught up in dreams of an ideal future when sober, sensible and attentive men would fall at her feet and provide equal pay for her work. Nettie, too practical to have her head turned by promises of heaven on earth, clearly held no such idealistic notions.

"I know you enjoyed the suffragette gathering last week," continued Eula. "The Women's Christian Temperance Union meeting will be even more inspiring. The speakers are so stirring. You know you want to come!"

Nettie Gordon watched two boys from her class chase several older girls across the field. She much preferred the classroom environment to her current task as playground monitor.

"Eula, I think you have the wrong impression. I'm happy you found kindred spirits at your meetings, but I'd much prefer going home, putting my feet up and embroidering to plotting to control the world." Nettie's corner room on the third floor of Mrs. Green's boarding house was her refuge. "Besides, I have papers to grade."

"That won't take long. Can't you imagine what it will be like once we have the vote? We'll have an equal say in what goes on in the world. It will mean an end to all social ills—drunkenness, smoking, child labor, prostitution, poverty; even dirty politics will all be wiped from existence."

Eula was Nettie's best friend and fellow teacher at Trinity Lutheran Church School. She taught fifth and sixth grades and Nettie taught first and second. The two women lived at the same boarding house on Bunker Hill. Their friendship seemed inevitable, a normal result of close proximity, but the women could not have been more different.

Having lived on a Wisconsin dairy farm her entire life, Eula was enthralled with all Los Angeles had to offer. She literally walked through the streets with mouth agape when she arrived last year. An uncle secured her teaching position at Trinity. Eager to leave her relation's house and control, Eula quickly moved into Mrs. Green's when Nettie mentioned there was a vacant room.

Eula's fondest wish in life was to find a husband although her individual goal had recently become subjugated by an avid pursuit of equality and justice for all women. Perhaps the fact she had few marital prospects also fueled her enthusiasm for matters political.

Gangly and tall, Eula appeared all elbows and knees, no small feat in the abundant layers of clothing women wore. Her dull brown hair was always tightly pulled into a bun on top of her head. She had a severely pointed chin, angular features and skin that blotched with the slightest exertion.

Nettie was entirely different, from her appearance to her temperament. Having grown up in nearby Pasadena, Nettie was never impressed with life in the City of Angels. Eager to leave home, she rode the street car as far as her money could take her, which was not far at all. At 16, she first took a job in a restaurant waiting tables.

If Eula's appearance made her stand out in a negative way, Nettie's appearance allowed her to blend in. Of average height, she considered herself quite plain. In fact, she prided herself in her average figure, average face and average hazel eyes. The only features that stood her slightly apart were her dark auburn hair and lightly freckled cheeks. Nettie considered these undesirable attributes in any case.

Her only real goal in life, besides making her own living, was avoiding marriage like the plague. Having five older brothers and a father back home, the youngest of six children was entirely fed up with men. Her mother worked herself to death before Nettie made her abrupt departure. She had no desire to suffer a similar fate. Men were dull, violent, bestial, lazy, repulsive fools.

Nettie's current life of teaching, church activities, reading and embroidery was her own modest dream come true. She found an outlet for her caring nature in her students and the luscious houseplants she tended on her windowsill. Her corner room provided a rare view of greenery in the midst of the city. Nettie made ample use of her proximity to Central Park and its lush tropical flora. Her bicycle was her most prized possession. She did not aspire to save the world.

Nonetheless, Nettie decided to accompany her dearest friend to the WCTU meeting that night to keep her out of trouble if nothing else. It was a decision that would alter the course of her life.

* * *

Nettie sat in the basement of the Vernon Congregational Church, filled to capacity on the warm June evening. Fervor for the Women's Christian Temperance Union was on the rise since the organization held their convention in Pasadena last month. Nettie would have to admit; the speakers were riveting. She listened attentively to the assertions women, being the far superior sex morally, were obligated to perform their duties as "citizen-mothers" to protect their homes and cure the ills of society. The goal of the organization was to create "a sober and pure world by abstinence, purity and evangelical Christianity."

The organization defined temperance as "moderation in all things healthful; total abstinence from all things harmful." Anything good in life should never be indulged to excess; anything fitting their definition of bad should be avoided completely.

The first example demonstrated how a family member's errant behavior could unintentionally affect their loved ones in derogatory ways:

> "Ned has applied for a job, but he is not chosen. He finds that the potential employer has judged him to be like his Uncle Jack. Jack is a kindly man but he spends his money on drink and cigarettes. Ned has also been seen drinking and smoking. The employer thinks that Ned lacks the necessary traits of industriousness which he associates with abstinence and self-control."

Innocent wives attested to have married kind and supportive men who turned to liquor and transformed into the scourges of their families. Women were forced to support their children and suffered the indignity of being wives of drunkards. Children were confused at the tears and sorrow of their mothers and at fathers who did not love them as Godly men loved their children.

Then came the story of a Mrs. Carse who became an activist after her son was killed by a drunken wagon driver. But it was the litany of personal accounts of sexual and domestic violence at the hands of drunken husbands that resulted in a hushed and horrified audience.

Liquor sellers were painted as no less than murderers. Nettie was certain liquor interests caused the failure of women's suffrage in many states. They used their political influence and money to defeat the movement, which was unquestionably a threat to their business. The Liquor Dealers League defeated suffrage as recently as 1896 in California. Women weren't about to forget.

The WCTU speakers effectively outlined the lack of women's civil rights. In many states, women did not have control of their property or custody of their children in case of divorce. There were no legal protections for women and children. Men were rarely prosecuted for rape. The age of consent was as low as seven in many states. Most political meetings occurred in saloons where women were not allowed. The speakers clearly outlined their agenda—once women won the vote, their lot in life would be greatly improved.

Nettie was impressed by the various charitable ventures the organization sponsored. They operated nurseries for children of working women, promoted Sunday schools, ran homeless shelters and homes for fallen women. As Nettie applauded at the end of the meeting, she had the undeniable feeling the polished presentation was lacking in some way.

Due to the lateness of the hour, Nettie was anxious

to head for home. Eula, however, vanished into the crowd of eagerly conversing women. Finally catching sight of her tall friend near the exit, Nettie made her way across the room to find an animated and excited Eula nattering away with other young ladies.

Grabbing Nettie's arm, Eula breathlessly declared, "We're going to pray. You must come."

"You're going to pray in the church?"

"No, remember when they spoke about the early days of the WCTU—the way women blocked entrances of saloons by kneeling in prayer at the door? That's what we're going to do."

"What a horrible idea. I want to go home and grade my papers so I can go to bed. It's almost summer vacation. Can't we pray in front of saloons next month when school is out?"

Eula linked her arm in Nettie's and started for the door. "We're going in the direction of home. We'll simply take some exercise along the way then we'll catch the Yellow Car. Here, I got a sign for us to carry."

Eula presented a hand-drawn sign nailed to a two-by-two. The picture on the placard featured a slovenly saloon owner laughing over the graves of his customers. This was hardly an appropriate sign to take to prayer as far as Nettie was concerned. She couldn't imagine why the barkeeper was laughing—he just lost his customers. Nonetheless, she reluctantly followed the group of enthusiastic women down the sidewalk.

Nettie noticed most of this group of ladies were younger than her. Nettie had been on her own for nearly ten years. Her maturity and self-reliance served her well since she moved away from home. Attempting to mull over her issues with the WCTU meeting, Nettie lagged behind the excited clutch of women.

She readily gave credit to the Union's various

charitable endeavors. They were generously providing for women's needs in communities around the world. She agreed women lacked the civil rights evident in the Bill of Rights. The right to vote would undoubtedly give them the voice they currently lacked. It was the group's insistence they knew what was best for everyone that proved concerning. She often heard sermons on the importance of moderation in all things. Nettie was not certain the prohibition of alcohol was wise.

Murder was prohibited, that hadn't stopped murder. Theft was prohibited, that certainly hadn't stopped robbery. Why did these women believe the prohibition of alcohol would stop drinking? In any case, she seriously doubted the Germans who populated her own church would willingly give up their beer.

After all, Jesus turned water into wine. The Bible did not contain a single verse about the evil of alcohol, only the evil of drunkenness and the benefits of moderation. If there was some percentage of the population who could not hold their liquor, why did everyone else have to give it up? Not that she cared much for liquor. Nettie surmised if the women of the WCTU got their way, law-abiding, God-fearing citizens would be made into criminals in short order.

As the group of ladies paused on the sidewalk in front of a saloon to kneel and pray, Nettie leaned against the corner of the building. She held Eula's sign and let her arm fall loosely at her side as she continued to sort out her opinions.

Nettie realized the WCTU blamed saloon keepers for the behavior of their clients. Personal responsibility did not seem to be the focus of the group as Nettie imagined it should. Every soul had the duty to choose between good and evil. It seemed the WCTU was trying to legislate morality. No sooner did Nettie feel comfortable with her conclusions than she heard the sound of glass shattering. Suddenly alert, she observed the ladies in her group dashing in all directions. A frantic Eula hurried past yelling, "Run!"

As Nettie turned to leave, a large hand tightly grasped her arm. Before she knew what was happening, a man pulled her down the sidewalk at breakneck speed.

Having just heard testimony of the wretched way women were treated, a shocked Nettie attempted to extricate her arm.

"Let me go! What do you think you're doing?" Short of collapsing, there seemed no way to deter her strong rival. Even if she did fall to the ground, he might simply drag her along the sidewalk. If he pulled her into an alleyway or some vacant building, there was little she could do to defend herself.

Nettie tried to strike his arm with the sign then attempted to dig her heels into the sidewalk but could not manage to stop his forward momentum. Considering she really ought to scream, Nettie caught sight of a police station ahead. Determined to put up a hue and cry in the hopes a kindly officer would come to her aid, Nettie was shocked when the brute pulled her right into the station.

"I want to file charges," proclaimed the beast.

"*You* want to file charges! Officer, this man accosted me on the street and brought me here against my will. I wish to file charges!"

"She vandalized my business. My front window is shattered. She's one of those temperance lunatics. Arrest her!"

Wide-eyed, Nettie stood uncomprehending. "I am *not* a lunatic."

"But you were among the women who blocked the entrance to my saloon."

"Well, I was but—"

"They broke my window and ran off. I happened to catch this one, Harvey. Lock her up. I'm pressing charges. I expect full compensation for my window and the lettering."

"I didn't break your window."

"You were certainly a party to it. Perhaps you'd like to fork over the names of the 'ladies,' and I use the term loosely, who accompanied you."

"I can't." Nettie was becoming angry. Being pulled down the street against her will brought back unpleasant memories of home and her rowdy brothers. She was tired and completely innocent.

"That's right, you women all hang together—everything for the common good. Selfless, stupid martyrs intent on ruining anyone's life who stands in your way."

"What's going on here?" inquired a distinguished-looking officer.

Harvey explained, "This lady broke Emmett's window."

"*I did not.*" Why was everyone here on a first-name basis? Nettie felt outnumbered and doubted justice would be done.

"Calm down now, lady. Let me explain to the chief," Harvey interjected.

"I'll be happy to explain," Emmett declared. "A bunch of temperance women blocked the door to my saloon. They broke the plate glass window in front—the big one with the lettering—and ran off. I caught this one. I'm filing charges. Arrest her."

The chief directed his next comment to the lady. "What is your name?"

A sudden dread came over Nettie. She could lose her job over this. "Nettie Gordon."

"Where is your husband? Can he come for you and clear this up?"

"I'm not married."

Emmett snorted, "That figures."

"Are you employed, Miss Gordon?"

"I am. Listen, I was simply following along after the WCTU meeting, waiting for my friend so we could go home. I didn't break the window."

"Perhaps you'd like to provide the names of the other ladies? We could investigate and find out who broke the window," the chief suggested.

"I don't even know those women." Nettie watched as the chief's eyes fell on the incriminating sign she held.

"What about your friend?"

Although Eula certainly got her into this mess, Nettie was reluctant to turn her over to the authorities. "I don't believe she broke the window either."

"But you don't know for sure, do you?"

"I don't know who broke the window. I think it must have been accidental."

"You can't possibly believe this?" Emmett could not appear angrier. "Throw her in jail. I want my day in court!"

"Just because your brother-in-law is a judge doesn't mean you'll have your way, Mr. Boyd," noted the chief.

Nettie's eyes widened in disbelief. This monstrous man clearly had the entire legal system in his pocket. She grasped the fact she was in serious trouble. "I don't want to lose my position over this. I didn't do anything wrong. I was simply standing at the corner waiting for my friend." Remembering the white ribbon that stood for the temperance movement was pinned to her collar, Nettie could not think of a way to discreetly remove it.

"Unfortunately, there are damages. I'm certain

Emmett doesn't mean for you to lose your job."

This drew a loud snort of derision from the furious Emmett.

"Can you make reparation for the damages?"

"You're asking me if I have money to pay for the window? My savings are meager. I support myself. I'm a simple school teacher."

"Nonetheless, charges will need to be filed unless you find a way to replace the window or turn over the names of the women who did the damage. Emmett, isn't Faith due to have her baby soon?"

"What does that have to do with anything?"

"She won't be working in the saloon much longer. Maybe Miss Gordon here could work off her debt." It was difficult for the chief to determine who bore the most profound look of horror at his suggestion, Emmett or Miss Gordon.

"But I have a job. I haven't time to work at another job!" proclaimed Nettie.

"Then I'll need to charge you with vandalism."

"She doesn't know anything about working in a saloon. What good could she possibly be to me? Besides, if you let her go now, she might never show up."

The chief explained, "I think the last thing you need is for this lovely lady to become a martyr for her cause. I'm quite certain she is trainable. If she writes her personal information on a card for me, I'll keep it securely in my desk as insurance she won't make an escape like some bandit in the night."

In the end, it was agreed Miss Gordon would work off her debt at one dollar per day, every Saturday from noon to 10 p.m. Emmett would provide copies of the bills for the window and lettering. Any disputes would be settled by a less-than-eager Officer Harvey. As the chief forced the pair to shake hands on their deal, he made a mental note to grab a beer on Saturday afternoon about four o'clock.

* * *

Nettie stomped out of the police station into the damp night air. The fog had come in. It would undoubtedly be a cooler day tomorrow. As she crossed the street, she was surprised to find Eula waiting around the corner.

"Some friend you are!" Nettie spouted, her pent-up anger apparent.

"Who was that man?" gushed Eula.

"What man?"

"The handsome man who took you to the police station?"

"Are you insane? He wanted to file charges against me. I'll have you know I could be sitting in a cell right now awaiting arraignment for your little stunt."

"He was so tall and strong. Nettie, he's about the most wonderful man I've ever seen. His shoulders were broad and his muscles bulged against his shirtsleeves." Eula looked upwards as if she could gaze at the moon through the fog.

Nettie shook her head in disgust. "I want to go home." She headed down the sidewalk. Eula hurried after.

When Eula discovered Nettie would be working for the saloonkeeper, she wished she was less adept at abandoning the scene of the crime.

* * *

Nettie gave a ponderous yawn as she watched her class at recess the next day. By the time she got home and graded papers, there was little time for sleep. She was in no mood for Eula. This obvious fact did not stop her friend from offering a greeting and beginning an inquisition.

"What do you think would happen if I gave myself up to the police? It's only right I should share your burden."

"Funny, you weren't so eager to confess last night."

"I was in shock."

"I think you're being shallow, Eula. You simply want to flirt with that vile man. It's certainly odd how you changed from temperance fanatic to willing saloon employee overnight."

"I was thinking. It's not fair for you to suffer through this on your own."

"What a dear friend you've become."

"What was it like when he held your arm? Were your knees weak? Did you swoon? I think you should have collapsed into his arms. Oh, my, how would that feel?"

Nettie glared as Eula hugged herself and swayed at the thought of being held by the repulsive saloonkeeper. "You can save yourself from further fantasies. Someone named Faith works at the saloon and is about to have a baby. It appears the object of your desire is married and soon to be a father." Nettie was not surprised when Eula suddenly remembered she had a prior commitment and would not be able to help.

* * *

A reluctant Nettie made her way to the Golden State Saloon on Saturday. Purposely dressed in her most prim and plain white shirtwaist and black skirt, only her face was visible. The high stiff collar of her blouse was buttoned right up to her chin. Buttons fastened her long sleeves at the wrists. She wore plain cotton gloves. Instead of her normal, fashionable hairstyle, Nettie braided her hair and wound it into a bun at the base of her neck. She removed all ornamentation from an old straw hat. There was no telling what rough sorts she might run into today. She appeared matronly and prudish and planned to protect her honor by any means possible—even going so far as to secrete her small switchblade knife in her reticule.

First taking a deep breath, Nettie opened the front door of the Golden State and feeling much like a sacrificial lamb, walked inside. She looked around in wonder. The establishment was quite refined, not at all what she expected. Although the lighting was rather dim—the fact the front window was boarded up undoubtedly contributed to the darkness—it was obvious the saloon was well-kept. The dominant feature was a beautiful mahogany bar extending across the entire rear wall. Heavy tasseled drapes hung at the windows. The walls were paneled. As many as 20 tables occupied the large room. It appeared a few were being used by card players. A pleasant aroma emanated from a lunch buffet.

Her captor stood behind the bar talking to a blond woman. When he noticed Nettie, he scowled before walking through a door near the end of the bar. The blond woman, obviously with child, walked toward Nettie. She appeared to be in about as dour a mood as her husband.

"So, you actually came. Emmett imagined you gave a false address and never intended to work off your debt."

In the haughtiest tone she could muster, Nettie replied, "It remains to be seen if this is my debt or not. Nonetheless, I am an honest woman and I am here on behalf of the Women's Christian Temperance Union to put things right."

"I suppose you don't know a thing about serving drinks?"

"I did once have a job as a waitress. I don't imagine this could be much different."

"That's better than nothing, I suppose. Come along. We'll get you an apron."

Nettie trailed along to a back room where two girls conversed across a table. The pair turned in unison to view the new, if temporary, employee. Nettie beheld identical twins. The girls were beautiful, fair-skinned blonds with blue eyes. They were primly attired but not quite to the same degree as Nettie.

"You two better get to work," commanded Faith. The girls immediately rose from the table and, glaring at Nettie, walked into the saloon without a word.

Nettie rightly observed the people who worked at the Golden State Saloon were rather hostile. Her expression apparently betrayed her thoughts.

Faith scowled, "Don't expect to be making any friends. Everybody knows what you did—the reason you're here. Hope and Charity may be about your age, but they don't have any use for your views."

"Hope and Charity?" This was too much of a coincidence. "They're relatives of yours?"

Faith nodded, "My sisters. This is a family business. We don't take kindly to anyone trying to keep us from making our living." She threw an apron at Nettie and slammed an order tablet and pencil on the table. "I wanted you to work the side room, but Emmett wants you in front. There's a menu on the bar. You can take a look. Food orders go through the bar to the kitchen. Aside from the buffet, the menu usually has about five entrees, which vary from day-to-day. Liquor orders are filled at the bar. What are you waiting for? You said you were a waitress."

Nettie tied the strings of the white apron and placed the pad and pencil in her pocket. As Faith walked out, Nettie quickly took the knife from her reticule and placed it in her other pocket. It was difficult to tell from whom she might have to defend herself, the patrons or her fellow employees.

The Golden State was one of the few saloons in Los Angeles to serve cold beer. On a hot June day such as today, business was truly booming. Although she had to ask a few questions of the belligerent twins, Nettie caught on fast, quickly reconciling her current duties with past waitressing experience.

No sooner did the lunch crowd let up than preparations for the supper crowd began. Determined to do a good job so no one could complain and tack time onto her sentence, Nettie was on the verge of collapse once the patrons left the barroom promptly at ten. She left her dirty apron on the table in the "closet" as it was called, grabbed her reticule and started for the front door.

"Be here on time next week," growled the beast behind the bar, who had not seen fit to acknowledge her presence in any manner since she arrived, on time.

Nettie did not give him the courtesy of a reply but quickly exited the building and walked toward the trolley. Having not worked so physically hard in some time, it was all Nettie could do to stay awake so as not to miss her stop.

* * *

"What happened?" asked Eula. "What was it like? Were you accosted?"

"Hush, Eula. I don't want anyone to hear." Nettie escorted the last of her Sunday school students from her room. She had the youngest class, three- and four-year-olds, and considered teaching the small children a nice way to introduce herself to future classes at school. From long experience, Nettie understood young children were eager to discuss private and even intimate details of home life. She didn't want them inadvertently repeating anything that might spill out of Eula's mouth.

"What did you do? Were there any brawls? What about shootings? How much do you owe?"

"There was nothing of the sort," admonished Nettie. "It's quite a respectable establishment from what I can see. There are house limits on betting so the poker players take part in friendly games. It seems they don't abide obvious drunkenness. Some men were rather loud, but that was the extent of their rowdiness. The window has not been repaired. I don't know how many weeks I'll be working. At least school will be out this week."

Nettie loved summertime ever since she was a little girl. Seemingly endless days stretched to a vague hint of productivity in the distant future. She enjoyed not knowing what day it was or what time, eating when she was hungry, sleeping when she grew tired. The only drawback since she was on her own was her lack of income. It was always a challenge to save enough to pay her room and board for those three months. No matter how diligently she prepared, how carefully she budgeted, the strain of making ends meet often troubled the glorious season. Nettie considered obtaining some temporary position, but what was the point of summer if one had to work? Now the trolley fare to the saloon would eat into her savings.

Although it was some distance, she considered riding her bicycle to the Golden State. She would have to be extra careful coming home. Reckless automobile drivers made navigating the roads of Los Angeles a challenge. The busy streets were a maze of trolleys, wagons, motor cars, trucks and horses. Attempting the roads at night might prove her undoing.

* * *

As a breathless Nettie parked her bike and entered the front door of the saloon, Faith grabbed her arm and directed her to the "side door," which was apparently where ladies, or ladies accompanied by gentlemen, could imbibe their own spirits. Not allowed in the main saloon, women were provided an identical experience. This was Faith's domain or at least it was up to now. She tended bar. Nettie noticed when Hope and Charity abandoned their posts in the main saloon last week, they were busily taking orders in back.

This Saturday, the Golden State was hosting a dance in the lady's area. It appeared a crowd was expected. Tables and chairs were tightly squeezed around the perimeter of the room. A band was setting up on the small stage.

"You did all right last week," admitted Faith, begrudgingly. "I need you to tend bar back here today. I have to leave for a while, but I'll be back. Emmett doesn't like the twins to tend bar." Faith paused to observe her captive employee. "I suppose you have moral qualms about serving liquor?"

"No, I certainly delivered enough drinks last week. This is no different."

"I thought you believed alcohol consumption was taboo, as if it were the 11th commandment—Thou Shalt Not Drink?"

"As I explained to Mr. Boyd when he dragged me to the police station, I accompanied my friend the evening the window was broken. I had nothing to do with it and doubt the other ladies caused the window to break, at least not intentionally."

"But you were at the meeting?"

"Yes, but I rather dislike when someone assumes they understand my opinions. I can assure you, I am not offended by someone taking a drink. I would be drummed out of my church for such an attitude—it's a German Lutheran church. Germans love their beer, although it seems hard liquor is the focus of the movement."

"Oh, I wondered why you were so afraid of losing your position over being arrested but not by working in a saloon."

Everyone here certainly seemed to know Nettie's business. "I'm not exactly working here. It's not as if I applied for a job or am being reimbursed. I consider it my contribution toward the charitable works of the WCTU."

Faith grimaced but quickly put her mind to the task at hand. After a brief 15-minute introduction, Nettie was the temporary manager and bartender of the side door at the Golden State Saloon.

CHAPTER TWO

Nettie found working behind the bar less taxing than being a waitress. For the first time, she had an opportunity to observe her surroundings. This was a side of life she'd never seen. Only a few couples ordered food. Most shared a beer and danced the evening away. Perhaps the crowd was a bit noisier than they might be at a church social, but they seemed to be having a wonderful time.

She viewed what appeared to be a lover's spat, which could occur anywhere. As the evening progressed, Nettie sensed a lack of inhibition. The dancers were definitely not as sedate as couples from church. She considered the possibility she was being lured into a life of sin and evil but quickly pushed the idea aside. After all, she would only be here until the window was paid off. What could it hurt to enjoy the music and observe a different way of life?

The saloon closed promptly at ten, to the disappointment of the dancers. Nettie wiped down the bar top one last time, returned her apron to its spot in the closet, grabbed her reticule and headed for the front door. At least she had sufficient energy to ride her bicycle home.

"Wait there," commanded the beast as he grabbed paperwork off the bar and walked swiftly toward her. "I have the bills for the window and lettering."

Nettie noticed the window complete with stained glass frame was replaced when she arrived. The lettering had not been accomplished. After viewing the totals on the two bills, her mouth dropped at the staggering sums.

"Is the window made of gold?" Her comment dripped in sarcasm.

"My father had that window made 20 years ago. I see no reason to settle for anything less."

"It will take me forever to pay this off!"

"I thought you were a teacher. I'm certain the mathematics do not translate into 'forever.' I'm crediting you a dollar a day for your services—certainly a decent wage for a woman. I'm being generous."

Nettie saw no point in arguing. She turned on her heel and marched out the door.

"Be on time next week," shouted the beast as she slammed the door.

Fury at the man's comments made for a quick ride home.

* * *

A thought took root in Nettie's mind. Perhaps a few of her precious summer days might be forfeited in payment of her debt. Determined to request more time at the saloon, Nettie decided to ask Faith to intervene. Although not friendly, the woman had been civil.

The next Saturday afternoon as Faith headed for the closet, Nettie saw her opportunity and quickly followed. She was surprised to find the older woman sitting at the table with her head down, crying softly. Nettie froze in place not knowing what to do. Faith looked up. Her cheeks were ruddy and damp. She wiped her face with the back of her hand and made as if to rise from the table.

"I'm sorry, I should have knocked," offered Nettie. "Don't get up on my account."

"Why on earth would you? No one knocks on that door."

"You stay here, I'll leave."

"I wish you'd stay. Have a seat."

Feeling entirely awkward, Nettie obliged.

"I can't talk to anyone about this. My husband doesn't understand." Nettie regretted having left her post as Faith waved her hand. "This place means the world to me."

"Why?"

"It's where I grew up. My father was a brewer. This saloon was his dream. My mother worked alongside him and us kids helped out from the time we were able. The Golden State means family to me, happy times, sad times, all shared memories. I want my baby; don't misunderstand. It's just that I won't be coming here anymore. This part of my life is over. The friends I have, my customers—my husband becomes quite furious when I try to explain. He thinks I should be happily devoted to our marriage and now, our family. He can't comprehend my feelings."

"But he works in the saloon too. Surely he sees how important this is to you?"

"What are you talking about?"

"Your husband, Emmett."

"Emmett's not my husband. I'm married to Judge Thompson. Emmett is my brother."

Nettie suddenly realized there was a family resemblance. Faith was an older version of Hope and Charity. Emmett shared their blue eyes, although his hair was a darker blond. There were definitely facial characteristics in common: the general shape of the nose and eyebrows. She'd been a fool not to see it, but then she avoided Emmett Boyd like the plague. She remembered a comment from the police station. It was Emmett's sister who was married to a judge.

"You really grew up here?" inquired Nettie once her thoughts were in order. Nettie handed Faith a handkerchief she kept in her pocket as the ladies took a seat.

"I know it doesn't seem conventional. I helped my mother in the kitchen then waited tables when I was 16. My older brother, Webster, and I had the best times. We were so close when he worked here too."

"What happened to Webster?"

"Oh, he developed a different career as an accountant. He's married and has three children. He still keeps the books for the saloon. We don't see much of him otherwise. He shows up for family dinners on Sunday once in a while. I miss him. I'm going to miss everyone." At this, Faith's waterworks began anew.

"It's not as if I'm moving away. The Judge's house is only a block from here. That's how I got to know him. He always came here for meals. It took him years to convince me he was earnest about marriage. I made him promise I could continue to work. He didn't take me seriously. The Golden State has been a source of conflict ever since we married. It's been five years already so you can imagine his delight when a baby came into the picture. He imagines his home life will now be all he ever dreamed."

"I'm sure you can come and visit once your baby is old enough." Nettie was beginning to think this outburst was more about overactive maternal emotions than anything of real concern. "I imagine you'll be so in love with your little one, this won't matter as much to you."

"Do you think so?" Faith seemed completely surprised at this suggestion.

"Of course! Why don't you go home and lie down for a while? I can manage here by myself. Maybe you're simply tired. When is the baby due?"

"In August, we think."

"You should be taking care of yourself. Tell your brother you can't work these long hours." This seemed the perfect opening. "I could fill in for you—work more days to pay off my debt. School is over now."

Faith nodded her head thoughtfully. "I don't care what Emmett says, you are a dear girl." Rising from the table, Faith walked determinedly to the main saloon.

Before the day was over, Nettie received a written note from the man in charge indicating she could work Wednesday, Thursday and Friday from 11 a.m. to 10 p.m. Wages for weekdays were somewhat lower, 75 cents a day. She was invited to initial the note and return it if she agreed to the terms. Frowning at her prospective remuneration and feeling she had little choice, Nettie applied a neat N.G. and returned the note by way of one of the twins.

The girls never styled their hair identically or wore the same clothes, but Nettie could not tell them apart. If one happened to say the other's name, Nettie took note of that twin's attire or hairstyle and so could call them by name for the day. Otherwise, she was at a loss.

As she walked out the front door that evening, Mr. Boyd called her back.

"Miss Gordon, I need a word." Nettie reluctantly approached the bar. "I forgot, next Tuesday is the Fourth of July. I would appreciate if you could work. It will be busy. Perhaps we could substitute another of the days you wangled out of my sister if that's too many."

"It won't be necessary. I can add Tuesday to my

Jean Jegel

workweek. What are my wages for the Fourth?"

"Seventy-five cents for weekdays."

"But this is a holiday and you said you'll be busy. I think I'm entitled to Saturday wages. I will work for a dollar on Tuesday, nothing less."

Her comment drew a dark scowl from the beast. "Very well," was his only reply.

"Perhaps I need some sort of written confirmation. Please give me an initialed note detailing our agreement." She stood by while Emmett angrily grabbed a receipt from a tablet and scrawled his initials on the back with 7/4/1905 and $1. He slid the slip of paper across the bar. Nettie picked it up to scrutinize it carefully before walking out the door.

* * *

"Nettie, why on earth did you agree to work? Just look at the *Herald*. Almost the entire paper is dedicated to activities for the holiday. Abbot Kinney's Venice of America Resort opens today. We could have gone! I want to see the canals. Too bad we don't have money to invest. We could buy one of those properties and live right on a canal. Look, the Cabrillo Hotel and the auditorium are open on the pier." Eula shook her head in disgust. "The beaches are going all-out to celebrate. There are fireworks, a camera obscura, even shooting galleries. To think I'll miss out on all this."

"I'm the one who will work the day away; I don't know what you're complaining about. If you have money to go to the beach, why don't you go? Where are your friends from the Anti-Saloon League and the WCTU? Oh, wait. Mr. Kinney made his money in tobacco, didn't he? Your cohorts would undoubtedly find the need to protest and might break windows. Then you'd be in the same hot water as me." Nettie chose to change the subject as she sipped the tea she brought up to her room. "Isn't there anything else of interest in the paper?"

"Not much," declared Eula. "There's a story about a beautiful woman, a fine cook, Mattie Ayres, from Lone Star, Texas. At 33, she has been widowed eight times, can you imagine? Her husbands' graves are all lined up at the same cemetery. She has a new husband of two weeks. I wonder how long he'll last? How could a body even manage to keep them all straight? Perhaps men are pretty much alike anyway. Maybe there really isn't much difference from one to another."

"I'm pretty sure they're all completely alike."

"How would you know? Every time a man comes around, you turn cold as a fish."

"Experience. I have five brothers, remember? I want nothing whatever to do with men. I can't imagine any woman being stupid enough to marry more than once. How did they die?"

"Shootings, consumption, old age. A tree fell on one of them. Oh, here's a tale of the tragedy of drunkenness. A Nellie Irwin filed for divorce. Her drunken husband tried to stick his daughter's head between the spokes of a wagon. There's a litany of abuse of his family by his hand. He broke his wife's nose; has beaten his children. He threatened to bash his wife's head in with a shovel!

"You can't be too careful in that saloon, Nettie, having all those drunks around. You better watch out for yourself. I will do nothing but worry about you today. Look here, though. Mrs. Irwin won her divorce. She has custody of her children and all of the property was turned over to her. That wouldn't be the case in most cities in this country. Los Angeles is a fair place for women to live."

Nettie turned her attention out the window toward the park as Eula rambled on. It was beautiful outside. The beach would be a temperate and exciting place to be. But she had an obligation to meet and few funds to support a trip to the shore. Sighing heavily, Nettie resigned herself to her fate but decided to treat herself to the street car on this hot summer day.

* * *

Because Faith had not made an appearance since she left for home last Saturday, Nettie was quickly put in charge of the side door saloon. She took up her position behind the bar and worked frantically. It seemed every woman in Los Angeles was eager for a cold beer to celebrate the nation's birthday. Many purchased beer to take home. From the noise in the main saloon, Nettie assumed business was equally brisk up front. Normally, there was a lull between the lunch and suppertime customers, but not today. Startled, Nettie looked up to find a radiant Faith standing on the other side of the bar accompanied by a tall, slender, older man. His arm was wrapped protectively around Faith's ample waist.

"Two beers, please, ma'am," requested Faith, who then gazed lovingly at her husband.

"Coming right up," responded Nettie, who promptly poured two mugs of beer and passed them over the bar. "No charge for soon-to-be parents on holidays," she teased.

"Judge, won't you save us a table? I want to talk to Nettie for a minute." Then more forcefully, Faith yelled across the room, "Charity, come tend the bar while I have a word with Nettie."

Charity has the lace cuffs today, noted Nettie. Hope had the braid around her head. She walked around the end of the bar and was surprised when Faith took her arm and led her into the closet.

"Have a seat. You look like you could use a respite. Oh, you should have poured a beer for yourself."

"No, it's all right. I'm not particularly fond of the taste of beer."

"Have you tried Emmett's beer?"

"What beer is that?"

"Why, the beer we serve. My father was a brew meister; Emmett learned the craft from him. He brews all the beer here. It's one of the reasons we have such loyal customers. Of course, it doesn't hurt that we serve our beer cold. The food is a big draw, as well. Even though our menu is limited, Marcel is a fine chef. There are other reasons our business is so brisk."

"I have nothing to use for comparison. Yours is the only saloon I've ever been in."

"You've seen how many uniformed gentlemen come in. They know our place is not rowdy. Policemen and sheriffs can relax and enjoy a beer or two without disturbance. Officials regularly come here from the courthouse. We have a peaceful clientele. The gambling limits keep riff-raff out for the most part. And then Emmett, like our father before him, keeps a close eye on what goes on. He's always been protective of his sisters. Customers know they will be promptly ejected if they don't behave. It's too bad saloon owners are being squeezed out."

"What do you mean?"

"It started almost ten years ago. It's becoming difficult for saloons to make a profit. First the city passed licensing laws. They greatly restrict our hours. We can't sell liquor at all on Sundays; we have to close by ten. There's a $13 a month fee for our license, paid to the police department. Not all establishments selling liquor are forced to pay the fee—restaurants for example. It's daunting.

"Now the citizenry is calling for stricter enforcement. At first, my father refused to pay the license fee. He claimed it was un-American for the government to single him out for what is essentially a tax or to tell him how to run his business. He was furious. He was a mild-mannered man but became so angry over what was being done to his livelihood, I believe it caused his heart to fail.

"The big breweries started running their own saloons. They have huge facilities and sell their wares at discount prices. All five of us are paid a salary for the time we put in here, according to our talents. For instance, I get extra for managing the ladies' saloon, Webster gets a salary for keeping the books. Then we split the profits five ways. Those have gone down drastically.

"The temperance organizations are taking a toll on business, as well. A day hardly goes by that their viperous accusations aren't featured in the papers." At this, Faith's eyes grew wide. "I'm sorry, I hope I didn't offend you. This is not what I meant to talk about."

"Everyone has a right to their opinion. Why did you want to talk to me?"

"To thank you. It made a world of difference for me to relax and stay home. As you can see, the Judge is quite happy at this turn of events. The twins ran the bar yesterday. They dislike working in back, they'd rather earn drinks as waitresses."

Nettie noticed the male customers in the front saloon often bought drinks for the twins. She'd seen the two girls—who evidently had quite a tolerance for spirits—tip their shot glass at a customer and down their whiskey.

"Your sisters seem to enjoy their alcohol."

"What?" Faith tried to decipher Nettie's comment then laughed. "Oh, it's not whiskey they drink. Heavens, we wouldn't be able to keep them from falling down drunk. Emmett keeps colored sugar water behind the bar in an old whiskey bottle. When a customer offers to buy a drink, the girls pocket the money and drink the fake whiskey. It amounts to making tips, but that practice is disparaged.

"Anyway, Emmett doesn't like them to tend bar. He can't keep an eye on them when they're in back. He certainly never minded when I did it. He'll have to get over that. We need to hire more help. I so appreciate you filling in. I can't tell you how much this means to me, but I better get back to the Judge. He was eager to please me by coming here today." After pushing herself away from the small table, Faith impulsively hugged her new friend. "Thank you again!"

Nettie watched through the doorway as Faith joined her husband. She felt a twinge of guilt at letting Faith believe the added workdays were for her benefit alone. She needed to be honest next time they chatted.

Nettie considered the way the twins teased and charmed their customers. This evidently resulted in the rather dishonest practice the girls used to make extra money. Tipping was frowned upon in general. There were those who thought the custom anti-capitalist. It was outlawed in several states. She rarely received a tip when she was a waitress. Nettie wondered if she might make extra money if she was a bit less rigid. Deciding to grab a bite to eat before she returned to her post, Nettie walked toward the kitchen. She might not be making the most of her entitlement to meals at the boarding house, but Faith was right. Chef Marcel was a wonderful cook and employees could eat all they wanted or, at least, all they had time for.

* * *

It became apparent the saloon was not as busy during the week. For the first time since she started at the Golden State, Nettie managed a conversation with Marcel in the kitchen. The older man emigrated from France. He apparently had an unfortunate tendency to drink too much, thus his attraction to the saloon. He took a great deal of pride in his work, however, and saved his drinking for after 8 p.m., when the kitchen closed. For a chef, he seemed rather slender to Nettie. His black hair was liberally flecked with gray. He kept a picture of a woman near his stove but changed the subject when Nettie inquired about her.

Bao Hang also worked in the kitchen. His father came from China to work on the railroads 30 years prior. Bao was a native Californian, proud of his heritage and the land where his family made their home. He seemed happy in his work, doing dishes and acting as assistant cook. Evidently Mr. Emmett paid well. Most Chinese found it difficult to earn a decent wage in Los Angeles. Nettie had witnessed the rampant anti-Chinese sentiment. She was constantly astounded by the words and actions of supposedly Christian people.

The sound of Bao and Marcel yelling at each other in their respective ancestral languages often wafted from the kitchen. Neither understood the other during these frequent outbursts yet somehow, the kitchen functioned perfectly.

The only other saloon employee was Charlie, who played the upright piano in the main saloon. The quiet negro man kept to his music. Nettie learned his wife and sister-in-law worked as cleaning ladies for the saloon and the Boyd household, which was located somewhere across the alley.

On Thursday night near closing time, Nettie paused

to watch Charlie play. As he finished his rendition of *Sweet Adeline*, Charlie greeted her.

"You like the music, Miss Nettie?"

"Very much. You play beautifully. I'm especially fond of the rags."

"Do you play?"

"I never had the opportunity to learn."

"I seed you tapping your foot when you wait on tables. You sing?"

"Not well, although my students seem to think I do."

"I heared you's a teacher. I'd like you to sing for me."

Somewhat nervous at the thought of singing in the saloon, she recognized the opening chords of *Meet Me in St. Louis, Louis* and she began to sing. Nettie's sweet, clear voice drew the attention of the few remaining patrons, but she didn't notice. She focused on the piano and Charlie's encouraging smile. Nettie was surprised at the appreciative round of applause and blushed quite charmingly before hurrying off to clear glasses from empty tables. She failed to notice the severe glower of the beast behind the bar.

* * *

Taking extra care with her clothing and hairstyle on Saturday morning, Nettie performed a self-appraisal in her mirror. Her hairstyle was the height of fashion—full and softly luxurious tresses were pulled into loose curls on top of her head. She wore her favorite shirtwaist with full sleeves. A line of gathered lace made a deep V-shaped pattern over the shoulders to the waist both on the front and back. Nettie wore her best blue plaid skirt. She might not be a beauty but was determined to earn her trolley fare in drinks today.

Assigned to waitress in the front while the twins ran the side door—an experiment in personnel placement—Nettie's friendlier-than-usual smile and fervent attempts to converse with customers did not produce a single drink offer. She understood the regulars enjoyed having the beautiful and gregarious twins perform the waitressing duties. Her attempts undoubtedly paled in comparison.

Nettie's enthusiasm waned as the afternoon turned to evening. After five straight days of work, she tried to focus on the dent she'd made in her debt and the next three days when she could do as she liked.

She noticed Emmett disappear into the lady's saloon—a frequent occurrence. Faith was evidently correct in her belief her brother did not trust the twins. Stopping to see if anyone at the back poker table was interested in another drink, Nettie grew alarmed when a hardened-looking customer grabbed her wrist.

"My luck's runnin' bad here, tootsie. I'll buy you a drink, but I need a good luck kiss. What do you say?" He pulled her toward his face and was stunned when Nettie smacked him soundly on the cheek. He did not let go. "That ain't very friendly."

The man pulled more forcefully. Prepared to defend herself, Nettie curled her fingers around the knife in her pocket when a deep voice behind her uttered, "Slow down there, Teddy. You'll have to leave now; you know the rules."

As Teddy released Nettie's wrist, she backed right into Emmett Boyd's broad chest. He moved her to the side, evidently intent on having a clear shot at his annoying customer.

"C'mon Emmett, it ain't like she's one of your precious sisters. Give a man a chance here."

"Get up Teddy. It's time to go."

Nettie, holding her wrist, looked on as a disgruntled Teddy picked up his few remaining chips and glowering, headed for the door. This seemed the prudent thing to do since Mr. Boyd had at least 30 pounds and a good four inches on the lanky Teddy. Nettie never really took note of Emmett's appearance aside from the day she realized his family resemblance to his sisters. She scrutinized him now as he saw to it Teddy left the saloon.

Emmett Boyd was a muscular man, at least six feet tall. He was immaculately attired in a striped shirt, white collar, bow tie and braces. She knew he sometimes wore a vest. His shoes and spats were the latest style. He had a square chin and was clean-shaven. Mr. Boyd cut a dashing and intimidating figure and had apparently seen fit to rescue her. She was somewhat surprised when he took her arm and forcefully guided her behind the bar as if she was in some sort of trouble.

"What have you got in your pocket?"

Nettie, fearing the man would not hesitate to put his hand in her pocket if she answered untruly, quietly pulled out her switchblade and opened her palm to show him. Emmett took the knife and released the blade then closed it and handed it back without a word. As Nettie returned to her duties, she heard, "I don't want to lose any more customers because of you."

A flood of retorts came instantly to Nettie's mind. Mr. Boyd's own sisters flirted outrageously. She did nothing wrong. She certainly hadn't led anyone on. Angrily, Nettie cleared the empty tables and left abruptly at 9:45.

Every head turned as Nettie slammed the door on her way out. All faces then turned back toward Emmett who announced, "Lights out in 15 minutes, fellas. You'll have to come on up if you want a refill."

He hid a smile as he wiped the bar down. Expecting

tears and hysterics, Emmett was impressed with Miss Gordon's deliberate reaction. The woman was actually willing to draw a knife in her own defense. If all temperance women were so prepared and self-reliant, he had a bigger fight on his hands than he ever imagined.

* * *

Nettie shook Pastor Arndorfer's hand as she exited the front of the church. "Wonderful sermon this morning, Pastor."

"Glad you enjoyed it, Miss Gordon. I need a brief word. I didn't have a chance to make an announcement at the service, but I expect the new vicar will arrive today. I was hoping to introduce him to our staff over supper. Naturally, Mrs. Arndorfer will be there. I was hoping you and Miss Stohr might join us."

"I can't speak for Eula. I haven't seen her this morning, but I'd be delighted to attend. Can I bring anything?"

"Well, I'd be lying if I didn't hope you might bring one of your delicious chocolate cakes," the pastor replied rather sheepishly. "It would surely help my wife. The baby is due in September and I did rather spring this meal on her out of the blue. If it isn't too much trouble?"

"Surely not." Nettie hoped her reply seemed heartfelt. Spending the hours between Sunday school and supper in Mrs. Green's hot kitchen was not the day she planned. "Maybe we can discuss the call list for the new third- and fourth-grade teacher while we're together."

"An excellent suggestion, Miss Gordon, as always," praised Pastor Arndorfer. He smiled his most engaging smile. His agenda for the supper table had nothing to do with teaching or preaching. There was an ulterior motive in his invitation.

* * *

Faith invited her family for supper on Sundays after church. It was the one chance they had to be together without the constant distraction of work. Having no desire to venture as far as the Golden State, Faith was firmly ensconced in her home of late. Even Webster was coming today although his wife made other plans for herself and the children.

Never comfortable with the role of lady of the house, Faith began to fill those shoes more confidently. She realized running the Judge's household was not so different from running the bar. Work needed doing and she was not in any condition to do it herself. If the cook and housekeeping staff were at all miffed by their mistress's sudden bold commands, they had the good sense to keep it to themselves. The Judge's reputation for generosity equaled that of the Boyd family.

As always happened when Webster joined them, everyone was eager to catch him up on the latest gossip and news from the Golden State. A modicum of business was discussed: rising expenses; ideas to draw in a bigger crowd during the week; how the free lunch menu might be enhanced; even the possibility of building one of the new and popular bowling alleys, which would require a major renovation of the saloon. Then the conversation turned to the temperance movement.

"I tell you Webster, we have one of the enemy amongst us," offered Emmett.

Webster glanced around the table, appalled at the thought any Boyd would sell out their own flesh and blood.

"Not here, you ninny," laughed Hope. "A woman from the WCTU broke the front window and Emmett caught her."

Charity continued, "She's working off her debt by waitressing."

"And tending bar," noted Faith. "Is this entirely legal, Judge? Nettie swears it wasn't her who broke the window."

"Leave me out of this," noted the Judge. "You know I don't like to get involved in the workings of the Golden State. I'm an innocent bystander trying to enjoy my meal." At this, the Judge lowered his head and shoveled a forkful of peas into his mouth.

"So, let me get this straight. You captured some temperance woman so intent on causing ruin that she actually broke a window and you're letting her wait tables and serve liquor? I think I need to come by and see this. Does she wear a white ribbon and carry a sign around the saloon? Is she some sour-faced old maid who preaches the gospel to customers? Do you have to lock her in the closet at night to keep her there? She must be scaring away more customers than she serves." Webster laughed at his own ideas.

"Nettie is no such thing," defended Faith. "I like her. She didn't break the window, having merely accompanied a friend who belongs to the WCTU. She was a completely innocent bystander and quite good looking as a matter of fact. Nettie is a teacher."

"I don't know what you see in her," complained Emmett. "She's nothing but trouble. I'm anxious for her to pay off her debt so she can be on her way. I lost a customer last night because of her. I'm quite certain Miss Gordon is busily confessing her sins this sabbath day. After all, she's now a party to drunkenness. I don't trust her."

"Well, I do and you should, too. Nettie is a decent, honest woman and has been doing an excellent job. You know I'm right and she isn't even getting paid. The

Judge and I owe her a debt we can only hope to repay before her service ends." This drew a warm smile from the Judge.

"She's probably a spy plotting to cause us ruin at her first opportunity," Emmet replied. "Your proper Miss Gordon was ready to stab a patron last night."

"That's ridiculous!"

The twins traded knowing looks. Perhaps this woman who fell into their midst was more interesting than they assumed. Anyone who put their older siblings at odds deserved immediate attention.

CHAPTER THREE

Vicar Haf seemed to be making friends with everyone in sight, save for Mrs. Arndorfer. To Nettie, that woman appeared to be on her last legs. The pastor's wife was normally a busy and efficient leader of her husband's parish. She taught third- and fourth-grade students and played the organ. She belonged to all the women's groups at church.

The fact she was soon to have a baby made the hot day a challenge. The fact her husband did not notice was causing more distress than the pastor realized when he dumped today's activities on his unsuspecting wife. Once she arrived, Nettie did all she could to help in the strange kitchen. When a red-faced Mrs. Arndorfer appeared to lose control, Nettie implored her to go to the back porch, have a cold lemonade and put her feet up. Nettie offered to mash the potatoes. She assured Mrs. Arndorfer God would not give her more than she could handle, but it didn't pay to test her limits.

Eula remained completely unhelpful throughout. Miss Stohr obviously set her sights on the new young vicar. The entire house could have fallen down around her and she wouldn't have noticed.

At the last possible moment, the pastor impulsively

added several church elders and their wives to his guest list. Nettie frowned as she transported various serving dishes to the dining table. By this time, she would have preferred to join Mrs. Arndorfer on the porch. She was hot and the thought of a heavy meal was not appealing.

"Where is Mrs. Arndorfer?" inquired the pastor.

"She's cooling off on the porch. I'll tell her supper's on the table."

"Please do. I don't want the meal to get cold as we wait to give grace."

Being certain no one could see, Nettie rolled her eyes in disgust as she went through the kitchen. Men were rude, thoughtless oafs. Not one of them could do anything to change her opinion. She had nothing but sympathy for the expectant mothers who needed rescuing so frequently. She certainly never intended to be one herself. Nettie cringed at the sound of Eula's laughter.

Dinner went well enough. No one but Nettie seemed to notice Mrs. Arndorfer's discomfort. As Nettie rose to clear the dishes, she loudly demanded, "Eula, come help so Mrs. Arndorfer can rest."

Pastor Arndorfer seemed rather piqued at anyone taking his wife's place and so proclaimed, "My wife will take care of the dishes."

"No, she's not feeling well. Perhaps it would be helpful if you escorted her outside where she could enjoy the breeze. Come, Eula. *Now*."

The good pastor was not accustomed to being bossed around much less by a female congregant. His wife was the most meek and deferential woman he ever met. Taking a closer look, she did appear on the verge of tears. The idea he was rather imperious in his demands today briefly occurred to him. "Would you like to go outside, my dear?" he finally inquired.

Unable to reply, Mrs. Arndorfer nodded her head, obviously emotional as her husband excused them from the table and assured he would return immediately.

An overly eager Vicar Haf stood and also began to clear. At first, Nettie thought the man was trying to make a good impression on Eula, but it soon became apparent he had his eye on someone else.

Nettie felt rather ornery when she decided to praise the vicar for his helpfulness since Eula had proven disappointing.

"Vicar Haf, you are such an able-bodied assistant. I can't tell you how refreshing it is when a gentleman such as yourself pitches in and provides much needed help." Her goal had been to goad Eula; the reaction she got was wholly unanticipated.

"Oh, Miss Gordon, assisting you is nothing but my pleasure. I hoped all afternoon to have a word with you. I noticed how you stepped in to aid poor Mrs. Arndorfer. Do you think she's all right?"

"I think she's hot and tired. She'll be fine. I'm sure she'll appreciate the fact we cleaned up her kitchen. I must be certain to explain how you've helped." At this, Nettie acted entirely against her nature and turning from the sink, flashed a smile at the vicar. It was Eula's angry reaction she sought and received. The woman glared at Nettie while the vicar appeared to have died and gone to heaven. He seemed completely captivated by her smile. Nettie imagined he would not hesitate to jump to her every command and understood she was in uncharted waters. Never having led a man on in any way, Nettie could not imagine how to discourage him and undo her smile. Were men truly so gullible?

She attained only a modicum of success in avoiding Vicar Haf for the duration of the afternoon. When he offered to walk the two young ladies home, Eula jumped at the opportunity and attempted to monopolize the vicar's attention as they strolled to Mrs. Green's. Nettie lagged behind, but the vicar found ways to include her in conversation.

No sooner did the front door at Mrs. Green's close than Eula turned on her friend. "What do you think you're doing? You don't even like men. I was doing quite well until you decided to put your two cents in. Why did you have to spoil everything?"

"Why didn't you help? Are you blind? Could you not see you were needed? You were rude, Eula."

"You know what I think? I think you're still mad because I abandoned you at the protest. I can't help the fact you can't run. This is your way of getting even!"

"Perhaps I am still mad at you," admitted Nettie. The pair parted on the worst of terms as Eula stormed up the stairs.

* * *

Nettie spent the next few days doing exactly as she pleased. This was the way summer was supposed to be. There was no trace of Eula. Surprised at her feelings, Nettie was relieved. Her room at Mrs. Green's had long been her refuge. She never before realized how much Eula intruded on her privacy. It was with regret she bicycled to the Golden State on Wednesday.

Entering the closet, she found the twins seated at the table, eager expressions in place.

"Good morning, Nettie."

"How are you?" inquired the twin with the striped shirtwaist.

This was more congenial conversation than she previously had with either twin. Nettie grew suspicious. "I'm fine, how are you?"

"We're wonderful," declared the twin with the

brooch pinned to her collar. "Have a seat. Let me pour you some tea."

Nettie sat down and took the cup of tea, too confused to feel at ease. "Thank you. This is lovely."

The brooch twin smiled. "Since Faith is gone, we felt it would be nice to get to know you better."

"After all, we work together."

The twins took turns commenting, one simply taking over where the other left off as if they shared a single mind. Nettie looked back and forth between the speakers as she would players at a tennis match.

"Yes, and we ladies need to stick together."

"Especially since Emmett is planning on hiring another bartender to work in the side saloon."

"He avoids that room like the plague and he doesn't like us back there together."

"He never trusted us."

"He is much older than we are—seven years."

"He still thinks of us as children."

"We know what we're doing in back."

"Yes, the receipts have been fine."

"Then again, he doesn't have us to flirt with the regulars in the men's bar."

"At any rate, we don't like working the side door."

"We make better money in front."

"I'm sure Emmett is missing all the business we bring in."

"It's true the register was a bit short in back last Saturday."

"I think you put money in your pocket when it should have gone in the drawer, Charity."

Ah, the hint Nettie was waiting for. The brooch twin was Charity.

"But that brings us to our question."

"Yes, Nettie, is it true you nearly stabbed a patron

on Saturday night?"

"We are disappointed to have missed that."

Finally pausing for a response, the girls looked at the object of their inquisition.

"I didn't try to stab anyone. Your brother simply asked what I keep in my pocket after a patron was forward. Nothing really happened."

Charity gave a subtle nod toward her twin and began their joint conversation anew. "Emmett always makes it clear ladies are to be shown respect in the Golden State."

"It's why we have free run of the place."

"No matter how much we flirt, no one ever gets out of line."

"You mean not anymore."

"Well, there were a few times when we first started. Emmett threw someone out."

"He even hit a man once."

"It was quite thrilling."

"Emmett was a rather wild boy when we were young."

"Yes, he was always in trouble. Fighting, drinking."

"Our parents were still alive then."

"We were, what do you think, Charity, around 10 or 11?"

"Yes. Father really was at his wit's end."

"But then he taught Emmett to brew beer. That is his true calling, his real passion."

"The saloon is simply a venue to him, a reason to make beer."

"He has a warehouse next to our house where he works when he's not in the saloon."

"All Emmett ever does now is work."

"He is incredibly boring."

"If he hires a bartender, he might spend more time in the warehouse."

"We wonder what that will mean to us."

"We'll have to see. For sure, he'll completely avoid the side saloon."

"Yes, surely. He'll likely never marry."

Nettie was befuddled by this comment. "Why do you say so?"

"Because he never has a sweetheart; not a real one. He only has projects."

"What is a project?" Nettie, although she had no liking for her captor, couldn't help her curiosity at the twins' conversation.

"Oh, it's a woman who needs help. Maybe she's down on her luck; maybe her husband beat her up; maybe she's a hopeless drunk. Emmett has always been a sucker for a project."

"It never ends well."

"Some of the projects improve and move on; some worsen and disappear."

"Projects are not the way to catch a wife."

"Emmett will be stuck in the bar selling his beer until he's an old man."

"Emmett doesn't like you."

"But Faith thinks you're a humdinger."

"Oh, look Charity, it's time for work."

"Yes, Nettie, we better go. Why don't you come early tomorrow?"

"We have so much to talk about."

"We want to see your knife."

Nettie followed the twins out the door, her head spinning. She noticed Hope and Charity never spoke at the same time and never interrupted each other.

Walking to the bar to get her assignment for the day, Nettie had little choice but to ask the odious

Mr. Boyd. She realized if he communicated through Faith, she did the same. Since Faith was completely out of the picture, the two would have to address each other directly. Nettie had a bone to pick, at any rate.

Without looking up from his paperwork, Emmett commanded. "I want you to work the side door today."

Determinedly, Nettie began, "I've come to understand work behind the bar draws a higher rate of pay than waitressing."

"Have you now? And how did you come across this tidbit of information? Has my sister decided to serve as your advisor?"

"As a matter of fact, Faith mentioned it to me in passing."

"Did she? Well this is a moot point. I hired a gentleman to manage the side door. He starts tomorrow. I'll agree to a credit of an extra 25 cents for your work today."

Doubting she could do any better than the extra quarter, Nettie accepted. "Fine," Nettie muttered as she tied her apron. At least she wouldn't have to put up with the beast while she worked in back.

"By the way, the twins will be up here today. They've pilfered through the cash register in back enough for this month. You'll also have to waitress."

Nettie glared at the elaborate lettering on the front window, wanting very much to throw a rock through it herself. But then she would remain in bondage forever.

* * *

With a loving smile for the small students in her Sunday school class, Nettie held the door as they filed out. She was surprised to find Mrs. Arndorfer waiting anxiously outside.

"Nettie, I must speak to you. Can I come in?"

"Certainly." Nettie waved her unexpected guest through the door. "How can I help you?"

"I wanted to thank you for all your help last Sunday. I was overcome by the heat and my duties and I've come to realize I'm in over my head. I was wondering if you could help."

"How?"

"I hoped you might take my place at some of the church functions over the next few weeks. Anything you could do would be most appreciated. You can let me know what's going on. The pastor likes to keep his thumb on the pulse of the congregation through the ladies' activities. My participation is important to him. I'm just so tired and I'd like to stay home." Tears welled in the young woman's eyes. "You understand, the pastor is 12 years my elder. His first wife passed away long before we met. I'm afraid he is somewhat, well, out of touch with my needs right now. I don't want to disappoint him."

"I'd be happy to help if I'm able. I have certain other obligations I need to meet, but I'm available on Mondays and Tuesdays or early morning other days. Let me know what I can do." Nettie felt obligated to help, but in the back of her mind, she realized her dreams of summer rest and relaxation were all but gone. And she wouldn't have a dime to show for any of it.

* * *

The next few weeks proved grueling for Nettie. Daydreams of taking a train to the beach continually occupied her thoughts, not that she could afford it. She had not laid eyes on Eula since the day they met the vicar. Mondays and Tuesdays were spent at church, working with the quilting guild, attending the weekly meetings of the altar guild, pot luck and Sunday School committees. She rose early to complete chores for the pastor's wife. Flowers for Sunday service needed to be ordered at the florist. The church required inspection to make certain the janitor—who had a tendency to drink too much—cleaned sufficiently. The printer required approval for the Sunday bulletin. On Friday mornings, Nettie stopped by the pastor's house to give a full account to Mrs. Arndorfer. Unable to afford trolley fare, she was bicycling more than ever. Ravenous, she took every possible opportunity to "sample" Marcel's cooking.

The new manager, Delmar, proved affable enough. He flirted outrageously with his female customers, even when they were escorted by a male companion. He seemed happy to have his new job. Although he never appeared inebriated, Delmar sampled the beer at the side door as frequently as Nettie sampled the food.

The only time Nettie made an appearance in the main saloon was near closing time. It became her habit, at Charlie's urging, to join him for a song. She sang popular tunes of the day, old favorites like *After the Ball is Over* and even an occasional hymn. Her performance became a trademark of the Golden State and marked the closing of the bar.

Nonetheless, she was surprised when Mr. Boyd, with whom she had not shared a word in several weeks, approached the piano carrying sheet music.

"Try this," was his only comment.

Charlie placed the music on the piano and played a few notes as an apprehensive Miss Gordon reviewed the words. The bawdy song *You'll Miss Lots of Fun When You're Married* had, no doubt, been selected to embarrass her. It was an appropriate song for a saloon in any case.

Determined to perform with gusto, Nettie sang a

rousing rendition of the piece, which drew ample applause from the larger-than-usual Friday night crowd. Reluctantly, the men headed toward the door, shouting approval her way as they left. Nettie smiled warmly and waved farewell until the last man exited. Glaring at Mr. Boyd, she stuck her nose in the air and walked haughtily toward the closet to retrieve her things, certain she bested him at his tawdry little game.

* * *

Nettie stirred awake. It was already hot. Her skin glistened with perspiration. Glancing at the clock only to realize she'd overslept, she flew out of bed. Her intention had been to arrive early at the Golden State to assist with an inventory project that would have earned her an extra quarter for only an hour's work.

"Drat!" she uttered aloud. Nettie quickly braided her hair and pulled it into a tight bun on the back of her head after she managed to throw on her clothes. She ran downstairs and bicycled at top speed, darting in and out between automobiles, street cars and wagons. She almost hit a pedestrian threading his way between congested vehicles.

As she rode, Nettie struggled to concoct an acceptable excuse for her late arrival. In truth, an argument broke out amongst the ladies of the pot luck committee at their meeting Tuesday night. She never imagined mashed potatoes could cause such commotion. When Nettie finally extricated herself from the unpleasant scene, she found Vicar Haf waiting. He insisted on walking her home, dawdling all the way as he steered her rider-less bicycle. They stopped at the soda fountain where he bought her an ice cream, which she ravenously consumed since she forgot to eat dinner. As the vicar bid her good night, Nettie became alarmed at the turn of conversation.

"Miss Gordon, I have a request," he began.

Nettie wished only to climb the stairs and crawl into bed. There weren't enough hours in the day to help anyone else, in any case. "What is your request?"

"I wish to ask your family's permission to pay court to you. I thought it only right to let you know."

Nettie grasped for some response. "Vicar Haf, I hardly know you."

"That may be, but I want your family to understand my intentions are honorable. It wouldn't be appropriate for me to see you without permission."

"My family doesn't live in the city. I haven't seen them for many years." She sought to throw an obstacle in the vicar's path. "What about Eula?"

"I certainly don't want to undermine your friendship. Miss Stohr is a lovely woman but—"

"Yes, I don't want to cause any problems. It's my understanding Eula is quite fond of you. In fact, I believe you may have been leading her on, perhaps unwittingly. You're asking me to proceed in a manner that might cause dissention between me and my dearest friend—the best friend I ever had. I think we need to consider this more closely.

"Oh, my! It's certainly gotten late. I have an early morning tomorrow. Good night, Vicar." Nettie was through the doorway to Mrs. Green's before the man could utter another word. She fell asleep mulling plans to avoid the vicar until Eula managed to step up her game.

Breathless as she approached the back of the saloon, Nettie found a glowering Mr. Boyd leaning against the warehouse wall, arms folded, disgust apparent. "You're late."

"Not by much," Nettie argued as she leaned her

bicycle against the saloon wall and followed her tormentor into the hot warehouse. "And I'm *never* late, by the way."

"You can't say that anymore."

Nettie hung her hat on a peg near the doorway and turned quickly, intent on making up the time she missed. Every penny she earned put her closer to a normal life. She felt an unexpected dizziness at her rapid turn. Mr. Boyd stood nearby, an odd expression on his face. She gulped for air, trying to clear her mind and regain her balance when everything went dark.

* * *

Nettie came slowly awake. She was lying on something soft. It was not her bed. Putting her hand to her eyes, she felt the rough texture of some sort of wet, cold cloth and pulled it away. She looked up to find herself in unfamiliar surroundings. The ceiling was ornately trimmed in fine millwork. An elegant crystal chandelier hung above her resting place. She'd never been here before in her life. Her arms felt cool. She wore nothing but her chemise above her skirt. Her feet were bare. She twitched when a man's voice uttered, "Oh, you're awake. Good."

Her breath came in quick spurts as Nettie tried to sit up. "What's going on here?" she demanded. "Where are my clothes? Where am I?" but she groaned as dizziness returned. Mr. Boyd unceremoniously pushed Nettie's forehead with the palm of his hand to force her back onto the settee.

"It seems you are a victim of your sex's frailty. You fainted."

"I certainly did not," argued Nettie, although she understood something happened to her. She disliked the wicked smile on the beast's face.

"I assure you, someone fainted and it wasn't me. I believed your corset was too tight as is usually the case in these instances. Imagine my surprise when I found yours was not tightly laced at all."

Nettie put her hand to her stomach. "Where is my corset?"

"Oh, I took it off anyway. It appeared to me you were overly heated from your ride. Your face was red. You were out of breath. This was no doubt caused by your inefficient and untimely arrival. What did you eat for breakfast?"

"I think I forgot to eat breakfast."

"I see. What did you eat for supper?"

"I think I forgot that too. But I did have an ice cream last night."

"That sounds like just the thing to tide you over on your wild ride here," Emmett sarcastically replied. "I can only assume it was a wild ride if my observation of your reckless approach in the alley was any indication. Sloth is such a difficult obstacle. I assure you, time cannot be overcome, no matter how one might wish it to be."

Nettie placed her hands over her chest above the chemise. "This is entirely inappropriate."

"Nonetheless, you're in no condition to continue on your way. You have not only been late and caused harm to yourself, you've kept me from my work. I think there will be some charge connected to your lack of diligence."

"There will not! Help me sit up." Emmett pulled Nettie to a seated position. "Oh, I truly don't feel well," she admitted as she fell back on the settee.

"Stay put while I go across the alley and see what Marcel might have to offer. Here, keep the wet rag on your eyes. Heat stroke is no laughing matter. Besides, I can openly admire your figure if you aren't watching," Emmett mocked as he placed the rag back on her face. "I'll be right back."

Peeking from beneath the bottom of the washrag, Nettie assured the vile man was gone before closing her eyes.

Emmett returned to his parlor carrying a tray of food. As he placed it on the side table, he could not help but admire Miss Gordon's fine figure despite his resolve to act as a gentleman should. She did not respond at his entrance; her hands rested at her sides. She must have fallen asleep. At least he hoped she was asleep; he did not care to call a doctor.

"Miss Gordon. *Miss Gordon!*" he yelled.

"What?" Nettie fumbled with the washrag and decided to place it on her chest—extra coverage from prying eyes.

"I brought you something to drink and some light fare. I think you ought to take it easy. We certainly don't want to upset your digestion in the middle of my parlor." Emmett placed his hand behind her head and offered cold water. "Only a sip at first."

"But I'm thirsty."

"I'm sure you are, but you need to go slowly." In an inappropriately familiar manner, he sat on the edge of the settee beside her and continued to offer water. He rather enjoyed Nettie's outraged expression.

"How did I arrive in your parlor?"

"I caught you before you collapsed and carried you here." Her displeasure was plain to see. "You're welcome. Try a cracker. You needn't be surprised. I have three sisters and had more than my share of lady friends in my youth. Yours is not the first shoulder I have glimpsed." Unable to contain his insufferable tendencies, Emmett continued, "I must make certain of one thing. After all, you did faint. There isn't any chance you are with child, is there? I would call a doctor if necessary. I have a telephone in the house. We use the Home Telephone Company and can dial direct."

Nettie choked on her cracker. Crumbs went flying in every direction as she gasped for air. Struggling to rebut the insensitive question, she ineffectively attempted to form words.

Emmett laughed a rich, full laugh. "Here now," he offered. "Have another drink of water."

"I can assure you," Nettie struggled, "there is absolutely no chance of that. I was evidently hot and hungry. How dare you imply—"

"I wasn't implying anything." Laughter still sparkled in his eyes. "I was simply touching all the bases as it were. I'll leave you to relax for a bit. I'll pull the table closer and I want you to sip the water and try to eat what's on the plate. I told Marcel to keep it bland. I'll be back in a while and we'll arrange to transport you home."

"But I was going to make a dollar today."

"Not today, Miss Gordon. Your debt will remain unpaid for one extra day. The end is in sight, however. I think you will be paid in full before the summer is up. I'll have to recheck my calculations."

I have my own calculations thought Nettie to herself. Nonetheless, she did as she was told. After the water and food were gone, she drifted back to sleep.

* * *

Emmett's mother often called him a rascal in his youth. The moniker fit completely today; he would attest to it if asked. He found great pleasure in Miss Gordon's discomfort. Having left his charge to her rest, Emmett appeared at suppertime to deliver a second plate of food.

As she scarfed it down, he noticed Miss Gordon lost weight since she first came to the saloon. Startled at his sudden feeling of concern, Emmett urged her to finish her meal so he could take her home. She barely spoke and glared when he offered to help her into her clothing.

"I assure you, I am capable of dressing myself," she huffed.

"I don't know. You were entirely unstable earlier. I think it would be best if I stayed in the room to assure you don't collapse again."

"Then at least turn your back." Emmett turned to face the doorway. Nettie didn't notice him watching in the mirror hanging beside the door.

Taking Nettie's arm in jest to steady her as she walked, Emmett discovered she was still shaky and would otherwise never have accepted his gentlemanly gesture.

"Where are we going?"

"To the carriage house. I'll drive you home." She lifted an eyebrow as he helped her into his new, dark blue, 1905 Buick. It was the latest in automotive technology, his pride and joy.

"Have you never ridden in an automobile before?"

"I have not."

"Well, you're in for quite a treat," he bragged. After giving sundry scientific facts about his most prized possession, Emmett obtained her address, started his car and drove into the alley. He decided to inquire about Miss Gordon's health as she rode in silent condemnation.

"Is there some reason you haven't been eating properly?"

"I can't see how my eating habits concern you."

"True. But my customers are used to your caterwauling at closing time and I wanted to assure them you would be back in form tomorrow night. I hoped a good night's sleep and an adequate breakfast would put you in fine fettle. There isn't any reason for you to skip breakfast, surely? Assuming you can drag yourself out of bed on time. Perhaps I should drop by in the morning to take you for breakfast and drive you to work. We don't want you to be late again."

"Oh, my bicycle! I can't return without it. I haven't any money for the trolley!" Nettie's face turned red as she realized her inadvertent blunder. "I mean, I have an engagement in the morning—an errand for my church. I'll eat breakfast at my boarding house quite early."

"Then I'll pick you up after your errand. There's nothing like an early morning drive. Perhaps we can do the inventory tomorrow." Emmett attempted small talk but failed to garner a comment from his passenger, neither of a friendly nor contentious nature. He parked the car in front of Mrs. Green's boarding house and offered his hand to help Nettie down. In a most courtly manner, he escorted a still unsteady Miss Gordon to the door, tipped his hat and departed, having procured the address of the flower shop where his bonded servant would perform her church duty.

Nettie stood on the porch to assure Mr. Boyd drove away then opened the front door to find Eula racing upstairs. "Wait, Eula! I need to talk to you." But Eula quickly disappeared. Nettie was in no shape to bound up the stairs after her.

* * *

"Thank you for assuring I was awake this morning, Mrs. Green." Nettie lingered over a cup of tea after breakfast. It was early. No other boarders had come down. Her good night's rest worked wonders. She never noticed how tired and hungry she was.

"No trouble at all, dear. You are such an easy boarder, I didn't mind one bit." Mrs. Green peered over her own cup of tea. She usually sat alone at this time of morning before her work began in earnest. "Who was the handsome gentleman that brought you home yesterday—the one with the grand automobile? Your friend Eula took off like a shot when she spied you two through the window."

Quickly taking another sip of tea, Nettie considered her response. Riding around unchaperoned was entirely improper. "That gentleman gave me a summer job. I wasn't feeling well and he offered to drive me home." She decided some superfluous information might throw off suspicion. "It's a family business. I was quite enthralled since I've never ridden in an automobile before. Eula has been rather stand-offish lately. She thinks I've cornered the market on men for some reason. Can you imagine anything so ridiculous?"

Mrs. Green smiled without reply. She couldn't help but wonder if it was the car or the man who enthralled her young boarder. As fine as the car was, that was one good-looking man.

CHAPTER FOUR

As Nettie finished the order, she turned to see who triggered the bell above the door. Half expecting the beast to come sauntering into the florist shop, she was taken aback as Vicar Haf approached.

"What are you doing here?" Nettie could not hide her alarm.

Surprise at the greeting was apparent in the vicar's expression. "Well, they told me in the church office you come here on Thursday morning to finalize the altar flower order. I wanted to speak with you."

Nettie glanced nervously through the shop window to see if she could spot Mr. Boyd's Buick. "I haven't much time. It might be best if we spoke later. I need to finish my transaction and must be on my way. Perhaps we could talk on Sunday?"

"Oh, we're done here, Miss Gordon," offered the florist, much to Nettie's dismay. Couldn't anyone take a hint?

"Wonderful!" Vicar Haf led Nettie toward the door. "I'll escort you to your next destination and we can talk on the way." He opened the door and waved her through.

Emmett, parked across from the flower shop,

perused the newspaper while he waited for Miss Gordon to appear. He took interest when the shop door opened and a slender young man escorted his employee out of the store. Miss Gordon seemed quite nervous as she spotted him across the street. She pointed toward his automobile as she conversed with her companion. Stunned silence was the man's reaction. He glared at Emmett, who tipped his hat in reply. Mr. Boyd's unusually mischievous mood from the day before returned in full force.

As the man escorted Miss Gordon toward the Buick, Emmett climbed down and offered his hand. Nettie had no choice but to release the other man's arm to take his, much to the chagrin of what appeared to be her suitor.

"I think I need to make introductions," Nettie falteringly commented.

"It's not necessary," noted Emmett as he helped her climb in the car. After cranking the engine, he took his own place. Tipping his hat once again, Emmett smiled and wished, "Good day," to Miss Gordon's unhappy friend. For some reason, Emmett felt immense pleasure at the man's befuddled and disappointed expression.

"I'll see you Sunday," Vicar Haf frantically yelled as the car pulled away.

"What happens Sunday?" inquired Emmett.

"I don't think it's any of your business," replied a harried Nettie. How did her life become so complex? Summer was supposed to be a time of rest and regeneration. All she did was run from pillar to post trying to avoid unpleasantness.

"My, my, such a caustic reply when I'm only here to provide transportation in your hour of need."

"This is hardly my hour of need. You forgot to bring my bicycle when we left yesterday."

"*I* forgot?"

"Well, I suppose I forgot as well. I wasn't myself."

"Correct. It was your hour of need."

If the man wanted to bicker over semantics, she would let him have his way. Nettie sat in sullen silence while they rode to the Golden State as the beast whistled a lively tune. She would admit, she enjoyed riding in his automobile.

* * *

It was another blistering day, but not as extremely hot as Wednesday. Nettie dabbed her forehead with her handkerchief as she scanned the inventory list she compiled. All that remained was to add her totals. She did not understand why Mr. Boyd wanted all the barrels and equipment in his warehouse counted, but if Nettie made extra money, why question his methods? She was anxious to return to the saloon where the two-bladed electric ceiling fans cooled the bar. As she paused in her addition, Mr. Boyd approached.

"Are we done then?"

"Almost. I have a question. What is that bag hanging in the corner? Was I supposed to add it to my list?"

"No, no. It's a piece of equipment I use. I became interested in boxing when I was young. Although my participation in the sport was short-lived, I developed a talent for the striking bag. The barrels are heavy when they're full and there's rarely anyone to help move them. Punching keeps me fit." Emmett walked over to the bag and gave it a few licks to demonstrate.

It looked easy to Nettie. "I recall seeing a demonstration at a vaudeville show. Can I try?"

After upending a crate for his assistant, Emmett stood to the side. "Help yourself."

Nettie stepped on the crate and took a swing, not realizing how quickly the bag would come back at her. She was startled as Emmett stopped the bag before it hit her in the head.

"Perhaps it's not as easy as I thought. Why were you interested in boxing?" Nettie considered the idea of two grown men punching each other beyond stupidity.

"I had the chance to see Billy Shannon box when I was young. I thought it was thrilling, but thought it much less thrilling the first time I entered the ring and got hit."

"How intelligent of you. That's an unusual quality in a male."

"Why, Miss Gordon, you've paid me a compliment."

"It was unintentional, I assure you."

Her comment was met by the rich laughter she heard the day before. It was never her goal to amuse Emmett Boyd.

"I would hate to elevate your opinion of me in any way so let me assure you, I got in more than my share of fights on an everyday basis. I was the bane of my parents' existence for several years."

"Yes, that makes much more sense."

"My pleasure. Anything I can do to reinforce your dire opinions." But Emmett rather liked tormenting Miss Gordon. All the pressures of running the family business and keeping his sisters in line while fighting off regulations and attacks on his profession took a toll on his temperament. He considered ways to cause some mischief. It was a long while since he found anyone amusing.

* * *

After Delmar asked her to get change from the front,

Nettie made her way to the main bar to find an eager customer addressing Mr. Boyd.

"Sir, I am told you are the brother and head of house of the lovely twins who wait tables. Is my information correct?"

Suspiciously, Emmett replied with a simple, "Yes."

Taking a deep breath of relief, the man continued. "We wish to court your sisters."

"Who is we?" inquired Emmett as Nettie stood slightly behind him. Curiosity had the best of her.

"My brother and I."

"Where's your brother?"

"Oh, he's not here."

"So how do you know he wishes to court one of my sisters?"

"My brother and I are twins. The moment I laid eyes on your beautiful sisters, I knew we were well-matched. My brother will be thrilled when I bring him back tonight."

Emmett gazed across the room where Hope was determinedly shaking her head no. "Fill yer boots," replied Emmett. "I have no objections."

"Thank you, sir!" The man eagerly shook Emmett's hand. "This is a day we won't forget," he declared as he turned and exited the Golden State.

At first Nettie thought the man meant he and Emmett, but she quickly surmised the "we" was the man and his twin. She would give anything to be in the main bar when the pair showed up tonight. After gathering her change, Nettie turned to leave as the twins descended upon their brother. Knowing the three shared the house across the alley, she could not recall ever having seen them converse. Their bond appeared more non-existent than acrimonious. She believed that was about to change.

Jean Jegel

* * *

As the dinner rush commenced, Nettie was thrilled when Emmett explained she would replace the twins in front and Delmar would handle the side door. She understood the twins had walked out after a loud and bitter argument.

Nettie was completely stunned as she turned at a tap on her shoulder. Before her stood two men, identical in every respect. They were of average height, about her own age with dark hair, blue eyes, handlebar mustaches and long sideburns. The twins wore identical clothing: brown suits and vests; bowler hats, white shirts, and matching blue bow ties. Even their shoes were identical. They each carried canes and individually would have looked quite dapper. Together, they seemed more a spectacle.

"Could you help us, miss?"

"We came to see the twins who work here."

"Would you mind getting them for us?"

Oh, no, thought Nettie. They even speak as twins. "I believe they've gone for the day. Did they know you were coming?"

"Did you ask them, Harold?"

"Well, I asked their brother."

"You simpleton. They didn't know we were coming."

"They have left for the day."

Although sorrow was apparent, Nettie had the undeniable desire to giggle. "Why don't you gentlemen have a seat and I'll see if I can find out when the girls might return. Can I get you a beer?"

"Splendid. My name is Harold."

"And mine is Lawrence."

"You can call us Larry and Harry."

Nettie bit her lip, afraid to say anything further lest

- 63 -

she burst out laughing. Emmett walked beside her while she placed two mugs of cold beer on her tray.

"Your future brothers-in-law are disappointed. They want to know when their lady loves will return. Do you have any idea?"

"I imagine they'll be back tomorrow. The lure of tips will be too much for them to resist. No doubt, they'll have some plan in place to deal with their admirers by then."

Happy to pass along the information, Nettie nodded and returned to her customers. She had a feeling this delay would not deter the men.

* * *

After her song of the evening, the popular new Welsh hymn, *Here is Love Vast as the Ocean*, Nettie was surprised to find Hope and Charity calmly seated at the table in the closet.

"What happened, Nettie?"

"Did that man come back?"

"Did he bring his brother?"

"What were they like?"

Nettie took a seat. "You needn't be dismayed. I actually think you might have a lot in common with these men. They returned and were crestfallen to learn you were gone for the day. I'm quite certain they'll return although I have no idea when."

"You talked to them?"

"What did they say?"

"We spoke only briefly. Their names are Harry and Larry. They're identical twins just like you." Nettie fought the urge to laugh when she said their names. "I don't think they'll go away until they're able to talk to you. You can't avoid them forever."

"We aren't avoiding them."

"Anything but."

"We're mad at Emmett."

"We want to cause him problems."

"He never listens to us."

"He never does what we want."

The twins looked at each other and spoke as one, "We're sorry if we caused you extra work."

"Oh, it wasn't so much extra work for me," Nettie confessed. In fact, she earned over 50 cents in tips. She pocketed the money, explaining she would purchase her drinks at closing time.

* * *

No sooner did Sunday school let out than Vicar Haf commenced his campaign. "Have you made any decision? Would it be all right for me to speak to your father?"

"This is hardly the appropriate place for such a conversation."

"I agree. What if I come calling this afternoon about two? I must attend a church council meeting right now and I won't be able to walk you home. Are you available?"

This would mean her only free afternoon would be gone. Nettie was certain her disappointment was obvious. Unfortunately, the vicar took her reaction the wrong way.

"Don't be disappointed, my dear. Two o'clock will be here before you know it." At this, the vicar boldly took her hand in his for a moment before he turned and walked away.

Nettie glared after him and caught Eula standing in the doorway of her own Sunday school classroom. She scowled at Nettie and quickly closed the door.

If anyone had a right to be angry, it was Nettie.

Feeling Eula's disdain was absurd, she marched down the hallway and opened the door.

"Eula, we need to talk. Soon, school will start and we'll be working side-by-side. If you're angry because of the vicar's infatuation, I assure you, I have no designs on the man."

"You flirted with him."

"Once. Only once. I can't wait to be rid of him. I have never been shy about the fact I don't want anything to do with men. I only smiled at him to irritate you because I was angry. I shouldn't have and I'm apologizing to you now for my anger." Nettie waited for an apology from Eula. It was not forthcoming.

"How can you lie right to my face?" accused Eula. "I saw you in the hall. You were disappointed the vicar wasn't going to walk you home. You can't wait for him to woo you right under my nose. He was interested in me before you cast your spell on him. I saw you with that saloonkeeper the other day. Shame on you, Nettie Gordon, taking up with a married man! You say you don't like men, but I can see with my own eyes you do. That makes you a liar in my book."

Another flare of anger washed over Nettie. She was not a liar. Instead of continuing the argument, she calmly replied, "First of all, Mr. Boyd is not a married man."

"You said his wife was having a baby! Do you mean to tell me you are seeing a man who fathered a baby out of wedlock! That poor woman must despise you!"

"Eula, stop talking and listen for one moment." She could see Eula was about to make further accusations so Nettie placed her hand over her friend's mouth. Eula's eyes flew wide as she pushed the hand away.

"Don't touch me!"

"Then be still and listen for a moment. The woman having the baby turned out to be Mr. Boyd's sister. He's not married. I was ill the other day and he drove me home. I assure you; I have no designs on him. I can barely stand to be in the same room with him." Nettie frowned. "He has an equally low opinion of me. He was only being kind when he brought me home. I was in no shape to ride my bicycle and I didn't have money for the trolley. I wasn't disappointed I have to wait until two to see the vicar. I *am* disappointed because I won't have the afternoon to myself. It was my only opportunity to do as I pleased this entire week and now it's gone.

"Listen, Eula, you need to make yourself available to the vicar. He could ask your uncle for permission to court you. When he shows up this afternoon, I'm going to make him understand in no uncertain terms that I'm not interested. I'll gladly point him in your direction. You need to step in before he sets his mind on someone else. Why don't we go home and I'll help you arrange a modern hairstyle?"

Eula primly patted her bun. "I don't know."

"Yes, you do. You can listen at the top of the stairs. When the vicar starts to leave, come down and stop him. You need to have a reason to detain him. We'll think of something while I do your hair."

The two women caught up on recent events as they walked home together. Nettie had her friend in stitches as she relayed the tale of Harry and Larry.

"So, the two men have been coming to the saloon for lunch and dinner every day since. They each order a beer for both meals, but it became apparent they were neither one drinkers so now they buy beer for fellow patrons. They rave about Marcel's cooking—it is awfully good. Apparently, they're affluent and Hope and Charity are starting to take an interest. I think it's only a matter of time before they go out. Can you imagine? I'm quite certain they'll go together. Most people would not like being gawked at, but I believe those girls will avidly anticipate the spectacle they'll make."

* * *

As Eula admired her hairstyle in the mirror, a burst of furious knocking commenced. Nettie opened the door to find a harried Mrs. Green. "You must come immediately."

"What's wrong?"

"There are men in the parlor waiting for you. They seem quite indignant and I certainly don't want any inappropriate behavior in my establishment."

"*Men*?"

"Yes, two men. They arrived at almost the exact same time. They both asked after you. You must come now."

Nettie turned and gave a curious smirk to Eula then the two women walked down one flight of stairs together. "Best to wait here," Nettie suggested before descending to the first floor. "One of the men is bound to be the vicar," she whispered.

Indeed, she spied the vicar sitting nervously on the sofa between the windows. He held a modest bouquet of daisies. Sitting next to him was Emmett Boyd; a sly grin lit his face.

Nettie smoothed her skirt as she stepped off the bottom stair and approached her visitors. "Gentlemen," she began as the two men stood. "Please have a seat. What are you doing here, Mr. Boyd?"

"Why, I've come to see if you would like a ride this fine summer afternoon. You did rather enjoy my Buick or at least it was the impression you gave at the time. Was I mistaken? You were overly appreciative as I recall. Or were you only teasing me, Miss Gordon?"

Nettie believed the vicar's eyes were about to pop out of his head. Mr. Boyd managed to couch her gratitude in an unsavory light. In her most severe and reprimanding teacher's voice, Nettie explained her position on suitors.

"Thank you, gentlemen, for your attention this afternoon, but I feel I must make something quite clear. I am not nor have I ever been interested in any sort of romantic entanglement. I would hate to lead you on or have you waste your time or finances. I wish to express my standpoint so as not to leave any doubt. If I have somehow given the impression I am interested in matrimony or any of the attendant ceremony or commitment involved, I apologize. My upbringing was such that I much appreciate and enjoy my freedom and I have no desire to change my current way of life."

At this, a scowling Vicar Haf rose and headed for the door. With perfect timing, Eula descended the staircase. She never looked so feminine or beguiling in her life and she played her part to perfection. "Oh, Vicar! Just the person I wished to see." Looking around the room, she innocently commented, "Am I interrupting?"

The vicar angrily responded, "No, Miss Stohr, there's nothing to interrupt."

"Well, if you're on your way out, perhaps I could accompany you and explain my dilemma." Eula gave the man no time to answer as she walked through the front door when he opened it.

That a girl, thought Nettie. You go right after what you want and don't give up. She abruptly remembered Mr. Boyd still seated on the sofa.

"You got rid of him nicely. Now we can take our ride." After sitting in his Buick waiting for the vicar to show up, Emmett was not about to be deterred by Miss Gordon's speech.

"How can you mistake my words so completely?"

"I don't think you meant what you said."

"Are you calling me a liar?" Nettie was outraged. If she was anything at all, she was honest. It was the second time today someone unfairly called her out for lying.

"Every woman longs for a husband and family. It's simply a fact of life. You're no different than others of your sex. To be clear, I'm not asking you to marry me; I'm asking you to go for a ride."

"Rest assured, Mr. Boyd, I have no designs on you or any other man. I know my own mind and I will not be held hostage by some arrogant male: cooking, cleaning, washing and playing foot maid while suffering through endless childbirth and likely being beaten in the process. My life is fine the way it is. Furthermore, I want nothing to do with you in particular. From the first day you pulled me down the street, I've had nothing but contempt for you and your nasty business. The minute my debt is paid, I will walk away and happily never lay eyes on you again. You are arrogant and insufferable and you do *not* know what I think or what I want. Am I being clear enough for you? You need to leave."

Evidently, Nettie managed to strike a nerve. She watched Mr. Boyd saunter out the door. No further words were exchanged. Nettie breathed a heavy sigh. Men always considered themselves some gift from God. They were all alike. The irony of her idea unexpectedly occurred. The rage she directed at Mr. Boyd was caused by his own belief all women were alike.

* * *

Eula, thrilled when the vicar offered to buy her an ice

cream, sat at the counter of the soda fountain completely entranced by his every word. She was the new and eager recipient of his bouquet, even if it was second-hand. He did not attempt to hide his disappointment at the afternoon's events. Eula was certain he barely noticed she was alive. But if Nettie was correct and she stuck this out, perhaps Vicar Haf would finally notice her. When conversation turned in an almost impossible direction, Eula doubted her ability to cooperate with the vicar's ideas.

"Was there something you wished to discuss, Miss Stohr?"

"Nothing of consequence. Go on. What were you saying?"

"I wonder if you would do me a favor?"

"Oh, anything for you."

He smiled and continued, "You see, I want to ask permission of Miss Gordon's parents to pay her court. She said they don't live in the city. Do you know where they live?"

Eula bit her lip. "I know they live in Pasadena or her father does."

"Perhaps you might be willing to obtain the address for me. Naturally, I wouldn't want Miss Gordon to think you aided me."

"But why do you want their permission? I was under the impression Nettie doesn't want suitors."

"Did you overhear our conversation?"

"No, no, I certainly did not. But she's spoken of her wish to avoid men for some time. Has she made an exception in your case?" Eula was racking up lies at an alarming rate. This couldn't be the proper way to win a husband.

"No, I can't say she has. But if I could obtain her father's support, I might be able to change her mind."

"I see," replied Eula. She appeared to devolve into deep thought. From the limited information she had of Nettie's past, she knew beyond doubt her father's opinion held no sway. Perhaps there was a way to get something out of this request.

"Vicar Haf—"

"Call me Clyde."

Eula smiled, the best smile she knew. "Clyde, yes, well, there is a way I might be able to get an address for you. Feel free to call me Eula. Let me see what I can do and we can meet during the week. We could even come back here. What day is best for you?"

* * *

It was with great trepidation that Nettie pedaled up to the alley entrance of the Golden State. Occupied by Mrs. Arndorfer's church duties, she gave little thought to her workday with Mr. Boyd since she provoked his exit from the boarding house on Sunday. She greeted Marcel in the kitchen and proceeded to collect her apron from the closet only to find Hope and Charity twittering away. Nettie's mouth fell open at sight of the two women dressed identically in pink-striped day dresses, hats and pink slippers. For the first time, as far as Nettie knew, the two girls had identical hairstyles. They were stunning.

"What do you think, Nettie?"

"Can you tell us apart?"

Never having been able to tell the twins apart even when they wore different clothes and hairstyles, she was completely honest in her response. "I can't tell you apart at all. What's the occasion?"

"Harry and Larry are taking us out for the day."

"We're going to the beach to play games and see the sights."

"But we think we'll be quite the sight ourselves!"

"Come and see, Nettie."

"The boys are also dressed alike."

"They're here to pick us up."

"Come watch and tell us what you think when we come back."

"All right, go on ahead."

The twins were correct, they were quite the sight as they walked onto the sidewalk with their new beaus. Nettie peeked through the window as onlookers craned their necks to get a better look at the two identical couples. Smiling at the spectacle, she turned her attention to the saloon.

Mr. Boyd managed to keep to his own business without addressing Nettie directly over the next two days, a remarkable feat considering the twins rarely showed up to work.

* * *

Determined to inform Mrs. Arndorfer she could not continue her current frenetic schedule, Nettie became concerned when they met on Friday.

"Are you all right?" The woman looked positively gray on the bright summer morning.

"Oh, I'll be fine. I wasn't feeling well and then I—lost my food. Perhaps I have some sort of influenza. I hope not, but it might be the case. If you'd rather not come in, I understand."

"I think I should go for the midwife. Tell me where she is. You need a knowledgeable person to review your condition." She could see the timid Mrs. Arndorfer was about to protest. "I insist. And I should let the pastor know you're ill. Did he know when he left this morning?"

"I told him I wasn't feeling particularly well, but I

urged him to go to work. What good would it do for him to be here if I have the influenza?" Mrs. Arndorfer wrote the midwife's address on a slip of paper.

"You go lie down. I'll be back in no time."

* * *

Nettie sat in the Arndorfer parlor. Any concern about being late for work seemed irrelevant. The next-door neighbor offered her telephone so Mrs. Arndorfer's family could be called. Relatives were starting to arrive. Nettie could leave now. Her intention was to slip out the front door unnoticed. It seemed incredibly difficult to stand up. As she opened the front door, Pastor Arndorfer stopped her.

"Will you still be helping out at church, Miss Gordon?"

"No. I'm certain there'll be abundant volunteers. I've had a difficult time keeping up and school starts in two weeks."

"The Lord giveth and the Lord taketh away," the pastor's words were meant to soothe. They only made Nettie angry.

Worn out from her frantic journeys of the morning and the drama of the day, Nettie knew she couldn't ride her bicycle to the Golden State and caught the trolley. It was almost dinnertime. People were headed home. She found it impossible to think. Nettie entered through the alley door and was waylaid by Marcel in the kitchen.

"Where have you been, woman? I need you to take this basket over to the Judge's house. Miss Faith is waiting."

"But I'm late. I need to go to work."

"Mr. Emmett knows this has to be delivered. You can make amends when you come back."

It was not Nettie's intention to make amends. Her

debt was almost paid. She grabbed the basket and walked out the back door toward the street. She delivered food to Faith several times over the last weeks. Although she never stayed long, Nettie always enjoyed chatting with Faith. What would she be able to say today? She knocked on the front door and was admitted by the butler.

"Right this way, miss."

Instead of taking her to the parlor, which was usually the case, the man led her upstairs. She soon found herself at a bedroom door. The butler stood aside and ushered her in.

"Nettie, so good to see you! Come and look what I have here."

Nettie walked toward the bed and found a tiny sleeping baby in Faith's arms. "Oh, Faith, your baby is beautiful! I'm relieved you're both fine!"

"It's a boy. The Judge is ecstatic. I'm surprised his feet touch the ground. The baby came last night. You were right, Nettie. I am completely smitten by my son!"

Nettie lowered her basket to the floor and stroked the baby's cheek with the back of her finger.

"What has Marcel made for me? I'm ravenous and they told me I shouldn't eat. But I must be hungry for some reason and I like his food best of all."

"I don't know what's in the basket. I'll take a look." Nettie bent over to remove the napkin covering the food, suddenly putting her hand to her eyes. Her shoulders shook as she sobbed.

"What's wrong, dear?" a concerned Faith asked.

"I'm sorry. You're so happy and I'm happy for you."

"Then why are you crying?"

"I've been helping the pastor's wife at my church. I met her this morning. Mrs. Arndorfer's baby was due next month. She didn't look well so I went for the midwife. There was nothing she could do. Nothing."

"Oh, my, what happened?" Faith feared the answer.

"She's dead and her baby girl is dead." Tears streamed down Nettie's face. "Her husband seemed to take it all in stride. I don't think he loved her at all."

"Oh, I'm sure he did."

"He only seemed to care about how her death might affect his work."

"Maybe he was overcome or sometimes when a person sees a lot of death, they don't appear emotional."

"How tragic for a woman to give her life to bring a child into the world and her husband doesn't even care? I talked to her this morning and now she's gone!"

"Nettie, I think you shouldn't go to work today. I'd like you to stay. I'll send word over to the saloon that I need you here."

"No, I've almost paid for the window. I need to finish." Nettie wiped her cheeks with the back of her hand and turned to go. "I'm happy for you, truly, and relieved you came through your ordeal. I'll be back to visit soon, I promise." Nettie headed straight for the saloon.

CHAPTER FIVE

Emmett frowned as he read a cryptic note delivered by the Judge's butler. There was no explanation in the message for Miss Gordon's strange behavior. She was hours late for work without excuse or comment. She did not engage the customers in her usual polite manner and seemed unable to focus on her work. He noticed she returned repeatedly to some tables but completely ignored others. Nettie delivered food incorrectly several times. At first, Emmett assumed this was some protest of his own standoffish behavior the last few days, but Faith's note implied some other malady was the cause of his lone waitress's atypical behavior.

He decided on a course of action last night while reviewing receipts. Perhaps this was the ideal time to let Miss Gordon off the hook. Emmett still bristled at the woman's remarks from Sunday. He could not deny she angered him quite thoroughly. In a serious and cold manner, he addressed her.

"Miss Gordon, I need a word."

Nettie wiped her hands on her apron and approached the bar.

"I went over the credit I gave you for the time you've been here and added an appropriate amount for the days you worked the bar. It turns out the window and lettering are paid in full. You're free to go. In light of recent comments, I imagine you're in a hurry to leave."

"I'd like something in writing to show my debt has been honored."

Emmett tore a page from an order pad and quickly wrote out the amount owed, the date and his name, scrawled "Paid in Full" across the bottom and handed it to Miss Gordon.

"Please leave now. You don't work here and women aren't allowed in the saloon." Nettie turned as if to bid Charlie farewell, but Emmett stopped her short. "Now, Miss Gordon. Please get your things and go."

Defiantly, Nettie headed for the closet, left her apron on the table, grabbed her handbag then marched toward the front door. She raised her hand in farewell to Charlie, who smiled back as he continued to play.

All eyes followed Nettie out the door then turned toward Emmett who stood behind the bar. He ignored the departure even though his customers obviously had not.

"What are you looking at?" he demanded. It wasn't as if the prim and proper Miss Gordon ever really fit in. He would admit she seemed to bring out the best in his customers. They never told bawdy jokes in her presence or even swore. There was some sweetness, some innocence about her that men respected. It was best she was gone. She didn't belong.

Nettie walked slowly down the sidewalk realizing there were things she would miss about the saloon: singing with Charlie, Marcel's delicious food, even the angry foreign language battles in the kitchen. She wanted to say goodbye to the twins. She might never see them with Harry and Larry again. At least she could find out if weddings were in the works when she visited Faith. Her footsteps slowed as she pondered the possibility of going through the alley to say goodbye to Marcel and Bao.

"Miss Gordon."

Nettie turned to find Mr. Boyd approaching.

"My sister sent a note. She wants you to return to her home. She's never been prone to melodrama or feminine dramatics so I trust her suggestion you are in some sort of need this evening." He could see tears well in Nettie's eyes. "If you like, I'll drive you home when the saloon closes."

Nettie did not trust herself to speak so simply nodded.

"There's one more thing. I seem to have been deserted by all my sisters and I'm in need of a waitress. I wish you'd consider staying on, Monday through Saturday. I'll pay you a dollar a day. I know you'll return to teaching shortly, but I'd consider it a personal favor if you'd work for me until I can hire new waitresses. You don't have to answer now."

Nettie's voice broke as she replied. "I could use the money. I'll be back tomorrow."

The ride in the car after closing was quiet. Emmett saw a side of Miss Gordon he never thought to exist. He might not know what caused her emotional upheaval, but he witnessed a chink in the prissy and sober armor of Nettie Gordon.

As he helped her down from the Buick, Emmett made a last comment. "I'd like to suspend hostilities—declare a truce. I realize you are not a fanatic. I relied heavily on Faith and I severely miss her presence at the saloon. It must be obvious I have no personal interest in you. That should have been clear the day you laid naked in my parlor."

A flare of anger flashed in Nettie's eyes. "I don't know why you feel the need for constant exaggeration. I was certainly not naked." Nettie was vulnerable to her own desire to make amends. She kept an exhaustive schedule over the past weeks and felt bombarded by the emotions of the day. A truce seemed a favorable way to begin her money-making venture although it ran against all prior instincts. "But yes, I would appreciate a friendlier dialogue. Good night, Mr. Boyd, and thank you for the ride."

Emmett tipped his driving cap and watched his employee disappear into the boarding house. She was intriguing if nothing else.

* * *

Eula was at a loss. Her friend took the death of Mrs. Arndorfer extremely hard. The dual funeral was set for Sunday afternoon so the congregation could attend.

The vicar conducted the rather lengthy church service, which concluded with a brief graveside interment. Eula felt tremendous pride as a composed and dignified Clyde performed his duties. New vicars were rarely so articulate. Nettie was unusually stoic and silent throughout.

The two teachers were expected to make an appearance at the Arndorfer home after the burial. Their attitudes about their visit could not have differed more. Eula relished her opportunity to waylay the vicar. Nettie never wanted to set foot in the Arndorfer home again and intended to make the briefest of visits. The women baked cookies to contribute to the potluck supper.

A thrill of pleasure ran from the tip of Eula's head right down to her toes when she spotted Clyde in the backyard motioning for her to join him. Although she was determined to stay at her dear friend's side, this was an opportunity she could not miss.

"I'll be right back, Nettie," she explained as she bounded off the porch and, floating on air, joined the vicar.

"Oh, Clyde," Eula gushed. "You did such a wonderful job today. I felt so inspired and consoled."

"Thank you, Eula. But I wanted to know if you were able to get the address for Miss Gordon's father."

Eula returned to earth with alarming speed. "Well, no, not so far. Nettie was busy this week and then she was quite disturbed by Mrs. Arndorfer's death. I have some ideas about how I might be able to obtain the address. What do you say we meet again sometime during the week?" This idea served to buoy Eula's spirts. "I might be able to have a look at Nettie's writing desk. She'll be gone almost the entire week. She ended up taking a job at the saloon where she was working off her debt."

"What did you say?"

"I said maybe we could meet again this week."

"No, something about a saloon?"

Eula realized she offered more information than intended. "Oh, um, Nettie was doing some volunteer work for the WCTU and—"

"At a *saloon*?"

"Well, no, not exactly. It's a long story."

"Are you telling me Miss Gordon has a job at a saloon?"

"Sort of, yes, but—"

"Eula, you must show me. I want you to take me there. I'll come for you on Tuesday afternoon."

"What time?"

* * *

Nettie impatiently rocked on the porch waiting for Eula

to return. She was ready to leave. They made their appearance. She would speak briefly to the pastor then this would be over. An apprehensive Nettie felt cornered when Pastor Arndorfer approached and took Eula's empty chair.

"I wanted to have a word, Miss Gordon. This seems the perfect opportunity."

Nettie only stared.

"I have the feeling you hold me responsible for my wife's death."

"Why would you think so?"

"Disapproval is difficult to overlook."

"I'm sorry if I seem—"

"I wish only to explain something to you. Perhaps it will make Mrs. Arndorfer's passing somewhat easier to accept. You see, I met my first wife when we were young. We were madly in love; perhaps as only young people can be. Life was difficult for us. I was at seminary; we had little money. Once I finished my year as a vicar, we were called to a church in Sacramento. We were well-matched. My wife relished her work in our small congregation. I came to depend on her completely. I can't tell you how vital it is for a pastor to have a wife willing to commit to his work. She made a happy home; she served our congregants at my side. I was devastated when she became ill and died unexpectedly.

"We were never blessed with children and I found myself alone in the world. I railed against God and strayed from my faith until I realized Edith had gone on to her reward, as we all will someday. How could I be mad at God for giving my dearest wife an eternal life in heaven? I came to understand I was simply angry to be left behind. It took many years for me to even consider remarriage.

"To my surprise, along came dearest Bess. I was afraid to love her as I did Edith. I never wanted to be hurt again. But she won me over with her complete devotion. She was my perfect wife, committed to our home, incredibly meek and deferential. I suspect I took advantage of her good nature more than I should have.

"God has taken her from me, but I learned from my experiences. I know I will join them one day and perhaps God will grant me another partner to share my earthly life. Don't mistake my determination to find joy in my loss for a lack of caring, Miss Gordon. I loved my wife and I miss her.

"Although I was never thrilled at the idea of being a parent as was Bess, I mourn the loss of my daughter, but I know she's in a place where there is no sorrow or pain, only joy. So, I have to do my best to live my life committed to my Savior and demonstrate what it is to be a cheerful Christian even when my heart is heavy."

"You didn't have to tell me this."

"No, I didn't. But I hope it makes this easier for you to accept, Nettie. You're a wonderful teacher. I believe someday you'll make a fine Christian wife and mother. I don't want your sorrow at my wife's death to prevent you from living your life as God plans."

Nettie had no intention of changing her attitude about marriage, but the pastor relieved much of her despair. "I am sorry for your loss."

Pastor Arndorfer smiled. "And we will both celebrate Bess's new life, although we miss her dearly."

The pastor was called away by others wishing to offer condolences. It seemed Pastor Arndorfer might have been a truer husband than Nettie imagined.

* * *

On Monday, Nettie took note of eager candidates lured

to the Golden State by a "Help Wanted" sign in the window. Nettie would admit, the women who applied seemed more suited to the position than her. Most were loud and gregarious. They would undoubtedly serve to fill the shoes of the missing twins more effectively than she ever could. Nettie was not surprised when the sign was gone on Tuesday and Mr. Boyd set her to work training two new employees.

Janie was the quieter of the two. She was businesslike and knew what to say to make tips. Louise was an outright flirt, bossy and brassy. It took her less than a day to make obvious overtures to her boss, who seemed quite pleased at the attention. Louise made no secret that she was available and Nettie imagined Mr. Boyd would not hesitate to take her up on anything she offered. The woman appeared such an obvious philanderer, Nettie thought her a rather dangerous choice in the saloon environment where men drank and jealousy might erupt. But Louise lavished so much attention on her customers, no one seemed to take offense, at least not so far.

The twins made the briefest of appearances at lunchtimes when Harry and Larry took their meals at the Golden State. Although Hope and Charity did little besides flirt with their beaus, Nettie imagined they were earning their regular pay. The two men appeared in the evening to usher their sweethearts out the front door. Mr. Boyd's customary scowl seemed to deepen whenever his sisters appeared. Nettie was certain he didn't expect much from the girls who symbolized his siblings' mass desertion of the family business.

Nettie was accepting when Mr. Boyd permanently assigned her to the side door. This actually suited her far better; it was similar to waitressing in a restaurant. Delmar was easygoing and cordial. When Nettie advised she might be late on Friday due to a meeting at school, Delmar promised to cover for her.

Nettie and Eula took the trolley to school in the morning as the summer day promised to be warm. Both women were astonished to find a stranger ensconced behind the desk in the small school office. Absent was a replacement teacher for Mrs. Arndorfer.

"Good morning, ladies. I am Mr. Pendergast, the new principal. Pastor Arndorfer meant to be here this morning to make introductions, but he was called away on an emergency." The man was shabbily dressed. His clothing was not pressed. He had a rather large belly but was slight in stature otherwise. He apparently held stock in a pomade manufacturing business.

"Principal?" inquired Eula.

"Yes, the school has grown so the elders felt it would prove beneficial to hire a principal. I will be taking the fifth- and sixth-grade class. Miss Stohr, you will take the third- and fourth-grade students. I hope this isn't an imposition so late in the summer. I'm certain you'll have ample time to prepare."

"I'll have little more than a week, Mr. Pendergast. I don't think there's sufficient time for such a change. I don't have lesson plans, I—"

"Let me assure you, there are others who would be happy to teach your class if you cannot prepare in a timely manner. My wife is a teacher. We are recent arrivals from Minnesota and she's eager to find employment."

Eula was dumbfounded. Nettie didn't know if she would recover in time to reply before her job was whisked away from under her.

Eula regained enough composure to suggest, "I'm sure Mrs. Arndorfer had lesson plans. I'll look in her supply closet to see what I can find."

"Excellent," replied Mr. Pendergast. It was obvious he thought her answer anything but. By the time the two teachers were released from the meeting, it was clear their new supervisor wished to replace at least one if not both of them immediately.

"How could they do this to us?" huffed Eula as the women walked away from the office. "That insufferable man is in charge of us even though he knows nothing about the school. I bet they pay him a hefty salary."

"Eula, you know men make more than women. That's life."

"But he's probably making a tidy sum to serve as principal aside from his teaching pay."

"Probably," Nettie sighed. "I hope he manages to mind his own business. I always loved my job here. I doubt we'll have the freedom to teach the way we want now. How are things going with the vicar?"

The abrupt change of topic startled Eula. How could she respond honestly? "Well, I don't think he's completely given up on you."

Nettie frowned. "Have you seen him lately, then?"

"Yes, as a matter of fact. I saw him briefly yesterday." Eula found it difficult to pay attention to Nettie's conversation as she reflected on her latest meeting with the vicar. At his insistence, she took him to the Golden State. He wanted to see for himself that Nettie worked in the saloon. They stood across the street near the corner until Nettie walked inside. The vicar was quite shocked.

"I told you she works there," chastised Eula. "Now you have seen with your own two eyes."

"Eula, it's more important than ever you get me her father's address."

"Why?"

"Because we need to intervene. Her father needs to

come and take her from the saloon before it's too late."

"Too late for what?"

"Her very soul is in jeopardy. If her father won't come and help, I'll have no choice but to take this information to the church elders."

"Oh, I don't think it's necessary. I assure you, Nettie's soul is in fine shape."

"Trust in me, Eula. I know what's best."

Eula bit her lip. She never intended to let this go so far. She had little choice but to do as Clyde requested.

* * *

After Nettie sang *In the Shade of the Old Apple Tree* on Friday night, she made her way to the side door. Nettie grinned as she passed Louise, who slipped her arm around Mr. Boyd's waist as the last of the customers departed. Louise teased him about his muscular torso as she fondled the buttons on his shirt. Mr. Boyd appeared completely enamored of his newest employee. A few minutes later, Nettie looked up from the ladies' bar to find Mr. Boyd approaching.

"Where did your lady friend go?" she inquired.

"I think she had an appointment."

"Oh, that's what they call it now."

Emmett laughed. "Don't misjudge her. She's merely putting on a show for the customers."

"Um, I'm sure it's exactly what she's doing. You seem to enjoy her company."

"Well, I am a man after all. After working with my sisters and a temperance maven, you can't exactly blame me for basking in a woman's attention. Why are you still here?"

"I was late this morning due to a school meeting. Delmar covered for me so I told him I'd wipe down the bar."

"I can give you a ride home if you'd like. It's nice outside. I just stuck my nose out the front door."

"Saying goodbye to the lovely Louise, no doubt."

"No doubt."

For the first time, Nettie relaxed and enjoyed the ride in Emmett's Buick. Emmett noticed her smile of delight. The cool night air was a welcome relief from the stuffy and smoky barroom. He asked about her school meeting. She obligingly responded, even adding details about the new principal.

"Next week will be my last week. Will you hire another girl?"

"I haven't decided. I don't know what the twins will do."

"Are weddings in the works?" Nettie could not help her curiosity.

"Not that I'm aware of. It's hard to say if they plan to come back to the saloon or not. I could have the new girls cover in back the way the twins used to do. Would you be interested in working Saturdays?"

"I think I would. My finances could use some help. I might manage to have a cushion in my savings for the first time in my life."

"You helped me make my decision. I won't hire anyone else for now."

"You must be disappointed. Faith told me how she loved the saloon because it meant family to her. Now all your family is gone."

"I suppose it was inevitable the girls would leave. I'm grateful Faith stayed as long as she did. When our parents passed away, we all worked together to try to make a go of things. My father never approved of Webster's marriage. I never understood then, but I do now."

"Why?"

"Father was upset because Webster married a Baptist. I didn't see a problem. I thought all that mattered was that he was in love and his wife loved him. Baptists are avid prohibitionists. My brother's wife never approved of him working in the saloon. It's the reason he left. She was so adamantly opposed to him taking his cut of the profits, he recently signed his fifth of the business over to me. She said it was blood money and she didn't want to profit from it.

"He still keeps our books but won't take any payment for his services. I know he feels guilty. Webster dumped all his responsibilities on me when he started his own business. If it was his wish to leave, I'd be more accepting. He wanted to go to the university when he was young. His wife wanted him to use his degree to best advantage, which served to get him away from the Golden State. He'd still be working here if it was up to him. Then Faith signed her fifth over to me when she decided to stay home. She's well-off, being married to the Judge."

"Why didn't they return their portions to the business to be split between you and the twins?"

"It would have given the twins two-thirds of the business. I would have been outvoted. Neither Faith nor Webster thought it was a good idea for me or the girls. So I can't really get upset when they pilfer from the registers.

"Tell me something. Since you've made your position on men so abundantly clear, how do you manage to tolerate the boys in your class? Are you the meanest teacher on earth?" Nettie laughed. It was the first time Emmett heard that delightful sound.

"You'll be surprised to hear, I'm quite fond of my little boys."

"I find that difficult to believe."

"No, it's true. I try my best to encourage them to be gentlemen, courteous to ladies, kind and thoughtful."

"How?"

"Well, there are vast differences between little boys and little girls. One would have to be quite dense not to notice. But the boys are eager to please and I hope I make a difference. Boys do require more discipline."

"And how do you accomplish that?"

"In my class, when a boy is naughty, they must take a trip to the cloak room with Little Oscar."

"Who is Little Oscar?"

"My paddle."

"Oh, I see."

"I rather imagine you are no stranger to a paddle, if your memory goes back far enough."

Emmett pursed his mouth and shook his head but admitted, "You could say that."

"One visit to the cloak room is generally enough to straighten out the most recalcitrant of students."

"You really give them a wallop, then?"

"Quite the contrary. We make a pact. They vow to improve their behavior and I give them a way to appear the brave and sturdy boy to their friends. I wallop a coat against the wall with Little Oscar—it makes quite an impressive sound—and the errant student, grim face intact, exits the cloak room without a tear, apparently having taken his punishment like a man."

"Then all these little boys fall madly in love with you?"

"Apparently. They are ever so much easier to handle then."

"No one has ever been hauled into the cloak room more than once?"

"Usually, the threat of Little Oscar is enough to make them toe the line."

"Do you use the same method of justice on the girls?"

"Oh no. An extra school assignment or writing a sentence 100 times is usually all it takes to set them on course. Tears and dramatic apologies are generated with little effort on my part."

"It sounds like you know your students well. Don't you miss them when they go on to the next classroom?"

"I used to be upset when school ended. I've come to appreciate the opportunity to teach new students each fall. Because I have first- and second-grade students, I also know, at least at recess, I'll see them in years to come. There were over 30 students in my class last year. Then summer is summer, for me as well. It's my favorite season."

"Why?"

"Freedom, Mr. Boyd, or that has always been the case before this summer. I must admit it was a frugal freedom."

"So, what if I were your naughty student; what would you say to me?"

"Mr. Boyd, you are not allowed to kiss girls at recess."

"But they dared me to kiss them."

"Even so, it's not appropriate behavior. Your punishment will be five whacks with my paddle."

"Five? Aren't you being rather extreme?"

"Five paddles for five kisses, Mr. Boyd. We must learn our lesson. However, I am quite fond of you. What do you say we make a pact? If you promise to never kiss the girls again, I will pretend to apply your punishment. Your friends will believe you took your whipping like a man and your new and appropriate behavior will please me. Have we a pact?"

"I don't know. I might want to take the paddling

instead."

"I can assure you, no boy has ever said that."

"Perhaps I'm simply more accustomed to your wrath than your favor. And I am no boy, Miss Gordon."

"I believe I would consider you to be the most wrath-filled between the two of us and I'm quite certain a paddling would not inhibit you from your desire to kiss Louise."

"You might be surprised to know Louise is not really my cup of tea."

"I would be quite surprised. Where might you find your ideal lady friend?"

"There are a number of women in hot pursuit at my church."

"Your church?"

"Yes, did you think because I sell liquor, I'm a godless man? Do you truly believe the wild accusations of the Women's Christian Temperance Union? My saloon might not be typical—I like to think it's exceptional—but I'm certain most saloon owners take their places at church on Sunday mornings with their families like the majority of Americans."

"To be truthful, I never considered that possibility. You have my apology, Mr. Boyd."

"Why don't you call me Emmett?"

"It wouldn't be proper."

"Why not? It's not as if we know each other from taking tea every afternoon. We work in a saloon."

"All right. You may call me Nettie."

Emmett pulled up in front of Mrs. Green's and walked around his car to help his passenger out. "It's been a pleasure talking to you, Nettie."

Nettie smiled, "It's also been a pleasure for me." And it had.

* * *

Nettie's life fell into a comfortable rhythm. She taught school on weekdays and returned to her embroidery in the evening. Her window plants suffered during the summer. Nettie meticulously pinched off the dead leaves and wilted flowers and resolved to coax them back to health. Eula surprised her with a new fern. When she delivered her gift, Eula was in an odd mood, as if she were making a peace offering.

Saturdays were spent in the side door of the Golden State. Nettie now recognized the regulars and looked forward to conversing with her customers. The women might not be considered friends, but Nettie enjoyed hearing about their lives. Several of the ladies relished Nettie's tales of her school day and asked about her students. When Nettie accepted the job, she viewed it as a commitment that would eat away at her free time, but she appreciated the extra income and newfound fellowship.

The side door underwent a bit of a remodel. Because so little hard liquor was sold in back, the bar was cut short to allow more room for tables and a larger dance floor. Only rarely did Nettie go to the front to fill an order for strong spirits. Those occasions were the only times she laid eyes on Emmett Boyd.

She was surprised to find the twins ensconced in the closet, sitting at the table drinking tea one Saturday morning. Weeks went by since Nettie saw the girls. The teapot was a sure sign they wished to have a conversation.

"Have a seat, Nettie."

"What are you girls doing here? Where are your beaus?" queried Nettie.

"We're mad at them."

"Do you know how delightful it feels to hold a

man's affection in the palm of your hand?"

"It's quite empowering."

"They send flowers daily."

"They come by the saloon and beg for our favor."

"It's quite delicious fun."

"We don't really know why we're mad."

"We believe the boys have bought us rings!"

"We are considering ways to make up."

"We're awfully curious about what the rings look like."

"So, you're working at the saloon again?" Nettie inquired.

"Only until we make up."

It appeared the girls were in no real hurry to make amends. Nettie was not surprised when the waitress named Janie quit. The twins and Louise hogged the customers in front and Janie could not make tips in the ladies' saloon.

One Saturday evening when Nettie needed to fill a whiskey order, she entered the main saloon to find a man standing on a chair in the middle of the room. He wore a clerical collar and carried a Bible.

The preacher shouted out pieces of scripture then pronounced, "Who hath woe? Who hath sorrow? Who hath contentions? Who hath babbling? Who hath wounds without cause? Who hath redness of eyes? They that tarry long at the wine; they that go to seek mixed wine. At the last, it bideth like a serpent, and stingeth like an adder. Thine eyes shall behold strange women, and thine heart shall utter perverse things. Yea, thou shalt be as he that lieth down in the midst of the sea, or as he that lieth upon the top of a mast. They have stricken me, shalt thou say, and I was not sick; they have beaten me, and I felt it not: when shall I awake? I will seek it yet again."

Emmett was angrily polishing a glass behind the bar while his customers snuck out the door. He seemed to be considering his options.

When he saw Nettie approach, he snidely noted, "I would say one of your cohorts has come to pay us a visit, but I know this man."

Nettie, sly smile in place, thought it might be amusing to throw a challenge at this particular man of the cloth. "You're quoting Proverbs 23, aren't you?" she shouted.

The man on the chair turned his attention to the cheeky woman approaching him. "Yes, sister. You know your scriptures."

"I do. I know enough to understand you are leading these men astray."

"Me? It is Satan's brew that leads them astray."

"The verses you quote concern the inadvisability of drunkenness. Nowhere in the Bible does it even hint that spirits should be forbidden. After all, Jesus turned water into wine, not the other way around. He partook of wine, Himself. He used it to administer His holy sacrament. If you wanted to give a talk about the inadvisability of drunkenness, I imagine most everybody here would agree." Nettie noticed a few men delayed their departure and paused at the door to listen.

"Women aren't allowed in saloons. I intend to report this to the police." The man was visibly angered by the impertinent woman who challenged his position.

"I work here. And if you wish to file a complaint, the police chief is seated in the corner."

Knowing there was no verse to refute her, the preacher snatched his Bible closely against his chest, descended from his improvised pulpit and walked toward the door. He stood in the doorway and offered one last Bible verse. "Be sober, be vigilant; because your adversary the devil, as a roaring lion, walketh about, seeking whom he may devour."

Nettie headed back to the bar to finish her errand.

"You were quite effective, Miss Gordon. I guess the next time a Bible thumper comes in, I'll come and find you."

"You said you knew him."

"He's the man who married my brother and his Baptist wife." Emmett turned to admire his Saturday employee as she returned to the side door. He was completely confused.

CHAPTER SIX

As Nettie entered the Golden State next Saturday, she was surprised when Emmett took her arm and led her through the kitchen.

"I wondered if you'd be interested in working in the fresh air today?"

"Why, have you decided to sell beer in the alley?"

They walked to the backyard of the Boyd house. "The twins are working today, all day. I need to harvest my hops and I have a feeling you might have more gardening experience than anyone else in the saloon. Do you?"

As Nettie went through the garden gate, she was overwhelmed by huge vines growing up supports and covering the entire yard. She had the impression there was a lot of greenery in the garden but never imagined a crop was being grown.

"I used to help my mother in her vegetable plot, but I don't know a thing about hops."

"I'll cut down the supports on this first row. If you go on the back porch, there's an apron and some gloves you can use. Be sure to use the gloves. The vines and flowers can irritate your skin." Emmett picked a flower off the closest vine and rubbed it between his fingers.

"See how dry and papery this is? That's what I want you to pick. This sticky yellow substance should be apparent." He stuck the flower under her nose. "This is the smell you're looking for." He then picked another example. "This flower isn't dry enough; it smells green. There's no lupulin." Emmett offered the flower up for comparison as a black cat emerged from nearby vines and rubbed against his leg.

Curious, Nettie observed the cat. It evidently felt at home in the garden and completely comfortable with Mr. Boyd. She could see her employer was uncharacteristically enthusiastic and paid no attention to his feline companion. Nettie's wonder must have shown in her expression, which Emmett interpreted as interest in his hops.

"I brew my own beer. I import Bavarian hops. They're what my father always used. But I started experimenting with my own a few years back. This is the first year I have a substantial crop. These brew a milder, lighter beer. I often use honey instead of sugar. If you don't want to do this, I can hire a day laborer. Not all the hops ripen at the same time, but most of them seem ready now."

"No, it's a beautiful day. I'd like to spend it in your garden, or field or whatever this is."

Emmett smiled an engaging smile. "You can fill this basket with hops then fill the crates along the wall. Whatever you accomplish today would be most appreciated. I'll persuade my family to finish up tomorrow before Sunday supper."

"What happens after they're picked?"

"Normally, they'd be taken to an oast house for drying. Since there isn't one around here, I spread them on screening in the attic of the warehouse and let them dry. I have to get back to the bar, but I'll return to see if you have any questions and to cut down the next row of vines. I can't leave the twins in charge for long or they'll rob me blind and send Louise packing."

"And you would miss Louise?" Nettie teased.

"She's reliable and the twins aren't. Louise is a good waitress." He noted Nettie's sarcastic smirk. "Louise is not what she seems."

"I'll let you be the judge of that."

Emmett grinned before walking across the alley. Nettie took a deep breath and headed for the porch, prepared to appreciate the outdoors on this glorious fall day.

* * *

Nettie rose from her seat and removed her gloves. Placing her hands on her hips, she stretched her back. It was finally too dark to see. Emmett's cat supervised the harvest but hurried away when Nettie stood. Although she took her time with her chore, she made considerable progress. Intending to grab dinner in the kitchen, Nettie planned to work the side door until closing. The saloon was hosting a dance tonight. These were always well-attended. Music floated through the garden for the past hour.

While Marcel generously filled a plate, Nettie glanced into the back saloon. The twins stood across the room near the bar. Evidently, they'd been stationed in back for the night. Once they caught sight of Nettie, they waved her over then put their heads together confidentially. They appeared quite amused with themselves.

As Nettie approached, one of the twins inquired, "Are you going to join us in back?"

"I thought I would as soon as I eat." The twin with the ruffled apron linked arms with Nettie and walked her toward the kitchen. Nettie noticed Emmett approach the twin with the plain apron.

Nettie's twin stopped abruptly once they reached the edge of the dance floor. "Oh, it looks like Emmett will haul us off to the front. I'd so much rather stay back here, watch the dancing and listen to the music."

A surprised Nettie was pushed toward Emmett. Looking up, she saw the other twin had given her brother a shove. Emmett grabbed Nettie's arms to steady her and stood staring at her face.

Quickly recovering his composure, Emmett managed, "Would you like to dance?"

"Yes, I would."

Emmett took up dance position and led Nettie around the floor in a two-step as the band played *The Ragtime Dance*. It was years since Nettie danced, but Emmett was an enthusiastic leader. She was swept up in the music and was breathless as the tune ended. Emmett, almost reluctantly, released her to clap.

"I have to go up front," but he didn't leave.

"This was lovely, thank you."

"Could I drive you home after work?"

"Yes," came her simple reply. Nettie headed back to the kitchen after Emmett hurried away. She remained distracted for the balance of the evening, enthralled by the memory of Emmett's embrace, his muscular arms and broad chest and the way his hand caressed her back. She decided Emmett Boyd would make quite a catch. He was industrious, a business owner, not to mention a handsome man. Louise would do well to capture him.

* * *

Nettie finished her closing song and bid farewell to customers ambling out the door. The twins made themselves scarce since the incident on the dance floor.

Louise put the last of the glasses on her tray and headed for the kitchen. Nettie noticed one man engaged in an intense conversation with Emmett showed no sign of leaving. Perhaps Mr. Boyd was too busy to drive her home.

She untied her apron and obtained her things from the closet. When Nettie reappeared, the man at the bar seemed unaffected by closing time and was apparently offering an apology.

"That's well and fine, Emmett, but there was no excuse for it. I apologize on behalf of my wife. This should never have happened. If it cost you any business, I'm happy to make amends."

"I don't think you can apologize on behalf of people. It doesn't work that way." Looking up, Emmett noticed Nettie pause to see if he was ready to go. "Look here, it's my Bible expert. Nettie, come and meet my brother, Webster."

Nettie approached the bar and shook Webster's hand. "It's nice to meet you." Webster was as tall as his brother but had a slighter build. He had brown hair, blue eyes and a definite family resemblance.

"Nice to meet you. I've heard a lot about you."

"Really?" Nettie raised her eyebrow and gave Emmett a sly look. "Good things, I hope?"

Webster laughed, the same rich laughter she heard from his brother. "I'd say there were mixed reviews until recently."

Nettie nodded her head thoughtfully. "I believe I can live with that."

"I must apologize if my wife caused you any distress."

"I don't understand."

"She's the one who encouraged the preacher to come here and spread the Word," Emmett explained.

"This has caused more than a little discord in my home. I came to apologize only to find my sisters have become engaged."

"Oh, Webster, I planned to drive Nettie home this evening. We'll talk about the wedding tomorrow at supper—you are planning to meet our future brothers-in-law?"

"I'll be there. Nadine and the children will come this week. Why don't you drive Nettie home? I'll stay and close up."

"I'd appreciate it. In fact, it would put us even."

"I don't think so. But I'm willing to leave it at that for tonight. It was nice meeting you, Nettie."

"My pleasure."

Emmett offered his arm in a gentlemanly manner, a pleasant change from his normal guidance. It seemed he was always pulling her somewhere. Nettie soon found herself climbing into Emmett's Buick in the refreshing night air.

"Did you hear, Wilbur Wright flew his aeroplane, the *Wright Flyer*, for over half an hour?"

"Does this mean you'll be buying an aeroplane next?" Nettie teased.

"I would if I could. I imagine it won't be too long before someone offers rides and I intend to be first in line."

Nettie thought this a foolish idea, typically male and a good way to get oneself killed. "When did the twins become engaged? They didn't say anything to me about it."

"It occurred after our dance when I returned to the front. The gentlemen were waiting to ask permission. I gave them my blessing."

"The girls must be thrilled."

"What makes you think so?"

"Wouldn't it be the normal reaction to engagement?"

"Normal, perhaps. But I doubt there is much that could be classified as normal concerning the twins."

"Why?"

"I have a sinking feeling the girls are more interested in putting on a spectacle than being wives."

Nettie would admit, the theatrics of the two couples were out of the ordinary. "I can't tell them apart."

"Harry is marrying Hope and Larry is marrying Charity. Does that help?"

"No, you assume I can tell the difference between Hope and Charity."

"You can't? I've heard you call them by name."

"Only after I had some hint as to who is who. I can't tell them apart. Can you?"

"Of course."

"Because they look different to you?" Nettie wanted to know if there was some telltale sign she missed.

"They don't look different, they look differently."

"You are not being one bit of help."

"The girls are amazingly alike; they always have been. Their dispositions are quite similar, which I don't think is normal in twins. I believe one twin is usually more dominant, one more submissive. My sisters are both completely devious. The only difference is, you can see Hope considering unpleasant opportunities in her expression while it does not show on Charity's face at all. They were small when my parents were trying to make a go of the Golden State. I'm afraid the girls may have suffered from lack of attention. They came to rely completely on each other, more than they might have otherwise."

"Is it why they talk the way they do?"

"What do you mean?"

"The way they talk, as if they were both thinking the same thing and the words take turns coming out of their mouths."

"I don't know what you're talking about."

Nettie rolled her eyes. Maybe Emmett was so used to their unusual speech patterns, he didn't even notice. "I'll take your advice and see if I can tell the girls apart."

"They have plans to marry in late October. It will be a church ceremony on Saturday, the 28th, as long as the church is available. They want to have a reception at Faith's house. The Golden State will be closed. I wondered if you would be available?"

"I could come and serve."

"No, you're mistaking my meaning. I want you to come—with me."

"Oh," Nettie, startled by his suggestion, was eager to see the two sets of twins marry. "Yes, I'd like to."

"Good!" Emmett's exuberance was apparent.

"Do you know if the girls are wearing matching wedding dresses?"

"I assume they will all dress as they have been, so no one can tell them apart. I believe they're planning on sharing the house the grooms currently share, at least initially. Who knows? Perhaps they'll even share a honeymoon suite."

"*Mr. Boyd!*"

Emmett laughed. "Is that beyond your imagining?"

"It is certainly inappropriate to suggest such a thing."

"Nonetheless, it does make you wonder. I've considered another idea. When the girls become bored with the twin they marry, will they switch husbands and hope no one notices?" Emmett could see his remarks were causing Miss Gordon's face to turn scarlet. He thought it best to return to a more conventional topic.

"I'm happy you're coming to the wedding. We'll have more opportunity to dance."

Nettie was piqued at Emmett's inappropriate conversation. "I'm surprised you didn't ask Louise. She seems interested in you and she's marriageable while you already know my ideas regarding matrimony."

"Who says I'm interested in marriage? And for someone who dislikes being categorized in any way, you are certainly judgmental."

"What do you mean?"

"I told you any relationship you discern between Louise and me is not what it seems. She makes extra money on tips, which she desperately needs. If customers are led to believe I have an overriding interest in Louise, nothing gets out of hand. She makes her tips and I have happy, pampered customers."

Nettie quietly contemplated the idea Louise might be one of Emmett's projects, to which his sisters referred. This made her uncomfortable about attending the wedding as his guest. Although their conversation became rather acrimonious, Nettie smiled sweetly and hurriedly stepped from the car when they arrived at Mrs. Green's. "Thanks for the ride, the dance and the day in your garden. See you Saturday."

Emmett tipped his driving cap in reply. Why was it so difficult to have a civil conversation with Nettie Gordon?

* * *

Nettie considered the possibility Tuesday might never end. Principal Pendergast imperiously announced his plan to hold parent-teacher conferences in order to nip any hint of trouble in the bud. Nettie thought his idea ridiculous and had not hesitated to voice her opinion. If she was not already on Mr. Pendergast's short list to unemployment, she certainly was now. Needless to say, her opinion held no sway. Nettie, trapped in her classroom all day, was nearly an hour behind schedule and wasn't the only one growing short of temper on the unpleasantly warm evening.

Although fall did not exist in Los Angeles as a season, Nettie always enjoyed the occasional brisk days with warm sun. Most autumn days were indistinguishable from summer days. Such was the case today. Her stuffy classroom wasn't doing anything to improve her disposition or that of increasingly irate parents anxiously waiting to go home. The principal scheduled meetings only 15 minutes apart in order to cram them all into one day. This caused a nightmare for Nettie, who had more children in her classroom than either of the other teachers.

As Nettie saw a set of parents out the door, she called for Mr. and Mrs. Brewer. Only Mrs. Brewer was present. Raising her hand to acknowledge her turn, the woman's face froze as she spotted her daughter Daisy's first-grade teacher.

Attempting composure, Nettie rushed the woman into her classroom and leaned against the door to make sure it was secure.

"Louise? What are you doing here?"

"I never knew when Daisy talked about Miss Gordon, she was talking about you."

"I didn't know you had children." Nettie took a deep breath to compose herself. "I think we should behave as if we didn't know each other. Do you approve?"

Louise nodded in agreement and took a seat in front of the teacher's desk.

"All right then," Nettie settled into her standard

meeting format. "Let me tell you, Daisy is a sweet girl and eager to learn. She's a joy to have in my classroom. I don't have anything negative to say. She does need help with her letters. Perhaps you could spend a few minutes when she gets home—oh, that's right, you don't get home until late. Perhaps Daisy's aunt—the one who picks her up from school—could spend a few minutes each afternoon having her write her alphabet. I don't have much else to say. I have a packet of her work here for you to take home." Nettie handed the packet across the desk to Louise.

"This isn't going to work."

"What?" Nettie uneasily replied.

"Pretending we're meeting here as teacher and parent."

"I think it's working splendidly."

Louise shook her head. "The truth is, I don't want Daisy or my four-year-old, Pansy, to know where I work. They think I'm a secretary at the telephone company."

"I see. Well, I won't say anything about knowing you. You don't have to worry. I give you my word. But if you want to be a secretary, why don't you try for that type of job? You could keep regular hours and spend more time at home."

"You don't understand," Louise looked into her lap where she nervously rubbed her hands together. "I can't read."

"Lots of people can't read. It's nothing to be ashamed of. But it doesn't lend itself toward obtaining a different occupation."

Louise focused on Nettie. "I have to explain."

"No, you don't. You don't have to tell me anything. We're here to discuss Daisy's academic progress and we have."

"I do need to explain. You see, my husband up and left us about two years ago. He said he couldn't take the pressure of providing for us. He wanted a different life. He didn't care if we could get by without him or not. I've had to provide and care for our two girls and his younger sister. To be honest, I couldn't have taken the job at the Golden State or any job at all if it weren't for Rae. Working as a waitress at the saloon has been a blessing; the best money I've ever made. For the first time since my husband left, I don't have to worry about paying the rent or buying food. I can't tell you how much I appreciate the opportunity Emmett gave me." Louise looked about to burst into tears.

"Don't be upset. Your secret is safe." Nettie was honestly sympathetic. "You have my word; Daisy will never know. She's such a sweet child. You're doing a wonderful job as a mother and have nothing to feel ashamed of.

"If you like, I could teach you to read. I wouldn't mind coming by the saloon occasionally after school. You could take a short break and we'll have you reading in no time. I don't know if it would open any opportunities, but I have no doubt reading would enrich your life."

"You would do that for me?"

Nettie nodded. "What if we start tomorrow? I'll ride my bike over after school and bring some introductory materials. It might be geared to children, but it's all I have. You can work at your own pace."

When Louise departed, she was filled with gratitude, both to her daughter's teacher and her newfound friend. Nettie watched her go, certain she must be Emmett Boyd's latest project.

* * *

The days went by all too quickly. The twins, busily making wedding plans, avoided the Golden State. Louise had her hands full waitressing for the entire front bar and filling in at the side door. She enjoyed unprecedented extra income since there was no one to compete for tips and so, urged Emmett not to hire another waitress. Emmett understood, if not for Nettie on Saturdays, he would be in serious trouble.

Emmett and Webster agreed to split the cost of the twins' weddings. The girls were not interested in economizing so Emmett was more than happy to do without an extra waitress until the weddings were accomplished.

The initial wedding strategy family supper proved quite challenging. Nettie obtained a full account from Faith. Webster's wife, Nadine, clearly attended against her will. Webster evidently laid down the law. Nadine gave a surly apology for the scene at the Golden State. Emmett accepted as a gentleman, but everyone knew he was angry at his sister-in-law, as were they all.

The family enjoyed a rare visit with their nieces and nephew while Nadine sulked in the corner. Since ongoing wedding preparations needed to be addressed, Webster and his family began a new habit of attending Sunday suppers, whether Nadine liked it or not.

Nettie made a trip to the Golden State each Wednesday after school to tutor Louise. She realized she misjudged the young mother, who was actually rather timid and sweet. The bravado she displayed for customers was truly an act. Louise was an eager student, but Nettie quickly noticed teaching adults to read was far different from teaching children. Children were not intimidated by their lessons and were open-minded. Louise was terrified of failure and convinced reading was beyond her grasp.

"I know the vowels are difficult. I understand there are more rules than you can learn at once. This is why we start with simple, small words and the sounds of letters that don't vary with usage. Trust me, Louise, you can do this."

Louise stared at her teacher in disbelief. "I don't understand. How can anyone possibly learn all this? Daisy will learn, but I never will! And I intend to pay you for your time. You come all the way over here on Wednesdays and help me on Saturdays."

"You need the money more than me. You have a family to support. Besides, I'm learning too. I never tried to teach an adult before. This is helpful to me as a teacher."

"No, I insist. I'll pay you 50 cents a week until I can read."

The two women bickered over money every week. In the end, Nettie accepted, not because she felt she deserved to be paid, but because Louise felt the need to take responsibility for her lessons. If nothing else, it made her a more focused student.

One Wednesday, Emmett caught the women together and angrily commanded Louise to the barroom to deliver an order. This marked the first time Nettie saw Emmett lose his temper since the day the window was broken. Although Louise clearly appeared guilty for taking a moment away from work, Nettie became angry and gave her boss the cold shoulder on Saturday. Instead of drawing his ire, however, he simply took her arm and directed her to his automobile after work. Her resolve to shun him dissolved with a ride in the motor car.

Things were quickly back to normal or at least what Nettie considered normal. Friendship, that was what she decided they shared. Emmett obviously wasn't romantically interested in Louise, who had her own husband, absent though he was. But Emmett understood Nettie's position on courtship and marriage. She was perfectly clear. There was no doubt he sought only friendship in return.

* * *

The Saturday before the weddings turned into one of the busiest days in the history of the Golden State. Perhaps the sign in the window stating the establishment would be closed in a week served to encourage business. It quickly became apparent Louise could not handle all the customers in front and Nettie's aid was enlisted. Emmett appreciated Nettie's speed and efficiency. She might not work the room as the twins and Louise managed to do, but she could take and deliver orders more quickly than all three of the other women combined. Nettie was trustworthy, as well.

Since the twins were no longer rummaging through the cash register, Emmett anticipated his profits would rise. This was not the case. He suspected Delmar was doing the pilfering now. Perhaps he needed to hire a bunch of temperance women as employees. At least they made honest workers.

Always attuned to customers who entered his saloon, Emmett observed an older man, probably in his 50s, standing inside the door. He made no move to either sit down or order a drink but peered about the room in search of something. As Emmett was about to ask him if he could be of help, it became apparent the man found the person he came to see. Emmett followed the man's stare to find Nettie carrying a tray of drinks.

As Nettie served the last glass and lowered her empty platter, the man walked up and grabbed her arm. No one was paying attention. The smoke-filled room was crammed with talking, rowdy men. Charlie played the piano. But to Nettie, the entire world became still and quiet as she glared at the man who delayed her. She tried to pull her arm away.

"Let go."

"I'm here to ask you to come home."

Nettie snorted in derision. "Let go."

"You're bringing shame on our household. This is no place for a decent girl."

"But it is a decent place for you?"

"Things have changed. You have a new mother. I want you to come home."

"Let go."

The man pulled her toward the door. "I won't take no for an answer. I'm your father and you will do as I say."

Nettie jerked her arm out of his grasp. Her tray clattered to the floor, drawing everyone's attention.

"Funny, you were never my father when I needed you to be. I'm no longer a child and I will not do as you say. I'm a grown woman, independent and self-reliant. I don't need you. You were always much too drunk to know I existed. I saw the things you did. I know what you are. I will never go home, old man, so you might as well leave. Don't come back. It will be a cold day in hell before I ever ask you for anything, you worthless, pitiful old drunk."

Nettie grew defiant as he raised his hand. She glared and lifted her chin. As his hand swung toward her face, it seemed to stop in mid-air. Nettie turned to find Emmett gripping her father's arm.

"We have rules here about how ladies are treated. You'll have to go." Emmett left little doubt he would make the man leave, peacefully or otherwise.

Hayes Gordon jerked his arm away and straightened his jacket, quickly realizing all eyes in the bar were directed toward him.

"You mark my words, Nettie, you'll regret this," he threatened as he walked toward the door. Nettie bent to pick up the tray and silently hurried to the side door.

When Nettie did not appear to sing the last song of the evening, Emmett assumed she went home and was surprised to find her counting out the drawer of the side door register. He joined her behind the bar.

"What happened to Delmar?"

"He wasn't feeling well. I told him to go home."

"He was into the whiskey, no doubt. I'd like to drive you home."

"No, not tonight."

"You have a gentleman friend coming to pick you up?" Emmett teased. He received a glare in response.

"I want to walk," Nettie admitted.

"It's late. All the saloons are emptying out. You better let me drive you."

"That's not a good idea, Mr. Boyd." Nettie left the money and her tabulations on the bar and went to retrieve her things. "I'll see you next Saturday."

"I'll pick you up. I have to be at church by ten, so I'll come about 9:30."

"Oh, the weddings."

Emmett could see Nettie was attempting to formulate an excuse. Her brows were furrowed; she appeared deep in thought. Evidently her mind was not working quickly enough. "Nine-thirty then," was her only response and she was gone.

Realizing he now had a piece of the puzzle of Nettie Gordon, Emmett wasn't clear how to use it. The woman mystified him. Whenever he expected hysteria from her, he got only stoicism.

She was friendly, polite and sweet to customers. She somehow came to belong at the Golden State. If he mentioned anything in the least negative about her to Faith or Louise, they about bit his head off. Even the twins liked her and they didn't like anyone except each other.

He hadn't attempted to befriend any woman in more years than he could count. He doubted Nettie was worth the effort and yet there was something about her.

If Nettie was the one who broke the window, Emmett believed she would have admitted it. Yet, she spent the entire summer working off a debt that wasn't hers. She defended a man's right to drink, on religious principles no less, but evidently had reason to hate alcohol. He certainly knew more beautiful women, but when Nettie smiled, her whole face lit up. For some reason, he wanted her to smile at him. She was a curious woman.

Emmett needed to keep his wits about him. Certain Nettie would try to get out of attending the wedding, he was determined to see she didn't.

CHAPTER SEVEN

Knowing Nettie made her usual Wednesday afternoon visit with Louise, Emmett gave a preplanned warm smile when she approached the bar.

"I need to talk to you," she began.

"I was sure you did."

"What do you mean?"

"It means you're here to tell me you can't go to the wedding." This comment drew a startled response.

The thought Emmett anticipated her conversation was unsettling. "Well, I—"

"There is no need for apology or feigned important obligations. I completely understand."

"You do?"

"Yes. You feel uncomfortable coming as my guest. I want you to rest assured, my invitation was only meant to grant the brides' wishes for their day. They're both thrilled you're attending. I'm sure you wouldn't want to disappoint them.

"Then there is the fact you cost me yet another customer last Saturday. I would imagine the least you could do is agree to be my partner in a few dances." Emmett paused to see if his dialogue was having the desired effect. Nettie seemed as uncomfortable now as when he began.

"I also realize you might not want to show your face after your argument in the saloon. I imagine you wouldn't normally make such a public display and assume you were too angry to control yourself.

"You owe me a thank you for interfering, which is so far unexpressed. I know from personal experience, it would have hurt had your father struck you. He's a good bit larger than you, after all, and you showed no sign of ducking. The wedding might prove a comfortable way to reintroduce yourself to society."

At this, Nettie's chest was fairly heaving. Emmett knew he reached the limit of his uninterrupted discourse. "Lastly, knowing you are a devout Christian woman, I understand unimaginative lies such as you need to wash your hair or aren't feeling well would be out of the question. Have I covered all the bases?"

"All but one. What if I find you insufferable and egotistical beyond tolerance? What if I simply don't like you?"

"No, that's not possible," the gleam in Emmett's eyes was unmistakable. "Let me prove you wrong."

"How?"

"I will show you at 9:30 Saturday morning."

* * *

Glancing in her mirror, Nettie wondered if her apprehension was obvious. She splurged on a new dress for the wedding. The only appropriate thing she had to wear was a white tea gown and she didn't want to wear white. She purchased a pale pink lace gown with elbow-length flared sleeves and a frilly deep V-shaped collar. The dress was the latest fashion and fell several inches short of the floor. Her shoes were clearly visible. The waist was fitted; the skirt hugged her hips unlike any garment she ever wore before. The top of her straw-brimmed hat was covered in ribbon loops; the back was filled with pink velvet roses.

She knew Faith was entertaining in her backyard, which was not a risky venture in this part of the country. October could be quite warm in Los Angeles and today was such a day. Although Nettie didn't plan to be out late enough to catch a chill, she quickly grabbed a shawl before heading for the door. It was 9:30 sharp.

Eula could not resist the opportunity to see her friend's new apparel so accompanied her down the hall toward the staircase. "Oh, Nettie, you're beautiful!" Her comment drew a frown.

"Be serious, Eula. Do I look ridiculously like summer?"

"No, I'm telling you, I've never seen you look so beautiful."

As the two women reached the second-floor landing, Mrs. Green hurried over. "Your young man is here!" she breathlessly declared.

This drew another glare. "He is not my young man."

"Well it's obvious he thinks he is," retorted Mrs. Green. She and Eula held back to let Nettie descend the last staircase alone. Hoping to hear what was said, they peered down the stairwell.

Nettie would have to be blind not to notice the appreciation in Emmett's gaze. She smiled woodenly and placed her lace-gloved hand through his arm.

"You look gorgeous." Emmett realized he must sound rather stunned because he was. He never considered Nettie Gordon a beauty. But then, he'd only seen her in severe, high-collared, long-sleeved shirtwaists other than the day she fainted. Her hair had never been so artfully arranged. Even the freckles peppering her rosy cheeks seemed to accent her auburn hair and the pink of her dress.

Nettie would admit, if only to herself, Emmett was quite dashing in his wedding clothes—a silk-lined, charcoal morning coat. His pocket watch was draped across a matching vest. He wore a long necktie with a white high-band linen collar, gray striped slacks and a top hat. A white carnation served as boutonniere. Nettie, intent on appearing uninterested, nearly forgot her wedding gifts.

As they reached the front door, she proclaimed, "Wait! I mean, I need my gifts."

"Can I get them for you?"

"Cer-certainly," Nettie stuttered. She needed to calm down, afraid to make a fool of herself. "They're in the market bag on the table." Emmett retrieved the bag and offered his arm once more.

Eula gazed wide-eyed at Mrs. Green. "What do you think?"

"I think there's another wedding in the works! Oh, I'm sorry. Were you interested in that young man? I didn't mean to overstep."

"No, I have my heart set on someone else, Mrs. Green. But you don't know Nettie. She's adamantly opposed to marriage."

"Nonsense! What woman wouldn't melt at the touch of that man?"

"Nettie."

* * *

"We have plenty of time; I'll drive slowly so the wind doesn't do any damage. You didn't have to bring gifts. I should have told you."

"I wouldn't consider attending a wedding without a

gift."

"I put your name on my gifts."

"Oh, how thoughtful of you." This revelation made Nettie uncomfortable. "But these are not extravagant in any way. I actually have a stash of gift items. I pulled something from there."

"You must be quite a shopper to be so well-prepared."

"Not really. When I was small, my mother insisted I have a hope chest. I started making things for it when I was probably six. I like to embroider so there are a lot of linens stored away. The chest was the only thing I brought when I left home. I threw my clothes on top and away I went."

"But isn't the idea behind a hope chest to save things for your marriage?"

"You're right and it's exactly why I don't mind pilfering from it for gifts. I will never marry. I chose some tea towels and a china teapot for each of the girls."

"Your gifts seem more extravagant than you let on."

"I tried to be thoughtful. My relationship with your sisters seems to have begun over tea."

Emmett kept the conversation light on the way to church and explained his plans for the day. "I'll be deserting you for a brief time. I'm giving Charity away. Webster will accompany Hope. Faith has been assigned mother of the bride duties. This is bittersweet for all of us. Our parents were still alive when Faith married. It was a traditional ceremony and reception, more formal than today will be. My mother was prudish about what constituted a proper wedding. The Judge was more than eager to concur due to his standing in the community."

"What was Webster's wedding like?"

"Well, it was much more stodgy than anyone on

our side of the family cared for. It was quite proper, no drinking, no dancing. Actually, my mother would be rather appalled at what her children plan for today."

"Why?"

"There will be beer aplenty, dancing in the latest scandalous tradition and music she would not have approved. Her offspring started making their own radical decisions as soon as she passed. We haven't stopped since."

"What would so appall your mother?"

"When my parents were alive, there was no side door for ladies although other saloons had those. There were no socials, no dancing in the saloon, certainly no rags, rarely music and only of a classical nature. Although a lot of regulars from my parents' time still come in, we appeal to a younger clientele now."

Nettie soon found herself seated in the first row of the brides' side of the church next to Faith, whose responsibilities obviously made her nervous.

"Would it help if I held the baby when the ceremony begins?" Nettie offered. She was soon cuddling tiny baby Luther, who quickly fell asleep. This allowed Nettie to give her full attention to the service.

The brides wore matching gowns. Nettie was awe-struck by their stylish choice. The dresses were white lace with hems that fell above their shoes, as Nettie's did. The gowns had cap sleeves and rounded collarless necks. There was no apparent waistline—the lace fell from the neck all the way to the hem in one fluid and seamless form-fitting piece, including the short, rounded trains.

The girls exuded elegance. It seemed to Nettie the twins thoroughly enjoyed the spectacle they made with their identical husbands. Wifely emotion played no part in the ceremony or the reception.

The bridal couples shared their own table but soon worked their way around the backyard, visiting friends, relatives, and Harry and Larry's business associates. Nettie discovered the two men were successful land speculators. She thought this a rather insecure occupation and wondered at the result should financial hardship ever become a marital issue.

Once luncheon was served and dancing commenced, the twins frequently returned to the family table. Nettie sat at the large round table beside Emmett, next to Faith and the Judge. Webster and Nadine were also seated there along with two cousins and their spouses.

A number of cousins were in attendance. One came from San Diego, one all the way from Sacramento. It quickly became apparent to Nettie, the twins frequented the family table because they didn't want to miss out on the fun. If there were no empty seats, the girls simply plopped in Emmett or Webster's lap, much as if they were still children. It seemed their husbands were quickly forgotten.

Jokes, insults, and laughter rang out frequently. The party got louder as the afternoon progressed. Hats, coats, vests, and gloves were discarded for comfort's sake.

Nettie never saw Emmett take a drink at the Golden State, but he imbibed freely today while celebrating his sisters' marriages. Emmett coaxed Nettie to sample his "pride and joy"—beer brewed especially for the weddings.

"What do you think?" he asked, offering a taste from his glass. He seemed so eager to please, Nettie hated to be honest.

"It's the best beer I ever tasted." This drew a huge smile. "But I still don't like it."

At this, their entire table dissolved in laughter. Her

opinion simply gave Emmett's sundry relatives more ammunition. He was the most frequent target of the barbs and teasing essential to the family's warm relationship.

Nettie knew Emmett was correct, at least in one thing. She did see him in a different light today. He always appeared the serious businessman. It was apparent he was a distinctly more fun-loving and affable man than she ever imagined.

Emmett frequently took Nettie to dance, perhaps to escape relentless teasing. It seemed his work ethic, propensity to lose at cards and his stature put him in the spotlight. Nettie was mesmerized by the family's antics, even the fact the twins did not hesitate to whisper in their brothers' ears. Nettie imagined if Emmett had a wife, she might be unhappy with the siblings' familiarity.

She noted condemnation written all over Nadine's face, but Webster's wife was unhappy throughout the day. Nadine obviously disapproved of Webster's two mugs of beer, the music and dancing. She sat sullen and quiet but this did not deter the Boyd family from their celebration.

Nettie briefly wondered if she appeared as dour as Nadine. She had not imbibed, except for the sip of beer. The music and dancing delighted her. Begrudgingly, Nettie realized the thing she liked most about this enjoyable day was Emmett Boyd. He was relaxed and happy. This made her happy, too. He held some primitive attraction for her. Past experience made Nettie feel more comfortable with men of her own stature. Emmett was a virile, strong and attractive man and she thrilled at his touch. He served as her protector on more than one occasion which made her feel unusually at ease.

Jean Jegel

Nettie pushed all thoughts of her father aside, intent on preparing for the wedding—first in avoiding it, then in making the most of it. But the fact her father came to the saloon was horribly disturbing. Had he walked in and found her there, to his surprise? He claimed he no longer drank so it seemed unlikely. If someone told him of her job at the Golden State, who could it be?

The thing she feared most was the possibility he could turn up somewhere else. Did he know where she lived? Did he know where she taught school and went to church? Somehow, her apprehension did not seem so daunting when Emmett held her in his arms or sat beside her. This proved a difficult idea to reconcile.

As servants hung mason jars filled with tapers, the yard became a fairyland of candle glow. White tablecloths reflected the light and stood in stark contrast to the evening darkness.

The last dance before the musicians took a well-deserved break was a polka. Emmett twirled Nettie around the wooden dance floor at a dizzying pace. She embraced him when the music ended to keep from falling over.

Using her handkerchief to wipe her brow, Nettie took a place on a blanket under a tree to wait while Emmett fetched punch and wedding cake to share. She imagined he'd grab another beer for himself.

Her suspicion was confirmed when Emmett approached. He balanced a cup of punch on the edge of a cake plate and held a mug of beer in his other hand.

"Can you take the punch before I drop everything?" Emmett requested.

"Thank you. Oh, it's nice and cold."

There was the smile Emmett wanted. "Your cheeks are still red. Are you cooling off? I'm sorry if—"

"Oh, there's no need to be sorry. I much enjoy

dancing."

Emmett sat down and sampled the cake. Although it was good, he believed the cold beer more refreshing so he handed the plate to Nettie. "You can have the rest."

"You don't care for cake?"

"Usually, but my beer hits the spot. I do believe the grooms are anxious to begin the honeymoon," he observed.

"Your sisters don't seem in any hurry. They're enjoying the celebration in their honor which is probably wise. Their marriage will last the rest of their lives; a wedding day is a unique event."

"I'm afraid it's a unique event in different ways for brides than it is for grooms." Emmett smiled as Nettie blushed. It was hard to imagine her cheeks could actually turn a darker shade. "I'll be honest. I would give pretty good odds my sisters will return home with me tonight."

"You're not serious?"

"I am. I don't believe they're particularly earnest about marriage. I doubt they've considered the consequences of their actions. It might seem they're worldly women. After all, they did literally grow up in a saloon. I can assure you they are quite innocent. They were never courted before Harry and Larry showed up. They have a great deal of bravado, which is basically an act. They've always been coddled and protected. Even I was surprised when I caught a glimpse of the bedroom they share last week. For all intents and purposes, an eight-year-old girl could move right in and feel perfectly at home. Dolls and toys fill the room."

"So, they're not prepared for marriage at all?"

"I wouldn't say that. Faith sat them down to have a talk before the engagements took place. I believe she was quite direct. I doubt the girls paid attention. When they don't wish to deal with reality, they simply ignore it, lost in their own little world."

"Your house will be quiet without them."

"I'd be lying if I didn't admit there were many days when I longed to be left to my own devices. But I'm certain I'll find the solitude strange until I adjust. Look, here come our favorite brides as we speak."

"What are you two doing over here all by yourselves?"

"You have to come and participate."

"Emmett, we're counting on you."

"It's bad luck if our garters touch the ground."

"You must be our champion."

Nettie thought this an odd comment. She never heard of such a superstition.

"And Nettie, we're going to throw our bouquets first."

Each twin linked an arm in Nettie's and walked her off to the throng of single women intent on becoming the next bride. Nettie allowed herself to be positioned in front of the group and understood she was being set up. Nettie knew she needn't worry. Ladies were always anxious to catch the bouquet. She stood with her arms at her sides as women contorted themselves in every manner possible to reach the bouquets. In the end, a cousin and Webster's oldest daughter, Susan, won the prizes. Nettie walked to the side as the single men took their turn.

Emmett, intent to bring his sisters good luck, did not notice when other bachelors slunk away from the high-flying garters. He managed to catch them both and held them above his head in victory only to receive laughter in response. Undaunted, he proudly slipped a garter on each shirtsleeve, adjusting them above his elbows.

The twins escorted him back to Nettie.

"Nettie, will you sing a song?"

Her eyes popped open wide, "Me?"

"Yes, we enjoy your singing at the Golden State."

"You must sing for us."

"It's our day."

"Don't be shy."

"Emmett will sing too."

Emmett gave Nettie a sly look. "It seems we haven't much choice."

"You're right."

"The musicians know what to play."

Emmett offered his arm and an anxious Nettie accompanied him. The twins selected an appropriate piece of music, *I Love You Truly*. Nettie began the song and Emmett joined in. She never heard him sing before. He had a fine voice.

The words seemed much too intimate. Although Emmett stared at her as he sang, she decided it best to focus on the newly married couples. Whether or not Emmett condoned the obvious romantic plotting of the twins, Nettie felt extremely awkward and quickly walked back to their table as the remaining guests clapped.

All too soon, it was time for the couples to leave; none too soon as far as Harry and Larry were concerned. The final farewells were for family so Nettie sat alone cradling a sound-asleep baby Luther. She watched the twins hug the Judge then their sister as tears began to fall. Next in line was Emmett, who lowered his face to whisper between the girls' ears. This caused an extreme case of waterworks. They desperately clutched at him but finally moved down the line to receive Webster's wishes.

Almost absent-mindedly, Nettie watched Emmett shake hands with his new brothers-in-law. She paid much more attention as the smiles on the twins' faces turned to alarm. Whatever Emmett said instantly drew the attention of both Faith and Webster, who turned to stare at their younger brother. The grooms moved quickly down the line, seemingly in more of a hurry to depart than ever.

Nettie was interrupted in her observations as Nadine sat next to her.

"Faith's baby is adorable."

"He is. Oh, you're his aunt; wouldn't you like to hold him?"

"No, the thrill of holding babies is long past for me."

"Didn't you want to go with the rest of the family to send the couples on their way?"

"Webbie will give my regards. Besides, those girls could care less whether or not I came today. They would probably have preferred I stay home."

"What a sad idea. I'm sure they're happy so many family members could be here."

"The only people on the face of the earth those girls care about, besides each other, are their sister and brothers. And I'm deliberately leaving their husbands off that list."

Nettie wished Emmett would return to rescue her from the awkward conversation.

"I believed I might have an ally in you when I heard you would be here today," Nadine continued.

"An ally?"

"Yes, someone who shared my view of the world. I thought you were a staunch member of the WCTU. I have nothing in common with my husband's family. They dislike everything about me. I'm only here because

Webster insisted."

"Don't you feel it's a good idea for your children to be here, to know their family? The Boyds are close-knit, nothing like my own family. I admire their loving relationships. Surely there must be things you have in common."

"I don't mind saying, I completely disapprove of the Boyds. I foolishly thought my husband could break away from his family and be content with his own. Until recently, he seemed to have done so. Now he's more intent than ever on spending Sundays here at Faith's and attending his boyhood church."

"Is that so terrible? Perhaps you could suggest trading off between his church and yours? There must be a compromise you could reach."

"I don't wish to compromise. I find everything about the Boyds quite repulsive. I'm certain they're all headed straight for hell, between their dancing and liquor, not to mention the card games they so relish. It would be one thing if they imbibed on occasion but Emmett continues the family business, leading others down the path to damnation. I'm certain you understand how distressing it is for me to see my children exposed to such behavior."

Nettie tried to be tactful. "I understand your views. I tried for years to reconcile biblical principles with the ideas of the temperance movement. Hard as I searched, the Bible simply does not forbid drinking. I think it admirable when a person chooses to refrain from alcohol, particularly those who seem prey to drunkenness. But biblical principles support moderation in all things. We must all decide these issues for ourselves. I don't think it's particularly beneficial to force your own views on others. I enjoy an intellectual debate as much as the next person, but I reserve the right

Jean Jegel

to make my own choices. The WCTU and similar institutions seek to force their ideas on the general population."

"Do not be deceived; God is not mocked: for whatsoever a man soweth, that also he shall reap," Nadine quoted.

"But each man gets to sow his own seeds and suffer his own consequences. The mob mentality regarding morals makes me uncomfortable. I don't believe it can lead anywhere beneficial."

"Of course, it will."

"Think about what it would mean if the WCTU got its way. People like your husband who enjoy an occasional beer would be made criminals. You can't be naïve enough to believe if drinking is illegal it will cease? When did making a law against anything wipe it off the face of the earth? It will only serve to criminalize what is usually a harmless activity. As I look around at the revelers at this reception, I don't think any of them deserve to go to jail. And if God frowns on their activities, it's between them and God."

"I don't think you're taking societal welfare into account."

"I think you're trying to control other people's behavior when it's your own you should be worried about."

Nettie became silent as Nadine's youngest child, three-year-old Rose, rubbed her eyes as she approached.

"What is it Rose? Are you tired?" Rose nodded in agreement. "Let's go get your father. It's time to go home." Nadine took Rose's hand and walked toward her husband without further comment, passing Emmett on the way. Nettie never intended the conversation to become so acrimonious.

"From the look on my sister-in-law's face, it's

apparent Webster's family will be leaving shortly. How did you manage to set her off?"

"It wasn't hard to do," Nettie admitted.

Emmett laughed. "You catch on quick."

"So, what was it you said to startle Harry and Larry?"

"Oh, I simply explained I have certain expectations. I want my sisters treated respectfully. I felt it necessary to be clear."

"They did leave for their honeymoons."

"But how long will they stay, Nettie? That is the question. What do you say we find that boy's mother and have another go at the dance floor?"

* * *

The last dance was a waltz, the haunting *Ashokan Farewell*. Once the musicians called it quits, Emmett asked if Nettie would mind staying so he could visit his cousins. This turned into a rowdy game of pinochle, lasting well past midnight.

Faith retired when the card game commenced and gave Nettie a sympathetic nod before going inside. The Judge, however, was in his element and proved himself a more than adequate competitor for Emmett and his cousins. Nettie was the only woman at the table, the female relations having retired about the same time Faith left. She decided to play the part of observer. The entire table broke into laughter when Webster returned, having escorted his family home.

"Why it's Webbie!" shouted the older cousin with the brown beard and bald head.

"Have a seat. Got rid of the old ball and chain, eh Webbie?" commented the cousin with the handlebar mustache.

Nettie was amused. Nadine's nickname for her

husband was apparently a family joke. She noticed neither Emmett nor the Judge joined in the ribbing.

Once the game finally broke up, Emmett escorted Nettie home. As the automobile accelerated, Nettie took note of Emmett's route.

"This is not the way home."

"We're taking a detour. I want to show you what my Buick can do on the open road. The 10-mile-an-hour speed limit in the city doesn't do her justice."

The road seemed rough at the higher speed, but Nettie found the ride exhilarating. She was disappointed when Emmett finally pulled in front of Mrs. Green's. He turned off the motor and faced his passenger.

"I know I kept you out later than intended. Thank you for coming. I had a lot of fun."

"I enjoyed the day, myself," Nettie admitted.

"And did I prove my point?"

"What point?"

"I think you do like me. It was the point of my invitation, remember? That and pleasing the brides."

"I believe you proved your point. You are a nice man."

"Nice. Well, it's not quite the endorsement I was hoping for, but I'll take it. I wondered if you might have pity on a poor, lonely bachelor and come with me to church tomorrow. Oh, it's in only a few hours. Can I come back for you about 8:30? I'm all alone in the world now, rattling around in my large, empty house. Feel sorry for me?"

"I certainly do not. You haven't exactly rattled around so far. Your sisters only just left. Besides, I think you have a companion already."

"Who?"

"Your cat."

"Oh, Hallie. She's not my cat."

"Whose cat is she?"

"She belongs to the twins. She was a black kitten they rescued on Halloween, thus the name Hallie."

"Are the girls taking her?"

"I rather doubt it. Hallie wisely has no use for the twins."

"Then I believe you are the pet owner and no longer alone in the world."

"Well, I would much appreciate you coming. As I mentioned before, there are these ladies at church who seem intent on capturing my heart. I'm not interested. The least you could do, as my friend, is let people believe we're a couple. Word will spread I took you to the weddings. If you accompany me to church, I may be able to avoid hurting anyone's feelings. Then there would be dinner at Faith's afterwards. My family will want to discuss the wedding and a couple of my cousins will be there. Everyone will have a good time. Maybe you could play cards instead of merely observing."

Nettie bit her lip in contemplation. "I suppose I could ask Eula to take my Sunday school class with hers tomorrow, er, later."

"Then I'll see you soon!" After helping Nettie from the Buick, Emmett politely kissed her hand at the door and bade her good night.

Humming the wedding march all the way home, Emmett entered his own front door only to find his twin sisters crying in the dark.

CHAPTER EIGHT

Nettie stood on the front porch of Mrs. Green's boarding house impatiently tapping her foot. Evidently, Emmett was too preoccupied to come for her after all. Although she would be late for her own service, Nettie headed for the trolley stop. Before she got half a block, she turned to see who was furiously honking their horn so early on a Sunday morning. Emmett's Buick pulled up beside her. Nettie glared and continued on her way.

"I'm sorry," Emmett yelled. "My sisters came home. I didn't even sleep. Won't you get in and let me explain?"

Nettie stopped and took a look. Emmett did appear rather rumpled. There were dark circles under his eyes possibly caused by the beer he drank at the reception. Her curiosity about the twins won out. Nettie climbed into the passenger seat and waited for further explanation.

Emmett paused to consider the terminology he wished to use. He was tired and didn't want to offend. It seemed things with Nettie Gordon might be improving. Although he was only interested in friendship, he didn't want to suffer a setback.

"When I drove home, the twins were there. They

didn't want to—their husbands were anxious to consummate the marriages, as was certainly their right. Those men should never have decided to go on a group honeymoon."

"Why?"

"There is power in numbers."

"What does that mean?"

"I'm quite certain countless women have decided marriage may have been a mistake once their wedding night was upon them. I'm equally certain countless men have persuaded them otherwise. Once the twins made a unilateral decision to return home, there wasn't much Harry and Larry could do to stop them. Eventually, they showed up to claim their wives. They weren't eager to do so as they felt I might prove a stumbling block."

"Why would they think that?"

"It might have been something I said. At any rate, I convinced the girls to depart for their honeymoons. I wouldn't be at all surprised if they took one room and sent their husbands to the other. I'm not sure if they will come home as wives or candidates for annulment, but that won't be for two weeks. I'm not going to worry about it. It's up to those boys to convince Hope and Charity they want to be married; I can't do it for them. I'm certain the convincing will prove expensive. They only just left. I changed clothes and hurried right over."

Emmett had a propensity to nod off during the sermon. He snored quietly on more than a few occasions. Nettie first tugged on the sleeve of his coat to rouse him then resorted to elbowing him in the side. If his intent was to announce to the congregation he had a lady friend, he more than succeeded. Nettie was certain he managed to draw the attention of every parishioner at the service.

After arriving at Faith's, they played a few games

of hearts before supper. Emmett struggled to stay awake. Nettie worried he might fall asleep while driving the car and kept a sharp eye on him all the way home. She wondered if he would make it to his own home in one piece.

"Are you going to stay awake?" she inquired as Emmett showed her to the front door of the boarding house.

"Why, are you inviting me up to have a nap in your bed?"

"How inappropriate of you, Mr. Boyd."

"I thought my name was Emmett now." He yawned, barely able to keep his eyes open.

"Not when I am vexed at you."

"Oh, you're vexed, are you?"

"I think you should leave your automobile here and take the trolley home."

"Why don't you drive me home if you're so worried?"

"I certainly don't know how to drive and I'm not at all worried about you. You're vain to think so."

"Hmm, what are you worried about then?"

"My paycheck."

Emmett laughed. "Leave it to you to put me in my place, Miss Gordon. See you on Wednesday."

"No, I don't work on Wednesday."

"I know you, Nettie. I'll find you holding court in my closet on Wednesday. There is no doubt of it," he yelled as he cranked the engine and climbed into the driver's seat.

Nettie turned to watch him drive away, much faster than was his habit. If he made it home in one piece, it would be a miracle.

* * *

Nettie attempted to make every holiday a special event for her pupils. Halloween was no exception. Many churches frowned on festivities related to Halloween, but her church did not. Nettie was free to celebrate as she liked, although she refrained from anything vaguely macabre. Her students' pictures of jack-o-lanterns and black cats decorated the room. She carved a large pumpkin for the corner of her desk. Nettie briefly entertained the idea of bringing Hallie to school but decided it might be difficult to control a cat in a classroom of 40 small children.

Nettie served cookies and punch after lunch. The children played games throughout the day, including blind man's buff, bobbing for apples, bean-bag toss and walnut shell boat racing. Although the children were unusually excited, she managed to control her class effectively. The afternoon's activities came to a close when Miss Gordon pulled the shades and turned off the lights to read a scary story by candlelight.

When class was dismissed, Nettie stood at the door handing out small salt-water-taffy-filled bags embroidered with jack-o-lanterns. She noticed Emmett Boyd leaning against the wall across the hallway.

"Whatever are you doing here, Mr. Boyd?"

"Would you believe me if I told you I couldn't wait until tomorrow to see you?"

"I would not. Try again."

"Well, I was hoping you weren't busy tonight. We're hosting a Halloween social at the side door and Faith thought it would be beneficial if I enlisted your help. I'm sorry I didn't ask earlier, but we've been preoccupied with the weddings. Would you care to join me? I'll pay you for your help."

Oddly, Nettie found the offer to be paid disquieting. She wished Emmett asked her as a friend.

Before she could reply, a grim Mr. Pendergast stuck his head out the office door and demanded, "Miss Gordon, I need to see you."

"I was on my way out. Could this wait until morning?"

"No, it certainly cannot."

"I'll wait here for you," offered Emmett, who was in a hurry to be on his way. Halloween at the Golden State had always been a family affair. The twins would be missed tonight. Faith and Webster were busy decorating the side door, which was presently closed. They planned to stay for the evening.

Emmett was troubled by the dour look on his employee's face when she emerged from the school office. Something of substance evidently occurred.

"Would you mind waiting for a moment while I collect some things?" Nettie asked.

"Certainly. Can I help?"

"Wait here. I'll be out in a minute. There's a box I need you to carry."

In less than ten minutes, the door to the classroom opened. Nettie pushed a box into the hall. She turned and gazed back at the room then closed the door as Emmett picked up the corrugated cardboard box. "What's this? You have a lot of papers to grade?" he teased, but he could see Nettie was not in a joking mood.

"Something like that." The ride to the Golden State was unusually quiet. Nettie stared out the side of the motor car, lost in thought.

Emmett decided to keep an eye on his friend. Initially distracted, Nettie was soon engrossed in putting her personal touch on decorations. He was certain not one Halloween item remained in the storage crates.

The barroom was dark save for the glow of candles

from a multitude of jack-o-lanterns. A "witch"—a pumpkin-head scarecrow padded with pillows—stood near the entrance dressed in a white nightshirt and black conical hat. Nettie helped set up food for a larger-than-normal buffet. Marcel outdid himself.

The side door was ready for customers at 6 p.m., sharp. Ladies were admitted for free. Gentlemen paid one dollar for unlimited beer, all they could eat and musical entertainment for the evening. Many of the revelers wore masks or costumes, from elaborate to simple, worn clothing.

Faith, dressed as a fortune teller, foretold risqué and riotous destinies in a tented corner, aside from a 45-minute break when she walked home to nurse the baby.

The ghost march was a yearly tradition. Unattached ladies were draped in sheets and auctioned off to gentlemen seeking a partner for the evening. The proceeds from the march were earmarked for a nearby orphanage.

A traditional "peanut carry" game commenced during a break in the music. Guests hurried across the dance floor balancing peanuts on the backs of their hands to fill a bowl on the opposite side of the room. The contestant with the most peanuts won one of Marcel's pumpkin pies.

Nettie never saw the side door so crowded. Hurrying to keep the buffet table stocked, she almost ran into Webster. He grasped her arms to hold her steady.

"We appreciate your help tonight, Miss Gordon, so long as you don't cause bodily injury to yourself in the process."

Nettie smiled a weak smile. "I'm surprised you're here tonight. I would think you'd want to be with your family."

"My wife feels any celebration of Halloween to be

a direct ticket to hell. Appalled as she is when I acknowledge this day, you can imagine her horror if I took the children to any festivities." Webster seemed affable enough at his predicament and smiled genially. He always appeared to be thoroughly enjoying himself. "The decorations have never been better. We're much obliged."

"I didn't do much."

"Nonsense. Leave it to a teacher to put everything in perfect order," he complimented but noticed his comment caused a frown to cross Nettie's features. "Did I misspeak?"

"No, certainly not. I need to go refresh the punchbowl." Nettie hurried away, leaving Webster perplexed. He wandered over to the bar where Emmett was busily filling beer mugs.

"Your lady friend doesn't seem herself tonight. What did you do to her?"

Emmett frowned. "What makes you think it's my fault?"

"I know you all too well, little brother. You are forever shooting yourself in the foot where decent women are concerned."

"You're making presumptions. First of all, I have no idea what has caused Miss Gordon's melancholia and second, you assume she's a decent woman."

Webster chuckled at this comment. "That must be your problem. You can't even tell a decent woman when you find one."

"Decency is overrated." But Emmett recalled the last time Nettie was absent-minded at work—the day Luther was born.

"Go ask her to dance. I'll watch things here," urged Webster.

"I believe I will."

* * *

Faith glanced through the opening in her gypsy "tent" to find her younger brother dancing with Nettie. Emmett seemed to be enjoying himself. Nettie struggled to manage so much as a smile. There were only a few minutes until the witching hour—10 p.m. at the Golden State. Faith believed this was the best-attended Halloween social ever and on a Tuesday night, no less. A rather inebriated gentleman bumped into Emmett as the dance ended.

"Hey, buddy, watch where you're going," accused the man.

"I think you've had a bit too much to drink, my friend," cajoled Emmett. "Why don't you have a seat and I'll get you a cup of coffee before you leave? Who is this bewitching lady you've brought?"

"What? You mean Sarah?" Sarah looked to be about as far gone as her husband.

"Why don't we get Sarah some coffee, too?" Emmett motioned for Louise to deliver coffee as he directed the pair to a table. Since the front bar was quiet tonight, Delmar was on his own up there. No sooner did Emmett turn from the table than he and Nettie were swept away by Faith.

"Farina, gypsy fortune teller extraordinaire, has one last fortune tonight." She noted Nettie looked none too eager to participate, but Faith continued, regardless. As the three took their places in the corner, "Farina" began, "Oh, I see a great love." Faith traced a line on Nettie's palm. "I see a tall, handsome, muscular, yet annoying man who spends too much time at work and not enough at play." Emmett frowned. "Never fear, it's not this man," she assured Nettie. "I see many, many children." Before Faith could continue, Nettie pulled her hand away and exited the improvised tent, obviously upset.

Faith stared at her brother. "I'm sorry, I was only joking."

"For some reason, Nettie isn't happy tonight. It has nothing to do with you."

"Does it have to do with you?"

"No. Why does everybody blame me for Miss Gordon's disposition?"

"Well, you should make it up to her, just the same."

Emmett glared at his sister then went to announce closing time. Nettie was nowhere in sight.

After the crowd reluctantly filed out the door, Emmett went in search of the illusive Miss Gordon, finally locating her in the alley. She leaned against the back of the building and did not acknowledge his presence. Emmett took a place beside her to share her observation of the tiny crescent moon perched above the roof of his house.

"It's kind of cold out here, isn't it? The twins are lucky the weather was so pleasant the night they married." Nettie was not inclined to comment. "Is something wrong?"

"No," came the too-quick reply.

"Oh, I'm glad to hear it." Emmett briefly wondered what he was doing. Nettie Gordon's problems, whatever they might be, were none of his concern. "If you're in a hurry to go home, I can drop you off before I clean up. You don't have to stay. Nettie? Did you hear me?" Emmett stood away from the wall, trying to view Nettie's expression in the darkness. "Nettie?" he asked again as he gripped her arms. He managed to make out her features in the dim glow of a nearby street light. She looked so gentle, innocent and vulnerable.

Without a single coherent thought in his head, Emmett leaned over to give a tentative and tender kiss. He pulled away and looked into Nettie's eyes. At least she didn't draw her knife. Surprisingly, she didn't resist and embraced him in return when he kissed her once more.

He was stunned as she stepped away and declared, "Don't do that again." Nettie disappeared through the kitchen door.

Taking a deep breath of cool night air, Emmett attempted to collect his thoughts. Why did he kiss her? Was he desperate for female companionship? He would admit it felt right to hold Nettie Gordon in his arms. He felt protective, almost proprietary. His thoughts proved unsatisfactory.

Determined to find her and try to talk, Emmett wandered through the side door into the main saloon. Despite constant interruptions, he eventually circled through the closet and made his way back to the kitchen.

"Have you seen Nettie?" he asked Bao.

"She leave right after you come in."

Emmett walked across the alley determined to inspect the box Nettie left in his Buick. It was gone.

* * *

Louise was obviously distracted on Wednesday night. Nettie failed to appear for their weekly meeting. Emmett also became concerned. Teachers were, after all, creatures of habit—completely dependable. Even though Nettie often confounded him, she was a reliable and trustworthy person.

He thought back to their kiss. In fact, he spent a good portion of the night thinking about that kiss. Why was he drawn to Nettie? Why did she allow him to kiss her? What did her warning mean? Lost in thought, Emmett overflowed the mug of beer he was pouring.

Before opening on Thursday morning, Louise walked through the front door and headed straight for the bar where Emmett was filling the cash register.

"Something terrible has happened."

Realizing Louise was not generally dramatic aside from her workday persona, Emmett paid attention.

"I need to explain. Nettie is my daughter's teacher. We neither one realized this until I went for a meeting at Daisy's school. When I got home last night, my sister-in-law told me Daisy was inconsolable the entire afternoon. Miss Gordon was gone from school and a Mrs. Pendergast has taken her place. All the children love Miss Gordon. She's the reason the school grew so quickly. I don't know what happened. My sister-in-law will try to find out when she picks Daisy up today. I'm worried about Nettie. Do you know anything about this?"

"I don't think we need to be melodramatic. I'm certain she'll show up for work on Saturday." Emmett imagined Nettie's strange mood on Tuesday could be the result of having lost her position. Even as he tried to quiet Louise's concern, Emmett felt an almost overwhelming desire to drive to Mrs. Green's and appease his own anxiety.

The fact the Golden State was understaffed was causing problems. Emmett was tied to his business ever since Webster left and he began to consider there might be more to life than work.

* * *

"Nettie, open the door, I want to talk to you," pled Eula. "I need you to explain what happened." Eula banged furiously on the door.

"Go away," came the flat reply.

"You can't stay in there forever. Nettie, you're my best friend. I want to help." No further reply was forthcoming.

Eula threw her hands in the air and stomped down the stairs. How could she help if Nettie locked herself away? She had not been seen since Tuesday. A more unpleasant thought occurred to Eula. This whole mess was likely her fault. How would she ever make amends?

Eula took a seat at the breakfast table.

"Did you get Miss Gordon to open her door?" inquired Mrs. Green.

"No. She won't talk to me."

"I'll leave a tray for her in the hallway again." Mrs. Green was not averse to delivering Miss Gordon's meals, although she merely picked at the food. Mrs. Green had other concerns. If Miss Gordon lost her position, the girl would need to find another place to live. She paid in advance for November and was always a good boarder, but Mrs. Green had her own problems.

She lived in grand style while Mr. Green was alive. Upon his untimely death, she was left with only one asset—her lovely home on Bunker Hill. It was her sole source of income.

Having retained the services of her gardener and housekeeper, she took on the cooking chores herself. She made only a meager profit and could not afford to house Miss Gordon without compensation. If the girl did not find work, Mrs. Green, of necessity, would have to evict her.

After breakfast was served to her guests—she always thought of her boarders as guests, it made life less mundane to imagine she had a houseful of company—Mrs. Green prepared a soft-boiled egg, toast and a small pot of tea. She carried the tray up to Miss Gordon's room and knocked softly at the door.

"Breakfast is here." As she turned and walked toward the stairwell, she noticed the door open. The tray disappeared inside the room.

Nettie, finally hungry, enjoyed the egg and toast. She savored the pot of tea and consumed every drop after taking her customary position—sitting on the floor beneath the window. She remained in her nightgown, having not bothered to dress since coming home on Halloween night. Breakfast and tea raised her spirits temporarily.

As Nettie turned her head to stare out the window, the calamity of her life came closing in. She loved and missed her students and would never see them again. She wasn't even allowed to say goodbye. There would be no references she might use to secure another teaching position. She realized fully this was her own doing, no matter how tempting it was to blame whoever informed the church of her job at the Golden State. That person was likely her father.

Mr. Pendergast made short work of terminating her employment. Nettie had no choice but to admit she worked Saturdays at the saloon. This was considered a morally inappropriate occupation for a school teacher. She was quickly shown the door without opportunity to plead her case.

The church elders reported her errant behavior to Principal Pendergast and left the matter to his judgment. He undoubtedly took the opportunity to provide his wife with a job. Nettie briefly contemplated a life where she stayed in her room forever tending her plants, but reality soon invaded her fantasy.

Having spent the money she made at the Golden State on wedding frippery, Nettie understood how desperate her situation was but failed to consider solutions. She could not focus long enough to read or embroider, basically having sat on the floor or slept for the past several days.

Tomorrow, she would have to find a way to drag

herself to work, the only work for which she was now suited. The Golden State never seemed much different than waitressing.

Teaching, her students and classroom—Nettie's heart ached over her loss. Perhaps she was simply tired. Pushing the empty tray into the hallway, Nettie crawled back in bed. Sleep seemed her only refuge.

* * *

Emmett stared at the *Herald* as he sipped his morning cup of coffee. Although he was anxious to see Nettie walk through the door, his attention had been diverted by the headlines. He was interested in the situation in Russia. The civil disorder caused by the Social Democrats was resulting in carnage on a scale almost unimaginable. Hundreds of Jews were murdered yesterday in a town named Kishineff. Only last week, the Czar agreed to an English-style government where he gave control to the people. They were not appeased.

The other big story was a terrible train accident north of San Luis Obispo. Emmett paged through the paper to find the bar and café at the Hermosa Hotel was robbed by an armed, masked assailant who actually fired at an uncooperative victim. The idea he should stow a revolver near the register was not new. Since there were often police or sheriffs in the saloon, he refrained from keeping a firearm. Perhaps it was time he put some protection in place.

Emmett shook his head. The news made him edgy. He admittedly felt relieved when he spotted Nettie in the side door. She must have come in through the kitchen.

Despite repeated attempts to converse with Miss Gordon, she managed to evade Emmett's attention. She looked haggard and unhappy. As far as he could tell, Louise hadn't managed to speak to her either. Nettie hurried away whenever anyone entered the side door. If the saloon was less busy, he would have pursued her no matter how quickly she managed to scamper off.

Emmett thought he finally found his opportunity when Nettie snuck up to the cash register to make change. No sooner did he finish serving a beer to a customer at the opposite end of the bar than the young man who paid court to Nettie at the boarding house came bursting through the door. "Nettie!" he called out as he scanned the saloon.

"I'm here," she answered from behind the bar. "What are you doing here?"

"I heard about your distress. They refused to let me see you at the boarding house. I had no choice but to try to find you."

Nettie, not wishing the clientele to know her business, hustled to the middle of the room where Vicar Haf stood. As she approached, the good vicar dropped down on one knee, much to Nettie's horror.

"I've come to redeem your honor," the vicar announced. "Nettie Gordon, will you marry me?" he pled as he grasped her hand and looked longingly into her face.

"Get off the floor, Vicar Haf. I assure you, my honor needs no redemption and I have no more plan to marry now than I did the last time you pursued me." All eyes were turned in her direction. Nettie's face felt hot; she could not imagine a more uncomfortable situation. Although she had no desire to embarrass the vicar, there seemed little choice.

"But Nettie, you're destitute. What choice have you but to marry? I can give you the respectability you lost. Please consider my offer," he begged.

Breathing heavily, Nettie stared down at the man who, against advice, remained on his knee. He was making a fool of himself and her, as well.

The vicar stuffed his hand in his pocket and fished out a modest engagement ring. He held it up to her expectantly.

"You don't even know me."

"Miss Gordon, I know you have a good heart. You've been dealt an unfair blow. I know you're a good Christian woman. What more do we need to begin life together? Many have started with less."

Nettie studied the expectant faces turned her way. It seemed obvious everyone in the saloon was rooting for her to accept, a supposedly happy ending to the vicar's ridiculous proposal. Even Louise appeared delighted. Only one face seemed less than eager. Emmett Boyd glared at her contemptuously.

Feeling dizzy and sick, Nettie pulled her hand away, untied her apron and dropped it on the floor. She turned and marched out the front door and down the sidewalk, leaving Vicar Haf kneeling in the middle of the Golden State.

Nettie ducked between two buildings and started for the alley. She didn't want the vicar to catch up, were he to follow. She had no money. Even if Nettie walked toward Bunker Hill, she didn't have the fare to take Angel's Flight to the top on the warm day. Three rides for ten cents seemed a stiff price to pay in her current situation, even if she had her reticule.

The faster she hurried away from the Golden State, the more she realized the need to return. Nettie walked through a vacant lot, crossed the street and headed for the next alleyway, certain no one would follow. Breathing heavily, she slid down against a wall and folded her arms on top of bent knees. Dropping her face on her arms, she began to cry. Remorse and self-pity welled up and finally spilled over.

Having left Louise in charge, Emmett hurried out the alley door to avoid drawing the vicar's attention. This proved a wise choice as he caught sight of Nettie scrambling down the alley to his left. He decided to keep his distance and follow discreetly but soon understood the woman was making good time and would lose him if he didn't hurry. Turning the corner of the second alleyway, Emmett found a sobbing Nettie sitting against a building. He walked quietly alongside and as she looked up to see who was there, sat down beside her.

"Having a rough week?" Emmett asked as Nettie dropped her face back onto her arms without reply. "I thought so. You've led me to believe you are an unemotional person. I have to admit, it comes as a great shock to see you crying."

"Go away."

Emmett pulled his handkerchief from his pocket and handed it to her. Without looking at him, she took it and blew her nose.

"I take it something dire has occurred. I heard a rumor you lost your teaching position." Emmett felt he was talking to himself but continued anyway. "I imagine this might have something to do with your work at the Golden State." He felt more than a little guilt at this idea. He never intended to cause Nettie to lose her job, even in the beginning. He was impressed by the love between teacher and students he witnessed on Halloween.

"So, you're out of work and destitute? I imagined you were something of a penny pincher with vast resources. What happened to the money you made since the window was paid off?"

"I spent it on clothes."

"Ah, a woman's true weakness, vanity. It's certain, a well-dressed woman does have a better opportunity to procure employment."

"I spent it on clothes for the weddings last weekend."

This admission added more fuel to Emmett's guilt. "What say we walk back to my house? You can relax and I'll have Bao bring over some dinner. Then I'll drive you home at ten. We can talk about the possibility of a new position since you're in need of employment and I'm in need of employees. I'm ready to send Delmar packing. He's been helping himself to my profits. I can't offer you a job in your preferred profession, but I assure you, I pay more than you would ever make teaching school."

At this, Nettie raised her pink, swollen eyes and stared at Emmett. He expected some form of gratitude. Instead he found defiance in her glare.

"I am not one of your projects."

"What does that mean?"

"The twins told me. You never have sweethearts, only projects—women who need help. I am not a project."

Emmett was shocked at the proclamation. What else did the twins say about him? "I assure, you are no project. I'm making a business proposal. I don't have projects."

"Would you be making this proposal if you didn't think I was needy? What about Louise? She's one of your projects."

"She is not. She's a good waitress, that's all. If anything, she's your project."

"How can you say such a thing?"

"You're the one who took her on, getting her to read and better her life. She's your project."

"Simply because she wants to learn to read and spend more time at home doesn't make her my project."

How had this discussion devolved into an argument? At least Nettie ceased crying. Emmett quietly reflected on her assertions.

"Well, I admit I always admired your work ethic. I never thought you would consider a fulltime job at the Golden State or I would probably have asked. I know this isn't a job you would seek for yourself, but as I explained, it could tide you over until you find a teaching position. It would help me while I find some trustworthy employees. I think it best to keep you at the side door as my manager. Men keep making fools of themselves over you in the front saloon.

"I know you're unhappy at losing your job, but as a Christian, aren't you assured all things work for your good in the end?"

"I seriously doubt God wishes me to become a bartender."

"It's a great mystery isn't it? And as far as being categorized as either a project or a sweetheart, I promise, I will not take you on as a project." The sudden relief he experienced when Nettie walked away from the vicar's proposal recurred. "So, I'm left with only one choice. I simply must consider you my sweetheart."

Nettie actually sputtered, completely appalled by his latest declaration.

"Those were your options. I'm simply accepting the least abhorrent choice." Emmett slid his arm around her shoulders.

"Don't you dare try to kiss me."

"This might be my perfect opportunity. I assume you are unarmed."

Considering his offer, Nettie used the handkerchief to wipe her cheeks. "I'll take the job. I can keep my room at Mrs. Green's while I try to find another position. I won't stay forever; I want to be clear. And you should keep Delmar. I'll encourage him to stay out of the cash register if you give me a week."

"Ever the reformer, aren't you? Very well. It's a deal. I think we should seal it with a kiss."

Nettie glowered at him but offered her hand to confirm their bargain. Emmett shook her hand then stood and helped Nettie up. She brushed off the back of her skirt and watched skeptically as Emmett slipped his arm around her waist, explaining, "You seem unsteady."

CHAPTER NINE

Curious about Nettie's church experiences in light of recent melodrama regarding her job and love life, Emmett decided to play detective. In a lull between lunch and dinner, he visited the side door to see how his new manager was faring.

"Do you need any help?" When Nettie did not answer, he continued, "Everybody missed you last Sunday. I should have asked if you'd like to join us." He could see the comment made her uncomfortable but pressed on. "Have you seen the vicar?"

"No, I haven't."

"He must have been home nursing his wounds."

Nettie's expression grew rather grim. "I'm afraid I was the one not brave enough to attend church."

"I see how awkward it might be. Not only would you run into your spurned suitor, people are undoubtedly curious about what happened at school."

His comment elicited even more distress. "I don't care much about running into the vicar. It's my students. How can I possibly explain? I don't want to lie to them or be a bad example.

"I resigned from my Sunday school position since they undoubtedly planned to exclude me. If I'm not good enough to teach school, I'm not good enough on Sunday either."

Although she did not tear up, Emmett could see she was distraught over the turn her life had taken. The fact Nettie felt herself to be a poor example because of her affiliation with the Golden State did not sit well.

"You could come to my church. You'll find no critics there. The Boyds have been active at church since my parents first moved here."

"Surely, there must be parishioners who sympathize with the prohibition movement?"

"If there are, they don't make it obvious. You'd be welcomed. You can come for dinner at Faith's. She'd love to see you."

Emmett's invitation provided a consistent opportunity to see Nettie away from work. It marked the first time the temperance movement afforded any advantage to Emmett Boyd.

* * *

Business as usual was anything but at the Golden State. Nettie took firm control of the side door saloon. If Delmar was surprised by her methods, he did not complain. She gave him absolutely no opportunity to approach the cash register. If she left the saloon for so much as a minute, she carefully counted out the drawer and made no secret the finances were under tight scrutiny.

Nettie began to keep meticulous records about the receipts, not only on a daily basis, but on an hourly one.

Emmett placed another help wanted sign in the window and quickly hired two new waitresses and a bartender. He gave supervisory status and a raise to Louise. She provided training and controlled the waitress assignments. The new bartender was an older man content to work short hours. For the first time in years, Emmett had the luxury of overseeing his business without the need to do most of the work himself. He reflected on the possibility he might now have too much help while understanding Nettie would not stay if she found a teaching job.

Profits increased as a result of Nettie's control of the side door. She might not be the best option as a waitress, but she was logical and businesslike. Emmett trusted her enough to run the entire saloon, but there was an ulterior motive in his current staffing. Mr. Boyd's intent was to take Nettie on outings.

* * *

The twins returned from their honeymoons and immediately visited their brother at the Golden State. It appeared to Nettie they returned as wives although they seemed so absorbed in each other, it was hard to imagine they had much time or passion for their grooms.

Moving their things from the Boyd home proved quite a tribulation. Emmett wanted everything gone. After all, the girls had a new home. The twins seemed to want a connection to their lifelong home and were reluctant to move so much as a piece of clothing. Their husbands, though not eager to move the toys and dolls, definitely felt their brides needed to sever all ties to the Boyd household and commit to their new home. Several loud but entertaining arguments broke out in the Golden State as a result. Both sets of twins yelled in their odd, shared speech patterns. Nettie realized the girls thought the saloon an extension of their home. The patrons came along with the territory. Anything the girls said was open for the world to hear.

Chauncey, the new bartender, proved a real find. He once operated his own saloon but was squeezed out by the large brewers. Emmett found in him a mentor, someone with vast experience and solid advice.

When Chauncey asked if there was a position for his old friend and fellow bartender, Johnny, Emmett decided to hire him. Johnny was an elderly gentleman much in need of income. He worked from opening at ten to 4 p.m., Chauncey took over at four until closing.

Emmett suddenly possessed all the time he desired for brewing and managing the Golden State. He'd be in fine shape when Nettie left.

Nettie steadfastly tackled what she considered the serious business of running the side door. She was accustomed to accepting responsibility and independently solving problems. Her endless auditing of the cash register resulted in interesting statistical information. She approached her boss—to whom she referred as Mr. Boyd due to their more serious business relationship—to report her findings.

Armed with pages of numbers, she explained, "Mr. Boyd, I have remarkably consistent evidence regarding the average amount each of your customers spends while visiting your establishment."

Emmett, amused at Nettie's solemn demeanor, decided to indulge her. "What have you discovered?"

"If you look right here, there is an average, by customer, for each day of the week. Monday through Thursday, the numbers are astoundingly constant. Friday is somewhat higher; Saturday is almost double. Although it's true, you can increase your profits by selling more product to the customers who come in, it seems to me, the secret of greater success is simply getting more people through the doors. I'm anxious to see how the next social affects these figures. But the wonderful thing is, as long as I know how many customers come through the side door, I can calculate quite accurately if anyone stuck their hand in the till without the need to continually count out the drawer. I believe these numbers would be higher here in front. It wouldn't be difficult for me to figure an average for you."

"So, you could actually leave the premises and know how much money should be in the register?"

"I could, as long as I know how many people come in."

"And how would you know, if you weren't here?"

Nettie smiled slyly. "I trained Delmar to keep a list. He believes we are attempting to increase attendance and the information he gathers is vital to the success of the side door. He makes a tick mark on a page whenever someone enters."

"What if he catches on you're merely keeping track of his honor?"

"I still count the money in the till frequently. I doubt he would make the connection."

"I don't know, Nettie. I don't understand why he doesn't get a new job, one where he can help himself to a bonus now and then. He's used to having extra income."

"You misjudge Delmar. All he needed was supervision."

"Have you made him fall in love with you? Isn't that your modus operandi?"

"Don't be ridiculous."

"Good, because I'm not anxious for anyone else to propose to you in the middle of my saloon. It's quite tedious. But I want to confirm something. You can leave the side door with confidence?"

"Yes, I believe I can."

"Then you have no excuses. I would like you to join me on an excursion Wednesday next."

"For business?"

"Of course."

* * *

Once they were on their way, Nettie asked, "What exactly are we doing today, Mr. Boyd?"

Emmett was happy to be outside on the brilliant November day. The air was slightly crisp, the sun was warm and cheering. "I need to make a purchase for the side door and want your opinion."

"What kind of purchase?"

"I've always enjoyed Charlie's piano playing in front. I think the side door could use some entertainment."

"You're purchasing another piano?"

"No, something more modern."

"You're not going to tell me, are you?"

"Why don't we enjoy the ride? You'll see what I'm up to soon."

They did enjoy the ride, even though the streets were crowded. On days like this, the 10-mile-per-hour speed limit seemed completely unattainable. Emmett was in no hurry to finish their errand and would have been content to wait for everyone in Los Angeles to pass in front of his automobile. Nettie looked at him suspiciously. He was unusually patient.

"Whatever became of your friend, the one who lives in your boarding house? The one who gets you in trouble."

"You mean Eula, who accompanied the vicar from Mrs. Green's that day," Nettie felt unexpectedly uncomfortable, "the day you came to call."

"So, he threw her over when he tried to make you his wife?"

"I don't believe so."

"Why not?"

"According to Eula, he still sees her."

"Does she know he proposed to you?"

"I don't think she does."

"And you didn't tell her? Isn't it your duty as a friend?"

"I don't want to hurt her feelings. I told her he's not good enough for her. She needs to send him packing." On the few occasions she'd seen Eula of late, her friend was unusually warm. Perhaps she truly was in love.

"Is she going to?"

"I doubt it."

Emmett finally parked on Broadway and helped Nettie out of the car. They entered a storefront advertising the Regina Music Box. Mr. Boyd evidently researched his purchase before their excursion since he quickly made his transaction. He asked Nettie to select music discs.

"I think we should have lunch before we return to the Golden State. There's so much traffic, it's hard to tell how long our journey might take. I'm hungry."

Nettie thought this the flimsiest of excuses. Short of taking a trolley back to the saloon, she had little choice but to consent. As they took a table at the nearby Grimes Delicatessen, Nettie inquired, "Why did you choose to make payments on the Regina Music Box?"

"It's a sales feature I wished to experience. How better to get first-hand knowledge?"

"I thought maybe you couldn't afford it. That music box was outrageously expensive."

"I assure you, Miss Gordon, I could have paid in full. I'm a businessman; I enjoy innovation."

The Golden State was a strictly cash and carry establishment. No one ever ran a tab. Nettie believed it a wise business choice and always assumed Emmett desired to simplify bookwork whenever possible and so she teased, "Are you planning to sell beer on an installment plan?"

Emmett chuckled. "Although that is a novel idea, I may not always be in the saloon business. One never knows where life might take them.

"I appreciate your advice about the music. I imagine the ladies will enjoy our modern melodic addition. I also wished to talk to you about something we can't discuss at work."

At this, Emmett reached his hand across the table and covered Nettie's. She was instantly suspicious. Total confusion prevailed once Emmett began his oratory.

"There's no ignoring the political reform movements in Los Angeles that began with the League for Better City Government almost 20 years ago. The Municipal League of Los Angeles formed in 1902 to unite all the reform movements in the city. They were instrumental in passing an ordinance limiting the number of saloons to 200 and prohibiting expansion into residential districts. The Anti-Saloon League has a firm grasp on many of the churches in the city and the moral sentiments of the majority of Angelinos. They make no differentiation between moderate social drinking and alcoholism.

"In the past, Webster and I unsuccessfully attempted to band together with other saloon owners to alter public opinion. The large brewers were uncooperative since they feel immune from the effects of the reformers. Small business owners proved impossible to organize, either because they doubted politics will have a long-term effect or because they simply aren't paying attention.

"The outlook for saloons is bleak. I believe public

opinion has been effectively swayed toward prohibition and you have suffered for this. I want to apologize. It's obvious your association with the Golden State has caused unwelcome upheaval in your life. It was never my intention for things to turn out so badly."

"You can't apologize for this. It's not your doing. I might not be working at the saloon if not for your broken window, but Mr. Pendergast was anxious for his wife to have my teaching job. He might have found some other way to fire me and then where would I be?"

Emmett gave a weak smile. Remorse didn't come naturally to him. She wondered if his recitation was simply an act intended to put her at ease. What if it merely provided him a way to touch her hand?

As she stared at Emmett's large hand still covering hers, she only felt discomfort. Her unease increased as he ran his thumb along her wrist when the waitress delivered their sandwiches.

Life was certainly moving in unexpected directions. She'd recently clung to the Bible verse, "All things work together for good to them that love God." She could not imagine how on earth her new job in a saloon could be in line with God's will.

* * *

"Nettie, I have a favor to ask. Tomorrow is Daisy's birthday. She talks about you constantly and she worries. She doesn't like the new teacher. I know you haven't been going to Trinity. I hoped we could meet somewhere after church so she could see you're all right. You did simply disappear from school."

"It was never my intent."

"Don't be angry. I know what happened. Didn't you say you live near Central Park? We could meet you at the gazebo, say about eleven? Would you mind terribly? It would mean the world to Daisy."

Nettie stopped wiping down the bar and looked at Louise, who was ready to go home. Nettie longed to say goodbye to her class. Not a day went by that she didn't think of them. She desperately missed teaching. If not for her new job, she would likely be wasting away on the floor of her room at Mrs. Green's. "Would our meeting be accidental?"

"No. I told Daisy I see you when I go to work. I told her you have a new job, but I never mention the Golden State. I want this to be a surprise."

"I can be there at eleven."

As Emmett escorted Nettie out of church the next morning, he was all smiles. "I believe we're having a croquet match at Faith's today. It looks as if the weather is in our favor. Do you play?"

"I have played croquet, but I can't go this afternoon."

Emmett's smile quickly disappeared. "You have another commitment?"

"I do. I promised to meet one of my students in Central Park at eleven. If you drop me off at home, I'll walk over."

Not wanting their day together to end, Emmett struggled to frame his request in an impersonal light. "Faith will be disappointed. I think she already drew up teams."

Nettie doubted Faith was so organized, but perhaps she was a rabid croquet enthusiast. "I simply must go. It's Daisy's birthday. She's Louise's little girl. I can't disappoint her." She looked up into Emmett's eyes. "I let my children down. This is the least I can do."

Emmett slowly nodded. "Well, what if I drive you to Central Park? I take it your meeting won't be lengthy? I can accompany you or wait in the Buick if you prefer. Then we can go on to Faith's."

"I don't want to ruin your Sunday."

"It would only be ruined if you left me without a croquet partner."

Nettie smiled. "If you truly don't mind, I agree."

"I truly don't mind."

* * *

Emmett looked on as Nettie considered her shot. This match was men against the ladies. Nettie took careful aim as she placed a foot on her yellow ball and proceeded to smack Emmett's orange ball into the distance. Feigning anger, Emmett tromped across the lawn.

Today already proved interesting and supper had yet to be served. Although Nettie requested he wait in his automobile at the park, Emmett was undeniably curious. He observed the reunion from behind a bush, certain Miss Gordon could not help but feel rewarded when Louise's daughter rushed to hug her. Nettie grasped the girl's shoulders and held her away to have a better look. She took a small wrapped gift from her pocket and presented it to the child. The two went to sit in the gazebo. It was difficult to see inside and Louise presented an obstacle as she lingered nearby. Emmett soon gave up and returned to his motor car. He slumped in the seat, pulling his cap over his face in an attempt to nap. Nettie appeared soon afterward and climbed inside.

"That didn't take long."

"It wasn't meant to."

"Are you all right?"

"Certainly."

Nettie was quiet after requesting a stop at Mrs. Green's so she could dress appropriately for croquet. Emmett found waiting in Mrs. Green's parlor quite tedious since the woman constantly peeked around the corner of the hallway at him. Nettie literally took his breath away as she descended the staircase in an elegant white tea dress. She normally wore modestly sized hats, but not today. The large-brimmed hat was festooned with white satin ribbon, feathers and millinery roses. Nettie's quiet demeanor remained unchanged until the croquet match began. Emmett couldn't tell if she was happy or distraught over her reunion with Daisy.

Once the match ended, Emmett placed his arm around Nettie's waist to guide her to the Judge's porch for refreshments. "Your cruel shot won the game for the ladies."

"Cruel? I thought this was a sporting match. All's fair in love and war."

"So, is this love or war?"

A precocious glint shown in Nettie's eyes. "I'm quite certain it's war."

Emmett tightened his arm around her waist as they climbed the porch stairs. "I'm not."

* * *

"I know it must seem silly to you, but I appreciate your offer to spend the night." Faith appeared embarrassed. "I've never stayed home at night alone. Not once in my entire life. My parents were always home, then I married and the Judge never went away before."

"Where did he go?" inquired Nettie.

Somewhat nervously, Faith rambled on, "Court was dark today so he took the opportunity to handle some business affairs of an elderly uncle who lives north of the city. He decided to spend the night and return early tomorrow.

"I'm so proud of the Judge. He was appointed as one of the first Court of Appeal justices in April.

Previously, he was a Supreme Court commissioner. He's extremely well regarded despite the fact he is comparatively young.

"I never dreamed being alone in the house would bother me so. I feel foolish. Here you are a woman of the world, used to being on your own."

"Nonsense," assured Nettie. She sipped her cup of tea as little Luther succumbed to his mother's relentless rocking. He'd been colicky and restless since Nettie walked over from the Golden State.

"You must be tired after working all day. I don't expect you to stay up. I simply find it reassuring you're here in the house. I could have gone and stayed at Emmett's, but it's so much easier to care for Luther here."

"I like to sit and relax once I get home from work, even when it's late. It helps me sleep better. You don't mind if I stay up a while?"

"I'd enjoy the company. If Luther stays asleep this time, I'll try to put him down." Faith bit her lip, temporarily lost in thought. "I suppose I've always felt protected. There was only one time I felt threatened even though I worked in the saloon all my life."

"How old were you when you started?"

"I was about 8. Naturally, I didn't work in the bar. My mother did all the cooking back then. We didn't have the house across the alley at the time. I don't know how my mother managed. She had three children and spent all day cooking. The twins came along later, after our house was built. I started out by helping in the kitchen. I didn't work as a waitress until I turned 16. Did Emmett ever explain why he keeps so fit?"

"No. I know he uses the striking bag in the warehouse and that he once took up boxing."

"There's quite a bit more to the story. A man

followed me home one night when I left the Golden State. I never worked past eight o'clock and after I said goodnight to my father, I went out through the alley. The man left the bar and walked down the side of the building to follow me. He grabbed me and put his hand over my mouth. I've never been so scared in my life. It was autumn, dark at eight.

"Who should come to my rescue but Emmett? He was in our backyard and heard what the man said to me. He was just a skinny, scrawny boy, no match for a grown man. But he was relentless and not about to let anyone hurt me. That child got beaten to a pulp and mind you, I tried my best to help him. We got in enough licks to prompt the man to run away.

"I think it was a defining moment in Emmett's life. He felt the need to be strong enough to protect his family. Then came his interest in boxing, although it lost its appeal rather quickly.

"Every morning, he goes and hits the striking bag. He's a formidable looking man, enough so most men don't care to try his patience. Emmett may appear dominating, but he's a kind and caring person. I'm proud of him. I'm proud of all my family. I've been blessed by strong and loving men in my life and I'd be quite a different person if not for them."

Nettie finished her cup of tea and bade Faith goodnight. She couldn't help but wonder how different her life might have been if even one strong man cared for her. Nettie was past that now. She learned independence. A product of her upbringing, she was sturdy and self-sufficient. But Nettie could not help but envy Faith's nurturing family, so unlike her own.

* * *

Nettie awoke to the sound of Luther crying fitfully. She

felt unusually refreshed. Even though it was still dark, she climbed out of bed and donned the robe Faith loaned her, ready to start the day.

Passing a grandfather clock on the landing, she noted it was only six o'clock. Since Faith would undoubtedly be busy with the baby for a while, Nettie continued to the kitchen, hoping to brew some tea before the cook arrived.

By the time Faith appeared carrying her happy little son, Nettie was seated at the kitchen table enjoying her cup of tea.

"Would you like some?"

"I would."

"What time does your cook start work?"

"She usually comes right before eight. That's when the Judge wants his coffee. He reads the paper then has breakfast. I wish Dulcie was as fine a cook as Marcel. Has he ever made breakfast for you?"

"No."

"Have you ever heard of eggs benedict? It originated at the Waldorf Astoria in New York. Marcel has his own version of the dish. It's simply divine. It makes my mouth water just thinking about it."

Nettie sipped her tea. Talk of breakfast made her stomach growl. "When does the Judge return?"

"He'll take the first train into town and go directly to the courthouse. He won't be home until late this afternoon. Oh, this reminds me. The Judge caught the heel of his boot in the bedroom curtain and tore the ruffle when he left. I wanted to have it mended before he came home tonight. Nettie, do you happen to sew?"

"My mother saw to it I mastered all the obligatory wifely skills. She was determined I catch a prosperous husband."

"I learned to cook—the extent of my training for

marriage. It doesn't look to me as if the ruffle would be hard to repair, but I'm no expert. Would you mind taking a look to see if you could sew it? If it's a difficult job, I'll send the maid to the laundry to have it mended, but I doubt it would be done today. I know; we could use my mother's sewing machine and then see if Marcel would make us eggs benedict. What do you say?"

"Sounds like a fine plan to me."

Once Nettie determined the curtain was easily mended, the ladies quickly dressed and met in the parlor. Nettie was surprised when Faith made as if to leave.

"Where are we going?"

"My mother's sewing machine is in the attic of Emmett's house. We have to walk over there. He likely isn't up yet, but we won't bother him. It's an electric sewing machine. Have you ever used one?"

"No. Is it in the attic because no one uses it? Is there an electrical outlet there?"

"My father thought my mother's purchase entirely frivolous. He never approved of her machine and didn't see why she needed it. She sold her treadle machine in order to buy it and sewed in the attic to keep it out of his purview. She never hesitated to explain what a wonderful invention it was and how much she enjoyed it. I'm certain it's not hard to figure out. My mother was not adventurous nor eager to incur my father's displeasure, but her machine was her pride and joy."

Faith thought nothing of breaking and entering her brother's home. It was the first time Nettie stepped inside the house, aside from her experience in the parlor. Full of curiosity as she climbed the stairs behind Faith, she was as quiet as possible so as not to wake the resident of the house. Nettie was soon seated at a table in Emmett's attic, busily experimenting with the sewing machine.

As Faith watched the Singer repair the torn ruffle, she became quite animated.

"I can't thank you enough, Nettie. I would have had to hang a sheet over the window and the Judge does like things in their place. He'll be pleased his house is in order and that his clumsiness didn't result in any permanent damage. I'll be certain you get all the credit."

"This machine is fun to use," noted Nettie. "Is the Judge truly concerned with every aspect of your housekeeping?"

"It's always been a bone of contention. As long as I worked at the Golden State, I'm afraid the household suffered. Servants need supervision. I must admit, I'm more comfortable running our house than I ever was before. It's not so different from managing the saloon. Luther has made a huge difference in our lives."

"Don't you miss the freedom you had when you were single?"

"What freedom? All I ever did was work. I'll tell you, Nettie, I've found more freedom being married these past few months than ever before. I need to run the house, but I have ample time to play with the baby and enjoy meals with the Judge. My life is less hectic. I feel fortunate. If not for the fact the Judge makes a good wage, I'd be doing laundry, cooking and cleaning. Don't you ever think about getting married?"

"No. I have no plans to marry."

"Why not?"

"Men are generally rough and crude. I would never put myself at the mercy of a man. I'm capable of taking care of myself.

"While I do clean my room at Mrs. Green's, it's quite manageable. I don't have to cook. The Chinese laundry is right around the corner. I have time to read and embroider and don't have to tolerate any grouchy man ordering me about."

"Well, I'll grant you men can be grouchy and occasionally imperious. But they do have their advantages too." Faith paused and broke into a sly grin. "Men are so, well, manly. There's nothing quite like crawling into a cozy bed at night with an attentive husband."

"Faith!" A charming pink blush lit Nettie's freckled cheeks.

"What's going on here?" asked a drowsy Emmett as he walked up the stairs to the attic. An uncombed head of hair appeared at the top of the stairwell. Quite disheveled, he rubbed his eyes as might a small child upon awakening and appeared to be dressed only in short-sleeved Porosknit summer underwear. The tight-fitting undergarment displayed his broad chest and muscular arms to full advantage and left little to the imagination. Faith sighed in relief once she saw he'd pulled on a pair of trousers.

"My nephew has come to visit!" Emmett walked over to the basket where Luther kicked and squirmed and retrieved the infant. "It's about time you paid me a call." Ignoring the two women, he sat down in a rocking chair near the dormer window.

As Emmett entertained his nephew, Faith kept an eye on Nettie. Completely comfortable with the care and handling of babies, Emmett's vast experience with Webster's brood and the countless offspring of their batch of cousins was apparent. Nettie might express disdain for marriage, but Faith could see, beyond a doubt, Emmett drew her interest. In fact, she couldn't seem to take her eyes off Luther's uncle.

"You are not properly dressed," noted Faith.

"You're lucky I'm dressed at all," responded Emmett. "I might note you ladies have broken into my house. I should call the police." He shook his head in disapproval. "Now you've gone and gotten Miss Gordon in trouble yet again, Faith. Whatever shall I do about this?"

"Well, we finished our errand. You could join us for breakfast."

"Who is we? Have you become the domestic your husband always longed for? I somehow doubt that. What are you doing there? And who's cooking breakfast?"

"Don't be rude. I have my share of domestic ability."

Emmett guffawed at her claim. "You know how to run a saloon, Faith. I'll admit you seem to be a competent mother. Aside from that, I don't believe you have any skills whatsoever."

"As if you have so many skills," jeered Faith.

"As a matter of fact, I do."

"You can hit your striking bag and pour beer. I believe we could train a monkey to do those things."

"I am a superb dancer. I won 100 percent of my matches in the ring. I am an astute and conscientious automobile driver and successful business owner."

"Wait, wait, wait. You boxed exactly one time. You only won because your opponent slipped and hit his head on the corner post of the ring after beating you into a bloody mess."

"Nonetheless, my perfect record is intact. But you never answered my questions."

"Nettie and I are going to see if Marcel will make us eggs benedict. And look, Nettie is quite the sewing machine operator. She doesn't seem to be lacking any wifely skills." Nettie gave her a glare. "We're going to hang the curtain while he prepares our meal."

"You mean, if he has time."

Faith rolled her eyes. "You know Marcel will do anything for me. At least someone appreciates me. You can go down to the warehouse and we'll meet you for breakfast in say, 30 minutes? It's the least we can do since we woke you up early."

"What is it you're doing for me?"

"Having your breakfast made."

"My chef is making my food out of my kitchen. It seems as if I'm having your breakfast made."

"Don't be rude in front of Nettie," who, Faith noted, hadn't spoken a word since Emmett appeared in the attic. "You should be thankful we're here to make your life more interesting. Heaven knows you're the most boring man on the face of the earth."

"I will be happy to host my nephew for breakfast. I'll take him down to the warehouse and you can have uninterrupted time to order my food and hang your curtain. I'm simply relieved you're not the one attempting to cook."

"I can cook, Emmett. You know I can."

"I would not call what you do in the kitchen cooking. You learned to be an assistant. You can chop, simmer and stir. I've tasted your cooking before, much to my dismay."

"Oh, Emmett, your skewed remembrances will bore Nettie."

"I seem to recall this turkey—"

"Hush. Mind your older sister."

Nettie continued to play observer to Faith and Emmett's lively banter over breakfast. She was almost disappointed when Emmett returned to the warehouse. "What does he do in there?" she inquired.

"He fiddles with his beer after using the striking bag. He's a creature of habit."

"Your childhood home is lovely."

"Charlie's wife and her sister keep the house immaculately clean. If you noticed, even the attic is well-kept."

"I saw an empty bedroom when we first came up the stairs. Was it the twins' room?"

"Yes, Emmett made them take all their things. I should have shown you my old room. Emmett and Webster shared a room. Emmett still sleeps there. My parent's room is at the back of the house."

"It must be awfully lonely living in such a big house by oneself."

Faith smiled at that comment. She knew the perfect person to help her brother fill it up.

CHAPTER TEN

Emmett noticed a stranger enter the Golden State. It seemed a fair percentage of strangers sought Nettie Gordon of late. Johnny pointed the man in his direction.

The man extended his hand, "Mr. Boyd, I've come by to see Miss Gordon. The gentleman behind the bar explained you would be able to help me."

"Certainly. Can I get you a beer?"

"It's a bit early for beer, but why not?" As he accompanied Emmett to the bar, he explained, "I'm Miss Gordon's pastor. I've come to check on her well-being."

Emmett faltered as he poured the beer. "I'm not certain she wants to see you."

"How much do I owe you?" asked Pastor Arndorfer.

"It's on the house," Emmett replied.

"Thank you. You know about her difficulties, then?"

"I know she lost her job because she helped me out here when I needed a capable and honest employee. I know she wasn't given any opportunity to explain. She's an excellent teacher."

"You don't need to convince me of Nettie's good

heart or her capabilities. I actually want to apologize. A serious mistake was made. She is sorely missed."

Emmett didn't know which held more distaste for him, the way Nettie was treated or the fact this man might take her away. "Come around the bar. She's in back."

After escorting the pastor to the side door, the men found Nettie reviewing receipts over a cup of tea. Emmett surrendered all paperwork over to her care, so intent was she to utilize her practical statistical information for the entire saloon. Clearly shocked, Nettie looked up as they approached the table.

Emmett offered, "If you need me, I'll be right over there." He pointed to the bar then took up his position and kept an eye on Nettie as she offered the pastor a chair.

"This is good beer," he began. "I should have complimented Mr. Boyd."

"Yes, it's probably the most important asset here. Mr. Boyd brews it himself."

"You must be curious about my visit. I obviously didn't drop in by accident for a cold beer."

"I didn't imagine so."

"Nettie, I've come to apologize." Nettie's heart raced. Could he be offering her a teaching job? Her hopes vanished with his next word. "Unfortunately, there is little I can do about this circumstance besides offer sincere regret. You see, the elders of the church were informed about your job here at the saloon. I would say most of them had no opinion whatsoever, but they felt the issue should be referred to the new principal. He was, after all, hired to attend to matters concerning the school. I'm afraid he made a rash and unpopular decision. Even though many felt his judgment in this issue lacked merit, the deed was done and another teacher hired in your place before anyone knew what happened.

"You're a wonderful teacher, Nettie, and sorely missed. I can't tell you how many parents have come to my office after vainly seeking retribution from Principal Pendergast. Several families even removed their children from the school. Your replacement has proven unsatisfactory and I'm afraid the school will continue to suffer through this fiasco for some time to come." Nettie's disappointment was obvious. She did not attempt a reply.

"I also want to assure you, as soon as a position becomes available, we would like to put this matter behind us and hope you'd be willing to come back to Trinity Lutheran."

"Is this a job offer?"

"I promise you, no one will be offered a position before you have the chance to accept or decline, as you see fit. You have my word."

Nettie nodded, realizing she would have to tolerate Principal Pendergast as a supervisor. "I would have to consider the circumstances, naturally."

"I understand. I would expect your careful deliberation and will honor your choice when the time comes."

Nettie made polite small talk and inquired after the pastor's wellbeing. She was heartened to discover someone at her church supported and believed in her.

Emmett watched carefully. He could only make out an occasional word but it was clear Nettie was not happy. Knowing it was a selfish thought, he felt relieved Miss Gordon would be staying at the Golden State.

* * *

Emmett was undoubtedly breaking every rule his mother

ever taught him about women, but these were different times. They lived in a city. Nettie had no watchful parents, no family parlor or tea house where he could commence a courtship. He was not content to be the object of rampant curiosity in Mrs. Green's parlor. The last thing he wanted was a chaperone. Churchgoing and Sundays with his family undoubtedly filled the requirements of early courtship, at least as far as he was concerned.

Although he spent all his time at work, Emmett was familiar with the new practice of "going out." He also knew these were normally public outings such as biking or hiking in a group setting. Chauffeuring Nettie in his Buick was undoubtedly socially unacceptable, even when he acted as her employer and not a beau.

He believed himself to be a more than adequate suitor, having both a fine home and the means to support a family. Emmett was intrigued by the aloof Miss Gordon and wished to test a different relationship.

Nettie was unquestionably a chaste woman, likely never romantically involved. Emmett also doubted he held any attraction for her. She never flirted, which was the common and accepted method women employed to express interest. To be honest, he imagined Nettie rather disliked him. He hoped an automobile excursion would provide a setting where he could showcase his merits.

Following the proper protocol of asking well in advance, Emmett nervously approached Nettie as she worked behind the bar.

"I wondered if you might like to come for a drive on Wednesday?"

"Do we have errands?"

"No. I thought we could spend a day motoring outside the city."

"That is highly inappropriate."

"You're right, it is." Emmett could not hide his disappointment. "It was unacceptable for me to ask. I realize your reputation has already been damaged and I understand completely."

Nettie was astounded. Emmett Boyd desired to appear the guardian of her virtue. She felt the urge to laugh.

Smiling, she replied, "Well, I am nothing if not a modern and independent woman. My honor, whatever it's worth, is probably damaged beyond repair. I would enjoy taking a drive in your Buick. What time?" Nettie was taken off-guard by Emmett's ready reply.

"I'll pick you up at nine."

"It might be best if I meet you here. I probably should maintain at least the illusion of decorum at the boarding house. After all, we wouldn't be going to church."

* * *

As Nettie walked through the alley behind the Golden State on Wednesday morning, she spied Emmett securing a large picnic basket and cooler in the Buick. Nothing seemed out of the ordinary since the day he invited her on this excursion so she was disarmed by Emmett's brilliant smile as he spotted her.

"Good morning!"

"Good morning, Mr. Boyd. Where are we off to?"

"We are off to see the sights. I have no particular destination in mind although I want to head in an easterly direction."

"Two gypsies in search of adventure, then?"

Emmett unexpectedly turned serious, "Does it make you uncomfortable?"

"No. I have no concerns about your character," but Nettie was intrigued by her employer's possible motive for this outing.

Emmett took Nettie's arm to help her into the passenger seat. Once he was seated, he handed her a small, expensively-wrapped gift.

"What is this?" she inquired, suspiciously.

"Open it."

As Emmett steered the car down the alleyway, Nettie carefully removed the wrapping to find six exquisite chocolates. She stared in wonder at the box. What could this mean?

"Th-thank you," she stuttered. "Why did you do this?"

Afraid to admit his true intensions, Emmett replied, "It's a token of my appreciation for your hard work and I want to apologize again because you lost your job."

"I see. I'm relieved to know our outing is platonic. I was starting to worry."

Emmett hid his grimace. Either he needed to be more direct or more deceptive. He decided to play his cards close to his vest and see how the day unfolded.

"I am appreciative of the fact you took over the side door so capably. I don't like working in back."

"Why not?"

"I prefer the male company in front. Against my better judgment I have, on occasion, been drawn into the lives of women who frequent the lady's saloon. I try my best to stay out of there."

Nettie observed her chauffeur. His confession lacked substance and piqued her curiosity. She recalled the twin's assertion their brother took on projects and decided to gently pry. "So, these women are friends of yours?"

"I would say they, well, no. I imagine you could categorize them as potential sweethearts."

Nettie raised her eyebrow. "I see."

"No, I don't imagine you do. They were women who saw me as the answer to their prayers. Someone who might protect them or offer them a better life than what they had."

"And how did you see them?"

"When I was younger, I suppose I viewed them as prospective wives. Over time, I learned women who frequent saloons unaccompanied often have problems beyond my ability to solve. I came to detest the side door as a result."

Emmett decided to change the subject. "I'm hoping to invest in property outside the city. I've heard a lot about Hemet, but it's a lengthy trip. I'm not certain we could make it there and back in a single day."

"What's in Hemet?"

"Water. Hemet boasts the largest dam in the west. It's made of granite and provides abundant water to the city and farmlands below."

"You're interested in farmland? I find that difficult to believe."

"I have interests beyond the Golden State. Since Webster started his own business, there hasn't been time to pursue other concerns."

Emmett proceeded on a course of formal and impersonal conversation. Distrustfully, Nettie was reminded of advice her mother gave about appropriate dialogue when a man came calling. Her attention lapsed as she struggled to recall details.

Women were supposed to test potential suitors by feigning illness or family tragedy to see how a suitor might react. Men were encouraged to send wildly romantic poems and letters to sweethearts, although in-person romantic overtures were discouraged.

Kissing was taboo, a sure sign of a loose woman. She already broke that rule when she allowed Emmett to kiss her in the alley but doubted he considered her a woman of low morals. The muddle of procedures seemed immensely tedious.

There was the possibility her chauffeur was simply a boring conversationalist. Wishing to put an end to the idle chatter, Nettie embarked on a different topic, hoping Emmett wouldn't notice her lack of attention.

"Why did you purchase your automobile?"

"Don't you like it?"

"Oh, I like it very much or I wouldn't be here. It's the most handsome motor car I've ever seen. Your lengthy explanations concerning the workings of the Buick never included the reason you chose a touring car. You seem more suited to a racing model."

"First of all, I believe the automobile is the way of the future. It's clean, easier to maintain than a horse, faster, and in time, will be even more reliable. Since my main objective is making my way around the city, the extra expense of purchasing a car built for speed seemed a waste. I like taking my family for rides. Webster's son, Jake, is enamored of automobile travel. I went all out to make the Buick as comfortable as possible. The shock absorbers enable a smoother ride. The wind curtain shields the passengers from dust and road debris and blocks the wind. I felt the bonnet was essential in California in order to shelter passengers from the hot sun."

Nettie noticed farmland and orchards had given way to areas of open desert. She was shocked when Emmett steered the car off the road, which made a turn to the north. "Do you know where you're going? What if there's some mechanical problem?"

Emmett laughed. "I assure you, I'm prepared for any difficulty. This is my first opportunity to take the Buick touring."

"Why didn't you stay on the road?"

Emmett imagined his route made Nettie uncomfortable. "I want to experience the freedom and spontaneity resulting from automobile ownership. The idea a chauffeur can plot a course in any direction, see any sights and appreciate vistas unknown to train travelers is appealing. I have spare parts and extra gasoline. I can repair tires. The first thing I did when the Buick was delivered was take it completely apart and put it back together."

"This comment made Nettie even more uneasy. "Why would you dismantle it?"

"So I can make repairs myself. Racing drivers usually take a mechanic on their journeys. I don't have that luxury unless you'd like to become my mechanic."

"Is this why you brought me along?" she teased.

Emmett briefly pondered his reply. Nettie made no secret of the fact she did not wish to be courted. Perhaps there was an explanation to suit her yet open the door to a closer relationship.

"To be honest, I feel the need to spend time away from work. I've been chained to the Golden State for years. My family may have deserted me, but my new employees appear trustworthy. Not only do I have a delightful companion in you, but your presence ensures I needn't worry about the female population, who seem inordinately eager to lasso any man who owns a motor car."

Nettie did not believe for a minute the motor car was Emmett Boyd's only fascination for ladies. "What if you come across a woman who interests you—romantically, I mean?"

"Then I will quickly explain you're my sister."

Nettie laughed. "I suppose I could play along." An overwhelming sense of relief came over her. What was she thinking? Emmett Boyd could certainly not be interested in her.

Nettie was amazed at Emmett's driving ability and his adventurous spirit. If their route proved impassable, he congenially turned around and tried a different course. When they came to a creek, he plunged right through and parked in a stand of white alder trees.

"This looks like a good spot to enjoy our picnic."

"You made lunch for us?"

"Of course not. Marcel made lunch."

Nettie served as hostess once Emmett laid out a picnic blanket. The wicker basket contained wonderful foodstuffs, two place settings of fine china, silver, crystal glasses and linen napkins, all carefully tied in place to withstand the rigors of a rough road. Emmett retrieved an ice chest that held lemonade and custard for dessert.

"Where did you find Marcel?" inquired Nettie. Always impressed by the man's cooking, she was enthralled by the unprecedented elegance of their picnic.

"My mother was French. Before Los Angeles started to grow, the French made up a good portion of the population. Once my parents became financially secure, they decided to hire a cook so Mother could help run the saloon. Marcel barely spoke English when he landed in California. I have vivid memories of my mother and Marcel sitting at the table in the kitchen, conversing in French."

"What was your mother like?"

"She was diminutive with dark hair. She was a human dynamo, always busy; always focused. In looks, we all took after our father, probably in temperament, as well. Father was even-tempered. We never knew what Mother said in French, but I'm certain there were more than a few expletives included, which was undoubtedly why she reverted to her ancestral language.

"Faith is the most like Mother. She has the same kind of drive, the same ambition and the same perspective on the importance of family. Faith kept us all focused after our parents were gone although she never had much patience for the twins."

"The twins are quite unique, but I do enjoy their company."

"Unique is a diplomatic and polite adjective. I appreciate your kindness."

Nettie laughed. "I admire your family."

"Tell me about your family."

"There's not much to tell. My parents were not happy people. My brothers were thugs. I enjoy the life I lead now. I appreciate my privacy and my freedom."

"And what if we should happen across a gentleman who appeals to your romantic side? Should I be prepared to pass myself off as your brother?"

"Oh, there's no need to worry."

"But women desire a partner in life and family. I find it difficult to believe you're immune to such longings."

"Rest assured, I know my own mind. Any maternal urges I have are affectively channeled toward my students."

"What about a woman's natural craving to be cherished and loved? Every unattached woman I ever met seemed bent on finding a mate and avoiding spinsterhood."

"Yet every man cherishes his freedom. You seem intent on such a course."

Emmett shot back, "Somehow, there are an equal number of grooms in the world as there are brides. It would seem your theory lacks merit. What makes all these men succumb to the institution you are so eager to avoid?"

"The answer is simple. Sex."

At this, Emmett choked on his bread and gasped for air. Nettie quickly stood and applied a series of hard slaps to his back. Emmett finally managed to take a breath and raised his hand to halt the beating he was taking.

"I'm all right," he asserted.

Nettie placed her hand on his shoulder and looked into Emmett's red face. "You're certain?"

Emmett nodded, coughing a few more times. He struggled to continue the conversation. "Why would you say such a thing?"

"I am unconvinced by Charles Darwin's theories, which are based on relationships between living organisms. In an attempt to categorize plants and animals, they've been logically classified into groups for study purposes. These similarities might encourage categorization but do not, in any way, prove living beings are actually related.

"It's no different than stating a bee is the brother of an eagle because they both fly. The categorized similarities are imagined by humans and have nothing to do with God's creation.

"Plants, for example, are first categorized by reproductive systems. One could just as easily sort them by size or leaf shape. How does either method indicate plants evolved from one thing to another?

"I can't imagine anything more ridiculous than the idea one creature bears a different creature, much as if a magician pulled it out of a hat. This notion should be an affront to any thinking man's intellect. Personally, I'm deeply offended at the idea anyone would consider me the sister of an ape. It is the soul that separates man from beast. But I do find a certain obvious similarity between people and animals."

Emmett sipped his lemonade in an attempt to clear his throat. "What kind of similarity?"

"The male of every species, including man, has an irrefutable hunger for sex. This urge ultimately results in marriage."

"That's a rather coldhearted theory. What about romantic love? Can men not succumb to emotion?"

"My ideas are rooted in undeniable fact. I believe men who extol the virtues of romantic love are disingenuous at best. The whole idea of romantic love is a relatively new concept, at any rate. Perhaps the notion was invented by men eager to find a sexual companion. The belief there are undeniable urges to which a person in love is helpless to resist comes instantly to mind."

"Then, you prefer the days when parents married off their children without knowledge or consent? A time when a suitor paid for his intended with a goat?"

"No. I prefer the current trend. Complete freedom for women who have autonomy to live the way they choose."

"The world might come to an end if all women believed as you do, not to mention the fact angry and frustrated men would populate the streets."

"As you noted, there's no shortage of women eager to wed. I am simply not one of them."

Emmett was unexpectedly reminded of the woman he pulled into the police station. Nettie was more of a firebrand than she appeared in recent months. A part of him felt his cause was futile but another part strove to accept a challenge. Nettie Gordon was an intriguing woman and he believed she was more passionate than she realized.

* * *

The going became difficult after lunch. The Buick suffered three flat tires in the space of an hour. At first impressed by Emmett's mechanical prowess, Nettie retreated under a nearby orange tree and read the book she kept in her handbag as he repaired the most recent flat. She was always prepared to read while waiting for a Yellow Car or riding to work. Her bicycle was abandoned since she made a better income.

"What are you reading?" asked an obviously irritated Mr. Boyd.

"The Sea Wolf. It's quite thrilling. Do you read?"

"Not often. I don't have the time."

"You'd like this book. It's about a sea captain who uses his superior strength to subdue his crew and force them to his will."

"What makes you think I'd like it?"

"It's basically geared to a male audience although there is a love interest."

"For the captain?"

"No, one of the weaker members of the crew, an intellectual."

"Oh, someone more your kind."

"I suppose you're right. I find myself most at ease with the less brawny of the male species."

"I don't believe you're being honest. You've never been intimidated by any male customers at the Golden State. You seem relaxed when we're together or are you deceiving me?"

Nettie bit her lip. "I agree. I don't feel intimidated by you, despite your size."

"What have I done to deserve your confidence?"

"I suppose it's because I've seen you in a family setting. Perhaps I consider you the kindly brother I never had although my initial impression of you was quite the opposite."

This was not what Emmett wanted to hear. The last thing he desired was to be thought of as a brother despite his cavalier inference he'd be willing to introduce Nettie as a sister.

After securing his tools, Emmett thought it best to turn toward home.

"We're headed back toward civilization?"

"Yes. I only have two inner tubes left. It's best we find a road and head back. There's no need to rush though unless you have another engagement this evening."

"There's no need to hurry. I enjoy riding in your car and seeing the countryside. Look, I stole an orange off the tree where I was sitting. Would you like some?"

"I would." Emmett enjoyed the juicy citrus fruit as Nettie slipped segments in his mouth while he drove.

As they neared the city, Emmett veered off toward a canyon. "I know this area. There's a good place to fish not far up."

"You're prepared to fish?"

"I am completely self-sufficient in my automobile. I can fish or hunt. I have cooking implements, even a tent for overnight excursions. There's a small loaf of bread left and butter in the cooler. What do you say I catch a fish and we have dinner here before we return?"

"You're not too tired? This has been a busy day."

"Certainly not. I feel invigorated by all the fresh air. I think you'll like this spot. It's a place my father used to bring Webster and me when we were boys. It's quite a change from the scenery we've enjoyed all day. Thick forest—amazing so close to the desert. Water makes all the difference."

"Are you disappointed we didn't make it to Hemet?"

"No. I imagined my goal was too lofty. We can

save that adventure for another time."

* * *

Emmett unpacked items from a trunk lashed to the back of the Buick as Nettie observed. Emmett used a small spade to dig some worms from a nearby patch of ferns. He made quick work of assembling his fishing rod and cast out his line.

Two boys stopped by to inspect Emmett's motor car on their way to the far side of the lake. They'd never seen an automobile up close and didn't hide their envy.

Nettie could see Emmett believed himself the rugged individualist, man against the elements, intent on providing supper against all odds. Smiling to herself, she realized he arrived at this pocket of nature in the most expensive and luxurious manner possible. He was armed to the teeth with every tool and modern convenience imaginable. Emmett was clearly a deluded city boy playing outdoorsman, but he was no less endearing for his fantasy.

After an hour spent reading, Nettie strolled around the lake to stretch her legs. As she completed her circuit, it became obvious Emmett was frustrated, unable to catch a single fish. The two boys headed home after their swim and the setting was serene, save for the echo of Emmett's occasional muttering.

Nettie spotted a hook and line abandoned on the beach and picked it up. Her next find was a piece of tin foil nearly hidden by a rock on the shoreline. She molded a strip of tin foil around her hook and threw it into the lake. In mere moments, a curious fish approached her bait. The fish struck and Nettie held firmly to her line, pulling the fish from the water as it wiggled furiously in the air, splashing her dress.

"*Look*!" Nettie screamed, clearly ecstatic over her

accomplishment.

"How did you do that?" Emmett asked after running to her side.

"I found a hook and line on the beach."

"So, the fish struck the hook?"

"No! Quick take the hook out of its mouth. It's bleeding."

An envious Emmett glanced at Nettie as he grabbed the fish. "You're the fisherman, you take the hook out. Here." As he tried to hand the fish to her, she backed away.

"I don't want to touch it. You do it. Then throw it back in the water." She looked away as Emmett manipulated the hook.

"Throw it back! Why would I?"

"I didn't mean to kill it. It will die if you don't throw it back."

"Nettie, this fish is our dinner. It's probably not quite enough for two helpings but it will have to suffice. I'm not going to throw it back." A look of abject horror crossed Nettie's face. "You would have eaten the fish if I caught it," he accused.

"True enough, but I don't think I can eat this fish. It's my fish."

Emmett rolled his eyes. "I suppose you'd take it home for a pet if you could manage?"

Nettie stared into Emmett's eyes, silently begging for the fish's life. Emmett stared back, noting the flecks of gold, blue, green and brown that made up her hazel eyes. But he was a practical man and shaking his head in disgust, Emmett headed for the Buick.

"What are you going to do?"

"I assume you don't know how to clean a fish?"

Nettie stood fast, not responding.

"I'm going to put this fish out of its misery, clean

and gut it then fry it in my skillet."

"I won't eat it," Nettie threatened.

"Fine. That's more for me."

* * *

Nettie sat against a rock, struggling to read her book in the shadows of the canyon. She didn't realize how quickly the light would fade. Soon, she only pretended to read while furtively glancing in Emmett's direction. He was more an outdoorsman than she imagined. He quickly made a fire, produced an iron skillet and was about to finish cooking her poor fish. Nettie contemplated her next move as Emmett retrieved the loaf of bread from the picnic basket.

Emmett had two things going for him. They were in the middle of nowhere and if Nettie was as hungry as him, she would at least come to share the bread.

As he sank cross-legged against the back of the Buick, the hem of Nettie's green gingham dress came into view. Looking up, Emmett grinned and sarcastically offered, "Would you like your share of bread?"

Instead of responding, Nettie sought Emmett's hand to make a graceful descent onto a patch of grass. She made quick work of her bread and watched surreptitiously as Emmett savored the fish.

"You sure you don't want half?"

"The bread is quite sufficient, thank you," but no sooner were those words out of her mouth than her stomach gave a noisy and unladylike grumble.

Emmett put a bite of fish on his fork and held it under her nose. The fish smelled incredibly good. Reluctantly, Nettie took a bite. She closed her eyes in ecstasy. Spending the day out-of-doors undoubtedly increased her appetite. She took the fork Emmett offered and eagerly finished the fish.

Leaning back, Nettie studied Mr. Boyd's expression. "I'm sorry," she admitted. "I acted childishly about the fish."

Emmett smirked. "I'm sorry, too. I coveted your fish."

"You did more than covet it, you stole it!" They both laughed.

"What kind of fish was it?" she inquired.

"It was a rare fresh water marlin," he replied, highly amused when Nettie's eyes grew wide. But no sooner did she fall for his joke than she realized there was no such thing.

"I see your understanding of fish equals your ability to catch them," she teased.

Emmett grimaced. "How did you catch the fish?"

"I told you, I found a hook and line abandoned on the shore."

"But what did you use for bait?"

"A piece of tin foil."

Emmett shook his head in disgust. "If you only knew how much I spent for my fine fishing rod."

"I can't help it if I'm a natural born fisherman," Nettie continued.

"You never fished before, did you?"

Nettie smiled back, "Correct."

"You never cleaned fish for your father or brothers?"

"My mother raised me to be a lady. She undoubtedly felt cleaning dead things might toughen me up too much, although I am a fine cook once things are dead—and clean."

"I'm sorry I didn't bring more food."

"Wait! We do have something else." Nettie gracefully stood and hurried over to the front of the Buick. She returned with Emmett's gift. "We can share the chocolates!"

"But those are for you."

"Well, this is an emergency situation. We must have dessert!" She gave Emmett first pick of her chocolates and sat down beside him.

"Are you sorry you came?" he inquired.

"Sorry! Certainly not. I enjoyed our adventure today. I'm sorry it's almost over."

"It doesn't have to be. We could stop by a soda fountain on the way to Mrs. Green's and share a milk shake."

"Two desserts? I don't know. Besides, I'm filthy and I think I smell like my fish."

"We flouted convention all day. Why stop now?"

* * *

After lighting the lanterns, Emmett started the engine. "Are you tired, Nettie?"

"I probably am, but I think a milk shake would hit the spot."

"It seems you've become a night owl. Saloonkeepers are people of the night."

"I don't think so."

"Think about it. When you were a teacher, your leisure time was spent in the evening. You work in the evening now. I imagine you get up in the morning, dawdle over breakfast, then do chores or leisurely activities before you come to work.

"It was worse when my parents were alive. Saloons stayed open late. Our family time was Sunday morning at church. We rarely had a meal together. I think when I have my own family, I'd like to sit down to dinner the way most families do."

"Do you give much thought to having a family? I can't picture you settled down with a wife and 10 children."

"It's something I've begun to think about. Perhaps it's a product of growing older and wiser."

"I suppose anything is possible. I hope you don't count on fishing to feed your children," Nettie could not resist one last barb.

CHAPTER ELEVEN

Business was not particularly booming at the Golden State on the drizzly December evening. Nettie sat in the corner, searching the newspaper for teaching jobs.

Disheartened at her latest rejection letter from a parochial school in Redondo Beach, she understood it was unlikely she would find a position before the school year ended. Unwilling to wait in perpetuity for a job at Trinity, she was willing to relocate, move from Mrs. Green's and give up the life she made in the city. She absently thumped her pencil on the table as Delmar approached.

"Miss Nettie, would it be all right if I left early? We're not busy and my sister asked me to help her out a bit. If I went now, I wouldn't have to go on Sunday."

"Surely. I'll grab an apron and tend the bar for this last hour."

Nettie took her paper along to the bar. Only three customers remained. She doubted anyone else would come in and wondered if business was as slow in front. Her curiosity was soon satisfied as Emmett peeked his head through the door. Spotting her behind the bar, he walked to stand beside her.

"Where's Delmar?"

"I let him go early since we're not busy."

"Oh, I was hoping you could accompany me. Things are slow in front."

"Accompany you where?"

"Out for dinner."

"It's a bit late, isn't it?"

"No. We're people of the night, remember?"

"Well, Delmar is gone so I can't leave."

"We could put Louise back here until closing," Emmett suggested.

"Where could we go for dinner at this hour?" Nettie looked over as the door opened. A man walked in; his wet rain poncho dripped on the barroom floor. He appeared to be alone.

"This is a lady's saloon," Nettie explained, but she took a step back when the man turned and showed a gun. Emmett quickly pulled Nettie behind him.

"No need for anyone to get hurt here." The thief laid a canvas bag on the bar top. "You folks over there, sit tight. I'll get to you in a minute and I'll be gone. You there, empty the cash register into this."

Emmett opened the register drawer to fill the bag. There was little inside.

"No, don't give him the money."

Emmett stopped his hand in mid-air at Nettie's statement then continued to place the money in the bag.

"Don't give him the money. This isn't right. It isn't his."

"It's all right, Nettie. Stay put," hissed Emmett.

"No, I won't." She moved from behind Emmett's back.

"What are you doing? Do you want to get somebody killed?" Emmett asked.

"The money isn't his. Don't give it to him."

"Shut up lady," yelled the robber. "Keep her still!"

he commanded.

"Nettie, stand still," Emmett urged as he pulled her behind him again. "We don't want to get anybody hurt. It isn't even your money."

"That doesn't make it any less wrong." She decided to direct her comments to the man in the black poncho. A bandana covered the lower part of his face. "You need to leave. There are police officers in front. All I have to do is scream and you'll be immediately overcome." She stepped away from Emmett's protection again.

"Nettie, be still."

Obviously agitated, the robber decided to take matters into his own hands. He walked to the back of the bar and took the bag from Emmett as he waved the gun to motion the pair against the wall. "You two need to shut up and you folks over there stay put." The customers were inching their way toward the door.

"Put the bag down on the bar," Nettie threatened. "I'm going to scream."

Knowing there were no officers in front, Emmett quickly put his hand over Nettie's mouth. "It's only money. Let him take it and go." Nettie struggled against him.

"I've had about enough!" yelled the robber, pointing the gun at Nettie as she pushed against Emmett's hand.

In one fluid movement, Emmett used the motion of the hand Nettie batted away to push the muzzle of the gun toward the back of the bar room. The gun fired harmlessly into the woodwork as Emmett overpowered the robber and forced him to the ground. Nettie retrieved the gun from the floor, placed it on the bar top and backed away.

"Go ring the alarm on the street," Emmett ordered as the man struggled on the floor. He was no match for the robust owner of the Golden State.

"The alarm's been rung," offered Chauncey as he and other men from the front came bursting through the door. Nettie stood back as the men pulled the robber from the floor and uncovered his face. The police were there in no time.

Nettie listened to comments of bystanders.

"What kind of low life robs the side door of a saloon?"

"There's no respect for ladies in this day in age."

"He probably thought there wouldn't be any men here to stand in his way."

"Good job, there Emmett."

Emmett did not respond and headed over to where Nettie stood. She was surprised when he took her arm and pulled her to the front. The large room was completely vacant.

"What the hell is wrong with you?" Emmett began. Nettie, wide-eyed, could only stare. "Why can't you let me help you? I was only trying to protect you."

"But—"

"The man would have taken the money and left."

"But it wasn't his money."

"You could have gotten me killed, or one of the customers. You could have gotten yourself killed. The money wasn't important."

"I just thought—"

"I want you to promise me you will never do a crazy thing like that again. Do I have your word?"

Emmett was so adamant, Nettie could only nod her head in agreement. She was astounded when Emmett pulled her tightly into his embrace. He was thoroughly upset; she couldn't imagine why. He certainly overcame the robber easily enough. She thought he was actually trembling.

"You're important to me, Nettie. I could have lost you."

Emmett quickly released Nettie as Chauncey stepped through the doorway and delivered a sound slap on his back. Soon he was being congratulated by employees and customers alike. Emmett smiled and offered a free round of drinks, but Nettie could tell he wanted nothing so much as to close the bar and leave.

After years of procrastination, Emmett purchased a pistol for the bar and stashed it beneath the cash register.

* * *

The congeniality Nettie and Emmett shared after their touring day subtly turned into something different. Emmett managed to overcome his aversion to the side door and could frequently be found in back. He blamed this on the fact Delmar had been ill.

Emmett's disposition seemed unusually sunny. He frequently served as bartender and did not hesitate to flash his appealing smile and compliment customers. He found reasons to converse with his manager, touching her arm, hand or back. His attention was artfully applied which led Nettie to wonder if his tendency to embrace her was new or if she simply didn't notice before. Comfortable with his touch, Nettie somehow came to welcome it.

Emmett's reaction to the robbery proved confusing to Nettie, who experienced an unfamiliar and unwelcome rush of excitement when he so ably forced the robber to the floor and when he so seriously demanded she accept his protection.

As Emmett placed two beers on a tray, he looked up to find Nettie staring at him from her usual corner table. She quickly returned to her paperwork when he caught her eye. He understood his initial assumptions about Nettie Gordon were wholly inaccurate.

From the moment he pulled her down the street to the police station, he believed her to be some timid, weak, witless female creature. He assumed, when he found she carried a knife, she was deeply afraid of something. She never ceased to prove him wrong.

Nettie was strong, capable, and efficient. She was logical and open-minded. She was not afraid to change her opinion. Even though she suffered for a short time after losing her teaching position, she recovered quickly and committed to her job at the Golden State. Nettie seemed not to be afraid of anything, even to her detriment.

She wasn't frightened of her father when he appeared in the bar. She was not intimidated by popular opinion, even if it caused her embarrassment. Nettie was not afraid of the thief and Emmett could not help but speculate what might have happened if he wasn't there during the robbery. Would Nettie have refused to open the register? Would she have drawn her knife? Could she have been killed? Emmett felt it necessary to treat the robber cautiously; he was more than willing to meet the man's demands. But when the gun was pointed at Nettie, he felt frantic to protect her.

Her unusual opinions on marriage proved more intriguing than off-putting. Emmett Boyd realized he had fallen hopelessly in love with a woman who likely felt nothing in return.

His sisters never hesitated to encourage his relationship with Nettie, but Emmett believed their ideas on how he should proceed too traditional. He found himself in quite a quandary. Aside from being polite and attentive, he felt his only real course of action was to monopolize Nettie's time, entertain her and encourage her trust. He wondered if he'd be able to earn her love before he was too old to enjoy it.

On Thursday, Emmett escorted his favorite employee to Venice Beach for the afternoon performance of Ellery's Famous Band.

They first strolled around the Venetian-style buildings beside the beach then walked along the canals admiring homes, both completed and under construction. After the concert, they dined at the St. Mark Hotel before returning to the city.

Emmett eagerly anticipated their excursions. It was obvious Nettie also enjoyed them. They spent every Sunday together. She undeniably felt a part of the Boyd clan as they discussed Christmas holiday plans. Each week, Emmett tried to take her out at least one weekday. Nettie's formal demeanor disappeared once they were away from work. She never hesitated to hold his hand. Today at the concert, Emmett placed his arm around her shoulders expecting her to scold him. She had not. Climbing in the Buick, he was in no hurry to go home.

"I don't think I mentioned how nice you look. Is this something new?"

Nettie never earned close to what she was making at the Golden State. Although she was careful to save as much as possible, she indulged in a few new dresses and the suit she now wore. Since Emmett frequently asked her out, she wanted to look her best. Her short double-breasted green shadow-check jacket was trimmed in black velvet. The simple circular skirt was of the same fabric. Nettie's practical side justified her purchase. She could use both the jacket and skirt for work if coupled with black or gray coordinates. Black kid gloves and a small black hat trimmed in green ribbons and peacock feathers completed her ensemble.

"Thank you, it is new."

"Well, I feel honored you dressed so exquisitely for

me."

Nettie grinned. "My new clothes are a result of your generous wages."

"Money well-earned and spent. You are a model of capitalism. I enjoyed our day together, Nettie. Would you be interested in going to the Electric Theater? I haven't seen a film in years and those were at the end of a vaudeville show. I understand moving pictures have come a long way. Have you been there?"

"I have but not since shortly after they opened."

"We'll make an evening for the theater, then."

"Only if you let me pay my own way."

"I assure you, Nettie, I can afford our outings. I haven't treated myself to any kind of fun in years. I appreciate the fact you accompany me. Your presence continues to categorize me as an unavailable male, which I much appreciate."

"Aren't all your new employees a drain on your profits? I thought your Buick was your primary source of entertainment. A motor car is an expensive luxury item."

"I use my automobile as an enjoyable way to get around the city. Although my payroll is larger than before, I own three-fifths of the Golden State. It isn't an issue. I'm afraid I became a complete dullard after Webster started his business." He was pleased Nettie accepted his explanation. Emmett wanted to be responsible for far more than her entertainment.

"It is convenient to take the Buick," commented Nettie. "You can go wherever you want, whenever you want. No waiting for trolleys or trains. Despite the obvious drawbacks, it is the ultimate freedom."

"I think the drawbacks are short-term. Most liveries and blacksmiths will soon be out of business. I foresee a mass conversion. Catering to motorists' every convenience is the up-and-coming trend. Gasoline, repairs and parts will be readily available. Travel by motor car will only get easier as time goes on."

"I'm not entirely sure about that. Many say automobiles are a fad and will never replace the horse and buggy."

"Do you believe them? From what you can see, I mean."

"I believe there are more motor cars on the road each time I step outside."

"There you have it. The consumers will have their way, likely much quicker than we imagine."

"What other predictions do you have? Are you a gypsy like your sister? Is your crystal ball handy?"

Emmett laughed but then became more serious. "My other predictions are not as pleasant."

"Why?"

"There was an article in the paper this morning. Despite pressure on the police commission, they granted permission for a liquor license to be transferred."

"It seems like a good thing for your business."

"A local saloon sold for $9,500 plus $500 for contents. Then the owner charged another $9,000 for transfer of the liquor license. The license is a commodity because they're limited. The commissioners made the case they should be the ones profiting from the transfer of the license, not the owner. In the end, the law states the commission has the power to refuse a transfer only if there's been a violation of the law. The argument will continue. Saloons are worthless without a license and there's no guarantee a new owner would be able to procure one. The decision had more to do with a feud on the police commission than abiding by the law. Times are bad for saloon owners and they'll only get worse."

"What will you do then?"

Emmett never intended their conversation to become so serious. "I'm not sure, but I'm determined to enjoy life for now."

* * *

Nettie and Emmett entered the large tent that was the Electric Theater, the first venue in Los Angeles to exclusively exhibit motion pictures. Nettie frowned at the pricy ten-cent entry fee. As they sat down, she slipped her arm through Emmett's, intent on keeping as warm as possible on the chilly evening. Emmett bit his lip to keep his smile to himself. It was the first time Nettie initiated a tender gesture. Although the program lasted only an hour, it included some of the latest in motion picture entertainment.

"What did you like best?" asked Emmett once the program ended.

"*The Night Before Christmas*. It must have lasted well over ten minutes. It completely replicated the Clement Moore poem and I was impressed by the technology they used to make Santa's sleigh fly through the sky."

"Even though there are apparently several moons circling our planet?"

"Well, I don't imagine many people noticed. I believe American films are finally catching up to the quality of French films. *The Night Before Christmas* captured my idea of a fantasy family celebration."

"Was it so different from your own family's Christmas festivities?"

"Yes, certainly. Why, are your childhood remembrances similar to the film?"

"My family was not as affluent as the one in the film, but we always got a toy on Christmas morning. My mother was fond of elaborate celebrations."

Nettie thoughtfully nodded her head.

Emmett then asked, "What did you think of *Rescued by Rover*?"

"I enjoyed it. That was certainly a clever collie. It was a much shorter film. Did you like it?"

"I couldn't help but take offense at the content."

"Why, you don't approve of dogs rescuing babies?"

"I didn't like the subtle slur. The crone who kidnapped the baby was obviously a drunkard. I can't seem to escape the presumed horror of alcohol even in my entertainment."

Nettie thought his offense ridiculous. "I don't think they meant any harm."

"Oh, quite the contrary. I believe their suggestions are insidious. The negligent nanny and her male friend were cigarette smokers. All the stereotypes fit perfectly into the tenets of progressivism."

Nettie rolled her eyes. "I won't argue, I'm having too fine a time." She took Emmett's hand as they strolled back to the Buick.

"There's a lot of competition for saloons nowadays."

"What kind of competition?"

"Saloons used to be the only entertainment in town. Now there are theatres, vaudeville and motion pictures. In Los Angeles, there are nearby beaches with vast entertainment options. How can I possibly compete?"

"You seem to be doing a fine job so far."

"I'm a forward-looking man, Nettie. I can't visualize the Golden State having a profitable future. There's too much against it."

"But the twins told me your true passion is brewing beer. What would you do for a living?"

Emmett was close to admitting he had a new passion. It had nothing to do with beer.

* * *

When Nettie took her coat and handbag to the closet on Monday morning, she was surprised to find Hope and Charity seated at the table ready for tea. It was the first time the girls came to the saloon since the day they moved out of Emmett's house and the first pot of tea they shared in a long while.

"Good morning ladies. What brings you here?"

"We need to talk to you, Nettie."

"We have several concerns."

One of the twins poured a cup of tea for Nettie and remembering she liked two lumps of sugar and cream, prepared her favorite beverage to perfection. Handing her the cup as Nettie took a seat, she continued, "First of all, we promised Faith we would confirm your appearance for Christmas dinner."

"She was troubled when you mentioned you had another invitation."

"My friend Eula's uncle entertained us at Christmas last year and invited us again," Nettie explained as she took a sip.

"You're not going there are you?"

"We need you to come to Faith's house."

"You *need* me to come?"

"Yes, we're quite adamant about it."

Nettie was perplexed. "Eula is a dear friend and I've seen little of her lately."

"Perhaps we should explain."

"We are in quite a quandary."

"You see, Charity is expecting."

"Oh, congratulations!" Nettie turned to the twin who was not speaking, assuming this was Charity. "You must be thrilled." Charity burst into tears.

"This is not the way things are supposed to be," explained Hope. Charity nodded her head in agreement.

"We do everything together."

This comment brought ugly notions to Nettie's mind, no doubt the product of Emmett's ideas about the twins and their husbands.

"We don't see how this is possible. We're alike in every way. Our husbands are alike in every way. How can Charity possibly be expecting when I am not?"

"How will we deal with this?" sobbed Charity.

Nettie frankly didn't see a problem, but the girls were definitely distraught.

"Well, you must accept this is nature's way. Charity will be a mother first and Hope will be the doting aunt. Once Hope has a baby, think how much fun your little ones will have, cousins living in the same house, no doubt close in age." Nettie hoped her encouraging words might serve to soothe.

"But what if Hope doesn't have a baby soon?" sobbed Charity. "We're simply not good at sharing. We tried once before."

Thinking it unwise to put pressure on Hope, Nettie replied, "You must trust in the fact God knows best. His way is not always what we might want, but He's doing what's right for us." Nettie knew this was a difficult concept for her to grasp, how could the twins comprehend it? "After all, it is your desire to have healthy, happy babies. Rest assured, this will work out for the best."

"See, Charity, I told you Nettie would help."

"Nettie, you must come for Christmas. We need your support when we tell our husbands."

"They don't know?"

"Not yet. It's our Christmas surprise."

Nettie was somewhat astounded at the "our" part of the surprise. "Oh, my. Well, yes, I'll come. You can tell Faith I'll be there." Nettie knew she would always be fascinated by the twins and their antics.

"And you are coming to our open house on Christmas Eve?"

"Yes, I planned on coming."

"Perfect!" Charity managed to stop crying.

"It means so much to have you there."

"You're like a sister to us."

"Not at all like Faith."

"Faith is mean."

"No, Charity. It's only because she's much older than us and now little Luther keeps her busy."

"Oh, Hope. Everyone will have a baby but you!" At this, both girls began to cry.

* * *

The Golden State was packed on Saturday, the night before Christmas Eve. The clientele seemed extremely festive. A dour Louise was banished from the front, temporarily assigned to wait tables at the side door where her ugly mood would matter less. Nettie had her hands full helping out when Louise disappeared completely. Having already checked the kitchen, Nettie found Louise in the closet bent over the table, her face buried in her arms.

"Louise, whatever is the matter? Is Daisy all right?"

Embarrassed, Louise quickly stood to return to work, using the sleeve of her shirtwaist to wipe her eyes.

"I'm fine," she explained.

"You clearly are not. Perhaps I can help."

"No, we need to go back to work. Poor Delmar is all on his own."

"Delmar will make do for a few minutes. Tell me what's wrong." It was unlike Louise to display anything besides eager congeniality at work.

"I can't tell you. You wouldn't understand."

"You might be surprised. Teachers are awfully empathetic. I doubt you have a problem unique to the entire world."

"It's not unique. But you're a decent woman and you wouldn't understand."

Nettie could see Louise was not going to divulge the source of her distress. "Maybe someone else could help. Why don't you ask Emmett?" This suggestion drew Louise's interest. "I'll go back to the side door. You go talk to him."

Louise nodded and walked to the front. Since the door was left open, Nettie paused to see if Louise would express her concern to her boss. Louise walked behind the bar and touched Emmett's sleeve.

He bent down to hear her comment in the loud barroom. Emmett frowned and made a reply. Louise, seemingly relieved, quickly disappeared through the door separating the two saloons. But Nettie noted Emmett ceased work to contemplate whatever Louise divulged. Nettie shut the door and returned to the back, only to be interrupted moments later as Emmett waved her toward the closet.

"Is something wrong?"

"No. I have to do an errand. I might not get back before ten." Emmett reached into his vest pocket to retrieve a stack of envelopes. "I have something here for everyone, a Christmas gift. I need you to pass these out. I gave Johnny his before he left. If I'm not back at closing, go ahead and lock up. You can go home and I'll clean up when I return."

"Where are you going?" Nettie asked suspiciously. "Is this about Louise's problem?"

"I can't explain now. I need to go. I'll tell you about it later." Emmett headed for the alley.

At eight, Nettie went to the kitchen to give Marcel

and Bao their envelopes. "Where is Bao?"

"He went with Mr. Emmett."

Nettie was even more curious. "Where did they go?"

"I thought you knew. I'm not certain."

"I don't know at all. And what aren't you certain of?"

"Well, I believe Mr. Emmett got Bao to take him to Chinatown."

"Why would they go there, especially when we're so busy?"

Marcel did not respond. "I have to clean up. I'm anxious to be finished tonight, aren't you?"

"I'm here for two more hours. If you want to leave, I'll clean up for you."

"If you're serious, I'll surely take you up on your offer."

"I am serious. Tell me why Mr. Emmett and Bao went to Chinatown."

Marcel untied his chef's apron, intent to spend the balance of the evening with his whiskey bottle. "I don't know any more."

But Nettie could see he had information he refused to share. Louise was right. Nettie didn't understand.

* * *

Emmett parked his Buick near a spot Bao assured was safe. The two men walked along the side of the Pico House. The building was once the premier hotel in the city but was now in decline.

Emmett could see the lights of nearby Chinatown as Bao led him to a staircase. They quickly descended a flight of stairs only to pass through a door and down another staircase. Emmett heard myths of a fantastic underground Chinese city. He frankly never believed it existed, but he now felt as if he had passed through the center of the earth and come up in China itself.

Chinatown was filled with average-looking buildings that sported Chinese script on the signage and housed shops catering to residents' needs. What now lay before him were rows of stalls decorated in a traditional Chinese manner.

Even though it was late on Saturday night, fish mongers sold their wares. Fabulous silks and metalwork were displayed. The pungent smell of herbs and spices assaulted his nose. Fans, jade, tassels, and clothing in richly embroidered, colorful silk lined many of the shops.

It appeared Chinese were living in small buildings at the edges of the cavernous area. Festive Chinese lanterns served to alleviate the perpetual darkness. He followed along as Bao located the tunnel Louise described.

Emmett was surprised when his presence did not garner more attention. Bao explained white men were often seen in the tunnels. Even women were not immune to the vices found in the underground city.

* * *

Emmett stood on his back porch, trying to decide if he wanted to tackle the work waiting for him in the Golden State. It was almost midnight. The saloon would not open again until the day after Christmas. Surely, he could find time to put things in order before Tuesday if he went to bed now. A light shining in the saloon's kitchen window made up his mind. Needing to turn it off, he decided to see what kind of mess was left for him.

Emmett found Nettie standing in the kitchen wiping dishes. He was enchanted by her look of delight as he entered through the alley door.

"You're back!"

"Yes. What are you still doing here?"

"I let Marcel go and told everyone else they could leave at ten. I cleaned up the bars and I'm finishing here."

"I don't think I gave you a big enough bonus," mocked Emmett.

"I think you gave me an extraordinary bonus. Thank you so much. I have Bao's here though."

"Yes, I forgot to take it out of the batch. He'll have to get it on Tuesday."

"Where did you go?"

"I went to provide the Christmas miracle, just as you directed." Emmett's demeanor seemed to sour at his comment. He was abruptly serious, almost derisive.

"I didn't direct any miracle."

"Louise told me it was your idea I help her."

"I told her she should go to you with her problem. She wouldn't tell me what it was."

Emmett appeared relieved at her admission. "I see. Well, let me drive you home."

"No, I want to know where you went."

"If Louise wanted you to know, she would have told you."

"She told me I wouldn't understand."

"She's probably right. Get your things. I'm tired."

"I can take the trolley home."

"It's late. You'll have to wait for the trolley. I should drive you."

"Then tell me where you went."

"I went to get Louise's husband."

"But that's wonderful! He's returned home, then? What a marvelous Christmas present for the girls."

"I doubt he'll stay."

"Why not?" Nettie remembered Marcel's belief Bao took Emmett to Chinatown.

"He is an opium fiend, Nettie. I hoped when I went for him, he might be able to recover, if only for a time. The man is skin and bones, so far into his habit, I don't believe he'll last long."

"You mean he's dying?"

"It appears so to me. Louise won't be back to work for at least a week. The joyous Christmas she envisions will never materialize. It will take at least a week to get the opium out of his body. He'll be very, very sick. If he survives, I have no doubt he'll head back to the opium den where we found him or someplace worse. He went to an old friend for money. The man told Louise where he was."

"Does she know about his tendencies?"

"I have a feeling this is not the first time she rescued him. I don't want to talk about this. Go get your things."

Nettie rode home in silence. Emmett had a grim look about him. It was Sunday morning, Christmas Eve.

When Emmett stopped in front of Mrs. Green's, Nettie put her hand on his arm to keep him in the automobile. Nettie shivered as she noted Emmett's curious stare. He was tired, as was she, and impatience showed on his face.

"What you did, was it dangerous?"

"No, not really."

"But the police could have come."

"I seriously doubt the police ever go there."

"Was it a tawdry and terrible place?"

"No, it was luxurious, even opulent. It's an experience I'll certainly always remember."

"It was kind of you to do that for Louise, especially because you don't approve."

"I didn't do it for Louise." It was his turn to observe Nettie. "Louise made it seem to be your idea."

"Why?"

"I would do anything for you, Nettie. Louise was clever to frame her request as yours. She picked up on my devotion to you." Emmett doubted Nettie comprehended the import of his comments. He intended to make things much clearer but not tonight. He stepped down from the Buick and escorted Nettie to the front door of the boarding house.

"Mrs. Green will likely have a fit if she's still awake," commented Nettie. "Merry Christmas!"

"Merry Christmas Eve, you mean." Emmett was delighted when Nettie reached up to kiss his cheek. "See you in the morning."

"Oh, I was planning to go to my church in the morning. Why don't you pick me up in time for the twins' open house?"

Shocked at the desolation he felt at not being included in Nettie's morning plans, Emmett recovered in time to offer an alternative. "Why would you want to go there alone?"

"I think it's time I put in an appearance. It's been almost two months. Besides, I rarely see my friend Eula. She goes to work early in the morning and I come home late. I've been spending Sundays with your family. I promised I'd save some time for her tomorrow."

"I don't understand why you'd want to go to your church when you're welcomed at mine, but I'd be glad to accompany you." Emmett would have to admit, if only to himself, how protective he felt. "We could take your friend Eula along." Nettie reflected on his offer. As usual, he had no idea which way she was leaning.

"I'd like that. I'm certain Eula would love to come. She's never ridden in an automobile."

"See you then," he commented as Nettie disappeared through the boarding house door. Somehow the events of the evening seemed less important. Emmett whistled *Deck the Hall* as he started the engine and returned home.

CHAPTER TWELVE

After the service, Emmett stood aside as various children and their parents approached Nettie in front of Trinity Lutheran Church. Soon, her line of well-wishers was longer than the one to greet the pastor in the vestibule. Emmett offered his hand when Pastor Arndorfer approached him.

"Welcome to our church, Mr. Boyd. Merry Christmas."

"Merry Christmas."

"I'm happy Miss Gordon joined us this glorious morning. Was this at your behest?"

"It was her decision. She's been attending my church, but she wanted to come here today."

"And you felt the need to accompany her? No doubt to protect her from persecution?"

Emmett chuckled. "Perhaps to keep her head from swelling with adoration."

"I told you she was sorely missed. What a treat for her students to be able to wish her season's greetings."

"Who's the couple at the top of the stairs? They don't look especially happy. Maybe my protective instincts were not in vain."

"I believe they'll be wise enough to keep their

distance. That's Principal Pendergast and his wife, the teacher who took Nettie's job. They're probably concerned her appearance today will stir the pot of discontent they brewed. Speaking of brewing, I never told you how much I enjoyed your beer."

"Thank you. Come by any time, Pastor. The beer's on me."

"Well, I doubt I can resist your offer. I'm afraid I have something of a serious nature to ask you, however. I'm aware Nettie is a woman alone, distanced from her family. I must inquire about your intentions. From what you say, you two are spending considerable time together. I wouldn't want your relationship to cast a bad light on Nettie's character."

"I can assure you, my intentions are completely honorable. We spend time with my family. I'd go so far as to say they consider her part of our family."

"Then I assume an engagement might be announced shortly?"

"As far as I'm concerned, I'd stand on the rooftops and announce it today. I doubt Nettie is quite so eager. She's a determinedly independent woman."

"Well, I wish you all the luck in the world. You two make a handsome couple."

"You have no doubts about my character? I own a saloon, after all."

"I see only a good man in you. I'm certain Nettie would never become involved otherwise. I trust her judgment."

"I don't know if she would characterize our relationship as any sort of involvement. Your approval is much appreciated, however. When the time comes, I doubt I'll be able to ask Mr. Gordon for Nettie's hand."

"If there's ever anything I can do, feel free to ask."

Having bade farewell to the last of her students,

Nettie approached the two men. After she greeted Pastor Arndorfer, Emmett inquired, "Where's Eula? I thought I would take you two out for brunch. Would you care to join us, Pastor?"

"Eula went to visit the vicar," Nettie explained.

"I'll get her," offered the pastor, who knew Nettie might find it awkward to see the vicar. Little went on at church that escaped his notice. "I believe there's just enough time between services for me to join you."

* * *

"I think Pastor Arndorfer likes Eula," Nettie reflected as Emmett escorted her to the twin's front door.

"What makes you say so?"

"The way he looked at her over brunch. I've never seen him so animated. He tried much harder to engage her in conversation than he did us."

"He's a preacher; he engages everybody in conversation."

"Truly, you couldn't see it?"

Emmett rang the bell and turned to admire his companion. Nettie wore an emerald green velvet dress and matching coat trimmed in black. She looked the picture of Christmas festivity right down to her stylish auburn hair and black hat. Emmett was dressed in formal black attire, complete with top hat.

He briefly wondered how she could interpret the pastor's modest attempts at conversation with Eula as infatuation when Nettie could not see his own blatant attempts to woo her.

From the moment Hope answered the door, having pushed the butler aside, Emmett and Nettie were caught up in the twins' first attempt at entertaining. The house was decked in layers of beribboned greenery. The most magnificent Christmas tree Nettie ever saw stood in the front parlor window. She was fascinated by the strings of electric lights illuminating the branches and the elegant glass ornaments.

All single partygoers were given a walnut and strict instructions to "guard it with your very life." Emmett promptly dropped his. It rolled under a console table in the entryway, much to Hope's dismay.

She grabbed his arm and hissed in his ear. "You must retrieve that walnut."

"Just give me another," he replied, unwilling to crawl on the floor in his finery.

"No, it has to be that walnut." Emmett glared at her as if she were insane. "Trust me, Emmett, you need that walnut. We're only trying to help you. Wait! I'll make the butler get it."

Emmett wandered off in search of Nettie, who proceeded to the parlor alone. Partygoers filled the house. He greeted various family members—his siblings and cousins who lived nearby. There were guests he recognized from the twins' weddings, business associates and friends of his brothers-in-law. Holding little Luther, the Judge sat in a corner of the parlor, his glass of beer perched on a nearby table. Emmett finally located a radiant Nettie carefully examining the lavish tree.

The reason Hope insisted her brother retrieve the walnut soon became apparent. As the first game of the evening commenced, all unattached gentlemen and ladies opened their walnuts. Each lady read a line from a nursery rhyme hidden inside and was quickly paired with the gentleman who had the answering rhyme for games and dancing.

Emmett, feeling certain he knew who held the reply to Nettie's verse, listened intently as she read, "Where shall the wedding supper be?" from *Froggy Went a*

Courting.

He did not hesitate to reply, "Way down yonder in the hollow tree." Catching what he thought to be Nettie's look of relief, Emmett approached and offered his arm.

"Happy to see me?" he inquired.

"I am."

"Why, I believe there are numerous eligible bachelors here. Perhaps you might have found your one true love."

"You know I'm not looking for a beau. It's what I love about you, Emmett. You understand me so well."

Perplexed at how to reply, he guided Nettie toward the music where they danced the night away.

* * *

Great care had been taken with both the food and arrangement of the buffet, although it was a bit picked over by the time Emmett abandoned the dance floor. The brides' festive celebration appeared to be an undeniable success. Emmett managed to find a chair for Nettie where she could eat a late supper. He sat on the floor beside her.

As the evening came to an end, many guests departed to attend late church services or to make an appearance at other parties. The Judge and Faith planned their departure in order to put Luther to bed and prepare for Christmas Day. Webster's family left early at the behest of his wife, who didn't approve of the wild Christmas Eve celebration.

While putting a last bite of au gratin potatoes on his fork, Emmett's attention was captured by the jubilant expressions on Harry and Larry's faces. The men proposed a toast to their wives' brilliant accomplishment. Faith paused to watch.

"We want to thank you for joining us in celebrating our first Christmas with our beautiful wives."

"We have exciting news."

"Come here, my dears," Harry requested as the two men drew their wives into their embrace. Both sets of twins were dressed identically. This became a habit left over from courtship days. They never failed to draw attention.

"My beloved Hope."

"And my beloved Charity."

"We have decided to sell this house."

"We've built identical homes next door to each other in the Wilshire."

"Merry Christmas, darling." It seemed obvious Larry anticipated his wife's lavish praise at this shocking announcement. Both men seemed dumbfounded as their wives' displeasure became obvious.

Relieved the twins were no longer his responsibility, Emmett watched attentively as the two women burst into tears. He briefly considered stepping in to provide the couples some privacy but decided to observe from the floor. This was not his problem. He flinched when Nettie nudged him with the toe of her slipper.

"Shouldn't you go and help?"

"Why?"

"Because your sisters are upset. The boys don't know what to do."

He found it amusing Nettie referred to the husbands as boys. They were likely several years older than her. Frowning, he handed her his plate, got up and approached the twins, putting his arms around his sisters' shoulders and directing them through the dining room and out to the solarium. Harry and Larry followed impotently behind. Faith stood in for the couples, assuring the remaining guests gathered their coats and wraps as she bid Merry Christmas on behalf of the hosts.

Admiring the Christmas tree as the house emptied out, Nettie gave her plate to a waiter and relaxed in her chair. Faith collapsed in an adjacent chair once the guests were gone.

"What a dramatic conclusion to the evening," Faith declared.

"Yes, I'm certain it will be remembered for years to come."

Both women looked up expectantly as Emmett returned to the parlor. "We should be going."

"What happened?" the women asked in tandem.

"Oh, the husbands are explaining all the advantages of living next door and giving the girls lavish budgets to furnish the homes. The girls don't want to live apart, even next door. It was difficult enough getting them to sleep in separate bedrooms. It also seems we're to welcome another baby into our family."

"Truly?" exclaimed Faith. "Who is expecting? Oh, they're not both expecting, are they?"

"No, and that seems to be another challenge to the mass marriages of our sisters. Charity is expecting. I don't know who's going to come out on the short end of this. Harry is desperate to appease Hope, who is devastated Charity is going into unexplored territory alone. Larry is desperate to pamper and reward Charity. I imagine before the evening is out, the budgets and dress allowances will be through the roof." Emmett shook his head, almost a shiver. "Those are two eccentric couples."

"Yes, but we love them," added Faith. "Wherever has the Judge gotten to? I need to find him."

"We should leave," Emmett declared as Faith

exited the parlor. He took Nettie's hand and led her toward the entry to retrieve their hats and coats. He paused as they passed through the archway dividing the rooms.

"Well, Miss Gordon, it seems you're standing right beneath the mistletoe. I didn't notice it before." He bent down and kissed Nettie on the lips. Since she did not put him off, he placed his arms around her and pressed her against his chest. His kiss became passionate, almost desperate. When he finally pulled away, he could not have been more pleased by the dreamy and sensual expression on Nettie's face. She kissed him back, whole-heartedly.

Faith stood near the staircase. Curiosity drove her desire to witness her brother's advances. He was so obviously in love. She made a Christmas wish his love would be returned.

* * *

Nettie leaned against the inside of Mrs. Green's front door, her mind reeling. Emmett kissed her goodnight on the porch. Even Nettie understood the kiss was not platonic, equally impassioned as his kiss under the mistletoe. As she unbuttoned her coat, she noticed Edra, Mrs. Green's housekeeper, clearing away dishes in the parlor. Mrs. Green hosted a Christmas Eve gathering, an especially thoughtful gesture given that many who lived in her boarding house had no nearby relations.

"My, Miss Nettie, has it grown warm outside? Your cheeks are fairly blushed full out. You ain't taken ill are you?"

Nettie removed her gloves and felt her cheeks. They were hot but not from the weather. "It must be from the cold night air riding in my friend's automobile."

"Oh, the fine-looking man is your friend?"

"Certainly," Nettie proclaimed as she walked toward the staircase.

"I don't know if friends spend so long at the front door doing what-all you were doing." Edra grinned as she picked up the tray of dishes. "You didn't get in the middle of the trolley car accident on Hill Street when you left did you?"

"I don't know anything about it."

"It was a wild sight. We could hear it all the way up here. I runned over there myself to have a look see. The street car comin' down Hill lost its brakes and slammed into two more trolleys. There was folks bleedin' and screamin'. I tell you, it was a mess I'll never forget. I'll see it in my sleep tonight. Folks at Mrs. Green's was right upset the whole night. You were lucky you were out with your beau."

"Goodnight Edra." Nettie thought the woman's account over-blown. No one at the open house mentioned anything about an accident. But it was Edra's assertion she had a beau that proved most disturbing.

Sleep seemed impossible once Nettie climbed into bed. Why did she allow Emmett Boyd of all people to kiss her? Why didn't she stop him? Slap his face? Why did he make her feel so unsure of herself, so— breathless? This simply would not do. What motivated him to behave in such an uncharacteristic manner?

His intentions could not be honorable. He understood she would not marry. He always seemed to appreciate the fact Nettie accompanied him, enabling him to get away from the Golden State and enjoy life. She contemplated the idea he was deceiving her all this time. She was a fool not to notice.

What benefit did she obtain from this strange relationship? The long hours at the saloon were grueling.

It was nice to get away now and then. Nettie abruptly recalled how frequently they were going out, several times a week. She came to think of herself as a member of Emmett's family. They certainly welcomed her, almost like a sister. They'd be shocked if Emmett proposed some illicit relationship. Or would they? If he continued to bring her to family dinners as his friend, perhaps he'd never have to admit his lustful ambitions.

She thought back to Emmett's occasional odd behavior. The night the robber came to the side door, Emmett seemed distraught when he hugged her. What did he say, something about almost losing her? That was the first of several peculiar comments. He'd been exceptionally generous. Was this all some well-thought-out plot to take her to his bed? Had she been incredibly naïve and trusting? Was she beholden to him in ways she never imagined?

Why did she cling to him and kiss him back? He was no more than a friend to her. He was a strong and attractive man. Was this simply some primal attraction? She certainly enjoyed his company and their excursions. When he held her, it seemed as if she could not think or move, mesmerized by his touch. Exhausted, Nettie's mind continued to circle round and round. The dawn would come before long. Determined to enjoy and revere Christmas Day, Nettie finally fell into a fitful sleep.

* * *

Sorry she'd been so agreeable about Emmett's holiday plans, Nettie contemplated ways to avoid him. Short of feigning illness, she doubted she could evade him entirely. Looking in her mirror, it seemed plausible to pass herself off as being sick. Dark rings circled her eyes. She was pale, although this was merely the result of a sleepless night.

She agreed to accompany Emmett to his church for Christmas morning services. Nettie was curious about the twins. Christmas dinner at Faith's house held the potential for high drama even though the girls divulged their surprise last night.

Emmett appeared at the boarding house on time, an eager expression in place. He was solicitous as he guided her into church and did not act inappropriately.

When Emmett suggested they go for brunch at Webster's house, Nettie requested he drive her home. Her fatigue was obvious. She also needed to deliver a few gifts on this most festive day. As Emmett expressed a desire to accompany her, Nettie skillfully put him off and was relieved when he left her at Mrs. Green's, promising to return exactly at four.

Emmett wished her merry Christmas as he held Nettie's hands on the porch before departing. Suspiciously, she gazed into the eyes of a man clearly smitten.

If Emmett Boyd had any nefarious motives, she would have to set him straight, Christmas or not. Why couldn't all these men propose to Eula and leave her alone? Eula would undoubtedly say yes to the first comer, whether she knew him or not.

* * *

Nettie was especially quiet as Emmett drove them to Faith's Christmas celebration.

"Are you all right?"

"I suppose I'm tired is all."

"Were you able to spend time with Eula? How's her romance coming along?"

"I'm afraid it's not much of a romance. I repeatedly explain the vicar isn't good enough for her. She continues to chase after him. She invited him to her uncle's home for Christmas dinner. I hope, for her sake, he shows up."

"It must be difficult to pine away for someone who isn't interested."

Nettie bit her lip. Was this the moment she was hoping for? Should she explain her position to Emmett now? No, not now. If she was going to ruin Christmas, best it be later. "I don't believe Eula truly cares for the vicar. She simply wants to get married."

Emmett nodded his head thoughtfully. Was this the moment he was hoping for? They certainly approached the topic he most wished to discuss. No, best to see how the day unfolded. "I had a nice time at Webster's house. His wife does not often entertain our family."

"So, it was a Christmas miracle?"

"You could say that. Actually, Nadine was in a congenial mood. She can be warm and charming when it suits her."

"Did the twins go?"

"No, they left church as quickly as we did. Charity was feeling queasy and wanted to rest before tonight."

"They are still coming then?"

"I believe so. Why, are they the highlight of your day?"

Nettie giggled. "You must admit, Emmett, your sisters are quite fascinating."

"That's certainly one word for them."

Once they arrived at the Judge's lovely home, Nettie looked around in wonder. Faith decorated her home to perfection. Her Christmas tree was every bit as opulent as the twins'. Nettie felt inordinately lucky to spend the holiday in such grand style.

Emmett, unimpressed by decorations, had eyes only for Nettie. She removed the same green coat she wore on Christmas Eve to reveal an elegant black taffeta dress with a scooped neckline, deep lace collar and short, full sleeves. The neutral clothing showcased her red hair in a manner she probably did not intend. Emmett wanted nothing more than to bury his face in her hair and kiss her as he did last night.

The festivities at the Judge's house were more solemn than Christmas Eve. Whether this was due to the somber reverence of the day or the fact the Judge was older and more settled, Nettie didn't know.

Faith was an eager hostess, excited for her son's first Christmas. Dinner was a formal and delicious affair. Even the twins seemed subdued in the stately atmosphere. Charity fairly glowed, the picture of maternal anticipation. Hope seemed to have reconciled her current fate, if only for the day. The husbands appeared pleased by this state of affairs. Nettie surmised those two men must enjoy a challenge. She was certain their life resembled a wild roller coaster ride with ever-present highs and lows unimaginable to the common man.

Webster appeared the devoted father throughout, intent on supervising his three youngsters but equally engaged in sampling their toys. Before leaving the dining room, he struck a teaspoon on his glass to draw attention. After clearing his throat dramatically, he announced his family was also expecting a new baby. There were more congratulations all around. Nadine appeared happily modest, unlike her usual abrasive and critical self.

Gifts were exchanged after supper. Nettie found herself on the settee next to Nadine as she sipped a cup of tea and enjoyed her pumpkin pie.

"I wanted to add my congratulations. How exciting it will be to have so many babies growing up together.

What a special Christmas this is for the Boyd family."

"It made Webster happy."

"Not you?"

"I believe I expressed my opinion on babies to you previously. But this was bound to happen sooner or later. Doesn't all this maternal bliss make you eager to start a family of your own?"

Nettie shook her head. "My only goal is to find a teaching job in the fall. I miss my students. Teaching is the life I long for."

"You mean you'd give up your lucrative career at the Golden State? All the money my brother-in-law pays you? I find that hard to believe."

"I appreciate my salary, but I work long hours six days a week. I'll be happy to return to teaching and the hobbies I enjoy." Nettie noted the perplexed look on Nadine's face. "Is something wrong?"

"I had you pegged as something of a gold digger."

"Me?"

"Yes. I thought you were taking advantage of Emmett. It's amazing what money will do to some women. I'm surprised to hear you have different plans. Or is this simply a ploy to get him to spend more money on you?"

"I assure you, it is no ploy."

"When I see the opulence in this house, I imagined you were looking for something similar."

"Faith's home is lovely, but this is not the life I see for myself."

"But Emmett could give you this."

"Emmett understands my ideas about marriage, probably better than anyone."

Nadine nodded thoughtfully. It appeared Nettie was being truthful. She decided to try a different tactic. "The Boyds have certainly embraced the current commercialization of Christmas."

"What do you mean?"

"You've seen how busy the stores were this season, how this sacred celebration has become little more than a reason to make money. Gifts and decorations like these were unheard of even a few years ago. My goodness, there was an article in the paper recently exhorting shoppers to stay calm and be polite. They say the poor spend as much as 10 dollars on Christmas. It's a week's pay for most families."

"To be honest, Nadine, I never experienced a Christmas so splendid in my entire life. I can't help but admire your family. If the Boyds can afford to celebrate in this grand manner, who does it hurt?"

As Nadine imagined, money was the underlying factor in Nettie Gordon's pursuit of her brother-in-law.

A sudden hush fell over the room as the twins, holding hands, headed to the center of the Persian rug to make an announcement. "We have one last gift this evening."

"Yes, it's for Emmett."

"Brother, we have decided to sign our portions of the Golden State over to you."

"You're the last of us to care for our parents' heritage."

"It's only right you should own it."

"Our husbands have encouraged us to do this."

"They're the bread winners for our family."

It was obvious Emmett was touched by the gesture. He approached the girls to give them each a kiss.

"You shouldn't do this."

"Yes, we should," the girls both laughed.

"You deserve it."

"You're the best brother ever!"

"We can't begin to thank you for putting up with us

all these years."

Nettie found the announcement amazing. First, the girls referred to their new families in the singular. Second, they acknowledged Emmett's importance in their lives. Perhaps they weren't as shallow as they appeared.

The Boyds were enthusiastic game players and so, parlor games commenced. Emmett hurriedly settled himself beside Nettie once Nadine vacated the spot. At the conclusion of the last game, Emmett explained, "I wanted to show you something. Faith has quite the plant collection in her solarium. I think you'd enjoy it in light of your fascination for horticulture."

Apprehensively, Nettie allowed herself to be guided to the solarium. She walked around observing the variety of exotic plants, including a rare orchid.

"I never knew Faith was interested in gardening."

"She always had an interest in exotic plants and has more time since she no longer works. Her life is changed."

Emmett offered a seat on the wicker settee in the corner and sat down beside Nettie.

"I have something I want to discuss."

Nettie bit her lip. She was certain this was the moment she feared. She took a deep breath and smiled, prepared to defend her honor. "This sounds serious."

"I wanted to tell you how much I enjoy your company. Our outings are the highlight of my life. I've come to care deeply for you, Nettie. I want something more than what we have now. I think you do too."

"What gives you that idea?"

"I believe you enjoy my companionship as much as I enjoy yours. You give me such pleasure, riding in the motor car, going to the theater, even doing errands for the saloon. I was thrilled when you kissed me. I believe my kiss had the same effect on you. The truth is, I want something more permanent."

Nettie was shocked. Did he actually intend to make some illicit pact? Was this to be a paid position, a business decision? Would he actually negotiate with her? She was certain her face was scarlet.

She was not prepared when Emmett got down on one knee and asked, "Will you marry me?"

"No," came the definitive reply. "What did you say?"

Emmett's mouth fell open. He appeared confused as he repeated, "Will you marry me?"

"I thought you said something else, but no, I won't. Get up from the floor this instant."

"No, you need to explain." Nettie inched forward on the settee as if to stand. "You can't walk away from me, Nettie. I'm not some boy you leave kneeling in the middle of the saloon." At this, he rose from the floor and took a seat next to her, grasping Nettie's arm to hold her in place.

"I already explained to you. I will never marry. Not you, not anyone, never. I don't know how to make this any clearer. I never dreamed you were going to ask me to marry you, of all things."

"What did you think I was asking?" Emmett demanded.

At this, Nettie's face turned an even deeper shade of red.

"It's not important."

"Yes, it is. Tell me."

"It's none of your business. I don't have to tell you anything. I don't have to talk to you. This is exactly why I'll never marry. No one controls me. No one tells me what to do."

Emmett could see Nettie was in a panic. He struck

a nerve with the usually calm, collected Miss Gordon. "Nettie, has someone hurt you?"

"No. What are you talking about?"

"Why are you so defensive? Did a man violate you?"

"Certainly not. How could you think such a thing?"

"Because I don't understand you. I, at least, deserve an explanation. What is it you so fear about marriage? Or is it me you fear?" His heart sunk at the possibility, but he needed to know.

"I'm not afraid."

"Yes, you are. Tell me what's wrong with marriage. Why won't you marry me? Is it something I've done or said?"

Nettie looked longingly at the door. She wished only to escape. She stared at Emmett Boyd. He appeared devastated. She never meant to hurt him. Perhaps he did deserve an explanation.

"It's nothing you've done."

"Then tell me why this is so abhorrent to you."

Nettie redirected her attention to the door and replied, "Men change when they marry."

"You think I'll be a different man if you marry me? In what way?"

Defensively, Nettie responded, "Did Louise know her husband was an opium fiend when they married? Would she have married him if so? Do you think she was so blinded by love she couldn't see the man for his true self? Or did he change after they married? Did he become something else? Was his marriage no longer important to him? Right now, she's struggling to encourage him to be the husband and father he vowed to be. You don't even think he'll manage.

"I know for certain my mother did not think to herself, I'll marry that man. He can beat me and my children and spend my egg money on liquor. We'll live in shame and poverty. This seems like a fine idea to me. I can assure you, she did not.

"Why would any woman sign onto such a life? I can only assume neither Louise nor my mother had any idea what would become of them. I certainly don't feel qualified to make a better decision than them. I can give you countless other examples. Do you think your sister-in-law would have married Webster if she knew then what she's learned since? She seems an unhappy and bitter woman. I don't even believe this is your brother's fault. Perhaps she would have been unhappy no matter who she married."

"So, it's the institution of marriage that is to blame?"

"Women lose what meager rights they have when they marry. They no longer control their finances or their occupation or even their body. How could you ask me to give my very self away, not to mention my children?"

Emmett sat dumbfounded. "Why do you think I'm like these other men? Nettie, everybody's different. There are women who do cruel things."

"But men still have all the rights."

"That's not true in Los Angeles. You read every day in the newspaper how women are granted divorces. They retain custody of their children and often their property. If you didn't think I was going to ask you to marry me, what did you think I was asking?"

"I thought you were going to ask me to be your mistress."

"And what were you planning to reply?"

"Certainly not. What kind of woman do you think I am?"

"I think you are a wonderful, loving, kind,

compassionate and confused woman." At this, Emmett put his hand in his vest pocket and pulled out a beautiful ring. Diamonds surrounded a sparkling garnet.

"What kind of man do you think I am? One who would beat you, subjugate you and treat you as some concubine? Do you know me at all? How can you think these things of me? I've never hurt you and I never would."

"You certainly have."

"When?" Emmett asked incredulously.

"You've been yanking me around by the arm since the day we met."

"Well, I thought you were a criminal." He looked down at his hand on her arm now and let her go as if he'd been burned. "I'm sorry. I won't do that again. And I'm sorry your family was so bitterly disappointing, but there are other kinds of families. You've seen mine.

"I'll grant you Webster's marriage isn't ideal, but it works. They love each other; they manage to get by. You and I could have such a happy life together. I don't want you to discard my idea over some ridiculous generalization. It's clear to me we're not ready for this," he held up the ring, "but I feel certain I can win you over. We work together—"

"I quit."

"No, you don't."

"Yes, I do. I quit."

"You're so afraid of me, you would give up a lucrative position to avoid my presence?"

"I cannot be bought, Mr. Boyd, if it's what you've been trying to do. Nadine hinted I'm overpaid. You've spent lavishly on me. How can I ever repay you? I don't wish to be further indebted."

As intent as Emmett was to remain calm, he knew he was about at the end of his patience.

"I assure you, I pay you what Faith made when she managed the side door and she didn't have a raise in quite some time. As far as our outings, it's normal for a suitor, or an employer, to foot the bill. Rest assured, I'm not keeping an accounting. I don't know what you consider lavish, but our outings haven't been expensive. You don't owe me anything."

He decided to change tactics. "I'm serious about this, about us. How many men would have walked away dejected once you said no?"

"The smart ones, surely."

Emmett frowned. "I'm convinced you're right for me. Further, I know beyond doubt I'm right for you and I'm going to prove it. This was meant as an engagement ring. I want you to consider it your Christmas gift." He took her right hand in his and held fast even though she tried to pull away. Sliding the ring on her finger, he continued, "I'll put this on your right hand until the day you tell me you're ready to wear it on your left. It's yours in any case."

"I'll never be interested in wearing it as an engagement ring. You're wasting your time and money. I tried to warn you about this before. It's now obvious to me you've been deceitful in your dealings with me, enticing me to come away from work, making me feel as if I was doing you some favor when all the while you sought to court me."

There was enough truth in her statement that Emmett couldn't deny it. "I love you, Nettie."

"I'm sorry you do."

"No, you're not. You love me."

"You're being ridiculous."

"I never thought I'd say this, but I wish you were more like the twins." Nettie's eyes grew wide in disbelief. "You could use some of their spontaneity.

You're so determined to stick by your ideas of men and marriage that you can't see the nose on your face. I'll prove you love me." Emmett pulled her into his embrace and kissed her.

At first Nettie resisted, but all too soon, she was lost—again—in his touch. She wrapped her arms around his neck and kissed him with a passion she couldn't deny. It was Emmett who finally ended the kiss.

"I'll make a deal. I'll kiss you once every day and when the day comes that you don't respond, I'll know there is no love in your heart for me."

Nettie, her pulse racing, considered this proposal. Surely, she could gird herself against his kiss one time and be rid of him. "Once a month. The last day of the month after work."

"I believe a compromise is in order. Once a week, every Saturday at the close of business." He offered his hand to strike the deal. Apprehensively, Nettie put her smaller hand in his and gave a firm handshake.

"What about our outings?" she inquired suspiciously.

"I'll ask you as always. You have abundant free will to decide if you want to come or not. It's up to you to determine if my intentions are devious. I will, as always, behave as a perfect gentleman."

"Perfect gentlemen don't make bargains about kissing."

"Perfect ladies don't either."

CHAPTER THIRTEEN

Faith wanted nothing so much as to telephone her brother and find out what happened in the solarium, but she knew she would likely be asleep before he arrived home. Besides, she didn't want some nosy operator listening in on their conversation.

She was ecstatic when Emmett shared his plan to become engaged. Before Nettie Gordon came along, Faith doubted Emmett would ever find a nice girl and fall in love. Nettie was like a sister and Faith wanted her officially in the family.

Obviously, the engagement did not come off as Emmett intended. He seemed pleasant enough when they rejoined the family. Nettie seemed hesitant. They were the first to leave the gathering, but the others followed shortly after.

Faith's curiosity had the better of her. Nettie must have said no, yet Emmett seemed more hopeful than distraught. Although Nettie did not show it off, Faith caught the flash of a beautiful ring on her right hand.

There was so much for which to be grateful. Her own little Luther lay asleep in the bassinette beside her bed. He was truly a miracle. The twins were married and on their own even if their lives were as dramatic as ever.

There would be two new babies in the New Year; hopefully a marriage. Faith surmised Mother and Father would have loved this Christmas Day. Perhaps they could see their family from on high. The thought gave her great peace as she drifted off to sleep.

* * *

If Emmett believed his relationship with Nettie would go on as it had before, he was sadly mistaken. Miss Gordon wasted no time asserting herself as the prim and proper manager of the side door and avoided him entirely. In time, he would wonder how she knew when to disappear at his approach. Whole days went by without so much as a glimpse of Nettie. Yet, the side door was managed to great effect, as it always had been on her watch.

Since New Year's Eve fell on Sunday, the celebration at the Golden State was planned for Monday. Emmett anticipated a fine crowd and wanted Nettie to accompany him to buy decorations. Applying persistence, he finally cornered her long enough to suggest, "I'm not certain what to purchase. I hoped you might come and help."

"I'm certain some streamers would suffice."

"But what color? How many? I think it's your duty to help. I also want the side door decorated. I've hired a band."

"Fine." Nettie disgustedly grabbed her coat and hat and reluctantly took Emmett's hand when he helped her into his automobile. She sat at the outside edge of the seat in order to stay as far away as possible.

"People fall out of motor cars. I wouldn't sit over there if I was you."

Pursing her lips, Nettie moved toward the center of her seat. This was the first time they were alone since

Christmas.

The streets were unusually full on this last business day of 1905. Emmett drove to a nearby mercantile store where he purchased an inordinately large quantity of streamers and rubber balloons in every color he could find. He bought a large boxful of paper hats, horns and noisemakers. Nettie stood impotently to the side. He obviously never wanted her opinion. This was simply a ploy to take her away from the Golden State for the morning. She was not surprised at his next request.

"We can grab some lunch across the street before we return."

"You go ahead. It's not far. I can walk back."

"As your employer, I insist you come. We need to strategize about decorations. Consider it a business meeting." He smiled and offered his arm to escort her across the street. Nettie had little choice but to comply.

After they were seated, Emmett shared his thoughts on how to hang the streamers and balloons and asked for Nettie's opinion on the best way to offer the horns and noisemakers. He wished the celebration at the Golden State to be loud and memorable. They decided to begin decorating at eight to entice the Saturday night crowd to return for New Year's Day.

Emmett imperiously ordered lunch for both himself and Nettie without asking what she wanted, which was not his habit. She glared daggers at him across the table and considered leaving her lunch untouched on the plate. But it proved tantalizing and she couldn't resist.

She sputtered when he proclaimed, "It's Saturday. I'm looking forward to our rendezvous this evening."

"It's hardly a rendezvous and you need to be quiet. Someone will hear." She was disappointed he planned to act on their deal, hoping he would be a gentleman and let her off the hook.

* * *

Nettie stood back to observe her decorations in the side door as the last customer left at ten. She was alarmed when Emmett poked his head through the doorway.

"I see you didn't follow my suggestions."

"No, I thought it boring to do the same thing in both rooms." She decided to string the streamers from the center of the room to the edges. "I like it," she asserted.

"I believe we should test it out," Emmett suggested. "Let's see if there's sufficient room to dance." He approached and took up ballroom position. Nettie, frowning, fell in place. Emmett twirled her around the room under the streamers. "They appear to be fastened properly."

"Of course, they are," Nettie stopped dancing.

"Well then, I think we need to get to the business at hand."

Emmett looked into Nettie's eyes and lowered his lips to hers. She stood still at first, determined this would be their last kiss. All too soon she disappointed herself entirely and succumbed to his romantic gesture. A wave of frustration encompassed her as he ended the kiss.

"I love you, Nettie. You can be as harsh as you like, but you love me too. I win."

"You win for this week," she breathlessly replied. "I will prove you wrong."

Nettie enjoyed his embrace and was content to stand in the center of the side door with Emmett's arms wrapped around her. Shocked at this idea, Nettie quickly backed away.

"I don't know why you have this power over me, but it will end."

"I'm only getting started," Emmett replied as she

turned her back on him and headed to the closet to collect her things. "I need you here at nine sharp on Monday. He received a glare in response. "I take it you won't join me at church tomorrow morning, nor at family dinner?"

"That's your family, not mine. I have other plans for church."

"You are so predictable. It will be Monday, then."

* * *

Emmett stood in front of the Golden State as Nettie approached from the trolley stop on New Year's morning. "Get in the Buick," he commanded.

"Why?"

"We have an errand to do."

Nettie reluctantly complied. She sat silently as Emmett climbed in the automobile and handed her a blanket. "It's cold this morning," he explained.

It shortly became obvious they were headed away from the city.

"Where are we going?"

"Ah, you can talk."

"Where are we going?"

"We're on our way to Pasadena."

"I don't want to go to Pasadena. Why would we go there?"

"Are you afraid I'm kidnapping you?"

"I wouldn't put it past you, the way you behave."

"You've successfully avoided me all week. Since you're no longer a willing participant in our outings, I find the need to be more sly. But feel free to jump out of the car. You'd surely make the headlines in the *Herald* tomorrow. It might even go national, right beside the litany of murders and suicides occurring daily. I can see the headline now—'Angry Woman Plunges Headlong from Buick—Found by Side of Road in Tattered Clothing.'"

"I don't want to go to Pasadena. Turn the car around."

"Pasadena is our destination, Miss Gordon. The Tournament of Roses will not change its course to accommodate you. Have you ever seen it?"

"Never. I'm quite certain I'll survive if I miss it this year."

"It's delightful—you'll enjoy it."

"Who will open the saloon? We can't be going to a parade."

"I assure you, the Golden State will do fine without us today. We'll be back in time for the evening crowd. Louise returns today."

"So, Louise is the answer to all your staffing challenges on this busy day? Have you lost your mind?"

"Not my mind, just my heart."

Nettie scowled. Why did Emmett Boyd's every conversation end with a proclamation of love? It was him who had become so incredibly predictable.

* * *

Emmett took off his knit scarf and wrapped it around the lower part of Nettie's face as she shivered in the cold. They managed to find a seat on the curb. Emmett spread one blanket for them to sit on and had another for their laps.

Greenery, bunting, flags and flowers decorated storefronts along the parade route. The parade was supposed to start at 10:30. Instead, a cold wind developed to chill the waiting crowd.

He couldn't complain. The day already exceeded his wildest expectations as Nettie plastered herself against his side, intent to find as much warmth as possible. She became distracted by the Tournament as soon as it began and seemed more herself than she had since his proposal.

From the moment the queen of the parade, Elise Armitage, appeared with her 24 princesses, Nettie excitedly pointed out all the floral displays as if he couldn't see for himself. Emmett enjoyed listening; it seemed he was the only one talking of late.

Decorated pony carts and wagons shared the parade route with equestrian teams and marching bands. Automobiles started appearing in the parade in recent years and they were well represented today. The undeniable highlight of the 17th annual Tournament of Roses parade was a fantastic self-propelled float, which seemed to drift down the route as if by magic. Only the wheels could be seen below an array of pastel flowers.

Despite a persistent drizzle, Emmett purchased sandwiches from a vendor shortly before the parade ended. As he handed one to Nettie, she seemed surprised.

"Isn't the parade almost over?"

"I believe so."

"Shouldn't we eat at the Golden State? Aren't you in a hurry to get back?"

"No and no. Who says we're going back?"

"Then where are we going?"

"To the chariot races." Since Nettie obviously enjoyed the parade, Emmett was disappointed at her eagerness to leave. "Are you in some kind of hurry?"

"I told you I didn't want to come to Pasadena."

"What's wrong with you?"

"Nothing." Nettie considered her reply. "I imagine I'm rather tired. Didn't you hear all the commotion in the street at midnight?"

"It only lasted a few minutes."

"Did you read the paper this morning?" Nettie asked.

"Yes, it's my habit."

"I'm certain you saw the article about the big temperance meeting at Blanchard Hall." Emmett scowled at her comment. Perhaps she could provoke him into taking her home.

Emmett replied, "It ended at midnight. Maybe the attendees joined the revelers in the street at the New Year. I'm sure there were more than a few flasks to be found for those who wanted to imbibe one last time. Why? Were you there?"

"I probably should have gone," Nettie goaded. "They say a lot of men took the pledge. I would have found the testimonials fascinating."

"No doubt."

"Mr. Murphy is a powerful speaker, I hear. Many men who signed the pledge last year reported on the joyful changes in their lives."

"I read the article, Nettie."

"Oh, so you said. I wonder if any of your customers signed."

"I'm not taking you home, not yet. But I am about to take my scarf back." His comment was met with silence. In no time, Nettie's attention returned to the parade.

The chariot races, also becoming an annual event, were well-attended. The crowd was horrified by a shocking crash at the end of the first race. The driver whipped his horses into such a frenzy, he wasn't able to control them at the finish line. Two of the horses bumped together and caused the cross bar to break. The chariot and driver launched into the air.

Aghast, Nettie drew close against Emmett as they stood to see what would happen. He slyly put his arm around her and held her tight. She was incredibly relieved when the driver, a Mr. Off, returned to wave at the crowd. His injuries proved superficial.

"He's the luckiest man in the world," Nettie commented as she clapped.

As Emmett stared down at her, he couldn't help but feel it was him who was the luckiest man in the world. If only he could make Nettie understand.

Emmett felt incredibly fortunate and wise when he drove past long lines of parade goers at the depot that morning. Many took the special train to Pasadena. Mr. Boyd and his guest only needed to make their way to the Buick to begin their homeward journey.

Noticing a hawker selling peanuts, Emmett kept Nettie close and struggled through the crowd to obtain a treat for the ride back. He felt Nettie lean against him once he stopped to make the purchase. He was surprised when the peanut vendor began to speak.

"I heared you took up with a fast crowd in the city, Nettie, and here you are, all dressed up fine. You even got a fancy man to pay your way."

Emmett couldn't believe his ears. He looked down at Nettie as she placed her hand on his chest and smiled up at him. "We don't need peanuts. Let's go home." She took his hand to lead him away from the vendor.

"Just run off. That's all you're good for. Pay no mind to them in need, you selfish slut."

Emmett, ever eager to defend his ladies, was not about to let that comment pass. He retraced his steps and before Nettie could react, took a swing at the vendor, hitting him squarely in the jaw. Peanuts flew everywhere as the man sprawled in the dirt. The crowd paused to watch this finale to their exciting day.

"That's not the way to speak to a lady. You got anything more to say?" taunted Emmett.

The vendor stayed on the ground, unmoving.

"I thought not." Emmett was in no hurry to leave, but Nettie pulled him into the crowd. "Who was that man?"

"It's not important."

"Yes, it is. Who was he?"

"You wouldn't understand." At this, Emmett stopped in his tracks. There was nothing Nettie could do to move him forward. She dropped his hand and hurried away.

Emmett kept an eye on Nettie's hat in the mass of people as he strode through the crowd behind her.

Dark thoughts plucked at his mind. Who was that man? Was she protecting the peanut seller when Nettie attempted to coerce him into leaving? Ugly possibilities speeded his step. They were nearly at the Buick when he finally caught up. He resisted the urge to grab Nettie's arm and instead, tapped her shoulder.

"I have a few questions."

"I'm sure you do."

"Who was that man?"

"No one of importance."

"Is he your husband?"

"*What?*"

"Are you married to him or were you ever?"

"Something evidently happened to your brain when you took up boxing. It doesn't work well. I'm ever astounded at the incredible twists and turns of illogic bouncing around in your head."

"It would answer a lot of questions if it was true." Incredulous, Nettie stared at him. "It would explain why you won't marry—because you already are or were."

"I can assure you, Mr. Boyd, I am not nor have I ever married. And I never will," she added emphatically as Emmett helped her into the Buick before climbing in without cranking the engine.

"Then who is that man?"

Nettie stared forward as if she didn't hear his question.

"We can sit here right until dawn if you like, but it will soon be much too cold for comfort. I won't leave for home until you tell me who that was."

"He's one of my brothers," Nettie stared at Emmett's shocked expression. "I can see you don't understand, which is the problem, but I'm not going to say anymore."

True to her word, Nettie did not make a sound until they pulled into the carriage house.

"Thank you. This was a fun and memorable day. But I won't be getting in your automobile again—for recreation or for work." Nettie climbed down and left Emmett behind as she quickly walked across the alley to the Golden State.

The reason for Emmett's leisurely attitude was quickly apparent. Faith and Webster filled in so their brother could spend New Year's Day with his supposed sweetheart. Nettie quickly took up her duties so Faith could go home.

From Nettie's serious and dismissive demeanor, Faith ascertained things did not go her brother's way, yet again.

* * *

The next weeks of winter seemed endless to Emmett. Although Louise put up an adequate front, she struggled through each day. Nettie successfully kept her distance. He caught only the rarest glimpse of his love. They never spoke. Short of running after her through the saloon and tackling her, he was at a complete loss as to how to get her attention.

He was surprised when Nettie came to him on Saturday at closing time. She submitted to his kiss and didn't resist. It became her custom to give herself fully to that one romantic gesture until he would end it. He tried everything he could to detain her afterward. She didn't respond to anything he said and would leave immediately for the trolley. No matter how long the kiss lasted, she never attempted to step away. He couldn't read her expression once he opened his eyes and saw her face. It could have been disappointment, perhaps regret.

He tried giving her a quick peck on the lips as if he was too busy to bother with their weekly rendezvous. He believed she appeared distressed, but perhaps she was only relieved. Emmett began to feel guilty when she initiated their kiss.

Their bargain became a source of anxiety and he frequently considered voiding their agreement. At other times, he pondered the possibility Nettie wouldn't resist no matter what he did. He considered the outcome if he took her to his bed, which might prove to be the only way to bind her to him. He quickly dismissed the idea whenever it occurred. It would be a deceitful and unchivalrous way to force a marriage. He took comfort in the fact Nettie was attracted to him. It was the only thing he had going.

Emmett became moody and sullen. His temper grew short. He rose early to use the striking bag. Missing the days of easy friendship with Nettie, he fantasized about putting her in the Buick and driving away.

Nettie's appearance changed. She returned to the austere clothing she wore when she first arrived at the Golden State. She wore her hair tightly braided and pulled in a prim bun on the back of her neck and seemed pale and unanimated. Emmett likened her to a flower that bloomed briefly and quickly faded.

Although he appreciated her elegant hairstyles and beautiful clothing, Emmett really didn't care how she looked. He fell in love with the being of Nettie Gordon, not her façade. It was her companionship and wit he craved and of course, the opportunity to make her his.

His family ceased to ask after Nettie. Emmett was certain they understood there was no improvement. Their solicitous and gentle demeanor only served to anger him further.

He believed Nettie's family must be the key to her behavior. Finding the peanut seller seemed a remote possibility. Looking for families by the name of Gordon in or near Pasadena was a definite option. Even so, they might not be willing to provide any insight. Emmett felt he knew Nettie better than anyone yet she continued to befuddle him completely.

* * *

Nettie was surprised to find the twins ensconced in the closet one blustery morning. They grinned slyly as she hung her things on their customary hook.

"What have you ladies got up your sleeves today?" Nettie couldn't help the note of suspicion in her tone. She was prepared for someone in Emmett's family to make an overture. They were a tight-knit clan. His unhappiness was apparent for all the world to see. She completely understood her role in his dour mood but could do nothing to change it. He chose to ignore her warnings.

"Have a seat."

"We will pour your tea." At least Nettie could tell the girls apart now. Charity wore a loose-fitting shirtwaist although the fact she was a mother-to-be was not particularly apparent.

Jean Jegel

"We have missed our teas together."

"We have exciting news!"

"We wanted to tell you in person."

"Hope is expecting!" The twins gleefully stared at each other. It was a completely personal moment and Nettie felt an outsider.

"Congratulations!" she offered. The twins, almost reluctantly, looked away from each other. "I'm so happy for you, for both of you, or for all of you."

"We are quite pleased, as well."

"You, more than anyone understood our dilemma."

Nettie smiled. She never understood, but if the twins needed to believe she sympathized with their imagined plight, so be it.

"How is life in your new homes?"

"We are not completely pleased."

"They are lovely homes."

"But we always lived together."

"It's so inconvenient to have to dress and go outside so as not to be apart."

"Once the husbands leave for work, we pick one house or the other and spend the day there."

"It is so tiresome to have to keep two houses."

"Then the boys come home and they want their own dinner."

"Although we often share our meal."

"One would think Harry and Larry would miss each other the way we do."

"They seem to like having their own homes."

"They are completely inscrutable to us."

"Men."

"Yes, men."

"Nettie, we want you to come and visit us."

"We miss seeing you on Sundays."

"Has Emmett somehow been cruel to you?"

- 251 -

"Men are so arrogant and determined to have their own way."

"Look at what our husbands have done."

"Nearly ruined our very lives."

"Now, the whole baby issue is ironed out."

"We are certain this was their fault."

"But we are still not happy about the houses."

Nettie offered, "You two live right next door to each other. Think what fun it'll be when the babies come." Although she felt prepared to ward off questions, Nettie was not equipped for the twins' direct assault.

"Enough about us." At this, Nettie nearly fell off her chair. Everything the twins ever said or did revolved around their own special world.

"Would you come on Sunday after church to visit?"

"We won't invite Emmett."

"We can go later to the gathering at Faith's house."

"Then you can see our houses and you will feel comfortable to tell us Emmett's faults so we can fix him for you."

"I'm afraid it's not that simple," Nettie admitted.

"We are quite certain it is."

"We have decided men are entirely fixable."

"There are things you can do."

"They are like putty in your hand."

"We could make suggestions if you tell us what the problem is."

"Sunday next, then?"

"No," Nettie firmly replied. "Naturally, I'd love to see your new homes, but I have other obligations on Sunday. I expressed a desire to return to teaching Sunday school and my pastor arranged for me to have the youngest children as I did before. I have a meeting afterwards.

"I appreciate your offer of help, but there's really

nothing to be done as far as Emmett is concerned. He hasn't done anything untoward. There is nothing to fix. Please believe me. It's best if Emmett finds someone else."

"But we like you."

"And Emmett does too."

"Don't you like him?"

"I do like him, but he's interested in a commitment I cannot make. I made myself quite clear. I was only interested in friendship and he didn't honor my wishes. I'm sorry if he's hurt by this, but my mind remains as resolved as it ever was. I'm afraid he and I can never go back to being friends."

The twins looked completely confused. Nettie excused herself to start her workday and promised again to visit the twins in their new homes. Relieved to make an escape, Nettie realized her odd and entertaining relationship with the twins was likely at an end.

Thoughts of Emmett came to mind as they often did. The man had some power over her she couldn't deny. She missed their friendship, their fun and exciting outings, his amusing way of thinking. Especially, she yearned for his touch.

She missed the thrill she felt when he held her hand or touched her arm, the undeniable passion she experienced when they danced or when he kissed her. Nettie felt truly sorry he was hurt, but she'd been nothing if not honest, right from the beginning. If he chose not to heed her words, she was not to blame.

Nettie frankly didn't understand why Emmett wanted her in the first place. She was plain, ordinary, and on the cusp of spinsterhood. Her only real interest was in her students.

More determined than ever to find a teaching job, Nettie asked Pastor Arndorfer to place her name on a call list. Hating to lose her to some other school, he reluctantly complied. Teachers would soon be giving notice or accepting calls for the fall term.

It seemed a good idea to move away. From the moment she left home, it was never her intention to settle so close to Pasadena. Now, her father knew how to find her. The last thing she needed was for relatives to show up looking for a handout.

The fact she needed to put space between her and Emmett Boyd occurred constantly. It was the best thing for Emmett. He could get on with his life. It was undoubtedly the best thing for her. Nettie could put all this ugliness behind her and start afresh. Emmett Boyd's touch could thus be banished from her consciousness.

Focusing on a grand new life, new students and an exciting locale, she was finally able to bring herself out of the doldrums she suffered since the encounter with Murl. Nettie could save her wages over the next several months and give notice. Teaching was the only life she wanted. There was nothing to stand in her way.

* * *

Emmett was always amazed when he found women happily dancing together to tunes from the Regina music box. Because unaccompanied men were not allowed in the side door, there simply weren't enough male partners to go around. Attendance was up in the ladies' saloon since the addition of the music machine. Emmett was not surprised to find the bar fairly bursting at the seams for the Saturday evening social.

Emmett hired a three-piece band; there was barely room to dance. Beer sales were brisk, so much so, he felt it necessary to help Delmar behind the bar. This afforded him a rare view of Nettie, who seemed formal and prudish in the midst of all the jovial couples.

When a young woman boldly asked Emmett to dance, he felt a sudden urge to elicit a jealous reaction and gazed across the room at his beloved. Smiling warmly at the young lady who identified herself as Marie, Emmett escorted her onto the dance floor. Uncertain if Nettie noticed him in the crowd, Emmett made a point of guiding his partner around the perimeter of the floor to ensure Nettie got a look. When the music ended, he managed to catch Nettie's eye while he clapped for the musicians.

Marie, who was more than a bit inebriated, touched his arm and lifted her face as if to speak. As he bent down to listen in the noisy barroom, Marie stole a kiss. Knowing he had Nettie's attention, Emmett planted a kiss on Marie's eager lips then laughed to give an impression of delight. As Marie hurried across the floor to join her giggling girl friends, Emmett glanced in Nettie's direction. He apparently succeeded in his quest. She looked positively furious.

* * *

Emmett hummed as he finished wiping down the bar. When Nettie didn't appear for their weekly appointment, he found her in the closet, ready to leave.

"Are you forgetting something?"

Receiving only a glare in reply, he attempted to put his arms around her. He was shocked when Nettie soundly slapped his face.

"Why'd you do that?" he inquired as he rubbed his cheek.

"You already got your kiss."

"I did not. When did you kiss me?"

"Oh, it wasn't me." Nettie was livid. "The little flirt on the dance floor supplied your romantic interlude for the week."

"Her? She wasn't part of our agreement."

"You were supposed to have a kiss and you got one. Good night."

"Wait just a minute." Emmett absent-mindedly grabbed Nettie by the arm.

"Are you going to drag me to the police yet again, tell them I haven't abided by your ridiculous agreement and demand retribution?"

"That was our agreement, not mine alone."

"I don't kiss men who plaster their lips on casual bystanders without thought or emotion. But perhaps I'm wrong. Do you love her, now? Have you already gotten down on one knee and proposed? I can see my concern for your welfare has been for naught. You didn't waste any time finding someone else. I was wise to turn you down, Emmett Boyd. You're nothing but a philandering, shallow male creature, exactly as I always suspected."

"You think you've been showing concern for me these past months? You're nothing but a cold-hearted, cruel and heartless snob."

"I am not a snob. You take that back."

"Well, we're in agreement. You are cold-hearted and cruel. But there was no doubt, was there?"

Nettie's cheeks were pink, her shoulders heaved in anger. "If you think for one moment I'll ever kiss you again since you've rubbed your mouth all over that trollop's face, you have another thing coming." At this, Nettie turned on her heel and marched out the door.

Emmett stood dumbfounded. Although he put himself into something of a hole, he would admit one thing. Fighting with Nettie was the best thing to happen in quite some time.

CHAPTER FOURTEEN

After the Sunday school meeting, Nettie and Eula caught the trolley at the corner of Spring and 7th. Roller rinks originated in the East but quickly became a fad along the entire West Coast. Ignoring critics who contended roller skating was the devil's own invention, the pair made a habit of visiting roller rinks around the city. These excursions resumed once Nettie was free on Sunday afternoons. The nearby Casino Rink recently opened.

Whenever Eula mentioned they might skate after school once Nettie resumed teaching at Trinity, she was always disappointed. Nettie didn't hesitate to proclaim she would be teaching in another city come fall, possibly another state.

"You're in an awfully good mood today," Nettie declared. "It would seem you don't need roller skates to glide down the sidewalk."

"You know me. I'm in love."

"You've been in love ever since you laid eyes on Vicar Haf. But he's traditionally been more a cause for sorrow than cheer. Has something changed?"

"I believe it has."

"Tell me."

"I suppose things changed on Valentine's Day

when I received a romantic postcard from a secret admirer. I'm certain it was Vicar Haf who sent the anonymous voucher of endless love."

"It doesn't really sound like him."

"You are too cold, Nettie. He's been caring and attentive of late. Things are going well."

"He's asking you out? Has he seen your uncle about this?"

"Well, no. He never asked permission. But we always met for ice cream."

"How do you know he's serious?"

"Nettie, even you know when a man is serious. You had the same experience with Mr. Boyd, but you were too stubborn to fall in love."

"You're not entirely accurate."

"So you *are* in love?"

"Certainly not."

"Then explain to me what part I have wrong."

"You don't understand. Tell me where you and the vicar have been going," Nettie requested, knowing Eula would be happy to discuss her true love.

Eula chattered on until they arrived at the Casino Rink. On-lookers watched skaters from bleacher seating. The huge wooden floor provided a perfect skating surface.

Eula and Nettie were dressed appropriately in ankle-length full skirts, elegant white shirtwaists and stylish hats. Double-clasping arms in front, they skated around the rink. The avoidance of inexperienced skaters provided their greatest challenge. Male skaters whizzed by at alarming speeds. A few couples did a two-step around the floor. There was no doubt roller dancing was the latest craze.

After circling the rink several times, Nettie was not prepared for Eula's sudden stop and went flying toward the wall. She grasped frantically at the rail and narrowly avoided crashing to the ground.

Ready to scold Eula for the sudden and unexpected move, Nettie turned to find Eula staring across the rink, unmoving. Nettie focused in the general direction of Eula's gaze and spied the object of her attention.

Stunned, she saw Vicar Haf coaxing a lovely young woman around the outer edge of the rink. The woman looked adoringly at the vicar. He laughed jovially as he almost carried her along.

Nettie skated over to her friend and noted her total devastation. Tears slid down Eula's cheeks.

"Let's go home," offered Nettie.

"No. I think I'll pay my respects."

"It's not a good idea to make a scene." But Nettie's advice fell on deaf ears. Eula skated across the center of the rink right up to the vicar, who quickly lost his smile.

"Eula, I—"

Before the vicar could attempt an explanation, Eula punched him in the jaw. Losing his balance, the vicar sprawled across the slick wooden floor. Nettie stood behind Eula, mouth agape. Curiosity seekers stopped to watch. The vicar's beautiful companion flew to his side.

"You horrid woman, look what you've done!" she declared as she knelt to assist her skating partner.

"I'd watch out for him if I were you," warned Eula, who turned and skated away. Nettie followed after.

"I'm so sorry, Eula. I know how much you care for him."

Eula wiped away her tears. Her complexion turned a blotchy red. She was intent on leaving at the greatest possible speed. The women removed their skates and exited the rink. Nettie fell further behind at Eula's every angry step. Her stride was simply not long enough to keep up.

"Wait, Eula. Hold up."

Eula turned momentarily then proceeded headlong down the sidewalk. Nettie managed to stay by her side. "I told you that man wasn't good enough for you. He's shallow and—and horrible. Mark my words, you'll find someone better."

Eula stopped and turned to her dearest friend.

"It's too late, Nettie. I gave myself to him. I'm ruined." At this, Eula continued her headlong flight toward home.

Nettie followed her friend right up the staircase at Mrs. Green's. Although Eula tried to quickly close her door, Nettie managed to slide through.

"Have you lost your mind?"

Eula stared defiantly. "Is that what you think? Nettie, I know I'm not a pretty girl. I have few prospects. I tried everything I could to charm Clyde. He was only interested in you. He thought you'd have no choice but to turn to him if you lost your job. He got your father to write to the church counsel."

"He *what*?"

Eula had definitely not meant that to slip out.

"How did he manage? Eula, did you help him?" Nettie could tell from her friend's shocked expression she must have been the one who aided the vicar. "How could you do that to me?"

Eula began to cry in earnest. "I wanted a husband. I thought the vicar was my best opportunity. At least he took me for ice cream. I would have done anything for him. I wanted to be the best wife ever. When he continued to see me because I helped him, I went along with his every wish. Finally, I offered everything, literally. I thought he was finally committed to me. How could I have been so stupid? What am I going to do?"

"How long has this been going on?"

Jean Jegel

"Two months."

Nettie's mouth fell open in horror. "Are you expecting?" It appeared Eula never contemplated this possibility.

"I don't know. I don't think so."

"Well, let's pray you aren't."

Eula, stunned, weighed the possibilities. "No, let's pray I am! Just think Nettie, he would have to marry me then."

"Oh, Eula, that's no way to start a marriage. How could you want to marry him now? He'd make you miserable for the rest of your life. He would make you pay for tricking him into marriage. He might never love you or your baby. You'd worry if he was with another woman whenever he was out of sight. He's simply not good enough for you, can't you see?" But Nettie could see, Eula clung desperately to the hope she might still capture Clyde Haf.

* * *

Nettie felt she was living a nightmare. Emmett purposely sought her out to complain. He tormented her until she lost her temper, which never took long. Memories of his kiss the night of the social fueled her anger.

Emmett accused her openly of jealousy. She gave up all hope of propriety at work. Even the customers lost interest in their endless bickering.

Nettie took to rising early to talk to Eula before she left for school. Ever hopeful she was a mother-to-be, Eula seemed irrationally euphoric. Nothing Nettie said managed to bring her back to reality.

Annoyed beyond measure, Nettie stood still as Emmett approached shortly before closing. She no longer attempted to avoid him.

"What exactly is this?" Determined to provoke her, Emmett waved several papers near her face.

"Perhaps if I were a bird, I might be able to see what you're flying through the air."

"This is an invoice for additional discs for the Regina music box. I never approved this expenditure."

"As manager of the side door, I took it upon myself to order new music. The ladies grew tired of playing the same songs over and over."

"This is ridiculous. Thirty discs? You have lost your mind."

"Evidently, yes. I work here, don't I? We already played them so you can't return them. If you find the need to take the price of the invoice from my paycheck, be my guest." Nettie was surprised she was able to remain so calm in light of her mood and the absurdity of the current complaint.

Emmett glanced around the room. Nettie had the full support of the female clientele. He needed to be careful or he might lose customers in his attempt to draw Nettie into their nightly argument. He should have waited until closing.

"It won't be necessary. I'll take on the full amount of the invoice to keep the ladies happy." He flashed a wicked smile at the few women who remained in the bar and drew smiles in return. "My pleasure ladies," he added for effect. Nettie rolled her eyes and attempted to sneak past him. "Wait just a minute. I need to talk to you."

"What now?"

Emmett's heart melted as he managed to capture Nettie's attention. He felt completely tongue-tied not to mention the fact he couldn't think of a single thing to argue about. "It's confidential, strictly business. Come and I'll explain."

An aggravated Nettie followed behind. Emmett closed the door of the closet as she walked through. As Nettie turned to ascertain his strictly business problem, she was taken by surprise as Emmett pulled her into his embrace and kissed her. She resisted, intent to push him away. All too soon, she was lost in his touch.

Once Emmett ended the kiss and looked into her face, he groaned, "I miss you so, Nettie. Surely you miss me? I want to talk to you and spend time together. I only meant to make you jealous at the social. When I succeeded so completely, I knew I found a way to talk to you, even if it was only to fight. I love you." He caught the glint of tears in her eyes when she unexpectedly pushed him away.

"You won't be tortured much longer. I'll soon have a teaching job and you can move on with your life." Nettie felt weak in the knees as she walked through the door to the kitchen and outside to the cool night air. What was wrong with her? She knew beyond doubt she loved Emmett as much as he loved her. She simply was not brave enough for the life he wanted.

After wandering back to the side door, she was surprised to find an ashen-faced Eula standing in the doorway.

"You can come in Eula. You won't be stricken dead because you step inside a saloon." But Eula didn't move. "What's the matter?" Nettie inquired as she walked toward the door.

Eula grabbed her hand and pulled Nettie out onto the sidewalk. She became hysterical as she explained.

"I was sick this morning. I'm certain I'm with child. I asked Clyde to meet me at our usual spot after dinner. He wasn't cordial. I did hit him the last time I saw him, after all. I listened to his complaints then he asked me what I wanted. I explained the situation to him. Oh, Nettie," Eula was sobbing so loudly, Nettie could barely understand. "He told me he didn't believe the baby was his. He told me there was no way to prove it was. He won't marry me!" Eula collapsed into Nettie's arms.

"I'm sorry, Eula. I don't know what to say. Somehow this will all work itself out; we simply can't see it quite yet." Eula only became more hysterical. "I'll get my things and we'll go home. You need a good night's rest and we'll make a list of solutions in the morning."

"What solutions?"

"I don't know. Maybe your uncle could help."

"I can't tell *him*!"

"We'll have to pray for God to show you the way. Everything happens for a reason, Eula. I know this is difficult, but I'm here for you and we'll figure this out."

"No, Nettie. There is no solution." Eula pulled away and wiped the back of her arm across her tear-stained face. "I'm going to have to take care of this myself."

"What are you talking about?"

Eula shook her head. "I'll see you at home." She turned and walked toward the street. Nettie followed after.

"Wait, Eula, I'll come along. Let me get my things and tell Emmett I'm leaving." But Eula was lost in her own miserable world and hurried toward the trolley half a block away. Nettie watched helplessly as Eula climbed aboard.

She folded her arms against the chill night air and turned toward the side door. A breeze moved a scrap of paper on the ground and Nettie bent to retrieve it. The note was written in Eula's careful script; she must have dropped it. Incredulous at the words on the scrap, Nettie grasped the wall, afraid to trust her legs to hold her up. This could not be happening.

By the time Nettie walked behind the front bar, it was exactly ten o'clock and the last customers were leaving. She put her hand on Emmett's arm to draw his attention. She was not surprised at the bitter look in his eyes. He was angry and hurt. Before he could yell at her, she quietly asked, "I need you. I need you to take me somewhere."

"Why should I help you?" Nettie could see the muscles play across Emmett's cheeks as he clenched his teeth.

"It's not to help me, but I'm desperate. I don't know where else to turn. Will you drive me? We have to hurry."

* * *

Emmett pulled up to the desolate, darkened building and stopped the engine. "This can't be right. What is this place?"

"You stay here. I'll be right back."

"I can't let you go in there alone."

"It's all right. Wait for me. I won't be five minutes, I promise."

Nettie climbed down from the Buick and drew her shawl closely around her shoulders. The door to the old wooden building was unlocked. She pushed it and walked inside. Oilcloth covered the windows to keep light from shining through. It was dank and dirty, a place of death. The overwhelming feeling of evil permeating the air was foreign to her. "Eula!" she yelled.

Although Eula didn't reply, a woman dressed as a nurse approached from a hallway. "Can I help you?"

"My friend is here. I need to see her."

"I'm afraid our patients enjoy their anonymity. You'll have to leave."

"Eula!" Nettie yelled again as she started down the hallway. Hearing a noise, Nettie hurried to the last door as the nurse followed quickly behind, urging her to leave.

"I'll call the police," she threatened.

Nettie turned and angrily replied, "I know what this place is. I'm certain you won't be calling the police." She was relieved to find Eula sitting on a cot, looking dazed.

"Eula, you haven't done this thing have you? Is it over?"

"No, nothing happened. But I need to sleep."

"Come along, Eula. *Eula*! Wake up, dear. Please say you'll come home now. Don't do this. You'll regret it forever if you even survive. Listen to me," Nettie, begged, "Please, Eula, please."

"She's taken morphine. She needs to lie down now. You'll have to go."

"*Eula*! Say you'll come home. You want to go home, don't you?"

"Le's go home," slurred Eula.

"There, you heard her. She's coming with me."

"I'm going to get the doctor. She doesn't get her money back."

"We don't care about the money, keep it."

At her proclamation, the nurse stood out of the way.

"Stand up, Eula," Nettie yelled. "We're going home now."

"I'll take her."

Emmett stood in the doorway of the pathetic, dirty room. He walked toward the cot and scooped Eula into his arms. Nettie trailed behind and gratefully opened the

Jean Jegel

door so they could put the horrid building behind them. She looked on as Emmett carefully placed Eula in the back seat of the Buick.

"You better ride back here," he suggested, holding Eula's head so Nettie could slide in. He closed the small back door. "What happens now?"

"Please take us home."

"You expect her to get up in the morning and go to work as if nothing was wrong? What will prevent her from coming back here?"

"She'll need to rest. I could take her class for the day if you don't mind."

"And when you go back to Mrs. Green's and she's not there, do you mount a new rescue?" He could see Nettie was upset and had no idea how to proceed.

"All I know is she didn't come straight here, she sought me out first. She wanted me to rescue her or she wouldn't have come to the Golden State." Nettie stared at the dark, foreboding building.

"You're taking on an awfully big problem here and it isn't even yours. I think I know what we can do." Disgusted with himself for playing the hero, Emmett climbed in the Buick and headed for home.

* * *

Nettie followed as Emmett effortlessly carried Eula up the stairway and placed her in Faith's old bed.

"Thank you. I'll see to it she's comfortable."

Emmett realized he'd been dismissed. It was late and he didn't imagine he'd be getting much sleep. Although not his habit, he went to his ice box and drew a mug of cold beer from a small keg. Dropping onto the settee with a stack of unopened mail, he removed his necktie and shoes. It wasn't long before Nettie came down.

She stood at the bottom of the staircase and began, "I don't understand what your plan was in bringing Eula here."

"It's simple. You can go and teach for her tomorrow. When she wakes up, I'll walk her over to Faith's house. Faith can keep an eye on her during the day. When you come back, she's your problem. Besides, it would have been difficult to explain if I took you to Mrs. Green's."

"I can't leave her here alone in the house with you."

Emmett lowered his chin and grimaced. "Do you think I'll ruin her honor? It seems to be missing already."

"It wouldn't be proper."

Emmett shook his head in disgust. "Well, you're more than welcome to stay here and chaperone us. But who will chaperone you? I'd offer to drive you home, but then your friend would be alone. You can go wait for a trolley or park yourself here and sleep in my parents' bed."

"No. I'll stay here in the parlor. You can go sleep."

"Are you telling me what to do in my own house?"

Nettie flinched at the accusation. She'd been through enough for one night. Her nerves were raw. Her head hurt.

"No, I—do what you want."

"Well, thank you, Miss Gordon." Emmett was obviously smarting from their last conversation.

"I want to thank you for your help tonight. I don't know what I would have done without you."

Belligerently, Emmett sipped his beer and replied, "You're welcome, I guess."

"You can tell Faith I'll be late after school. I plan to talk to Pastor Arndorfer before I return."

"You're going to butt in more than you already have and share Eula's secret with someone else? What exactly am I supposed to relay when she wakes up tomorrow morning?"

"Simply tell her everything will be fine and I'll explain when I return."

"And you're going to magically fix her life?"

"I don't know what I'm going to do."

"That's not very godlike of you. I thought you temperance women knew what was best for everybody."

"If you're so eager to help, why don't you marry Eula? She got herself into this mess because she desperately wanted a husband. You want to get married. I think it's the perfect solution. Ask her."

"Be serious, Nettie. You can't transfer affection from one person to another. It's you I love, not Eula. Besides, you were wildly jealous when I simply kissed that strange girl, think how it would affect you if I married your best friend right under your nose."

"You're free to do as you choose."

"You mean, except as far as you're concerned. Oh well, you're a risky venture anyway. You always have your knife at the ready. Were you planning on fighting your way out of that building if they didn't let you take Eula?"

"It never occurred to me."

"Good, because it's one thing to wave your little knife under someone's nose and it's something entirely different to stab them."

"I know."

Emmett snorted. "Because you've stabbed so many men?"

"I stabbed a man—once."

"Truly? Who did you stab?"

"One of my brothers."

Emmett was appalled at this admission. "You aren't serious?"

"I'm perfectly serious. I didn't hurt him badly, but it definitely got his attention. It bought me some time."

"What do you mean?"

"It gave me the opportunity to plan my departure."

"You're not making any sense."

"I don't need to. I don't owe you anything."

At this, Emmett stood and walked toward Nettie. He intentionally grabbed her arm and drew her back to the settee. She bounced slightly when he pushed her into the seat then sat down beside her.

"I need to understand something. You owe me an explanation. I want to know why you left home and what it has to do with me."

"I'll save you some time. It has nothing to do with you."

"No, I think it does. Explain. If you want me to leave you alone, you need to explain."

"There isn't much to say. I wasn't happy at home so I left."

Emmett drew her into his embrace. "I won't let you go until you tell me the truth." She struggled against him.

"Don't."

"Why, are you afraid you'll get carried away like your friend upstairs?"

"What a cold thing to say."

"It's the truth, though, isn't it? You're attracted to me and you don't want to be. I think you love me. You certainly don't kiss me as if you are appalled."

"That's absurd," but Emmett could see she was lying. He pulled her tight against his chest and kissed her. When he stopped, she soundly slapped his face, but he didn't let go.

"I can do this all night. I don't care if you slap me. Tell me what's wrong."

Nettie's chest was heaving; she felt trapped. "I don't want you. Is that honest enough?"

"I think it's a start. Tell me why."

"Because you're overbearing and pushy and because you're just too big."

Emmett snorted in derision. "What's that supposed to mean?"

"I don't have a chance against you, not physically."

"Why would you need to?" He could see honest fear in her eyes. "Why are you afraid of me?" He was appalled at the idea, but he believed he was finally getting to the root of their problem. "You told me before your mother should never have married because your father beat her. Did he beat you?"

"No. He slapped my face a few times is all."

"But he beat your mother?"

Nettie nodded.

"Why? Do you know?"

"He was a drunk, the town drunk. We lived a poor life. My mother raised chickens to make enough money to feed us. She came from a wealthy home. Her family disowned her when she married my father. She couldn't go back no matter what he did to her." Nettie got a faraway look in her eyes as if she were looking at her life from some distant place.

"She was my rock, my protector. She taught me about culture and etiquette, how to speak, what to write. If not for her, I would have turned into some animal like my brothers. Do you know what it was like to see how truly helpless she was? I watched while he beat her, kicked her. She would collapse on the floor, curl in a ball to try to protect herself. There was nothing she could do. She was my protector and she couldn't even help herself.

"The more my father beat my brothers, the wilder they got. By the time they were grown, they were monsters. I was the curiosity. I was the odd man out. And when I became a woman, they looked at me differently. My mother died by then. I was on my own.

"One day, my brother came back to the house early in the afternoon. Pushing me up against the wall, he pinned my hands above my head and told me he could do whatever he wanted. If I didn't cooperate, he'd get our other brothers to help. He groped me. I was completely helpless until I managed to bite his arm. He let go of my hands to grab his arm and I stabbed him with my switchblade. That gave him something to think about. I decided it was best if I left before he could plot some revenge against me. I wasn't safe there, not in my own home."

Nettie emerged from her reverie, seemingly shocked she said those words aloud. She glared at Emmett.

"I suppose in the grand scheme of things, I was lucky. Nothing horrible happened to me, but I will never put myself under the control of any man, much less one so physically strong as you. I wouldn't survive."

"Nettie, I'm not that kind of man. You must know I would never hurt you." He was incredulous as she stood and walked toward the staircase.

How could he ever make her understand? He didn't know how to combat her fear. Certainly, his forced embraces and kisses hadn't furthered his cause. Appalled at her family and angry she'd been treated so wretchedly, Emmett tossed and turned throughout the night, unable to sleep.

* * *

As the sky lightened, Emmett attempted to see what became of Nettie. He found her asleep in a chair in Faith's room, keeping guard over her friend. Emmett proceeded to the kitchen and put a pot of coffee on the stove. The beverage tended to have an invigorating effect on him and he'd need all the stimulation he could get to stay awake today.

Before the coffee was done, Nettie poked her head through the kitchen door.

"I'm going now. I need time to stop at home and prepare for school. Thank you again." She disappeared before he could manage a word, which was probably just as well.

Emmett spent his sleepless night considering options. He understood he should probably leave Nettie to her inevitable spinsterhood and get on with his own life. He also realized he was not about to let that happen. Incredibly attracted to the stubborn and opinionated Miss Gordon, he knew she delighted and challenged him as no woman he ever met. He enjoyed her company and conversation. He wanted to be her partner in life and longed for the opportunity to love and cherish her.

Analyzing in detail the story she told him last night, he remembered she divulged pieces of her past before. He largely ignored her previous admissions, but no more.

Nettie mentioned his size. It was true, he was much taller than her. If she was looking for some man she could overpower, her pool of potential husbands was severely limited. Although she might claim his size was intimidating, he never previously used his strength against her, nor would he ever. She purported to be afraid of him on some level, but he doubted this was true. She didn't hesitate to lean into him as if for protection when they came across her brother on New

Year's Day. She never shrank from his touch. In fact, her enthusiasm for his kiss only encouraged that behavior. She never seemed intimidated by him on their outings nor was she afraid to be alone with him.

Of course, her family was completely unsatisfactory. He rather doubted the peanut vendor was the brother that attacked Nettie; he seemed too mousy. The thought of a girl so afraid in her own home that she would carry a knife for protection was abhorrent. Having experienced a happy and secure childhood himself, he could not imagine Nettie's perspective on marriage and family. He was certain this was her real problem—the surrender of her security to any husband.

Emmett entertained methods to overcome this obstacle. He was always at ease with Nettie and felt it disingenuous to appear anything other than the man he was. But he could certainly be more of a gentleman. No more impulsive embraces. No more kissing for now, planned or spontaneous. There could be no forced or deceitful outings. If she needed to be lulled into a sense of security, he was happy to oblige.

Knowing this was a long-term project, Eula's predicament served to give him extra time. He doubted Nettie would accept a position unless she could remain at Mrs. Green's. Once he was done, Nettie Gordon wouldn't be able to face life without him. He envisioned the day when she would beg him to move his ring to her left hand.

* * *

Nettie, tired and angry, stomped through the Golden State in search of her boss. After being informed he was in the warehouse, she crossed the alley on the beautiful spring day. Taking a deep, soothing breath, she stopped briefly to feel the sun on her face and enjoy the fresh air, lightly scented by the irresistible fragrance of sweet peas growing wild along the back fence of Emmett's house. She paused to get her bearings once she stepped inside the dim warehouse and was startled when Emmett greeted her.

"Why are you back so soon?"

Frowning, Nettie launched into an angry explanation of her morning.

"That ignoramus, Mr. Pendergast, did not see fit to let me teach, even for a day. He managed to find another substitute teacher and dismissed me at lunchtime."

"Did you tell him Eula was ill?"

"Yes, but she has a week to pull herself together. It's Easter vacation. What happens afterward is up to her. How was she, when she woke up?"

"Embarrassed. She was more than willing to go to Faith's and rest. I don't think you need to worry about her going back there. I imagine last night's drama was an act of desperation and she has returned to sanity."

Nettie bit her lip, wondering if Emmett's observations were accurate.

"Do you mind if I go see her for a moment?"

"I'm quite certain the side door will continue to function without your immediate appearance." Emmett smiled warmly. "Take your time. I'm sure Faith would enjoy a visit."

Nettie strained her eyes to get a better look at Emmett in the dim light. There was something peculiar about him. He was being much too congenial.

"Thank you. I think I will."

CHAPTER FIFTEEN

"Eula, you must listen to me." Eula, tall though she was, appeared a little girl in the bed of Faith's guest room. "You and the vicar might have made this baby, but God has provided a soul. Your baby is a person with a right to life. If you succeeded in your plan last night, I know you would regret it had you managed to survive."

"I know Nettie. I can't thank you enough for finding me."

"You need to thank Mr. Boyd. I never would have made it there in time or got out the door with you in the condition you were in."

"I will, I will."

"I simply don't understand, Eula. How did you let this happen?" Nettie doubted Eula would remain cooperative and contrite and took the opportunity to confess. "I have something to explain. You may get angry."

"Never, Nettie. I know you have my best interest at heart. I was so disappointed and distraught. I trust you completely."

"I told Pastor Arndorfer about your plight."

"*You what?*"

"I think he's trustworthy and you need help."

"But Nettie, I didn't want anyone to know. First you told Mr. Boyd. Now his sister knows and you've gone and blabbed to the pastor. How could you?"

"I didn't tell Mr. Boyd, but your problem became obvious. The pastor does need to know. Vicar Haf is under his guidance. He's unfit to lead a congregation after the way he behaved. Beyond what this means to you, it was my moral obligation to inform him."

"Are you certain it's not revenge for what Clyde did? It would seem so to me."

"That's beside the point."

"Is it? I'm having trouble believing you."

"Are you actually defending him after the way he treated you?"

"No, certainly not." Eula primly straightened her covers.

"Well, then, Pastor Arndorfer has some suggestions. He wants to meet with you in his office on Sunday after Bible class. It's kind of him to take the time considering it's Easter Sunday. He said I could come and I'll be happy to support you if you wish. You can go to your uncle's later. He won't mind."

"Yes, I want you to come."

Nettie could tell Eula was angry, but she was equally angry. Eula demonstrated an intolerable lack of morals. Now Nettie was drawn into the resultant fiasco. The fact she wasn't allowed to teach for even a day still rankled as she made her way downstairs.

Faith served tea as Nettie played with little Luther, who was sitting up quite sturdily.

"Nettie, do you have plans for Easter?"

"Oh, Faith, it's simply not a good idea."

"This isn't for Emmett. In fact, he doesn't know I'm asking."

"Truly?"

"Yes, Nettie, I wouldn't lie to you. We all miss you and the twins especially would be delighted if you came. I'm certain you and Emmett are mature enough to have Easter supper together as friends."

Anxious to have some distance from Eula and her problems if only for an afternoon, Nettie accepted.

* * *

As usual, churches overflowed with lilies and ladies carried small bouquets of flowers to Easter services. Passengers crowded on trolleys. Young men rode the rails outside the cars to provide seating for women and children within.

A delighted smile lit Emmett's face when he caught sight of Nettie entering the Judge's house on Easter afternoon. If Faith plotted this circumstance to surprise him, she could not have done a better job. Nettie looked radiant in the finery she wore to the twins' weddings. The flower has a second life thought Emmett, as he observed from a corner of the parlor.

Nettie was inundated with greetings, especially from the women of the family, and was put in charge of Luther. The twins joined Nettie on a settee as Faith walked toward the dining room and grabbed the sleeve of Emmett's coat to pull him along behind her.

"I need to have a word," she hissed, rather severely.

"Yes, ma'am," Emmett followed submissively. He owed her a debt for managing to deliver Nettie on this blessed holiday. He was prepared to offer his earnest thanks.

"I watched you pine away for Nettie for months on end and I want it to stop." Emmett was speechless at her harsh words. "She agreed to come today on the condition you would behave as a gentleman and not annoy her. I expect you to respect her wishes. You managed to make her a part of our family and we all miss her. Don't ruin today!"

"I have no intention of ruining anything. You might take my part. You are *my* sister after all."

"It was you who managed to drive her away. I can't imagine how. She's the only woman you've ever been serious about."

"She's not seriously interested in me; did you ever ponder that possibility?"

"Well, what have you done to disinterest her? Honestly, Emmett, you're a good catch. You're tall and fit, not unhandsome. You're a prosperous businessman, hardworking—you even own an automobile for crying out loud. What girl wouldn't be interested in you?"

"Evidently, Nettie Gordon."

"But why? What did you do?"

"I proclaimed my undying love and asked her to marry me."

Faith gave him a curious stare. "I avoided this topic until today, but you simply must do something about this situation. It's entirely unsuitable—for you, for Nettie and for this entire family. Get your wits about you, Emmett Boyd. Whatever your tactic has been in the past, it isn't working."

"You're telling me."

"Don't be impertinent."

"Faith, I'll do my best to be a gentleman and attempt to woo Nettie Gordon, which is basically a discouraging activity. But I assure you, I'm not giving up although we may be quite elderly before there's any progress. Any help you can provide would be most appreciated. For instance, a seat beside her at supper might prove beneficial."

"I believe that can be arranged." At this, Faith hurried toward the kitchen. Emmett took a deep breath and returned to the parlor, intent to remain aloof as long as he was able.

* * *

"Why Miss Gordon, it appears we are to be tablemates," Emmett gushed as he held Nettie's chair. "It's lovely you could join us today. You made my sisters quite happy. Thank you."

Nettie took her seat, a crooked smile on her face. Whatever was Emmett up to now? Once he was seated, she placed her hand on his arm and was startled by the adoring look he unsuccessfully attempted to hide.

"I need to talk to you after supper."

"My, you sound rather scandalous, Nettie. Is it something improper?" Emmett rolled his eyes in disgust. Why was it so difficult to be a gentleman in her presence? "I'm sorry. That was inappropriate."

"No more so than most of your comments. Are you going to start a fight next?"

"Certainly not. Why would you say such a thing?"

"Experience."

Emmett could see this was not going the way he intended. "Look, Nettie, I think it might be best if we started over. I'm trying my best to impress you."

"Well, you're failing miserably, but I do appreciate your efforts."

"So, you would also like a fresh start?"

"Of course not. What a ridiculous idea." She could see she was making him quite wretched, but it was nothing new and was never her intent. "Before you proclaim your love and get down on your knee again, perhaps we could simply agree to suspend hostilities for today and see how things go. I have exciting news to share, but it's of a rather personal nature so it must wait for now."

Certain Nettie must have taken a job, Emmett feared her exciting news.

Webster, seated across the table beside his children, launched into a controversial topic.

"Emmett, did you catch the article in the *Herald* this morning about the barmaids in London?"

Emmett frowned. "I imagine that will gain traction here soon. Although the delightful Mrs. Savory seems to be the object of misinformation."

Webster laughed. "I particularly enjoyed her husband's explanation we string publicans up in the West if they attempt to hire a woman to serve liquor. Do you think he misled her on purpose? It does make her look the fool."

"I didn't have time to read the paper this morning. What are you talking about?" asked Faith.

Eager to pursue the topic, Webster continued, "This American woman was shocked to see barmaids serving liquor in London pubs. She started a crusade against it. She says she's not interested in the temperance movement; she simply thinks it's immoral for women to serve liquor. Believing no bar stateside would ever hire a woman, she held up America as the model for her beliefs. She claimed women only drink on the sly in America because they're ashamed. The article was lengthy."

"If she's from America, doesn't she know it's not the case?" Nettie inquired.

Emmett replied, "I don't think women serve liquor on the East Coast. It's different out west. Next thing you know, your temperance friends will try to pull you out of the Golden State to save your soul. Then again, you could profess working in the saloon hasn't managed to damage your morals, but I doubt anyone would listen. That point of view is not popular, true or not. Or perhaps you'd agree your soul is in tatters due to your experiences in my establishment?"

Nettie could see the topic was disturbing to Emmett, yet another assault on his business.

"Do all saloons have women attendants?"

Webster took the question, "Most do. I suppose it started like ours—women family members worked under the watchful eyes of husbands or fathers. Women always worked in the Golden State. It didn't seem unusual when you came along. Every woman at this table has served as a barmaid. Here's to moral degradation!" Webster laughed as he poured another glass of wine.

"Since your wife isn't here to rein you in today, I'll be glad to fill in for her," explained Faith. "You've had enough to drink. That's your last glass."

As conversation turned in other directions, Nettie leaned over and asked her tablemate, "Where is Nadine today? She didn't want to spend the holiday here?"

"I think she would have come if she was able. She's not been feeling well. In fact, I'm driving Webster and his two youngest to the train in the morning. He's taking the children to San Francisco to stay with Nadine's parents. They offered to keep their grandchildren for the next few weeks, hoping Nadine will improve. Susan's in school. They didn't want to interrupt her studies. She's staying here."

Possible showers had been the weather prediction for the day, but a breeze blew the clouds away and Easter Sunday could not have been more perfect. The Boyd family enjoyed the end of the lovely afternoon in Faith's backyard.

Although Luther wasn't old enough to participate, it was Faith's habit to prepare games for Webster's children. The men in the family were easily cajoled into competition.

Faith paused to observe Nettie. She cheered for Emmett, who was on his knees, coaxing an Easter egg along a narrow paper ribbon with a spoon. Although he held a substantial lead over both Webster and the Judge, the twin husbands were giving him a run for his money. If Emmett's egg rolled off the ribbon, he'd be eliminated.

Nettie seemed delighted at the game. Faith noticed her apparent loyalty and knew beyond doubt Emmett was crazy about this woman. From all she could see, Nettie was a woman in love. She captured Emmett's attention at dinner by gently touching his sleeve. When she looked at him, it was with warmth and affection.

She knew the pair hadn't been getting along since Christmas, but they certainly appeared happy together today. Faith felt confused as she stared at Emmett's ring, still on Nettie's right hand. What obstacles were they facing? Why were they not already engaged? Admittedly, it took five years for the Judge to persuade her of his love and devotion.

Faith was eager to see her younger brother happily married. Perhaps it was because all the Boyd siblings were now wed except Emmett. Perhaps she had an undeniable urge to play matchmaker.

As Nettie hurried to congratulate the winner of the egg race, Faith continued to watch. Nettie drew Emmett toward the back of the yard to engage in private conversation. Her expression appeared eager and happy.

"Propose to her again," Faith whispered under her breath, as if she could plant the idea in Emmett's brain from across the yard. She had no way of knowing that was exactly the wrong course of action.

* * *

Emmett was completely smitten as Nettie took his arm and sought a private place where they could not be overheard. As the sun sank in the sky, the air took on a pink glow that showcased Nettie's beautiful complexion. He took in the details of her face: her petite, rather pointed chin, her long, slender neck and lovely smile—directed at him, for once.

"You absolutely will not believe what happened today!" Nettie began. "I accompanied Eula to meet with Pastor Arndorfer. He explained he met with the vicar to urge him to do the right thing and marry Eula. Although he didn't go into detail, I got the impression the vicar either denied his responsibility entirely or simply refused to marry. So, he sent the vicar packing! His report to the synod will, of necessity, be completely unfavorable.

"Then the pastor listed options Eula might consider including going home to her parents, placing her baby for adoption and so forth. He even identified a couple who might be willing to take the baby. He was so kind and matter-of-fact.

"This could easily have been awkward and embarrassing for Eula. But then he offered to marry Eula himself! It was truly shocking. Neither Eula nor I could quite believe him. He mentioned how beneficial it was for a pastor to be married, how Eula and he were both committed to the church and would work well together. He even explained how drawn to her he was since the day you took us all in the Buick for brunch. Believing their love would grow in time, he knows he's much older and hopes it won't prove too daunting a challenge for them to overcome.

"Emmett, I think it must have been Pastor Arndorfer who sent the Valentine to Eula.

"Willing to take the brunt of gossip, he even

worked out the details so as to spare Eula any controversy. He intends to hint they've been married for some months and kept it secret due to the impropriety of marriage so soon after his wife's death. Now there's a baby to consider, thus the need to make their marriage public. His clear intention is to protect his new wife and child.

"The pastor also mentioned he felt partly responsible for what happened. Thinking it advantageous for Vicar Haf to start his career as a married man, he deliberately introduced the vicar to likely candidates for matrimony, including Eula and me. When the vicar seemed to have turned his attention to Eula, the pastor believed his matchmaking was successful. He felt he might have contributed to Eula's unfortunate problem although I doubt he really had much to do with it."

Emmett was surprised at this turn of events. "What did she decide or is she mulling it over?"

"As you know, Eula wished to marry for some time. She was completely swept off her feet. They decided to leave on the train for San Diego where they'll marry and return on Tuesday to take up their life together."

"They don't even know each other."

"Well, I suppose that's true, but I know the pastor is a good man. He certainly understands the role of a husband. I know Eula is more than eager to be a proper wife. The pastor will no doubt provide a steadying influence. Incredibly, I think this all worked out for the best."

"Nettie, I am a good man," Emmett seriously stated.

"I know you are, Emmett." A wealth of emotion overtook Nettie as she stared into his eyes. "But I know you'd be better off without me. I simply am not able to marry. Now Eula is settled, I'm free to take a teaching job. I think it's best if I leave the city."

"I want you to stay, Nettie. Give me the opportunity to show how much I love you."

"I can't—"

"I don't care if you leave the Golden State; it might be best. But promise me you won't leave Los Angeles. I love you and I believe you love me."

Nettie didn't reply and looked nervously at the ground. Putting his hand under her chin, Emmett lifted her head in order to see her face. "All I want is the chance to prove we could be happy together. All I want is time."

"That's not all you want."

Emmett chuckled. "It's all I want for now." He stared into her eyes. "Promise me this, nothing more— only time."

"All right." Nettie expected a kiss to seal her promise; instead Emmett offered his arm to walk her back to the house. She didn't anticipate her intense disappointment. She longed for his kiss, more than she imagined possible. Nettie clung to Emmett's arm and smiled weakly while they strolled across the yard to join the others. Emmett nonchalantly asked her opinion on what she thought would happen when the new Mrs. Arndorfer returned to the city.

* * *

Emmett lay awake, waiting for dawn to lighten the sky. His life seemed to be taking a turn in the right direction. Easter went well. Nettie even allowed him to drive her home. After he deposited Webster and his niece and nephew at the station yesterday morning, he found a smiling Nettie, who served him a morning cup of coffee before opening. She chatted about her hopes for Eula's unlikely new marriage. The past several months of acrimony seemed magically swept away.

Doubting he'd be able to fall back to sleep, Emmett sat up and turned on the light to see what time it was. His pocket watch on the bedside table read five o'clock, too early to get up. But if he went out to the warehouse now, he could shave and dress later and have Marcel make him a hearty breakfast.

Finding his way downstairs in the dark, Emmett turned on the kitchen light to make a pot of coffee. He grabbed his newspaper from the porch and opened it on the kitchen table as the dishes in the cupboard rattled. He felt the sway from a rolling earthquake and paused to see if it intensified. Feeling no further motion, Emmett sat down to read the news and wait for the coffee to percolate.

* * *

By the time Nettie arrived at the Golden State, word of the devastation in San Francisco had spread like wildfire through the city. Los Angeles, as in every other city in the country, was abuzz with rumors and supposition about the disaster unfolding in the City by the Bay.

Nettie had never seen the saloon so packed with men as it was this morning. Crowds were gathered around telephone and telegraph offices to read the latest dispatches as they were posted. As quickly as news hit the wire at the Western Union offices, it spread across the city as if by some spider web of communication. Extra editions of the newspaper sold out as soon as they were printed. People stood in the streets conversing. Almost no one was working.

Even though the saloon was full, few were drinking. After Nettie dropped her things in the closet, she peeked in on the side door, which stood empty. Evidently women sought information in other ways. She walked behind the bar in front, leaving Delmar to keep an eye on things in back. Emmett stood stony-faced behind the register, listening to the buzz of information. Nettie suddenly remembered—Emmett's family was in San Francisco.

"Oh, my. Emmett, have you heard from Webster? Has Nadine?"

He silently shook his head but finally replied, "I doubt telegraphs are working in the city from what's being reported. Maybe we'll hear before the day is out."

Nettie could see Emmett's concern. "Perhaps you should monitor the telephone in your house."

"I can't sit and stare at the telephone. It would drive me insane."

"I'll go if you want me to. Send someone for me if you need me up here."

For the first time, Emmett looked away from the crowd. "I'd appreciate that. Let me know as soon as anyone telephones."

Nettie hurried across the alley and through Emmett's back door. She took a place near the telephone. Although she wouldn't know what was going on, at least she felt useful.

After staring at the phone for some time, Nettie took a book from the cabinet and attempted to read. Unable to focus, she started to pace and was relieved when Emmett appeared carrying a plateful of lunch.

"I take it the telephone hasn't rung?"

Nettie shook her head and took the plate.

"I would have told you to help yourself to food in my kitchen. I'm afraid there's not much there so I brought this."

"Have you eaten?"

"I'm not hungry."

"Come and sit beside me and we can share."

Emmett may have been distracted but he wasn't dead. Any invitation from Nettie was welcome. He sat down and nibbled at the food. Nettie dropped the plate as the earth began to shake. She threw herself into Emmett's arms.

"It's all right," he soothed. "It stopped."

"Oh, so it has." But she hated to let go. They could hear the shouts and screams of panicked people outside. "Now I've done it," she proclaimed as she peered at the cold cuts, bread and deviled eggs she spilled. Reluctantly, she got down on the floor and piled food on the plate while searching for stains on the carpet. Emmett knelt beside her to help.

No sooner was their task complete than the earth shook again. Nettie screamed, a jumble of nerves as Emmett grabbed for her. They knelt in a tight embrace until well after the temblor subsided. Pandemonium erupted outside.

Emmett smiled. "If we're going to die, I want one more kiss." He slowly lowered his lips to hers. There was no resistance. It was several moments until he finally pulled away. He put his hands on Nettie's waist and moved her onto the settee then picked the plate and food up off the floor.

"Will you be all right while I go check on things at the Golden State and bring back a fresh plate?"

Nettie, too stunned and breathless to reply, nodded her head. As he headed toward the back porch, she yelled, "Wait. First tell me what's happening."

Emmett grimly replied, "Large areas of San Francisco are on fire. There's panic everywhere. Streets have sunk or bulged, there are huge fissures. I heard a bad report about the Valencia Hotel where Webster planned to take a room. Nadine's parents purchased tickets to see Enrico Caruso in *Carmen* last night so Webster was supposed to drop the children off this morning, then head back home."

"Tell me."

"They say it simply sank into the earth. I don't know how he could have escaped with two small children in the dark." It was clear Emmett believed the worst.

"Maybe he didn't stay there. You can't know for certain. We must remain optimistic. Is someone with Nadine?"

"Faith stopped by the saloon on her way over. She'll stay."

"Don't you think you should go, too?"

"I'll go later. Nettie, will you come?"

"Shouldn't one of us stay here?"

"This isn't important. I need you."

"Certainly. I'll come. Whatever I can do to help." Once Emmett left, Nettie returned to her knees to pray.

* * *

Emmett put Chauncey in charge of the Golden State when he showed up for his four o'clock shift. There was a rumor that saloons might stay open past ten o'clock so the populace could continue to share news. Emmett promised to return by ten.

Once he pulled up in front of his brother's home, Emmett seemed reluctant to get out.

"What's wrong?" nudged Nettie.

"This won't be pleasant."

"I know. I'm here."

"I'm sincerely grateful for that. I need you, Nettie. Thank you for coming."

Nettie held tightly to Emmett's hand once he

helped her from the car and the pair approached the house together. Faith threw open the door before Emmett could knock.

"Any news?" he inquired.

"Nothing."

"How is Nadine?"

"I called the doctor. She's been sedated and is sleeping. Mrs. Skapmore from church came by. She offered to keep a vigil during the night so we can all get some sleep. There were other women at church who volunteered. I don't think it's a particularly good idea for the twins to come. I'll return in the morning."

"Go on home, Faith. We'll stay until nine."

"Susan is staying next door with her little friend, Toni. She has everything she needs."

Faith hugged her brother and Nettie, collected Luther and headed for home. No sooner did Faith depart than Nadine could be heard upstairs.

"Faith? Is that you?"

After taking a deep breath, Emmett halfheartedly climbed the stairs. Nettie followed behind. Smiling, Emmett poked his head through the bedroom door.

"How are you doing?"

"Has there been any word?"

"Not so far. But it's early. I don't believe people can send personal telegrams yet. Most of the lines aren't even working. I know Webster will send word as soon as he's able."

"Yes. He wouldn't want us to worry."

"Maybe tomorrow." Emmett could see his sister-in-law was on the verge of panic. Her eyes darted around the room as she fidgeted with her covers. "Should we call for the doctor?"

"No. no. I'm fine, truly. I need to rest is all." Nadine's breathing seemed labored.

"I'll be right back," declared Emmett as he hurried toward the door. "Can you take care of things here for a moment?"

Nettie nodded. She took Nadine's hand in hers.

"Thank you for coming, Nettie. I know it means the world to Emmett."

Nettie was surprised Nadine was sensitive to Emmett's plight.

"He's pining away for you, surely you must know?"

Nettie smiled. "I think you need to rest. You have a baby to think about." Nadine seemed calmer.

"Have you heard much news about what's happening in San Francisco?"

"Not much. I was attending to the telephone today."

"What time is it? Is Susan home from school?"

"Yes and she's with her friend Toni. She's probably oblivious to all the current events."

Nadine took a deep breath. "She might be all I have."

"It's much too early to draw such conclusions. Webster is resourceful. I'm certain he's doing his best to let you know he's all right. He probably needs to leave the city to do so. Probably everyone is trying to leave."

"My parents. No one has heard from them either?"

Nettie had forgotten this part of Nadine's tragedy. "Not as far as I know. Do you have other family here in the city who might have heard?"

"No, no one." Nadine considered her next words carefully. "I wish I could see Webster once more. There are things I'd like to say. I know I've been a difficult wife. I wish I could apologize. It might not seem so, looking at us from the outside, but we've been happy together.

"I'm afraid I let details of our lives get in the way. I tried much too hard to control Webbie instead of letting him be himself. I did fall in love with the original version, after all.

"Nettie, if you have a chance for love, you must be sure to take it. Life is short. I have regrets now I wouldn't wish on anyone. You must listen to me."

Nettie could tell Nadine was losing control again. It was at this moment Emmett appeared with the doctor, who lived only a block away.

"There now, Mrs. Boyd, how are we doing?" was all Nettie heard as Emmett pulled her from the room.

Nadine watched the doctor open his bag.

"Wait! Emmett, you must make me a promise."

Emmett waved Nettie downstairs. "I'll be right there. He'll likely drug her again."

Nadine asked, "I want you to go to San Francisco, Emmett. I need you to go. I need to know what happened to my family."

"I plan to go, Nadine. You rest now."

"Not yet." She held her hand up to halt the doctor. "When will you leave?"

"If we have no word by tomorrow, I'll go. I give you my word. I won't return without Webster and the children."

Nadine relaxed against the pillow as her sedative was administered. Soon she was asleep.

"How can you make such a promise?" the doctor inquired.

"One way or another, I'll find them," vowed Emmett.

CHAPTER SIXTEEN

Once Nettie and Emmett were in the Buick headed for the Golden State, Emmett explained his plans.

"I know this may be for nothing. If we hear from Webster tomorrow, none of it will matter, but I'd prefer to tell you what I can tonight. It'll be less to think about later."

"What are you talking about?"

"I promised Nadine I'd find Webster and the children."

"You can't go there. It's too dangerous. The city is in shambles and all on fire. It's chaos. Emmett, they're shooting people they believe to be looters. Anyone could be shot. San Francisco is a big place. It's like trying to find a needle in a haystack."

"I know where to begin my search and I'll be able to find out where survivors are being housed."

"And where the bodies are kept? Are you going to do that, too?"

"Yes, if need be."

Nettie was appalled. "This is too much. Nadine can't ask this of you."

"It has nothing to do with Nadine. She wanted me to go, but I already planned to. I'll take The Owl tomorrow night if we have no word. This is my family, Nettie. I must do everything I possibly can."

"But I don't want you to go!" Nettie seemed alarmed those words came out of her mouth. She sat back against the car seat, not knowing what to say next.

Emmett looked at her curiously. "What did you say?"

With more assurance than she thought possible, Nettie replied, "I don't want you to go. I want you to stay here with me."

"I don't think you can possibly imagine how I've longed to hear that."

"Then you won't go?"

"No, my darling Nettie. I am going, but I'll come back. I promise you."

Once they arrived at the Golden State, there was a flurry of activity. Emmett closed the saloon at ten, as usual. Then he made a list for Nettie.

"My safe is in the house. I'll show you. Here's the combination. I need you to run the saloon until I come back. I know you're perfectly able. I'm counting on you." He glanced at her, only to find her in a state of complete bewilderment. "I use the safe on Friday and Saturday since the banks are closed. You know how to do the deposit."

"Maybe you won't have to go."

"Maybe not, but I need you to take care of things for me here if I do. I know I won't have to worry about you or my business and I can focus on my search without distraction. Until I come back, I want you to stay in my house. You can bring your things tomorrow before I leave. I'll feel better knowing you're here. You wouldn't mind?"

Nettie quietly shook her head.

"Is that a yes or a no?"

"I'll stay here."

All too soon the saloon was secured for the night and Emmett took Nettie's arm to guide her across the alley and through his back door.

"I never lock the doors, but it might be best if you keep them locked while you're here. I'll get you a spare key out of the safe. Faith can help if you need her and Chauncey ran his own saloon. You can ask him for anything."

"It feels like you're leaving now. Don't talk this way."

Certain he would be going, Emmett put his arm around Nettie's shoulders. "This is good information even if we don't use it now. I'm sure there'll come a day when you might have to serve as my replacement. Hopefully we'll hear from Webster tomorrow."

Surprisingly, Nettie put her hands around Emmett's neck and pulled his face to hers. She kissed him passionately, completely. He dropped his list and pencil and rubbed his hands across her back, lost in her kiss.

Nettie quickly found herself prone on the settee. Emmett made quick work of the buttons on the back of her shirtwaist. Her corset was somewhere on the floor. Emmett lay over her, supporting his weight on one elbow as he kissed her, gently touching her.

Swept away in his passion, Nettie uttered the only thought in her head as he kissed her throat, "Don't stop. Don't stop."

First trying to pull her chemise strap over her shoulder, Emmett unbuttoned the front when unexpectedly, he stopped and looked into Nettie's eyes.

Breathing heavily, he whispered, "I can't. We can't do this."

Nettie's breath was coming in quick bursts, "What?"

Jean Jegel

"This isn't right. It's not what's best for you so it's not what's best for us. Nettie, this is too dangerous. What if I left and never came back? I don't want you to be subject to scandal as Eula was. I want to do this the right way." He sat up and pulled Nettie's feet across his legs, stroking her ankle as he continued, "I want you more than anything on earth. I love you. But if I'm going to be the head of our household, I have to make good decisions for us. Putting you in a compromising position would be irresponsible. I need to show you I would never hurt you."

Nettie put her hands over her eyes and sobbed.

"I'm sorry," Emmett admitted. "I should never have let this get out of hand."

"You must think me a harlot! I should have been the one to say no."

"I can't tell you how happy I am you didn't! Marry me, Nettie. We'll do everything honorably when I come home. I'll ask your father for your hand in marriage."

"Oh, no you won't," Nettie blubbered.

"Oh, yes I will. And if he says no, I'll ask Pastor Arndorfer."

"Here!" Nettie moaned as her hands flailed through the air.

"Here, what?"

"Here's my ring. Put it on my left hand."

"You're not afraid, are you? You've been running into my arms out of fear, not away. But I need to know you're serious. It's not only the earthquake or because I might leave?"

Nettie dropped her hands to her sides. Her face was red, her cheeks wet from tears.

"I'm not afraid of you, Emmett, and I do want to marry you. It's not because of the earthquake, but today has made me wake up. I love you. I trust you enough to promise myself to you and you know how difficult that is for me. It doesn't mean this will be easy. I'll undoubtedly test you."

As Emmett took her left hand in his, she froze in place.

"Wait! Stop. Let me sit up." She awkwardly pushed herself into a seated position. "We can't tell our children you proposed while I was lying on your settee half naked." She buttoned the lower portion of her chemise, took Emmet's ring off her right finger and handed it to him.

Emmett took a place on his knee in front of the settee.

"We can leave the half-dressed part out of the narration. Nettie Gordon, will you marry me?" He slid the ring on her left hand.

"Oh, yes I will." At this she launched off the settee pushing Emmett back onto the floor. They lay on the carpet locked in each other's arms and sealed their promise with a kiss.

"There is one problem," stated Nettie, matter-of-factly.

"Already?"

"I don't want to go home. I don't want to be alone."

Emmett nodded. "I understand. I think I have a solution."

The future Mrs. Boyd spent the night in her fiancé's bed, locked securely in his embrace, wearing only her chemise and drawers.

* * *

Emmett lay awake as the sun shone through the bedroom window. Nettie still slept soundly; a contented smile curved her lips. Sleeping beside Nettie in his bed proved both impossible and uncomfortable. If this was one of her tests, he was barely passing. To think, this had been his bright idea.

He was filled with conflicting emotions. Jubilant that Nettie agreed to marry, Emmett did not look forward to his unpleasant and difficult journey. All he could do was pray word would come from Webster before The Owl left for San Francisco tonight. As he ticked off preparation plans in his mind—to keep it off his sleeping companion—he didn't notice Nettie awoke until she snuggled against him.

"You're awake at last."

"Didn't you sleep well?" Nettie inquired as she looked at him.

"I most definitely did not."

"You're worrying about your trip."

"That was not my problem with sleep." Emmett pressed his hand against the small of Nettie's back to draw her closer.

"Oh, *oh!*" She scrambled off the bed. "I'm sorry," she apologized, but it was clear she thought his predicament amusing.

Emmett propped his head on his bent arm to have a better look. Nettie seemed oblivious to the transparency of her undergarments as she stood in front of the window. The top of her chemise remained unbuttoned. Her knee-length, lace-bedecked, wide-legged drawers left her lower legs completely bare and available for his perusal.

"Yes, well, if this was your first test of me, I can assure you it was the most difficult trial I ever endured. I'm surprised you find this amusing. Shouldn't a proper lady appear innocent and shocked?"

"You're always making presumptions of me," she scolded. "I have five older brothers from whom I garnered my despicable ideas about men. Let me simply state, I'm not unfamiliar with the male anatomy."

"All I can say is, I hope you're agreeable to a short engagement."

"I'm agreeable. We'll make plans as soon as you come back or tonight if you don't have to go. We could elope."

"Yes and it would eliminate the need for me to visit your father. But that couldn't have anything to do with your suggestion, I'm certain."

"Of course not."

"Nettie, are you beginning our life together with a tall tale?"

She sat on the edge of the bed. "How could you think such a thing of me?" she teased.

"We'll be completely proper, except for this— whatever this was. I wish we were already married."

"This wasn't proper and I need to get dressed. No one will know I was here, will they?"

"No. But I'll relish the memory of this night forever even if it was completely frustrating. Give me a kiss before you dress."

"No, I think I've tempted you enough and you have surely tempted me. What will I say if someone asks where I was?"

"Hopefully it won't come up, but if it does, say you slept at Faith's. I'm certain she'll cover for you. When I see her, I'll be sure to let her know your visit here was strictly platonic. Besides, she'll be so thrilled you've agreed to marry me, she won't care."

But Emmett was wrong.

"Emmett Boyd, I am extremely disappointed in you! Whatever were you thinking? You'll ruin Nettie's reputation."

"No, I won't. All you have to do is say she spent the night with you if it should come up and I'm reasonably certain it won't."

"I swear, I thought you had her best interests at heart. If Mother was alive, she would box your ears."

"Yes but—"

"Don't but me. It's no wonder Nettie won't marry you. You never behave as a gentleman should and you know better."

"But Faith—"

"Of all the stupid, thoughtless—"

Emmett finally placed his hand over her mouth so he could get a word in. "Faith, we're to be married. Nettie said yes!"

Faith's eyes widened in surprise. She pulled Emmett's hand from her mouth and smiled broadly. "Well, I suppose it's all right then, at least it's better. You're certain you behaved in a gentlemanly manner?"

"More or less."

Faith couldn't keep her joy to herself and applied a bear hug.

"I'm so glad you finally did something right!"

Emmett rolled his eyes. "I love the way women in my life are supportive of my character. But seriously, Faith. I think we should keep this to ourselves at least until things are settled with Webster."

"Certainly. But I can't wait to see the twins when you tell them!"

"Have you got things arranged for Nadine?"

"I'm going over there shortly. Will you see her before you leave, if you leave?"

"I'll go by on my way to the train."

Faith hated the way their family circumstances dampened Emmett's happy news. "This will all work out."

Emmett nodded. "You'll keep an eye on Nettie while I'm gone? I know she'll be fine as far as the

Golden State, but I won't worry if I know you're watching out for her."

"Oh, you wouldn't be able to keep me away!"

* * *

When Faith's mother passed, she did not hesitate to take on the role of family matriarch. She felt it her duty to keep her brothers in line, even though Webster was her older brother and married. She offered advice, tried not to be overbearing—except perhaps where the twins were concerned—and kept them together as a family. Overall, Faith felt her efforts proved successful. It was this role that emboldened her to take control of Webster's home.

Her relationship with Nadine was never warm. Nadine's efforts to draw Webster away from his family had proven effective to varying degrees. Their recent return to Sunday family dinners was undoubtedly a failure of Nadine's endeavors.

Faith intended to set a few matters straight. If Nadine thought her cruel, she was prepared to endure any consequences.

As Nadine finished her meager attempt at consuming breakfast, she laid back against the pillows.

"Faith, I need to see the doctor. I'm feeling uncomfortable and nervous."

"What's wrong with your breakfast?"

"I'm not hungry."

"Well, you have a baby to feed. You need to finish your egg and toast. Sit up and dig in."

"What about the doctor?" Nadine was out of her element. Webster catered to her every whim since she became ill. She wallowed in compassion since the earthquake yesterday and had no reason to suspect her sympathetic care would cease so abruptly.

"There'll be no doctor today. You need to stay

alert."

"No, I don't. I want to sleep."

"Feel free to sleep. I won't stop you."

"But it helps when the doctor administers his sedative."

"I'm certain it does, but I won't call the doctor for you. You have a baby to care for and a daughter who needs you. No matter how long the doctor makes you sleep, you'll have to face your life at some point. You can't leave Susan next door forever. She needs to come home."

"But she knows I've been ill."

"Susan needs her mother. I'm certain she knows something is wrong and remembers her family went to San Francisco. You must explain and help her. Whether you like it or not Nadine, you're a Boyd woman and Boyds don't hide away from the challenges of life. If you expect Emmett to go to the hellhole of San Francisco, you can surely put your own worries away long enough to be a mother to Susan."

"You're harsh, Faith. I always knew you were a cruel woman."

"Think me cruel if it pleases you. It doesn't hurt my feelings one bit. We don't know what you've lost at this point, if anything, and I think you need to put the best possible face on this and wait to see what happened. I assure you, our family will not hesitate to support you, but you won't be coddled or pitied, Nadine. It would be the worst thing we could do.

"Finish your breakfast. I'm going to get Susan and we'll attempt to put your household in order."

Faith grinned as she hurried out the door. Nadine needed something to think about besides her worries. She was prepared to channel Nadine's thoughts in more constructive directions, even if that included hatred of her sister-in-law.

* * *

The reporter made his way through The Owl, taking down names and stories of frantic passengers desperate to locate friends and relatives in San Francisco. He finally took the empty seat next to Emmett, pencil and tablet in hand.

"I'm certain you've heard I'm from the *Herald* and I'm documenting the stories of travelers on this train. Every car is filled with distressed folks. I'm trying to put names in the papers in order to locate loved ones."

Emmett doubted names published in a Los Angeles paper would do much to sort out the missing hundreds of miles away. It seemed to him the man was falsely raising hopes for the anxious passengers and wouldn't hesitate to dramatize his information to sell papers.

"I have nothing to say."

"You're not looking for loved ones? What about property? Many are anxious to see what's become of homes, businesses—are you a businessman on the brink of ruin?"

"I am a businessman on the brink of ruin but not due to the earthquake—due to reporters such as you who print any atrocious accusation in order to sell a paper."

Without comment, the reporter rose and went to the next car.

Emmett pulled his hat over his face to get some sleep. Not wanting to think about what might happen once he got off the train, he focused on Nettie.

She clung to him passionately when they parted and begged to go to the train station. He held her face and wiped her tears with his thumbs as he explained it would be easier on both of them to say their goodbyes at his house. Emmett considered her long-held determination to resist him, how she sought his embrace for protection, and especially the way she filled out her undergarments that very morning.

He greatly admired how Nettie's mother managed to raise her to be a lady under difficult conditions. Nettie graciously held her own in conversation, whether speaking to the Judge or Bao in the kitchen. She was not intimidated or put off by social position or title. She never hesitated to use the proper utensil at Faith's often ostentatious Sunday suppers, always used proper English and obviously had a way with children. He was eager to see if her claimed housekeeping ability proved an honest self-assessment. Even if she couldn't manage to find a dust bunny with a telescope, he could not be more thrilled to claim Nettie as his fiancé.

Emmett considered their life together and knew he needed to make changes. Although he never hid his head in the sand about popular opinion and its effect on his business, there were harsh realities on the horizon. Finally managing to fall into a fitful sleep, he awoke when the train stopped as close to San Francisco as it could travel.

Emmett stepped off the train to complete pandemonium. Screaming people crowded around, denied access to the train because they hadn't a nickel for the price of a ticket. The refugees were wild-eyed; some nearly naked. Emmett thought this complete idiocy. Who wouldn't want the survivors to vacate the disaster zone as quickly as possible?

He stepped to the side of the ticket window and angrily inquired, "Why aren't these people being allowed to leave?"

"We can't do nothin' about it, mister. Nobody has give us permission to load them on the trains."

Emmett frowned. He didn't bring much in the way

of supplies—only some emergency provisions in a knapsack slung over his shoulder. He was well prepared to pay outrageous sums to bring his family to safety. Deciding he could well afford it, Emmett fished a $20 gold piece out of his vest pocket.

"Give me 400 tickets," he yelled over the uproar. At least he could help a few of these poor souls. Certain of his own lunacy by heading toward the calamity instead of from it, Emmett rented a carriage to take him the final 15 miles to Oakland.

* * *

Faith made a point to stop by the Golden State and keep Nettie abreast of what was happening. She made a daily pilgrimage to check on Nadine, who was out of bed and managing her household. Nettie was amazed at this turn of events, but Faith seemed fully supportive of her sister-in-law and gave Nadine ample credit for her fine attitude and faith in God. Faith did not mention a healthy fear of her husband's sister played no small part in Nadine's improved mindset.

Faith assured it was too soon to hear anything from Emmett and Nettie believed that to be true. Newspaper stories emphasized the brutal environment caused by the earthquake. Nettie found the reports disturbing. Knowing all Emmett wanted was for her to watch his house and manage the Golden State, she longed to accomplish something more personal.

Nettie could find no household chore requiring her attention. Charlie's wife and her sister kept the Boyd home in perfect working order, from the carefully polished silver in the drawer to the sparkling clean windows. It was their custom to clean the saloon at 6 a.m. They worked until almost ten, opening time, and often could be found having a cup of coffee and a pastry with Marcel in the kitchen before they walked across the alley to keep Emmett's house. There, they worked for two or three hours, cleaning, doing dishes, taking care of laundry and ironing. The women said nothing about Nettie sleeping in Emmett's bed. The linens held his scent, which she found comforting.

Nettie knew Emmett paid a premium for the excellent service he received. Having a complete understanding of the bookkeeping in the Golden State, she wondered how he managed financially before his siblings gave him their shares of the family business. But then, she quickly realized all he ever did was work before they started going out. She imagined Emmett must have savings. How else could he afford his expensive automobile?

Although Emmett rarely used his back porch, Nettie settled on that area for her home improvement project. There were lovely pieces of wicker furniture with cushions badly in need of new covers, a sturdy porch swing and a wooden table and chairs.

Determined to keep careful watch over the Golden State, Nettie decided to take a few hours to do some shopping. After all, Emmett could often be found in the warehouse since he hired Chauncey and Johnny. Certainly, Nettie could take some time away.

She selected an orange and gold leaf print upholstery fabric and a mustard cotton gingham for a tablecloth. Nettie purchased a variety of paint: cream color to freshen the wicker furniture, golden yellow for the table and chairs and a warm terra-cotta for the swing, all of which complemented the yellow house.

Nettie stopped by the Payne Nursery on Broadway and purchased plants and terra cotta pots to decorate the porch. Over the next days, she sewed late at night on the cushion covers and rose early to plant and paint. The project kept her mind off Emmett and his ordeal. Her sudden burst of domestic energy served as a reminder this would soon be her home.

A final touch was a bonnet-covered basket. Nettie sewed a cushion out of leftover fabric and placed it inside. It had a place of honor near the corner by the steps. Hoping Hallie would abandon the chair where she usually slept, Nettie was delighted when she found the cat napping inside.

She gave her promise to Emmett and would shortly sacrifice her freedom. Nettie vacillated between two hopes: wanting Emmett to stay away to give her time to adjust to the idea of their life together; and wanting him back immediately to ease her anxiety. As the days went by, Nettie understood more than anything, she wanted Emmett home, safe and sound. Having retrieved her houseplants from the windowsill in the boarding house, she gave them a new home in Emmett's kitchen window in an attempt to come to terms with her future.

* * *

Tired from an exhausting and dramatic week, Nettie sat on the porch, reading the paper. She was intrigued by businesses advertising fundraisers for earthquake relief. She put a sign in the window of the saloon, the same window that was broken the night she met Emmett. It read "All Saturday Receipts Will be Donated to Aid Earthquake Victims." Faith thought her plan brilliant.

Nettie hoped Emmett would not be upset when he returned to find his beer supply diminished and his receipts so light. Perhaps the gesture of good will would serve to generate more income during the coming week. Emmett would surely be home by then.

Nettie decided to attend church at Trinity in support of Eula and her sudden marriage. The day was set aside for prayer. It was hard to believe Easter was only a week ago—so much had happened.

Taking a place in her accustomed pew near the side aisle on the left side of the church, Nettie noticed the gossips were at work. Both ladies and gentlemen were discussing Pastor Arndorfer's inappropriate marriage, obviously accomplished before an acceptable period of mourning was up. Nettie frowned disapprovingly whenever one of the gossips looked her way. She found it hard to believe this was more important to the congregation than the disastrous events occurring to the north.

She was not prepared when a stately and self-assured Eula took a place beside her. The woman looked positively radiant and smiled sweetly at anyone who looked her way.

"Are you quite all right?" whispered a curious Nettie.

"I have never been better. Bert says we must put a happy face on our marriage. If we refrain from conflict, no one will have cause to find fault."

"So, you imagine they'll want to share in your joy? Is this joy real or feigned?"

"Oh, Nettie. I've never been so happy in my life!" Eula gushed.

The good pastor jubilantly announced his marriage at the end of the service. He guided Eula out of church to join him in the vestibule so the happy couple could be congratulated by the congregation. Nettie could see the pastor's plan seemed to be working splendidly. Even the most dour old German seemed glad to greet the delightful couple. Nettie even caught wind of a plan to have a potluck dinner next week so the congregants could express their best wishes. It was a good thing. There seemed far too little cheer in the world right now.

CHAPTER SEVENTEEN

Lotta's Fountain was located in what was left of the financial district. It served as both a meeting point for people searching for loved ones and an information exchange point in a city bereft of communication.

Slumped against the fountain, Emmett rubbed the stubble on his chin as he observed an all-too-rare reunion of a man and what appeared to be his wife. Spending a few hours a day at the fountain had become his habit.

After a brief stay in Oakland among survivors, Emmett took the ferry to San Francisco—the only way in and out of the city. Horrified at the devastation all around, he was amazed how quickly he became inured to the gruesome scenes. The city was still on fire when he arrived. It was the dead and bloated horses littering the streets, the acrid smell of smoke and the constant explosions that first captured his attention. Soon he noticed the charred remains of bodies scattered everywhere. He watched as a man was shot and killed trying to pillage jewelry from a body across the street from where he stood.

First making his way to the site of the Valencia Hotel, Emmett learned the entire building simply sank into the ground moments after the earthquake occurred. Evidently only the top floor poked from the remains. For two days and nights, a rescue effort proved effective and about 40 people were plucked from the subterranean floors before fire swept through what was left of the building. Many guests of the hotel from the lowest floors drowned due to a burst water main. Emmett questioned people in the vicinity who witnessed the fire hours before he arrived.

Drinking water was the biggest problem in the city since water mains were leaking underground. Emmett saw supplies of alcohol destroyed by law enforcement officers trying to stem the threat of mob violence despite the fact there was no water to be had. Food was not much easier to obtain.

Firefighters strung hoses from the bay and used salt water to fight the conflagration. As the fire made its way inland, dynamite was used to make firebreaks in hopes of halting the fire's advance. A cantankerous old miner Emmett met in a bread line claimed the firemen were inexperienced in the use of dynamite and, "didn't know what the hell they were doing." Their efforts likely caused more fires than they stopped.

Citizens rightly believed insurance would not cover earthquake damage and were torching their own homes to make a claim against their policies.

The din of explosives rocked the city day and night, adding to the distress of survivors already unnerved by the multitude of aftershocks.

Uneven and twisted thoroughfares made walking difficult, but it was the only way around the city. Crowds gathered to watch buildings burn, which also made it difficult to traverse the streets.

Emmett searched through city parks, Golden Gate Park and the Presidio where survivors were housed in tents. He carried a picture of Webster and his children, asking everyone who would pay attention if they had seen the family in his photograph, to no avail. He went to Mechanic's Pavilion to search through unidentified bodies although he refrained from inspecting burn victims. As far as finding his family, Emmett considered only three scenarios. Webster and the children drowned, managed to escape, or were rescued before the building burned so Emmett spared himself that horror.

Desensitized to the plight of people wandering aimlessly through the rubble, he no longer thought it odd to see deranged inhabitants sporting dazed expressions, senselessly dragging furniture or some other vestige of their belongings. The constant sounds of crying and prayer punctuated the air with a symphony of sorrow.

At least he didn't often need to stand in long lines for food, having cash for the meager fare he found. There were always opportunists who sought to make a dollar any way they could and Emmett was prepared to use his funds to spend his time effectively.

Since leaving the fountain yesterday, Emmett had the uncanny feeling he was being watched. The eerie sensation had not dissipated. There was the possibility someone noticed he carried money, sought to rob him and simply waited for an opportunity.

Propping his arms on bent knees and dropping his head to rest, Emmett considered his next move. Even though some telegraph lines were reconnected, he didn't want to wire disappointing news. He felt a complete failure.

Emmett cringed as the hair on the back of his neck stood on end. He could barely make out the shadow of someone standing nearby in the waning daylight. The shadow was still. Quickly looking up, he saw a boy turn and run.

Jean Jegel

Emmett leapt to his feet and bounded after the youngster, who darted in and out of the crowd surrounding the fountain. It took Emmett several minutes to catch up. Curious to discover why he was being watched, he grabbed the boy's shoulder and spun him around.

The child was smaller than he first imagined. Emmett peered into the filthy face, covered in soot. He was dressed in ragged, dirty pants that fell below his knees and what looked to be a pajama top. He was barefoot. But as Emmett looked closely at the boy's eyes, he was stunned.

"Jake! Is it you? Oh, thank God!"

The boy appeared hesitant, unwilling to reply.

"It's me, Uncle Emmett. Don't you know me?" He knelt and hugged the boy. "Why didn't you come to me?" Emmett looked into the dirty face when there was no reply. "Can you talk? Are you hungry? Here, I have food and water."

From his knapsack, Emmett produced a whiskey bottle he found in the rubble of a saloon. He filled it with water each chance he got. Jake went straightway for the water.

"Here, not too much at once. Take a few swallows at a time. Don't you want some bread? I have jerky." The boy only sought to quench his thirst.

Myriad questions hurried through Emmett's thoughts as Jake kept his silence. The boy undoubtedly experienced horrible tragedy. "Let's get out of the street." Emmett picked Jake up and was relieved when the child willingly wrapped his arms around his uncle's neck. "Are you hurt?"

Jake shook his head then dropped it against his uncle's shoulder. Emmett was intent on finding shelter for the night. By the time he walked to the nearest park,

Jake was sound asleep.

* * *

Not having slept well in more nights than he could count, Emmett spent a virtually sleepless night in the tent. Jake snuggled against him for warmth but also flailed wildly, frequently flinging arms and legs at his dozing uncle with unimagined strength. As dawn lightened the tent, Emmett realized he needed information to determine how to proceed. He smiled, attempting to exude confidence and good cheer when Jake awoke and rubbed his eyes.

"Are you hungry?" The boy nodded in reply. Emmett gave him water and a piece of bread. "This will tide you over until we find something else, but it'll likely be more bread. Jake, I need to find out what happened." The question Emmett most needed to know was the most difficult to ask. "Where are your father and Rose? Do you know what happened to them?" He waited for a reaction. Jake chewed his bread but finally looked up at his uncle.

"I don't know where they are."

Relieved the boy could speak, Emmett urged him on. "Can you tell me what happened during the earthquake? Where you saw them last?"

Jake took another drink of water and wiped his mouth on his pajama sleeve as words came tumbling forth. "We were at the hotel to meet Grandma and Grandpa the next day. Rose wanted to be up high so Daddy took a room on the top floor. He was grouchy because Rose wouldn't go in the elevator and he didn't want to walk up all the stairs to the fourth floor.

"We were asleep and the room started shaking so hard, we fell out of bed. Everybody was screaming; the shaking was noisy. It felt like the whole building was about to bust apart. When the bad shaking stopped, Daddy got up and looked out the window. He grabbed us and we crawled right out the window onto the ground. The street went all the way up to where our window was.

"Daddy put me on his back and told me to grab tight. He held Rose in front.

"People was screaming and crying and running all around like crazy. They was even naked. Daddy said we was heading right for the ferry to get us out of that place quick. When we got to the ferry, there was folks pushing and shoving and screaming and yelling. It was a sight. He told me to hold fast and I tried real hard, but folks was fighting to get on the boat. I did try real hard, Uncle Emmett, but they grabbed at me and tore me off. I fell on the ground and screamed for Daddy, but he got pushed away by all the people.

"I could hear him yelling my name for a while. Then I had to get away 'cause people was stepping on me. A lady fainted beside me and people walked right over her. I couldn't see Daddy by then. People was clawing and grabbing and I figured I better get out of there 'cause Daddy sure couldn't see me where I was so I slunk back the way we came.

"By that time the boat left, but people just kept coming and I never found Daddy. He didn't come back for me."

Emmett was incredulous at his nephew's factual and unemotional recitation. "What did you do then?"

"Well, I walked around some, looking for something to eat. Daddy cut his feet on the broken glass and he was bleeding pretty bad by the time we got to the ferry so I be'd careful and watched where I was going.

"I see'd terrible things, Uncle Emmett. I seen buildings burn down. There was a lady carrying a birdcage full of kittens and a parrot on her shoulder.

"I saw a man trapped bad in the bricks and wood. Men was trying to get him out, even policemen, but they couldn't budge him and the fire came and started to burn his feet. He screamed for them to kill him so he wouldn't burn up and a policeman took out his gun and shot that man right in his head. He stopped screaming then."

Emmett closed his eyes in dismay but understood he needed to keep steady and make everything as normal for Jake as he could manage.

Since his nephew was only five, Emmett hoped he wouldn't remember as time went on. He asked, "How did you find food?"

"After some while, people was giving away food. The lines were long, so I decided to creep up behind a lady near the front and pretend like I belonged to her. After she got her bread, I'd take some too and then amble off. Nobody ever called me out for it.

"Later, I found some other boys who were lost and we stayed together. We all shared our bread or whatever else we found. One boy found a bottle like the one you got and I tried the brown stuff in there, but it was awful. I spit it out.

"We found a place to sleep figuring we'd be safe together, but that building burnt down, too. We couldn't find another good place to sleep. That was when I saw you by the fountain."

"Why didn't you come to me?"

"I wasn't for certain it was you. I never see'd you with whiskers before and all the grownups are acting pretty bad. I was scared so I followed you. I want to go home, Uncle Emmett."

Emmett could not help but notice the irony. After seeing all the horror in the aftermath of the earthquake,

Jake was afraid of his own uncle.

At least he could make a plan. Webster, no doubt, was forced onto the ferry by the crowd. Emmett would take Jake and catch the ferry today. They'd make a stop in Oakland and then he could take his family home.

* * *

Oakland was a mass of miserable humanity. Literally every home in the city housed refugees from across the bay. Although Emmett was able to purchase food and some ill-fitting but pricey clothing and shoes for Jake, he knew he could not take time to make a thorough search for his brother and niece.

The trains were transporting food, water, and supplies and recently started taking refugees to the destination of their choice free of charge. If Webster's feet were cut as badly as Jake believed, he'd never be able to walk to the train tracks and likely had no money for a ride. Emmett could only hope his family was someplace safe in Oakland.

Intent to deliver his nephew home, Emmett planned to make a return trip to find Webster and Rose. For the first time, there was real hope they managed to survive.

* * *

It was after 4 a.m. when The Owl pulled into Los Angeles. An exhausted Emmett stepped onto the platform carrying a sound asleep Jake. His head wobbled on his uncle's shoulder. Knowing he should take Jake immediately to his mother, the thought of Nettie waiting in his house proved an irresistible attraction. It was the middle of the night, why not let Nadine sleep? He could rest for an hour or two, have Nettie clean Jake up and return him before breakfast.

Emmett managed to catch a trolley for the short

ride home but felt almost too weak to walk up the porch stairs. He tried the door then remembered he told Nettie to keep the house locked in his absence. He fished in his pocket for the key and let himself in.

Assuming Nettie slept in Faith's old room, he was surprised to find her asleep in his bed. After unburdening himself of his diminutive load, Emmett could not resist clasping Nettie's shoulder and shaking her gently. He was charmed by her enthusiastic greeting when she clung to him, pulling him across the bed.

"Oh, thank God, thank God! I thought you were never coming home."

Exhausted by the past days, Emmett confessed, "I failed, Nettie. I only found Jake so far. Actually, he found me. What am I going to tell Nadine?"

"You found Jake?" she exclaimed. "Perfect! He's the only one missing. You didn't fail, everyone is home now. You're a hero!"

"What are you talking about?"

"Last Sunday afternoon, Nadine's parents showed up at her house. Her mother remains quite distraught from their ordeal. They stayed in San Francisco as long as they could, watching the fire come closer to their home each day. They buried some belongings in the backyard and had the means to buy their way out of San Francisco. Oh, Emmett, they watched firemen use dynamite to blow up their home."

"But what about Webster?"

"That's the fortuitous part. The Sheratons rented a carriage to take them from Oakland to the train. Mrs. Sheraton attempted to avert her eyes from all the tragic refugees walking alongside the carriage, but then she noticed a little girl who looked familiar. Emmett, it was Rose.

"Webster was trying to carry her to the train. His

feet were badly cut. He could hardly walk. When his in-laws urged him to join them in the carriage, he tried to get them to take Rose home so he could go back to San Francisco and find his son. But he lost a lot of blood. There was infection in his feet and he had a terrible temperature. He couldn't go back so they brought him home."

"Is he all right?"

"The doctor removed glass from his feet. Can you believe it? He walked around with glass in his feet all that time. After the doctor left, Faith made him stick his feet in salt water. I was there, I thought he'd pass out from the pain. But Faith makes him soak his feet daily, she even found more glass. The salt seems to be doing the trick and he's starting to heal.

"His temperature finally came down. All he talks about is going to find Jake. He blames himself because he couldn't hold onto the boy in the crowd.

"Oh, Emmett, I was starting to think you wouldn't return without them and would stay forever rather than come home empty-handed. Look what you've done!" Spotting Jake at the end of the bed, Nettie tenderly smoothed the boy's hair off his forehead.

"Thank God," Emmett muttered, "I thought I'd have to go back to that hellish nightmare."

Nettie, concerned at Emmett's fatigue, urged him to be still. "You can sleep. I'll telephone Nadine as soon as the sun is up and we'll get Jake home. Are you hungry?"

"I'm famished, but I need to sleep. It's been so long—"

Almost before the words were out of his mouth, Emmett's breathing deepened in exhausted slumber.

* * *

Opening his eyes to the dim light of sunset, Emmett

- 319 -

thought he might be dreaming as he looked around the bedroom. It seemed an eternity since he was home.

Still dressed in the clothes he wore to San Francisco, he realized his feet were bare. His body lay at the strange angle where he collapsed next to Nettie. Jake was gone from the end of the bed.

Emmett's stomach gave a noisy growl. He'd never been so hungry in his life. Light-headed as he sat on the edge of the bed, Emmett watched his bedroom door slowly open.

"You're awake!" Nettie proclaimed as she walked across the room and settled beside him.

"Where's Jake?"

"He woke up this morning not long after you came. I don't think he suffered from lack of sleep the way you did. He was ravenous so I made him breakfast and stuck him in the bathtub. I found some boy's clothes in the attic. I can't believe how well-kept your house is. The clothes in the trunk were actually clean and pressed."

"I'm starving. Can we continue this downstairs?"

"If you wait a moment, I'll scramble you some eggs."

Emmett looked unsteady as he stood up so Nettie grabbed his arm and accompanied him down the stairs.

"I'll heat the water for your bath while you eat."

"You didn't answer my question."

"Once Jake was ready to go home, he expressed a desire to ride in the Buick. I thought it only right you take him to his parents, but I couldn't wake you up. I really tried." Nettie set a frying pan on the stove and lit the burner. "I took Jake on the trolley to relieve his parents' worry as soon as possible. Emmett, they were ecstatic. They owe you everything. It was all I could do to keep them from coming over here immediately. If you're up to it after you eat, you should drive over there.

Jake's waiting for his ride."

A curious Emmett watched Nettie melt butter in the cast iron pan then fry random items she pulled from the ice box. What appeared to be diced ham, green peppers and onions were soon joined by four fresh eggs. Nettie stirred the whole mess and topped it with cheddar cheese. She quickly served the plateful of food, handing him the salt and pepper shakers as she poured him a beer from the small keg.

"I don't think I've ever tried beer and eggs before," he noted, gleefully. "Is this my reward?"

"I guess so. I would have baked you something, but I've been over at the Golden State all day, only checking on you from time-to-time."

Skeptically, Emmett tried the egg dish and was amazed how good it was. He knew he was starving; anything would taste good. It appeared he was about to marry a fine cook, much to his delight. He scarfed down the eggs and drained the beer in short order.

Avoiding mention of San Francisco, Nettie filled the tub and brought clean clothes. As Emmett lolled in the tub, he nearly fell back to sleep.

* * *

Nettie tossed and turned in her bed at Mrs. Green's. This was only proper, she kept repeating in her head. She missed Emmett's house, the way the sheets on his bed smelled, her pleasant mornings in his kitchen having tea, her delight at her accomplishment every time she walked across the porch. Nettie conceded she was simply sad to be back home.

Another idea wiggled through her mind. She missed Emmett more than she cared to admit. Her joy at his return was a difficult thing to concede.

Nettie finally rose before dawn and prepared for the

day. If she was early, perhaps they could share breakfast on his porch.

* * *

Emmett awoke to the smell of bacon. His stomach growled at the irresistible aroma. Scratching at the heavy growth of beard on his face, he crawled out of bed, grabbed a pair of trousers and headed for the kitchen. He was delighted to find Nettie working over the stove, wearing one of his mother's aprons.

"Good morning."

Nettie flinched, startled at his appearance, but then she turned and smiled. "Good morning. Are you all rested up?"

"I doubt it. I feel like I need to sleep for a week. What are you cooking?"

"There will be flapjacks in a minute. I have coffee here and bacon. Do you want eggs?"

"That sounds wonderful. What are you doing here?"

"We didn't have much of a chance to talk last night. Are you going to work?"

"No, I think I'll let my capable staff run things one more day. I believe I'd like to spend some time with my fiancé, but I have an errand to do first."

"I'll bring your food to the porch. Your newspaper is out there already," Nettie suggested. Once she served his breakfast and coffee, Emmett tore into the hearty meal.

"What happened out here?" he asked.

"Do you like it?"

"Yes. Is this your doing?"

"It was my way of saying thank you for letting me stay in your house."

"Not your way of taking possession?" he teased.

Nettie actually blushed. "It's pleasant. I'll definitely spend more time out here."

"Hallie evidently approves of the improved porch. She left me a present at the door while you were gone."

"A dead mouse?"

"Only the skull. I'm afraid Bao now considers me a hopeless sissy. I made him come and pick it up."

"Nettie, if you could choose anything you wanted to do tonight, what would it be? Dinner and dancing? An evening at the Electric Theater? A vaudeville performance?"

"Actually, there's a roller rink over on 12th and Main. It's called Dreamland. They have a band and the paper says you can skate the length of a whole block without turning a corner."

"I wasn't aware you liked to roller skate. I've never been to a roller rink."

"I'll teach you," Nettie offered.

"Little you are going to hold me up?"

"Well, I can help," she suggested.

"Roller skating it is then. I want you to write your father's address down for me."

"I don't see any need," Nettie shot back.

"I do. I want us to marry as soon as possible. I told you I'd ask your father. This isn't new. Let's get past this so we can make our plans."

Nettie went into the kitchen and retrieved a small tablet of paper she found in a drawer. She scribbled the address and handed it to Emmett.

As she sat down and put a bite of flapjacks on her fork, Nettie asked, "Aren't you going to tell me about San Francisco?"

"No. I don't even want to think about it. I'll only give credit to Jake who is quite a brave, inventive and steady young man. He's a true survivor, especially in light of the fact he's only five years old. I think he takes after his uncle."

"Oh, you mean the Judge," Nettie smiled slyly.

"You know exactly who I mean, Miss Gordon. Watch out or I'll skate rings around you tonight."

"That is highly unlikely for a novice. Your fate will be entirely in my hands."

* * *

After stopping at his brother's home, a suited and shaved Emmett took his nephew for a ride in the Buick. He decided against visiting last night, having telephoned instead. Emmett found his family's gratitude tedious and happily escaped his brother's house. Nadine's mother appeared completely depressed. He didn't know if his lack of sympathy was due to the complete devastation he witnessed or whether he was still tired.

Jake was probably too young to understand the enormity of his recent experiences. The ride in the automobile seemed as magical to him as ever. Taking pleasure in the memory of Jake's delighted expression, Emmett commenced his journey to Pasadena on the glorious spring day.

Nettie went to work at the Golden State after breakfast, intent to spend the day as she would had Emmett not returned. He let her believe his intention was to visit family. She never imagined he planned to travel to her girlhood home.

Mr. Boyd was accustomed to the curious stares and attention his mode of transportation provoked. Automobiles, though more common than ever, were still a novelty. There was more than curiosity apparent as Emmett pulled up to a dilapidated house near the railroad tracks on the outskirts of Pasadena. He decided to use his locking device to ensure the Buick would be waiting for him when his visit concluded.

Emmett approached the ramshackle building and turned to close the front gate behind him when a surly-looking man appeared on the porch. Perhaps it was only Emmett's imagination, but the man bore some resemblance to the peanut seller.

"Can I help you?"

"I'm looking for Mr. Gordon."

"Well, you've come to the right place. There's a lot of those here. Look, Grayson, here's a dandy come to see us." Another man came outside. He was dark-haired with stubble on his face. Both men were dirty and unkempt.

"I'm looking for an older Mr. Gordon," Emmett added, "the father of Nettie Gordon."

"Well," said the second man, "he don't live here no more."

"Do you know where I might find him?"

"I reckon I do, but what's in it for me?"

"Nothing much. I'll be on my way and you can get on with whatever it is you're doing."

"You know what I think?" said the first man. "I think you all are Nettie's fancy man. We heared about you from Murl."

These two were apparently more of Nettie's no-good brothers. Emmett wondered if it was one of them who attacked her as the men strode toward him. They were smaller in stature than Emmett but clearly believed they presented a menacing combination. Emmett was not intimidated.

"If you can't give me his location, I'll be on my way." As Emmett tipped his hat, one brother charged. Using the man's momentum, Emmett diverted him into the fence, which loudly crashed onto the sidewalk.

The second brother approached more cautiously.

When he managed to take a swing, he was quickly introduced to Emmett's knuckles. The man flew backward and hit his head on the bottom tread of the porch stairs. He appeared stunned, perhaps unconscious. Emmett turned his attention to the dazed brother still lying on the sidewalk while keeping a careful eye on the front door to see if more brothers emerged.

"Maybe you'd like to give me that address," Emmett suggested, nudging the man with the toe of his shoe.

"It's four blocks south. A blue house with white trim—the only blue house on the block."

"Thank you. Your help is most appreciated." Emmett stepped over the fence, got in his motor car and quickly drove away.

In moments, he approached the blue house. The mailbox sported the name GORDON.

The neighborhood improved dramatically on his four-block drive. The bungalow was neat and tidy; the yard was nicely kept.

Emmett walked across the wide front porch and knocked on the door. A tall and angular older lady answered. If he could apply a face to the temperance movement, this severe-looking woman perfectly fit the bill.

"Good morning. I'm looking for Mr. Gordon."

"He's not here. He's at work."

"I hate to impose, but I need to talk to him. Could you possibly provide his work address? My business won't take long and it would save me another trip to Pasadena. I wish to speak to him about his daughter."

The woman took careful note of Emmett's attire and looked past him to see the Buick parked in front of her house.

"You can come in. He'll be home for lunch

shortly." She offered him a seat in her parlor. Though hardly opulent, the house was orderly. "I'm Mrs. Gordon, the second Mrs. Gordon."

"Pleased to make your acquaintance. I'm Mr. Boyd."

"Can I offer you something to drink while you wait?"

"A glass of water would be greatly appreciated." Emmett hadn't been able to ease his thirst since he came home.

Once Mrs. Gordon returned from the kitchen with a glass of water, she seated herself opposite her guest. She seemed far more curious about Emmett than he was of her.

"You know my husband?"

"No, but I met him once."

Before the woman could formulate more questions, the front door opened and Nettie's father entered.

Emmett rose and offered his hand. "Mr. Gordon, I'm Emmett Boyd. I'd like a word."

Mr. Gordon took his hand and gave a firm handshake. "Do I know you?"

"You came into my saloon looking for Nettie." Emmett would have paid dearly for a photograph of Mrs. Gordon at that moment. Aghast at his occupation, her mouth fell open. With nothing to lose, he proceeded. "I know you're home for lunch. I don't wish to take up your time so I'll come to the point. I'm asking you for Nettie's hand in marriage."

Mr. Gordon stepped away, staring in what could be disbelief, but Emmett didn't know the man well enough to read his expression.

"Have a seat, Mr. Boyd," Mrs. Gordon requested. "Sit down, Hayes," Mrs. Gordon demanded.

At least the woman had a sense of decorum,

Emmett thought as he took a seat. Mrs. Gordon commenced an inquiry, evidently feeling she had free rein to satisfy her curiosity.

"Why should my husband give you his consent?"

"Well, I love her. I have the means to support her. I own a home and have a profitable business. I want to spend my life with her. Is there anything else I can offer to ease your mind?" Although Mrs. Gordon asked the question, Emmett directed his reply to Nettie's father.

"How do we know Nettie wants to marry you?" came Mrs. Gordon's next query.

"You don't. She'd hardly walk down the aisle with a man she didn't want to marry. She's sure of her own mind, not some timid, witless or coddled woman. But it's my impression you've never met your step-daughter. Am I incorrect? You'd hardly be in a position to understand anything about her.

"I can tell you, she didn't want me to come here, or rather to her ancestral home down the street where I believe her brothers reside. She doesn't know I'm here."

"Then why did you come?"

Mr. Gordon remained completely silent.

"It's the proper thing to do. I'm sorry I didn't have the opportunity to ask your permission to court Nettie. We worked together and our courtship hasn't been conventional. We were in love before courtship became an issue."

"You hardly deserve my husband's daughter for a wife, leading Nettie down an immoral path—working in a saloon—serving the devil's brew. Folks like you are headed straight for perdition."

"Hush woman!" Mr. Gordon broke his silence.

Although Mrs. Gordon did as she was told, there was a definite defiance in her manner. No doubt Mr. Gordon would get an earful upon Emmett's departure.

"Nettie always took after her mother. Our boys were wild, more than she could handle. She put all her efforts into Nettie. That girl thought she was too good for the likes of us and she took off."

Emmett bit his lip. Nettie was too good for them, but he knew it wasn't why she left.

"You can have her. Help yourself." Mr. Gordon abruptly left the parlor and headed for the kitchen and his lunch.

Emmett smiled at the dour Mrs. Gordon. "Well, then, I'll be going. Thank you. It's been a pleasure."

The more politely Emmett behaved, the more austere Mrs. Gordon appeared. But he felt extremely jovial. Despite the slurs on his business, he had what he came for.

CHAPTER EIGHTEEN

Emmett didn't anticipate his warm reception at the Golden State. It was taking much longer to collect Nettie than he hoped. The patrons were curious about what he saw in San Francisco and inquired about the rescue of little Jake. He frankly didn't want to discuss his journey and allowed his inquisitors to drift off into their own ruminations regarding the earthquake.

Once Emmett finally caught sight of Nettie, he decided to address her in the most severe and reprimanding manner possible.

"Miss Gordon!" Everyone got the idea Miss Nettie was in some serious trouble and grew silent as Emmett made his way behind the bar. Giving a sly wink, he admonished, "I need to see you. Right this way." He directed her through the closet and kitchen, then out to the alley. "I believe we have an appointment. Are you ready to skate?"

Nettie was relieved there was no problem, despite his wink. "I'm ready, but I don't understand why you'd go roller skating. You understand, it is quite physical. Aren't you tired? You only got home yesterday. I didn't expect you'd stay so long at Webster's."

"I admit I'm tired, but the thought of roller skating

Jean Jegel

kept me going all day. Shall we go?"

"Let me grab my shawl first. It's chilly tonight."

"Is it in the closet?"

"No," Nettie replied sheepishly. "I left it in your house." Assuming Emmett would think it forward of her to leave belongings in his home, she was surprised at the smile her comment drew.

It wasn't long before the Buick was parked near the corner of 12th and Main. Emmett rented two pairs of skates. Nettie demonstrated how to apply the metal skates and proceeded a few feet out onto the rink, turning to offer encouragement. Smiling furtively, Emmett stepped boldly onto the wooden floor, wobbly as he awkwardly managed to push himself into Nettie's waiting arms.

"You'll get the hang of this. Shall we try going around the perimeter, close to the wall?" Nettie, holding tight to Emmett's waist, clearly believed she was effectively guiding him along.

"Oh, I like this," but what Emmett really enjoyed was the public display of intimacy.

After taking a few spins around the huge rink, he suggested, "People are dancing on the skates. Perhaps we could try."

"They're doing a two-step. Those are sophisticated movements. I think you're better off keeping to the side for now."

She was shocked when Emmett abruptly pulled away, skated a few steps and made a sharp turn, his hands behind his back as if he were ice skating.

"You told me you couldn't roller skate!"

"No, I told you I'd never been to a roller rink. This is an even, smooth surface, not at all what I'm used to. Skating was my favorite boyhood activity. Anywhere we could find pavement, Webster and I used to race other boys through the streets of Los Angeles." He skated toward Nettie and made a quick stop, holding his arms out in dance position. "Shall we?"

It was obvious Emmett felt himself quite the expert and was immensely pleased at having fooled her.

"I don't know. There are some awfully handsome men here. Perhaps I should wait and see if one of them asks me to skate." Nettie stuck her nose in the air and thoughtfully patted her index finger on her chin.

"Oh, no you won't." Emmett grabbed her waist and took her hand. "Let's see how good a skater you are, Nettie Gordon." He whisked her quickly around the rink, rapidly spinning and turning. Nettie couldn't help but laugh. This was by far the most fun she ever had roller skating. Since she was mostly skating backwards in dance position, she couldn't see where they were going and couldn't gauge their speed as properly dressed ladies and gentlemen went by in a blur of color.

Emmett skillfully wove his way around the slow skaters. Having used extra hat pins, Nettie felt secure she would not part ways with the newest chapeau in her wardrobe.

Nettie knew Emmett accommodated her smaller frame by shortening his stride when they danced. There was no need for caution on the roller skates. The wheels on her skates spun as quickly as his.

When the music stopped, Emmett made a quick turn to halt their progress. Nettie almost crashed into him, but he held her steady.

A breathless Nettie declared, "We're not in a race, you understand? They'll throw you out if you don't slow down."

"Well then, we'll drive to the next rink. Perhaps we could attain some record for most ejections from roller rinks in a single night."

As Nettie assumed, after an hour of wild abandon on the rink and several warnings, Emmett Boyd and his fiancé were soundly ejected. This did not diminish Emmett's enthusiasm in the least.

"Did it occur to you they were clapping because you were leaving, not because of your skating prowess?"

"Certainly not. We provided thrilling entertainment. We didn't even knock anyone over."

"Just the same, your salute to the crowd was rather ostentatious."

"Nettie, you simply don't understand how to appeal to the masses. We'll be remembered for all time at Dreamland."

"Yes, I'm sure we won't live down being escorted from the building. We can never skate there again."

Emmett shook his head in disgust. "I'm certain they'll welcome us with open arms when we return."

"I never realized how egotistical you are, Emmett Boyd."

"Egotistical? I simply have a thorough grasp of my abilities, which are profound. Should I list them for you? Some you might find extremely rewarding—for you."

"No, that's quite all right."

Nettie considered Emmett's newfound zest for life might be a result of his recent experiences. She pulled her shawl around her shoulders after they took their places in the Buick.

"Your shawl is pretty. Is it something new?"

"No, I knitted it. It's actually old. You've seen it before."

"I especially like that you keep it in my house. I like having your possessions there. I noticed your plants in the windowsill."

"I should take those home."

"Why? We'll soon be sharing the house. You

should move more of your things." He could see her expression had grown serious. "We need to make plans for our wedding."

"Isn't it rather soon?"

"Nettie, I've never been more certain of anything in my life than I am of you—of us. After seeing the devastation in San Francisco, I know life is short. A person can't gauge how much time they have. I want to spend my time with you, all I can get. You haven't changed your mind, have you?"

"No. I gave you my promise." Nettie knew how thrilled and thankful she was to have Emmett home. She also understood how his experiences might skew his thinking. "I feel there's no reason to rush is all."

"I seem to remember some half-dressed girl—what was her name? She was awfully eager to sleep in my bed. In fact, she crawled right in. She was anxious to marry me. I wonder what's become of her?"

Nettie bit her lip and stared at Emmett.

"I have to tell you something. I asked your father for your hand this afternoon."

"I see. What did he say?"

"He gave me permission. He doesn't live in the house you used to live in."

"Then how did you find him?"

"It seems your brothers, or some of them, live there now. I got your father's address from one of them."

"How friendly this all sounds."

"It was friendly enough that I got what I wanted."

"Why did my father consent?"

"I don't know. I imagine he didn't have a reason to decline. He doesn't know me, but he doesn't really know you either. I think this would be a good time to reach out and ask him to our wedding."

"*No.*"

Jean Jegel

"It doesn't do any good to hold a grudge, which takes more effort than it's worth."

"I don't hold a grudge."

"Then why not ask him to come?"

"This is too hard for you to understand. You have a nice family. There was love in your home."

"I understand forgiveness."

"My father never asked for my forgiveness."

"Nonetheless—"

"Look, Emmett. I don't wish any ill will on him. I don't wish him harm. I simply don't want anything to do with him. I'm happy to live and let live. He lost the right to be honored or respected when he beat my mother. I will not relent on this."

Emmett's dubious expression reflected his lack of understanding. She needed to make her point. "I'll go so far as to tell you, if my father appears at our wedding, I will leave."

They rode in silence until Nettie inquired, "Were my mother's roses blooming in the front yard?"

"There wasn't much of anything but dirt in your front yard."

Nettie stared at him in disbelief. "My mother had a beautiful garden. Her roses were her pride and joy."

When they came to the corner where they should have turned, Emmett continued straight.

"You weren't serious about going to another roller rink, were you?"

"No. But I do think we should kidnap a rose."

"What is wrong with you tonight? Are you determined to persist in reckless pursuits until you get arrested?"

"No. But I am determined to make you happy." He could not gauge her mood. After driving several blocks, he introduced a new topic. "Nettie, I want to make some changes. I've decided to sell the Golden State."

"Why would you do that? It's your life's work."

"No, my beer is my work. The saloon was my parents' dream."

"But why would you sell? What would you do? Why would you give up brewing beer if it's what you love? I don't want you to do this on my account. This could prove a bitter way to start a marriage."

"I can see nothing but trouble ahead for saloons. I don't want our life to revolve around popular opinion. And I have no intention of giving up brewing."

"I don't understand."

"I think we should move outside the city, start a different business. I'm interested in property in the San Fernando Valley. I'm thinking we could have a farm, raise citrus trees and keep our own bees. I could control the quality of more of my ingredients. I can grow hops there and brew as much beer as I like.

"It's close enough to the city so we can visit and shop or even roller skate. It's a better place to raise a family.

"The saloon business is changing. There was almost no stigma attached while I was growing up. I don't want you or our children exposed to public disdain because of my living."

"So, you're letting the prohibitionists drive you out?"

"I'm making a business decision that enables us to live a less complicated life. The hours at the saloon are long and I don't make enough money to compensate for that. It's one reason I never encouraged Webster to stay when Nadine urged him to leave.

"I made money as a bartender and got my fifth of the profits, which was fine for me. Webster had a family to support. Even when we gave him a bigger salary and called him the manager, it wasn't enough."

"You don't think you'll make enough to support a family?"

"Oh, I make enough. I always made enough. I never counted on my income from the Golden State."

"Then what income do you count on?" Nettie could not imagine what he was talking about. Aside from their excursions, all he ever did was work. She'd seen the ledger book. Even though Emmett now owned the saloon outright, it wasn't especially lucrative.

"My brewing income. I sell my beer." He could see she didn't understand. "I have patrons who buy my beer. Haven't you ever seen me leave the bar with a customer?"

"I suppose so."

"I have quite a following, some of the wealthiest and most influential men in the city who enjoy a truly excellent glass of beer. I save my best for them. They'll continue to buy whether I brew my beer here or in the Valley." He drove on as Nettie considered his declaration.

As they approached her old neighborhood, Emmett parked the Buick a couple of blocks from her childhood home. That way, her brothers couldn't hear the car and it would be parked in a slightly better area. After helping Nettie down, Emmett rummaged in his trunk.

"What are you doing?" Nettie felt uncomfortable. She hadn't been near her home in the years since she left except for their New Year's visit to Pasadena.

"I'm getting the small spade I keep to dig the wheels out of the mud."

A cheery Emmett took Nettie's arm and guided her along the sidewalk. They made quick progress and soon stood in front of her old house. She halted where the fallen fence still covered the sidewalk. Lights were on inside. The sound of men laughing and talking emanated from within. There was enough light from the street lamp and the moon to see the dirt and weeds in the front yard. If Emmett could have better seen his fiancé's expression, he might have been alarmed.

"Where were the rose bushes?" he whispered.

"They were along the fence mostly, and near the porch. There were a lot of hydrangeas, too."

Emmett stepped across the fence, then held Nettie's hand to help her into the yard.

"Let's check around the corners of the porch. Maybe there's something left."

No sooner did they round the corner than they came face-to-face with a large, dark-furred dog. The dog crouched and bared its teeth. A sinister growl rumbled in its throat. To Emmett's horror, Nettie dropped his hand and approached the dog.

"Hush, Runner," she hissed. The dog immediately quieted but seemed as wary as Emmett. But then Emmett made out the dog's tail wagging as he greeted Nettie. "Good boy." She petted the dog, who was evidently happy to see her. "Good old boy." She slapped his back and put her arms around his neck, burying her face in his fur. The dog followed obediently behind when Nettie covered the short distance to where Emmett stood.

"An old friend?"

"A very old friend. I'm surprised he's still alive." Then she turned her attention to the pitiful and scrawny remains of her mother's roses.

In the end, the spade proved unnecessary. Nettie took her knife and cut the two healthiest canes from two remaining bushes. She patted the dog once more and bade him goodbye as they retraced their steps away from the house.

Jean Jegel

"What do you plan to do with those?"

"I'm going to pot them up. It seems silly to put them in the ground if we're going to move."

"Will they grow?"

"They should." She looked toward Emmett as they walked. "Can I keep them at your house? They'll get more sun in your yard than they will on my windowsill."

Emmett was clearly delighted to be the keeper of Nettie's newest possessions and relieved she accepted his idea about moving.

As he kissed her cheek, he replied, "I think there's room at our house."

Once they were on the way home, Emmett, who enjoyed himself thoroughly the entire evening, noticed Nettie's reserve.

"I have a question for you," he began. "Would your mother approve of me?" Emmett expected a speedy reply and was surprised as Nettie carefully considered his query.

"You expect me to be honest?"

"Of course."

"Then I would have to say no. She would not approve."

Emmett was stunned. "Why would you think so?"

"I don't think. I know she wouldn't approve."

"Why? Because of the saloon?"

"My mother arranged for me to attend a cotillion. She used connections to get me invited. I was 14 and she took me to a big house she said belonged to a 'Cousin Virginia.' Mother stood on the sidewalk as I approached the front door. She somehow scrimped and saved to buy me a proper dress. I looked quite the young lady, but I felt awkward. She told me I knew everything I needed in order to find a society husband and she expected no less of me. This was the first of many opportunities she intended to provide.

"I came to understand Mother groomed me to fit into the life she had before her marriage. So, no, she would not approve of you.

"Mother died so there were no other opportunities for me to charm the husband she envisioned. You, Mr. Boyd, are no society gentleman, although you are a gentleman—usually." Nettie graced him with a tentative smile, sorry she wasn't able to supply the answer he sought.

"Did you want a society husband?"

"Emmett, you well know it was my sincere intention to avoid husbands altogether."

Mulling over the events of the evening, the two remained quiet as they made their way to Mrs. Green's.

As they neared their destination, Emmett noticed Nettie's furtive attempts to hide her tears and could only speculate as to the cause. It could be her disappointment at the state of her childhood home, her dreary family relationships, mourning for her mother, fatigue, disappointment at their imminent parting, or the one he most feared—dread of their impending marriage.

* * *

Alone in the side door, Nettie counted the money in the cash register for the third time. It was almost 10:30 and she was tired. Fatigue was not the cause of her present mental lapse.

Emmett didn't hesitate to share wedding news with anyone who would listen. The often-cited relationship between bartender and customer had been reversed. The bartender was now doing all the talking.

No such discussion occurred in the side door. If gossip traveled to the female customers, they were evidently waiting for Nettie to bring up her impending marriage. She had not. Although imminent nuptials were normally heralded by friends, family and the community at large, Nettie felt her wedding was immensely personal. The thought they should have simply eloped frequently crossed her mind. She knew this fervent desire would not be fair to Emmett's family.

Thankfully, news of the earthquake was still the main topic of conversation. Los Angeles was deeply involved in charity work and the wedding of Emmett Boyd and Nettie Gordon was comparatively inconsequential.

Her counting was interrupted by a gentle knock at the door. Disgusted, Nettie threw the money back in the register drawer and slammed it shut. She flung open the door to find a disheveled woman clutching a small child of about four years of age.

"Please miss, can I come in?"

"We're closed."

"But I need help. Please, just for a few minutes. My husband is following me. I'm afraid."

Nettie placed her hand on the woman's shoulder and guided her into the saloon. She turned to press the door closed when it swung forcefully open, knocking her backwards against the wall and onto the floor.

Stunned, Nettie sat up and covered her mouth in horror as a man descended upon his wife, who cowered near the corner. He struck her face, yelling epithets.

Nettie scrambled to her feet and hurried to the front saloon. Not only was it emptied of customers, Emmett was nowhere to be seen. Nettie felt in her pocket for her knife. When she considered the burly man who was attacking his wife in the next room, she knew the knife would be of little help. She precipitously recalled an item that would give her a decided advantage.

* * *

Emmett stood on the sidewalk in front of the Golden State. His longtime customer, Earl, was showing off his recently purchased automobile, a white 120-horsepower Mercedes. The car was snappy—a racing model.

"I want to race, Emmett. What if you sign on as my mechanic?"

"I don't know anything about your fine motor car, Earl."

"But you could learn. You figured out your Buick in no time. I'm certain we could break some records."

"As eager as I am to have a ride, I'm going to be a family man soon. I don't think racing is in the cards for me. If you're serious about setting distance records, you need a real mechanic."

"You're keeping to your slow touring car? I can't entice you?"

As Emmett shook his head, the sound of a gunshot jolted him. Knowing the sound came from the saloon, he gasped, "Nettie!" and ran toward the door. "Use the call box!" he shouted at Earl.

Finding the saloon as empty as when he left, Emmett bounded toward the side door and found a truly disturbing scenario. Nettie trembled visibly, not from fear but apparently from rage. She held a pistol in both hands, pointing in the general direction of a tall, stocky man. No one appeared to have been shot. A woman and child cowered beneath a table near the corner.

"*Coward*!" Nettie screamed at the man as she stepped in his direction. "You're a sniveling, worthless coward!"

"*Stop*!" yelled Emmett as he walked across the room. "Don't get too close, he'll grab the gun."

Nettie never took her eyes off her intended victim but stopped her forward motion.

Emmett stepped beside his fiancé, wanting to take control of the wildly swaying weapon.

"What are you doing?" he calmly inquired as he noted a prominent red mark on Nettie's cheek. A flare of anger almost overcame his resolve to remain composed. If Nettie had been hit, he would shoot the man himself. "Give me the gun."

"*No!*" Nettie yelled, then continued her rant. "How does it feel to come up against someone who has power over you? How do you like it when you're the underdog? Get down on your knees!" she yelled.

The man, obviously perturbed, complied. "Look, lady, what happens between a man and his wife is none of your business."

"What did you say to me? How dare you? I saw you hit her, a defenseless woman. You're a bully, a coward, too afraid to take on someone your own size."

Emmett feared his beloved was on the verge of becoming a murderess should she manage to aim her shot. He never imagined she was capable of such blind rage.

"Nettie, you're about to shoot an unarmed man you don't even know. Give me the gun. He's not worth it. Look at me."

Emmett kept an eye on the kneeling man as Nettie turned to face him.

"Give me the gun." Although she didn't move, Nettie didn't resist as Emmett removed the gun from her hands and stuck it in his belt.

"Get up," Emmett commanded, but no sooner did the man come to his feet than Emmett punched him in the gut and then in the face.

The man keeled over, moaning.

"I don't ever want to find out you hit your wife again. Should I ever hear such a rumor, I'll beat you within an inch of your life. Do you understand?"

Groaning, the man could only nod.

The wife emerged from under the table and leaving her dazed child behind, crawled across the floor to her damaged husband.

"Don't hit him anymore!" she yelled at Emmett. "Danny, are you all right?"

Danny managed to speak. "Oh, darlin', I'm so sorry. You know I didn't mean to hurt you. I'll make it up to you, I swear I will."

"I know, I know," the woman bawled as she cradled her husband's head in her lap. "This is all my fault."

Stunned at this turn of events, Nettie wanted nothing so much as to escape. She turned toward the doorway to the front saloon to find it full of police officers, who hurried down the street in answer to Earl's call. Quickly changing course, she made her way outside. Shaking violently, Nettie set a swift pace down the street.

Absently crossing at the corner, Nettie froze when an automobile honked and swerved to avoid her just as someone grabbed her arm and pulled her toward the curb. Barely cognizant of the danger she was in, Nettie looked toward her rescuer. Emmett crushed her against his chest, angered by her reckless flight.

Expecting hysterics, Emmett was astounded when Nettie pushed him away as if to continue her headlong flight. Despite his resolve to quit pulling her by the arm, he held tight as she struggled to free herself.

"Let go."

"No. I intend to walk down the aisle with you. We can't if you commit murder or suicide. Of all the ways I imagined you might try to escape matrimony, I never considered these possibilities." Nettie trembled with emotion and tried to catch her breath. "Sit on the curb and calm down."

He held fast to her arm and took a seat, pulling Nettie beside him. Wanting nothing so much as to yell at her for her carelessness, he knew anger would only alienate her. Emmett considered the possibility he was not equipped to deal with such intense hostility.

"I'm happy you finally took my advice and abandoned the knife as your primary armament, but it was never my intention to steer you to more formidable weaponry. Can you explain what happened? Nettie, please talk to me. Did that man strike you?"

"No. Why?"

"Your cheek is red."

She put her hand to her face and winced. "I was standing at the door when he came in. The door hit me and I fell."

Emmett didn't comment, hoping she would continue to explain. Nettie stared toward the street, now devoid of traffic.

"The woman knocked and when I answered, she told me her husband was pursuing her. As I let her in, he must have seen her and he pushed the door in. I used the gun to stop him."

"Your first inclination was to shoot him?"

"No. I went to get you, but there was no one in front. Then I remembered the gun you keep in the cabinet under the cash register."

"Did you fire at him?"

"I fired at the ceiling to get his attention."

Emmett nodded thoughtfully. "That seemed to have worked although my saloon is getting shot up rather frequently since you came along. Would you have shot him?"

Continuing to stare into the street, Nettie

considered her answer. "I wanted to."

"But you didn't. Why not?"

"I don't know."

"Then tell me why you wanted to shoot him." He could see Nettie still struggled for breath, but as she considered his comment, she calmed down.

"So, you don't want to marry me now?" Nettie inquired as she used her thumb to twirl her engagement ring around her finger.

"Oh, no. You're not getting off so easily. I think I need to be more cognizant of how well to arm myself though."

Nettie didn't react to his attempted humor. Her trembling subsided and Emmett stood and took Nettie's hand, urging her to stand.

"Let's go home. We'll get you warm and comfortable and we can talk. Besides, we have a business left with doors wide open. We better make sure the general populace is not helping themselves to free beer."

Questions churned in Emmett's head as they quietly made their way to his house. Nettie refused to go inside while Emmett secured the doors of the Golden State. Instead she curled up in the swing on the back porch and pulled an old quilt around her. The porch reflected her efforts in his house. She felt at home there.

Emmett wanted her promise to stay until he returned, but she appeared so settled in, he refrained. Nonetheless, he made quick work of locking up and wasted no time perching himself on the swing beside her. Nettie nestled against his side and placed her arm across his chest.

Enjoying the chill night air and Nettie's proximity, Emmett almost hated to break the silence.

"Are you all right?" He felt her tense at his

question.

"Why?"

"You were so angry. Have you ever been that angry before?" Emmett waited patiently for her reply.

"A long time ago."

"Maybe you should tell me about it."

"It's all in the past. What good would it do?"

"It might help me understand. I'm about to marry you, after all. You told me you weren't angry at your father, but I wonder if you're being honest."

"You're accusing me of lying?"

"No. Maybe you don't understand either."

"Do you think they put that man in jail?"

"I'm certain they did not."

"Why?"

"Because it didn't seem to me his wife would file charges. She felt sorry for him. I've seen this before. She undoubtedly feels her husband isn't able to control himself. He doesn't hesitate to appeal to her sympathies. In any case, except in divorce, a judge wouldn't take her accusations seriously. The courts don't generally intervene in what occurs between a husband and wife. That's what bothers you, isn't it?"

"Why did you hit him?"

"Because I wanted to."

"You consider your behavior appropriate?"

"No. But he hurt you and he hurt his wife. I wanted him to think twice before he hit her again and to understand there could be repercussions he might not enjoy. I don't know if it will make any difference. It probably won't. You might not understand, but there are women who, quite incomprehensibly, seek out brutal relationships and find excuses to keep them."

"Maybe they simply fell in love with the wrong man."

"Then why would they stay?"

"Because they have no rights; they have no money; they have no job."

"That might be true in some cases, but I'm sure most women have relatives who would help. You managed to find a job when you needed one."

"What if they're too embarrassed to ask for help? The stigma of a broken home is more than many women can bear."

"Nettie, I know you would never stay if I mistreated you."

"I have self-confidence. Most women don't. They're trained from birth to be submissive and obey."

"Perhaps women are by nature more submissive. Most women enjoy being cherished and coddled even if they are self-sufficient. I understand why you'd be upset by what occurred tonight, but I don't understand the intensity of your anger."

"Make the swing go," Nettie requested. Emmett used his foot to move the swing slowly back and forth and he waited.

"I will tell you the story of how I won my knife. I told you my mother protected me. In all my memories, she never attempted to shield my brothers from my father's wrath. I don't know why. They hated me all the more because I seemed to be the favored child, spared from the punishment they so frequently endured.

"One morning when I was about ten, my mother and I were alone in the house after breakfast. My father came in from a night of drinking and sat at the kitchen table. When I walked over to hand him a dish of oatmeal, I knocked over my glass of milk. It spilled in his lap. He was furious. He slapped me and told me I was clumsy, that I would never marry. I knew his comments would break my mother's heart.

"He came after me and I crawled under the table. Predictably, my mother inserted herself between us. She received the beating meant for me. I watched in horror from under the table, feeling helpless and guilty, but she trained me well through the years. I was not to interfere."

Nettie clutched frantically at Emmett's shirt as her memories spilled forth. Although her voice was even, he could see she was crying.

"I imagine he forgot why he was so angry after a time. He staggered to the parlor where he passed out on the settee. My mother lay helpless on the floor. I tried to aid her. Tears streamed down her cheeks from pain, but I could see she was ashamed. It was the worst beating I ever witnessed.

"Instead of gratitude for my help, she was angry. She told me to go to school, insisting she was fine and I was dawdling. 'Get out,' she screamed, 'or you'll be a no-good like your brothers.' And so, I went to school.

"I've seen your sympathy for those who are slaves to alcohol. There's a terrible stigma not only for them but their families. Everyone at school understood I was the daughter of the drunk who lived near the tracks. I had friends, mind you, but there were always those who took every opportunity to belittle me. On this particular morning, the biggest boy in school—his name was Aaron—decided to taunt me.

"I ignored him at first, but the more he tormented me, the angrier I got. He was a bully and I had enough. I turned and punched him right in the stomach. He was shocked; he never thought I would fight back. He wanted to make me cry and he'd never been able to do that. All my fury and frustration were directed at him.

"He collapsed to the ground so I put my foot on his chest, dug the heel of my shoe in and warned him never to speak to me again. His prized possession was a knife he kept in his shirt pocket. He used it to impress the other boys in school. I reached down and took it, half expecting he would come after it.

"For the rest of the year, he was the big boy who let a girl beat him up. Aaron's family moved away that summer, but I kept the knife. The other bullies at school left me alone afterwards.

"When I left home, for the first time in my life, I was free. There were no drunks, no beatings, no threats. I had peace and quiet and time to do as I pleased. No one knew my family. No one knew my shame.

"Since the day I met you, you have bullied me, pulling me to the police station, relentlessly dragging me here and there, even holding me to your kissing agreement. You were disingenuous and purposely ignored my wishes. You've repeatedly shown yourself to be a violent man. All this was offset by your better qualities and my attraction to you, but how do I know what you will be once we wed? Your record to date is rather flawed."

"It was never my intention to be a bully, except perhaps on that first occasion. I might not have resorted to deceit if we had a more traditional courtship."

"So, it's my fault?"

"Certainly not. I'm not trying to make excuses."

"It sounds to me as if you are."

Although he felt Nettie's opinions were tainted by her past, he better understood her reluctance to wed and her derogatory ideas of husbands. Her knife was a trophy and symbol of her strength.

"I can't change the past any more than you. I'd certainly change your past if I could. All I can do is assure you it's my life's work to be the kind of husband you deserve and to give you a happy future.

"Believe me, Nettie, I'm being completely candid. I never wanted anything or anyone the way I want you. I promise you'll never have reason for regret. After all, you first came to me for help. I don't think you would have if you didn't trust me and know I would share your view of what happened. Somewhere deep inside, you understand I'm an honorable man who would never hurt you."

He waited for her response, eventually realizing she fell asleep wrapped in his embrace. Closing his eyes, Emmett knew the proper thing was to take Nettie home. Instead, he fell asleep.

* * *

It was Faith's habit to come and go from her family home by way of the back door and so she unexpectedly discovered her brother and his fiancé asleep on the swing. She approached Emmett and poked him in the shoulder with her fingernail. His dazed and confused expression upon coming awake almost garnered her sympathy, but Faith quickly quelled that emotion. Mother would not approve.

"What do you think you're doing?" she hissed.

Emmett absently rubbed his injured shoulder as he yawned. He was reminded of boyhood days when his sister was in charge of getting him to school on time.

Noticing Nettie was still asleep, he held his index finger in the air to quiet his sister and gingerly slid out of the swing. Gently lowering Nettie's head, Emmett pulled the quilt over her shoulders, then shooed Faith toward the kitchen door and braced for an assault.

"What is wrong with you?" Faith began.

"Apparently more than I ever realized," Emmett responded. Faith ground coffee from the wall dispenser into the strainer and began a pot of coffee as was her usual morning custom before she married. "If you don't mind, I'll use the water closet before you begin your diatribe." Faith didn't answer as she put the tea kettle on to boil.

"Nettie will need a cup of tea when she awakens," Faith murmured.

Once Emmett returned to the kitchen, he took a seat as Faith gathered three cups and saucers and the sugar bowl and placed them on the table. She busied herself filling the creamer and absent-mindedly took a place opposite her brother. She gazed across the table struggling to remember why she came.

"Oh, Mr. Tuckson, the milkman, had the most astounding thing to say this morning, but first I feel the need to reprimand you quite severely."

"Go right ahead."

"How can you be so careless and negligent? Your fiancé's reputation should be your primary concern."

"I assure you, Nettie's reputation is of little concern to her."

"I don't imagine for a minute that's true. Even if it were, she's soon to be your wife and mother of your children. Her reputation should matter to you."

"I have the greatest admiration for Nettie Gordon's reputation. It is entirely intact."

"Well, no thanks to you. First you tell me she actually spent the night here after the earthquake and you expect me to provide an alibi if it should become necessary—"

"Did it become necessary?"

"Well, no but—"

"Then go on."

Faith frowned, "Now I find you've spent the night with her again. What's more, any inquisitive neighbor would be able to see for themselves."

"No one has been as inquisitive as you. The warehouse blocks the view on one side and the fence does the same on the sidewalk and alley sides. I believe you're the only nosy neighbor I need to worry about."

"You know this is not appropriate. Mother is turning over in her grave this very moment."

"I assure you, my pants have remained in place throughout. There's no need for concern."

Faith's eyes flew open in shock. "That's certainly no way to talk to your sister."

"Well, it's what you're worried about, isn't it?"

"Even so, you know you should have taken her home last night. Oh, last night! I heard Nettie shot a man in the side door! Is that true?"

"No. It's ridiculous."

"I'm so relieved."

"She did shoot my ceiling though and she certainly would have liked to shoot the man who hit his wife in the bar."

Faith's eyes flew open once again. "What are you saying?"

"I said she shot my ceiling. Are you going deaf in your old age?"

"I am not old, but I am your elder and I must insist you treat me with an appropriate amount of respect."

"Very well. I apologize."

"Have you behaved inappropriately in other ways? Are you telling me everything? You've been kissing, haven't you?"

"You know perfectly well we've been kissing." Emmett almost laughed at Faith's shocked expression. He knew it was feigned.

"How would I know?"

"You watched us kiss as long ago as Christmas Eve. I saw you standing there. I wonder what Mother would think of your voyeurism?"

Faith sputtered, "You're imagining things."

Emmett cocked his head as Faith squirmed. "You won't have to worry about me or my future wife much longer. We'll soon be married. I give you my word, I will behave with a proper amount of decorum until then."

"Much better. Now explain what happened in the saloon."

Emmett smiled as Faith poured his coffee. Life was about to be good indeed.

* * *

In the end, a simple family wedding was planned in the Judge and Faith's garden on May 5 with an elegant meal to follow. Pastor Arndorfer presided. Eula stood up for Nettie, Webster stood up for Emmett but only briefly. Although the best man succeeded in wearing shoes, standing proved difficult.

The original plan was for Emmett's family to gather around for the brief ceremony. It soon became obvious that idea was impractical. Faith had a baby. Every other woman in attendance would shortly follow suit. Emmett hoped the fecundity of the wedding-goers didn't immediately rub off on Nettie. Not eager to share her attention, he anticipated having his wife to himself for a time.

Emmett realized their hasty marriage would likely cause gossip. The scandalmongers would be quieted once they understood the Boyd marriage was not scheduled from necessity.

Believing a wedding dress was an unnecessary expense, Nettie decided to wear her white tea gown. She borrowed Faith's wedding veil and carried a bouquet of white sweet peas and roses. Emmett thought she looked angelic.

He was stunned at a Bible verse the pastor read before the vows. Did Pastor Arndorfer actually know Nettie this well?

"'There is no fear in love; but perfect love casteth out fear.' Emmett Boyd, do you take Nettie Gordon as your wedded wife, to have and to hold from this day forward, for better or worse, for richer, for poorer, in sickness and in health, to love and to cherish, till death do you part, according to God's holy ordinance?"

"I do."

"Nettie Gordon, do you take Emmett Boyd to be your wedded husband, to have and to hold from this day forward, for better or worse, for richer, for poorer, in sickness and in health, to love, cherish, and to obey, till death do you part, according to God's holy ordinance?"

Nettie stared into Emmett's eager face. She never imagined a man would look at her with so much love and caring. Nettie took her vows seriously and considered their import as she paused to reflect.

She was, after all, signing away her rights, her possessions—meager though they were, her very being, and her right to any children they might have. She did not believe in divorce and felt marriage was a holy sacrament.

Would she go the way of so many women before her, choosing poorly, spending the rest of her life abused and tormented, watching her children ill-treated or even beaten, making the same mistakes her mother made? She could still walk away, even now. It was obvious her hesitation made Emmett uncomfortable.

"Nettie, are you all right?" asked Pastor Arndorfer.

EPILOGUE

Wyatt Boyd was an extremely calm baby. He absently patted his head. Only last week, Papa took him to the barber shop for the first time. He watched in the mirror as his red hair fell on the cloak. Wyatt was perfectly still, shedding nary a tear. Now, his papa approached to take him from the car.

"We're home, Son."

Wyatt deliberately placed his sucker stick in his mother's hand before lifting his arms toward his papa.

He toddled off toward the house as Emmett helped his wife from the Buick, then hurried off to supervise Wyatt as he climbed the porch stairs.

Nettie noticed her shadow on the unusually warm winter morning. Placing her hand on her belly, she was amused by her misshapen silhouette, which reflected her current expectant condition so perfectly. She looked up at the new house. It took much longer to sell the property in Los Angeles and find the right acreage in the San Fernando Valley than Emmett anticipated.

Rubbing the small of her back, Nettie paused to consider their new home. She knew this was not the life she ever wanted or expected. God's plan was much different than she imagined. She shouldn't have been surprised. His plan was always far superior to anything a simple woman could dream up.

Emmett watched Nettie stretch in the sunshine after the long ride. She always had a grace about her, even now when she was heavy with his child. He enjoyed the view as Nettie untied her hat. The copper highlights of her auburn hair gleamed in the sun.

Emmett considered all the changes that occurred since their marriage. The Boyd siblings launched their own population explosion. Nadine first delivered a healthy baby girl. Faith had a new baby daughter. The twins seemed to be competing to see who would bear the most offspring. Hope was soon to be the mother of three children, Charity had two.

Motherhood agreed with the twins in ways no one could have anticipated. They both matured and were devoted to their babies and even to their husbands. Although they weren't as close as they had been historically, the change seemed beneficial for all concerned. Perhaps it was the sad stillbirth of Charity's second baby that served to commit the girls so completely to their young families.

Eula's little boy was his father's delight. Both the pastor and his wife were happy with their small family and their church work.

But no one was more strongly affected by motherhood than Nettie. Emmett thought back to the early days of their marriage.

There were times he would admit Nettie wasn't cut out for marriage, as she always asserted. Believing Nettie's tests came before their wedding, he was astounded to find her most daunting trials actually came after. Emmett felt devastated when the idyllic life he anticipated seemed so far from reality.

Emmett understood, in retrospect, he should never

have rushed her to the altar. Nettie's apprehension and his enthusiasm quickly led to discord. Her deep distress at being married became obvious. Nettie's moods were mercurial. She was a bundle of conflicting emotion; from passionate to prudish, eager to reluctant, happy to somber.

He refused to lose his temper—as best as he was able—remaining gentle and loving throughout, when in reality, he had never so wanted to wring anyone's neck as he did his wife's. They suffered in secret, determined to hide their disastrous marriage from the outside world and especially from Emmett's family.

He remembered the day their lives changed. When it was clear she was with child, Nettie suffered grim moods. Emmett planned to announce Nettie's expectant condition on a Sunday afternoon at Faith's house.

That morning, Nettie rose from the kitchen table and knocked over her glass of milk. Emmett jumped out of his chair to avoid the liquid as it dripped off the table. He grabbed the glass to set it upright. His quick reaction surprised Nettie, who took a step backward and stumbled over her chair. Emmett caught her arm to steady her and avoid disaster but thought nothing further of the incident.

After cleaning up the table, they proceeded first to church, then to Faith's to make their announcement. If anyone noticed Nettie's lack of enthusiasm, they were too polite to comment.

As Emmett rough-housed on the grass with Jake— the two shared a strong bond since their experience in San Francisco—Emmett caught Nettie staring at him as if he was a stranger. For the first time, she looked through the curtain of her prejudices about men and saw her husband clearly. Understanding neither she nor her baby were in harm's way, relief flooded over her.

Nettie appeared so emotional, Emmett took her home. His family assumed they were beholding a new mother's weepy outburst when in actuality, they witnessed the rebirth of Nettie Boyd.

Emmett offered to go for the car, but Nettie thought it ridiculous since they only had a block to go. He soon regretted his decision. She became so hysterical, she could barely place one foot in front of the other.

"What's wrong with you?" he asked, probably more gruffly than he intended. He missed dessert.

"I love you," Nettie blubbered.

"I can appreciate that. It's been difficult to tell lately. Why are you crying?"

"When you and Jake were playing, it all seemed so clear." She could see he didn't understand. "I just feel like—like—I know you would never hurt me or our baby."

Emmett stopped walking and stared into her face as realization dawned. "You thought I was going to hit you this morning, didn't you?"

Nettie only stared in response.

"I can't believe this. You love me enough to marry me, but you've been afraid of me all this time?"

"I'm not afraid of you," Nettie belligerently retorted.

Emmett shook his head disgustedly. Nothing she did or said made any sense.

"I thought I was like other women. I fell in love, against my better judgment I might add, and then I expected you to turn out like other men—like my father or my brothers, even Louise's husband. But I realized while you played with Jake, you aren't like them at all!"

"Thank you so much for noticing," he sarcastically replied. Then, as they walked up the front porch stairs, the gravity of what she admitted dawned on him.

"You've been waiting for me to turn into some kind of ogre?"

Nettie nodded. Emmett stared into her puffy, wet, red eyes. Women were truly inscrutable. As they walked through the front door, Emmett took her in his arms.

"Do you love me enough to make dessert?" he asked as he kissed her face. She laughed, relieved at his attempt to lighten the mood. "I love you Nettie Boyd. You are stuck with me, you understand?"

"I want to be," she admitted.

Their marriage became all he dreamed and more, not that it was any kind of picnic. They were both strong-willed. There were arguments galore, especially over the new house and property.

His idea to sell beer brewed from fruit on their property was a current source of conflict. But their marriage was sound. They were partners in life, best friends and lovers, who knew beyond doubt they would meet all challenges together.

Although his family was disappointed when Emmett announced his plan to sell the Golden State, he remained committed to his decision. Splitting the money between them served to smooth ruffled feathers. Feeling it dishonest to transfer the liquor license when it might be revoked at any time, the property was eventually sold to a developer. The family saloon would soon be demolished to make way for new construction. Charlie found a daytime job playing piano at a roller rink. Bao, Louise and Marcel opened their own business—a diner located a block from the Golden State.

Believing there was no acceptable future for his family in Los Angeles, Emmett was not bitter. After all, if not for the temperance movement, he would never have met Nettie Gordon.

"What are you doing, my dear wife?"

"Just looking."

"Well come here so I can carry you over the threshold."

Wyatt giggled and toddled behind as his parents made an unconventional entrance into their new home.

* * *

The Anti-Saloon Public League suppressed all public drinking in Los Angeles County by 1910.

In 1917, three years before national prohibition, the people of Los Angeles voted to prohibit hard liquor and close all saloons.

It took until December 5, 1933, to realize the folly of prohibition and rescind the 18th Amendment.

ABOUT THE AUTHOR

Author Jean Jegel lives with her husband, Carl, in Santa Clarita, a suburb of Los Angeles County. A lifelong Californian dedicated to marriage, raising three children, and working for the Man, Jean now enjoys quilting, gardening, sewing, reading and, of course, writing.

California as it used to be serves as Jean's inspiration and the background for her vintage romantic novels. Love of research is the catalyst for the rich details of historical eras she portrays. Visit jeanjegel.com for book excerpts, giveaway information, Jean's blog and the latest news. Come home to a simpler time and fall in love.

WORKS BY JEAN JEGEL

Truer Beauty

By Light of Day

A Keepsake Love

Catching Nettie Gordon

A Home on Carroll Avenue

What Money Can't Buy
    Book One—The New Saleslady
    Book Two—Family Ties
    Book Three—Character
    Book Four—Brotherhood
    Book Five—Trust
    Book Six—Love